# Dark Tangled Truths

C.S. BERRY

Copyright © 2026 by C.S. Berry

All rights reserved.

No part of this book may be reproduced in any form or by any electronic or mechanical means, including information storage and retrieval systems, without written permission from the author, except for the use of brief quotations in a book review. 21326

**NO AI TRAINING:** Without in any way limiting the author's [and publisher's] exclusive rights under copyright, any use of this publication to "train" generative artificial intelligence (AI) technologies to generate text is expressly prohibited. The author reserves all rights to license uses of this work for generative AI training and development of machine learning language models.

AI was not used in the making of this book or cover artwork.

Cover design by Pretty in Ink Creations

# Author Note & Content List

Dear Reader,

Thank you for choosing Dark Tangled Truths. First thing, this is a continuation from Whisper Pretty Lies and Brutal Little Secrets. If you really want to be confused, start here. If not, Whisper Pretty Lies and Brutal Little Secrets are also on Kindle Unlimited.

This has been a crazy ride. What started out as a duet (what I can write short *eyeroll*) turned into a trilogy. But I wanted to give this creative little director and her hockey playing men a fleshed out story. It's kind of sad to say goodbye, but maybe we'll see them in someone else's story in the future.

A side note: S. Massery let me use her NHL team for my book. If you like dark hockey romance, hers are *chef's kiss*.

This book contains darker themes, which can be found on my website csberry.com/lust-liars under content warnings. Your mental health is important. If you're concerned, you can always reach out to me.

Evan and her guys will find their happily ever after!

XOXOXO
C.S. Berry

AUTHOR NOTE & CONTENT LIST

Content warning:
Dark themes including bullying, blackmail, chasing scenes, consensual somnophilia, kidnapping, and stalking. It also includes attempted sexual assault.

# CHAPTER 1
## Hawk

ANNIE'S HURT, and I try to take in what happened. Her wet hand is washed of blood, but blood still accumulates on the wounds. Blistering wounds. Little pinpricks of blood everywhere. My stomach twists, but I focus on figuring out the cause. The time for panic is later.

I glance around the black box theater, trying to get my thoughts under control. Annie trembles in my arms, too focused on the pain to talk to me. She needs me, and I have her.

There's a rose lying on the desk, forgotten, along with some papers with spots of blood dried on them. The rose thorns must have cut her. It's the only sharp thing nearby. A rose thorn shouldn't burn unless Annie is allergic. Maybe? Or else there's something I can't see that cut her or something on the rose that's affecting her.

Annie is my priority. I need to get her to either the urgent care or the hospital as soon as possible. But I also need to secure what hurt her so we can figure out what it is.

A group of actors stands nearby, watching us. Their eyes are wide and worried. Jason stands next to them. There aren't many people here. Most are using the break. Jason seems like a good guy, and I need to trust someone to make sure nothing is disturbed until we can figure out what happened.

"Jason, stay here and don't let anyone touch anything on this desk until Keira gets back."

"Got it." Jason looks worriedly at Annie, but he takes up the post.

My next problem is transportation. I only have my motorcycle. I don't think she can ride in her current state.

We need a driver. Almost everyone is doing fuck knows what during the long break. I carry her out into the hallway. Maybe Mark or Mia can give us a ride. But I'll take pretty much anyone at this point. I head out to find someone, anyone.

"I've got you, Annie." I study her tear-streaked face.

Annie's gone silent except for the occasional whimper. Her hand is tucked against her body protectively. She's focused inward on the pain.

"What's wrong with her?" Chase straightens from the wall. Just what I need to deal with, this dick. He must have a brace on his knee under his pants because he's been walking stiffly all rehearsal.

I pull her tighter against me. She's still whimpering in my arms, and my chest aches at seeing her hurt. She's stopped mumbling, but I can tell she's holding in the pain.

"I don't know," I grit out. He's the last person I want to ask to drive Annie anywhere, but if he's our only option, I'll have to take it. I won't let Annie be in pain just because of some pissing match between Chase and us.

It's not ideal. But we need a ride. The sooner the better.

"Hey." Mia hurries to my side from behind me. She's got a bunch of paper towels. "Keira said Evan's hurt. Fuck. That doesn't look good. Mr. Watson will be a minute."

I blow out a breath. Annie's fingers are red and swollen. Her good hand shakes as she takes the napkin from Mia. She drapes it over her wounded hand with a hiss, careful not to press on it. When the blood seeps into the napkin, Mia pales.

"You got a car?" I look at Mia. I'd rather deal with her than the asshole any day.

When I glance at Chase, he watches Annie with a worried expression. Is it fake? For all I know, he's the reason she's hurt. Payback for what we've done. Fuck, what if we're the reason she's been hurt?

A fist squeezes around my heart, but I can't deal with my own emotions right now.

Mia nods and pulls out her keys. "Let's go. Where's the closest emergency services?"

"There's an urgent care a few blocks away. The hospital is on the other side of town." I follow her to the parking lot, glad to be moving.

"Hawk!" Mr. Watson yells behind me.

I glance over my shoulder. Not pausing, I call back to him, "We're going to the urgent care on Clarkson. Can you tell her mom?"

He nods and pulls out his phone.

Mia holds open the back door of her car. I get in with Annie and strap her in. Tears stream relentlessly down her face and she rocks slightly, hunched over her hand. I want to fix this for her, but there's not much more I can do.

The fact she's not insisting we go back into rehearsal tells me this is bad. Nothing gets in the way of her rehearsal.

"What happened?" Mia says as soon as she starts the car and puts it in gear.

"I don't know." I pull out my phone and text the group chat. "She hasn't said much except that it's bleeding and it burns."

> ME:
> Annie's hurt. Something on her table during rehearsal

Annie inhales sharply and glances at me. Her eyes are strained. Her lips pinched, but she bites out, "The rose. Thorns. Burning."

I tear my gaze from her and focus on the text. My insides scream to hold her and tell her everything is going to be okay, but I know we need to find out what actually is hurting her. We can do that, and then I can focus on her.

> ME:
> Someone needs to come get the rose and anything else on her table
>
> Find out what hurt her
>
> On our way to urgent care

> CAM:
> I'm on it

When Annie leans against me, I wrap my arm around her shoulder. My hand trembles.

"I've got you," I whisper softly into her hair, wanting to hold back everything that could ever hurt her, but knowing something got by on my watch.

Cam was home, but at least he saw my texts. Damon is probably training. I don't know when he'll find out. Hopefully, he doesn't come storming in when he does.

"Take a left on Lucas," I say.

Mia turns and goes as fast as traffic will allow. Her knuckles are white on the steering wheel and she glances at us in the rearview mirror, but she keeps her focus on the road.

Whoever did this... I can't even finish that statement in my head. This fury swirling inside me begs to find a target. But right now, I need to concentrate on getting my girl the help she needs. I'll deal with whoever did this after I'm sure she's taken care of.

---

## Cam

"Oh good. Another of EvanAnn's fuckboys is here."

I glare at Chase. He stands with his phone in his hands just outside the doors to the black box theater. Part of me wishes the fucker would have taken the out and joined the other play. I don't like him having any access to Evan.

But I also know Evan thinks he's the best for the character.

I walk past him through the doors and resist the urge to fuck him up, even if he didn't do this. Anger boils under my skin. Someone fucked with my girl, and this asshole is just begging to eat my fist.

Decking Chase is out of the question though. Mr. Watson has been at practices lately and there's probably a security camera pointed this direction in the hallway. While I really want to wipe that smirk off Chase's face, I don't want to get suspended and a lecture from my dad.

So instead, I ignore him as he scoffs and follows me into the theater room. I passed the other play rehearsal on the way in. It's happening at the same time in the smaller room. Meaning there are twice as many suspects.

Chase walks over to the seats where other students wait for their parts in the play.

I don't bother trying to sneak in. Hawk and Annie left about ten minutes ago for urgent care with Mia. The cast is back to rehearsing, but down two major players and the director. The show must go on.

Keira stands near the table she and Annie sit at, overseeing the rehearsal. I walk to where the rose still sits, along with its bloody thorns and the papers it's on. Keira turns to me.

"I haven't touched anything. The papers look like EvanAnn's script and notes, but the top paper doesn't look like something she'd use." Keira talks softly as Mark Green gives a speech on stage. "I didn't see who put the rose there. I didn't even notice the rose until after EvanAnn touched it."

The top paper has some blood on it, but it's folded over and has a jagged edge like someone tore it. Knowing the blood is Evan's makes my insides boil hotter.

I take a few pictures with my phone before sliding it into my pocket.

Using the tongs I grabbed from the lab on campus, I pick up the rose and slide it into the plastic bag I was carrying. There's no telling what's on it, but if it hurt Evan enough to send her to urgent care, I'm not taking any chances.

I use the tongs to lift the note by the corner too. It opens as I slide it in. After I seal the bag, I pick up the script with another plastic bag and slide it inside, just in case. "Until we figure out what the fuck is on this or it's cleaned, I recommend not touching the desk in this area."

Keira nods. Her green eyes are wide as she looks up at me. "Will you text me when you find out what happened? And let me know how EvanAnn is?"

"I can do that. I need a list of everyone who's at the school today. This rehearsal, the other one, and anyone else fucking around. Can you get me that?"

She nods and stares at the bag. "What does the note say? Honestly, I was afraid to touch anything on the table."

It's probably a good thing she didn't. Something is toxic on this shit. I glance at Keira. It's hard not to think about carrying her limp body at the party a week ago. Yeah, both of them being hurt at the same time would have been awful. I lift the bag with the note and read it through the plastic, tipping it so she can read it too.

> Enjoy your men, pretty girl.
> They'll only leave you burned.

"What the fuck?" Keira narrows her eyes as she looks around at the cast as if she'll be able to pick out who left it here. I don't know what all Keira knows about Evan's situation, but maybe it's time to read her in. She might notice something we haven't. But I'll wait and see what the others think.

I take a quick picture of the note.

"There are too many people around." I shake my head when she glances my way. "Whoever did this was careful not to be noticed. It's easier to hide in a crowd."

"We should really have cameras set up." She squints up at the corners of the ceiling.

Damon said the same thing after Chase stormed into rehearsal last weekend. Chase could have been suspended for how he came at Hawk, not that Evan wants one of her leads to be suspended. But putting wireless equipment in the theater room might interfere with the audio equipment. Evan didn't want to risk it.

Now I wish we had. Then I'd know who targeted my girl. Not that we don't know.

Jackson Riordan. It has to be him. Evan said he called her pretty girl at the game. The problem is, I can't see him going unnoticed as a stranger on set. Is someone working with him? Someone on her play?

Or could it be Chase paying us back for fucking with him in the woods? Or is there another threat out there we aren't aware of? Girls can be more fucked up than guys when they want something another girl has.

"If you see or hear anything, let us know." I nudge Keira's shoulder with my own to get her attention.

She blinks a couple of times and then looks at me. "Of course. I just don't know who would have done this. Or even when they might have put the rose on the table. They would have had to wear gloves or something, right? If something was on it?"

She stares at the rose like it will give her information. I glance over the table and chairs to see if I notice anything else Keira might have missed, but there's nothing else on them.

"We'll figure it out." I nod to her and head out.

The great thing about a school like Deimos is if I need a specific nerd, I have one on speed dial. And Mike Duncan happens to like me. I get him tickets to the hockey games and invites to the best parties, and he tests the shit that goes around school to make sure it's not corrupted with something toxic.

The hallways outside of the theater wing are empty on the weekend, especially on the Deimos side of the building. Sundays are usually a day off for sports. The Anteros side is busy with students, practicing or working on projects. Busy little ants.

I make my way to our science wing, a gift from some donor years ago. When I get to the chemistry lab, I knock on the door and wait.

Mike opens it and gestures for me to come in, like we're doing something nefarious. Usually we are, but not this time. After he closes the door, he looks at the baggie in my hand with the rose and the note.

"What have you got for me?" He pulls on some latex gloves and holds out his hand.

I pass him the bag. The rose has tons of thorns. Some have poked through the plastic on the bag. Hawk said there was a lot of blood. Fortunately, someone had cleaned up the floor. I don't like the idea of Evan bleeding that much.

"My girl got stabbed by the thorns, but the pain was intense. She said it burned and she got blisters from whatever got in the wounds."

"Hmm, allergic reaction or chemical?" Mike studies the rose inside the baggie with an intense look. "The stem is shiny. Maybe there's something coating it. I can run a few tests and see what we're dealing with."

"How long?" I step to the sink and wash my hands to be on the safe side.

"An hour or two, depending on which tests give me results." He's already working. "We just got a new liquid chromatograph I've been jonesing to use."

Mike takes a clipping from the stem with some of Evan's blood on it and puts it in a petri dish. He hands me back the bag. "You might want to take this to wherever your girl is. They might need to confirm my findings."

Mike begins preparing his workstation. I study the rose. It's evidence, but we'll have our own results to go off. He makes a valid point though. I'm surprised Mr. Watson didn't call the police to come investigate, but he probably didn't suspect someone of actually tampering with the rose. Just that Evan had been cut and it was bad.

He'll have to fill out a form at the school for the injury. Mr. Watson wasn't in the room when I went in to get the rose. Hawk can find out what Mr. Watson knows and if we need to do damage control.

"You've got my number," I say. It's not a question.

Mike nods, but he's not really paying attention to me at this point. He's got a mystery to unravel, and I've got a girl to see.

## CHAPTER 2
## *Cam*

WHEN I GET to the urgent care, Mia sits in the waiting room. I look at the doors to the back and know they probably won't let me in to see Evan. Hawk must be back with her. He wouldn't have left her side. I head over and drop into the seat next to Mia. I waited with Evan last weekend and then for her. I guess I'm doing that again now.

Except my skin crawls with the need to go and make sure she's really okay. My stomach is tied in knots. Someone fucked with our girl.

"Do we know anything?" I ask. My knee bounces as I stare at the door. I already texted Hawk about the flower and he said the doctors don't think it was anything too toxic. She's already doing better.

Mia shakes her head. Her face is pale and her lips tight. "She had blisters on her fingers. Maybe we should have taken her to the ER."

She looks about two seconds from bursting from her seat and storming back there to get Evan and take her to the hospital instead.

"This was closer. Hawk says she's doing better." I blow out a breath and rub my hands together. I didn't see our girl before they took her back, but if Mia is worried... Fuck. "If they thought she needed the ER, they would have sent you right away."

That's for Mia, but I need to hear it too. It wasn't bad enough for the ER.

Mia nods and rubs her hands together. "Who would do this? I would have noticed if Jackson slipped in. Wouldn't I?"

That question comes out shaky. She seems just as worried as me.

"He might have someone on the inside." It's what keeps going through my head. Who does he know at our school? Anyone could be bought, or someone could be jealous of Evan or us.

Fuck, it could be Mia. She's been friendly enough and even handed over her phone without hesitation. But she could be playing us. This could be her game to get Evan out of the picture so she can fuck us.

Girls have done crazier things for stupider reasons.

It would be better if we knew the real motive, but all we can do right now is guess.

"Brandt's play was going on at the same time. I saw Abby during the break. We were chatting. She really doesn't like Evan." Mia releases her breath and leans back in her chair. "But I can't see anyone doing this to her intentionally. Yes, making snide remarks or bitching about her. But to physically harm her? That's fucked up."

"You're new to this school. Anteros is super competitive about everything." I train my gaze on the doors to the back. "There are plenty of people who would stab you in the back to get your part."

Mia shakes her head.

The outside door bursts open. A woman similar in features and build to Evan races up to the front desk. I sit forward.

"Can I help you?" the receptionist asks.

"EvanAnn Ward. She was brought in. I'm her mother." Her hands shake and there's this anxious air around her.

After a second, the receptionist says, "She's in the back. I'll buzz you in."

"Thank you." Mrs. Ward goes to the door, and it buzzes, letting her back.

Heather Ward. At least she shows up when it matters.

"You can head out if you want," I say to Mia.

She shakes her head. "I've got nowhere else to be, and I want to make sure she's okay."

I get my phone out and text the group chat.

> ME:
>
> Fair warning
>
> Evan's mom is here

---

# Hawk

The nurse comes in to irrigate the wounds another time and to check how Annie is doing. Glancing at Cam's text message, I sit in the chair next to her bed, holding her other hand. Annie's mom is here, but I'm not pretending I don't give a shit about Annie. I've probably lost a few years off my life between her and Damon's accidents.

I'm ready to wrap her in Bubble Wrap. Or better, tie her to my bed for the rest of our lives to protect her. It's not rational, but fuck, I need to find a way to keep her safe. Damon tracks and records her, but I'm the one who ends up having to save her.

"Does it still burn?" The nurse doesn't look up from what she's doing.

"Not as much." Annie's voice is soft and a little hoarse. She watches the nurse intently like she can see what was in her wounds. It took time for the pain to become more manageable. Every minute was excruciating, watching her face contort with pain and not being able to do anything to help her.

The door opens, and everyone turns to see Annie's mom in the doorway. Her face is pale and she seems braced for the worst possible news.

"Evan, are you okay?" Heather looks at the nurse and wrings her hands, like she's afraid it's something much worse. "Is she okay?"

"She's fine." The nurse finishes and wraps the wounds in bandages. They're too close for Band-Aids, so they're currently wrapped in gauze. "Some sort of irritant was on the thorns that cut her. We treated her for an allergic reaction and flushed the wounds."

The nurse straightens on her stool. "She should be fine, but we can go over her discharge instructions again if you'd like."

Heather turns and sees me. Her brow furrows when she focuses on me and my hand holding Annie's.

The nurse stands and says, "I can print those out for you."

Heather nods and checks over Annie before returning her gaze to her hand in mine and then her bandaged hand. Heather swallows slightly. "Are you okay?"

"I'm fine," Annie's voice is shaky, but she makes sure to meet her mother's gaze. Her face is pale and streaked from tears. She's exhausted, and I just want to tuck her in my arms and never let anything bad happen to her again.

"I'll be right back." Heather examines Annie for another moment before she releases her breath and follows the woman.

Annie takes her hand from mine with a small smile and touches her bandages. "Mom doesn't do well with hospitals or doctors. We spent a lot of time in them during Dad's illnesses because of the treatments."

I bring her hand to my lips and press a kiss to her knuckles.

When she lifts her gaze to mine, I ask, "Is it better now? How do you feel?"

She blows out her breath. "Sore. Still burns a little, but nothing like when it happened. It felt like my hand was on fire, burning and melting from the inside out."

I touch her hair, tucking it behind her ear. "Cam's got someone looking into it, but we can also get the rose to the police."

"The police?" Heather says, catching the tail end of our conversation when she returns. She looks me over again, noticing how I'm still holding Annie's hand.

I don't let go and I'm not going to. I'm done pretending Annie's not mine.

Heather presses her lips together and narrows her eyes on me. "You're one of Damon's friends?"

Annie closes her eyes and takes a deep breath, like she doesn't want to deal with this. I'm not going to make this a thing like Damon would, but I'm also not going to deny that I love this girl.

"Yes, Hawk Wilker," I say, but I don't move away from Annie. She may not be ready to say I'm her boyfriend, but I'm not about to pretend

I don't care about her. "I'm part of EvanAnn's cast. I was there when it happened."

Heather stands near the door. Her arms wrapped around her middle. She's almost as pale as Annie. She focuses on Annie. "I still don't understand. You picked up a rose and the thorns cut you, but they treated you for chemical burns and an allergic reaction? You aren't allergic to anything."

Annie swallows and glances at me before returning her gaze to her mom. "Someone left a rose on my desk during the play. I picked it up to move it out of the way, and it cut me. But it wasn't just a prick. It burned and the wounds blistered. The pain was intense and I couldn't even think. We didn't know what was happening, so Hawk had Mia drive me to urgent care. The staff couldn't figure it out either, but there must have been something on the stem that got into the wounds. The actual cuts aren't severe. Just a lot of them. There was some swelling and blistering so they wanted to make sure I wasn't having an allergic reaction."

Heather steps into the room. She still seems really off. Like something is bothering her about the whole thing. Like she's missing a piece to the puzzle.

"Isn't Chase in your play?" Heather asks. "I'm surprised he didn't help you. He always seemed so nice."

Annie gives me a wary glance before meeting her mom's eyes. "Did you get my text, Mom?"

She smiles and waves her hand. "Yes, you two broke up. That happens in high school sometimes, but it doesn't mean you two don't care for each other still. It may come back around. Maybe he gave you the rose to apologize?"

"If he gave me the rose, it didn't work. Besides, I don't think we're going to get back together." Annie glances down at her hand.

She doesn't *think* they'll get back together? What the fuck? What all was in that text to her mom? Just that they broke up? Not all the shit Chase put her through? All the reasons they shouldn't be together? Obviously nothing about us.

Because if Heather knew what Chase had done, she'd be the worst mother ever if she wanted her daughter to get back with that asshole.

And while Damon's opinion of Heather is low, I don't know what to think about her.

Heather cocks her head. "Do you want to talk about the breakup?" She glances my way. "Maybe later? We could watch our favorite movies and have pizza on the couch." Her eyes sparkle and she smiles as her eyes light up, which makes her look more like Annie. "Just the two of us tonight. What do you say? Girls' night. It's been forever."

When Annie turns to me and gives me a smile, I return it and squeeze her hand. We take what we can get from our parents. Her mom wants to spend time with her. Besides, I need to fill Damon and Cam in on everything, and we need to figure out who targeted our girl.

"I need to get going anyway. I'll text later." Standing, I run my hands over my jeans. Every instinct wants me to lean in and kiss Annie goodbye. Honestly, I don't want to leave her, even if it's with her mother. I blow out a breath and turn to Heather. "It was a pleasure, Mrs. Ward."

She gives me an odd, assessing look. "You can call me Heather."

I nod and with a quick look back at Annie, I head out.

---

## Damon

I grab the towel to wipe the sweat off my face and pick up my phone. There are multiple texts on the group chat with the guys. And more recently, a few from Evan.

I click on the ones from Evan first.

> LITTLE DEVIL:
>
> I'm okay
>
> Hanging out with my mom tonight

My brow furrows. She was at rehearsal and should have been home an hour ago. Dinner isn't for another half hour. I grab my water bottle and head upstairs while opening the texts from the guys. A rock settles in my gut with every text. Evan was hurt at rehearsal, and Hawk took her to urgent care.

Cam has someone looking at the rose that apparently hurt her so severely she needed to go to urgent care. What the fuck.

ME:
Come over

HAWK:
On our way

I walk out of the gym and make my way through the house to where I know Heather and Evan will be. I just need to see her with my own eyes.

The movie is loud and the lights are dimmed as I walk in the back of the rec room where I showed Evan my blackmail. She's curled into the corner of the couch under a blanket. Something happens on screen and they both laugh.

My gaze flicks to Heather, who sits close and has everything within reach for Evan. She's taking care of her daughter after ignoring her for weeks. My lips press together.

The need to scoop Evan up and take her upstairs where I can check over every inch of her is almost overwhelming. My gaze zeroes in on the bandages on her hand. She turns suddenly and locks eyes with me. Her smile is soft and happy, not begging me to save her.

She's good. It doesn't stop the need to check her over, but I can let it go while I find out from Cam and Hawk what we know so far.

I give her a small nod before I go up to my room and take a quick shower. When I walk into my room, the guys are on my couch with sodas, watching a game. I quietly dress in the background.

When I finish, I sit at my desk and lean forward with my elbows on my knees as they turn off the TV.

"She good?" Hawk leans back and watches me, like he knows I've already checked on her.

I nod and scrub a hand over my face. "What happened?"

Hawk goes through the whole incident. Cam lets me know what happened when he got there. Chase just happened to be there for everything. It was rehearsal and he's an actor in the play, so it's not necessarily suspicious. It could have easily been anyone else in the cast who happened to be in the hallway, but it wasn't.

"You said Brandt's play was also meeting?" I glance at them. So another whole set of suspects. My mind is working on everything, trying to figure out how anyone could have gotten in the room. Who could have placed the rose? What everyone's motives could have been.

"A lot of ants work on the weekend. Not just the drama students." Hawk runs his hand through his hair and glances at the doorway toward Evan's room. "But that also means someone who shouldn't be there would stand out more. There's no way Jackson snuck in and out of that practice. Someone would have seen him and thought it odd."

I nod. "But that doesn't mean it wasn't his idea."

"No, but why hurt her?" Cam taps his foot, like he wants to spring up and pace the room, but holds back. "Why would anyone hurt her?"

Evan shouldn't be a target to anyone. I drag in a breath. Unless we made her one.

"Chase." It makes sense. "We struck him hard with the catfishing."

Neither of them deny it. From that edge of guilt around their mouths, they both must have thought it.

"He doesn't know about Jackson though. At least we don't think he knows about Jackson." Cam puts his hands on his knees. "The note had *pretty girl* on it. That's what Jackson calls Evan."

"Do we have anything with Chase's handwriting?" Hawk asks. "We could compare it to the note."

Earlier, Cam texted us the pictures of the rose and the note.

I want it to be Jackson because then it's his fault. If it was Chase, then it's possible he's retaliating against what we did. Whether it's to get back at us for taking Evan in the first place or because of the other shit we've done to him, it would be our fault for kicking the hornet's nest. I don't think any of us believed Chase would strike out at Evan.

"It may not be his handwriting, but I'll see what I can find," Cam says.

"We need to narrow down the suspect pool," Hawk says.

A noise comes from Evan's room. I lift my head and watch for her. She'll come to me. She always does.

## CHAPTER 3
## *EvanAnn*

WITH A FULL BELLY and a light heart, I head up to bed after taking some pain meds and getting a fresh ice pack. The burning pain has faded to almost nothing, but Mom insisted on the meds. Just in case.

I didn't really explain any more about the breakup or Chase to her. Or why Hawk was holding my hand. A few times I thought Mom might ask, but then she didn't. I don't want to tell her about the guys or why Chase and I broke up. That he was cheating on me and everyone knew except me.

It's embarrassing. I still don't know if she'd move my room away from Damon's if she knew about us. It wouldn't really change anything. It's not like *she* has a nanny cam watching my every move. Only Damon does that.

But there's a possibility she'd want to move out to get me away from Damon if she knew.

At least Chase can't weaponize my mother's ignorance about our breakup against me now. The rose? Pretty sure Mom thinks it was an accident of some sort. Even the doctor didn't seem overly concerned. Just some irritant and a reminder to be careful picking up thorny roses.

They don't know about the texts or the car. There's no reason for them to be suspicious. I'm hoping the guys have something. It seems obvious that it's from Jackson, but maybe it's too obvious?

My head still feels a little fuzzy.

I walk into my room and hear voices through the bathroom. I'm already in pajamas. My pulse increases and warmth builds inside me just knowing they're near. Locking my door, I walk through to Damon's room.

"Hey, baby girl." Hawk holds his hand out to me, and I go to him, letting him draw me down onto his lap. Cam reaches over and takes my injured hand delicately. He looks over the bandages like he can tell if everything was done correctly.

"Goody." He lifts my fingers to his lips and kisses my fingertips delicately, one by one. A little shiver of awareness rolls down my spine.

My guys are all here. I can breathe.

I turn to look at Damon sitting at his desk. His expression is closed off, but I can tell he's angry. Not at me, but for me. His love shines in his eyes and fills me with warmth.

"It was capsaicin," he says. "On the rose. It was covered with chili pepper oil. The same thing they use in pepper spray."

I look at my fingers. They're considerably less swollen now than at the clinic. Chili pepper oil explains the burning. It seems so innocuous. Maybe the cuts made it worse? If you touch your eyes after touching peppers, it burns. Same concept with an open wound?

"There was a message on your desk. Did you notice it?" Cam asks.

I shake my head and rest it against Hawk's shoulder. Once the pain started, the world could have ended around me and I wouldn't have noticed. My head is heavy and I feel more tired than I did a few minutes ago.

I struggle to stay focused on what we're trying to figure out. Someone wanted me to hurt. Who wants to hurt me? Jackson? I didn't think he wanted to cause me pain, but those texts were aggressive. Finishing what he started?

A shiver crawls down my spine.

Even if it was him, how did he get into the school without being seen? Especially when not many students were there today.

A stranger in the building would have been noted by someone. Jackson isn't the type of guy who can hide in a crowd. He's tall and built like my guys. I can't imagine him sneaking in without being spotted.

"It read, *Enjoy your men, pretty girl. They'll only leave you burned.*" Cam rubs his hand over my knee to comfort me but also like he can't resist touching me. I put my hand over his, and he threads our fingers together. The need to be connected is mutual.

"Jackson," I say softly. The note's words send a chill through me as I consider them. The author definitely burned me. "He calls me pretty girl, but how would he have gotten into rehearsal?"

"He could have someone at our school working for him or with him," Cam says. "He doesn't have money, but he has some influence. At least people might think he does because of the school he attends and his hockey record."

"What do we know about Brandt Stanwell?" Damon leans forward with his hands clasped between his knees.

"Brandt?" I ask, a little confused and kind of sleepy. It's like all the energy just leaked out of me. I try to force myself to make sense of this train of thought. The other play rehearsal was happening at the same time today. They had the smaller theater room. So, Brandt would have been at the school. But what does he have to do with this?

Someone came after me hard. If anyone can figure out who it was, it should be the four of us.

Right now, I'm safe, and Hawk is so warm. Everything in me just wants to curl up against him and go to sleep. But I also want to be present for this conversation.

"Brandt's got money and connections," Cam says. It almost sounds like he's reading a file instead of pulling it from his memory. "An ant. Director of *The Crucible*. He doesn't make waves. Attends parties every now and then. Thinks he's the shit because of his famous parents and will tell anyone within earshot who his father is. But mostly, he does whatever it takes to win. Overall, I haven't heard anything too salacious about him."

"Would he go this far to sabotage Evan?" Damon's words are fading.

Sabotage? That's ridiculous. This is clearly Jackson from the note, and it didn't do anything except make me miss one rehearsal. Definitely not sabotage level. Besides, why would Brandt try to sabotage me? He already knows so many more industry professionals than I do. My eyelids are growing heavy. I need to pay attention. But I'm so tired, and the pain meds are making everything fuzzy around the edges.

"If it was something he wanted, maybe. It's questionable. His family has connections. He's going to make it one way or the other. He's in the fall showcase and there's an opportunity attached to it. But he's already set for success. The win won't matter in the long run. What would he really get from hurting Evan?" Cam brushes his hand over my hair, and a smile tugs at my lips. "She needs sleep."

"I have to go home." Hawk shifts me on his lap. I snuggle into him. "Both my parents are there and want to pretend to be a family. This morning Dad said we needed to talk."

I open my eyes. When did I close them?

"Mine too." Cam stands. "Or not exactly the same, but Dad wants a status report on my studying and grades, so kind of the same."

When Damon lifts me against him, I wrap my arms and legs around him and rest my head against his chest, inhaling his earthy scent and letting my whole body relax into him. Crazy as it is, he's my safe space.

Maybe he coerced me into being his, but now he's mine.

"I've got her." His words burrow into my heart and make a little home there.

I don't open my eyes as he walks with me to the door and locks it after they leave. I mumble my goodbyes at some point, but I don't even know if they're still here when I do. I wake up on his bed a little disoriented. When I try to turn, I'm drawn in closer to a body. My face is pressed against his warm chest and I release my breath.

"Go back to sleep, little devil."

My mind feels foggy. I try to wake up to think clearly, but the room is dark, and he's so warm beneath me. There's something he was talking about. Something I needed to ask. I want to understand his reasoning.

Oh, yeah...

"Do you really think Brandt is involved in what happened?" I ask.

Damon releases his breath and rubs his hand over my back. "He mentioned both Chase and Olivia at the party. It's like he was whispering in their ears about what they needed to do this year. Meaning you and me, respectively. The way he was talking felt like he was trying to get into my head too."

"Mmm, sounds like Iago."

"Iago?" He rubs my back soothingly.

"The manipulative character in *Othello* who causes everyone's death." I release my breath, not really thinking about what I'm saying. "That's who Chase wanted to be. His machinations are what drive the plot. His jealousy over Cassio..." I sigh, and the bed drags me into it.

"Sleep, little devil." Damon pulls me in tight against his warmth, keeping me safe.

I touch his face with my good hand and pat his cheek. "You're a good boyfriend."

He chuckles and takes my hand to rest it on his chest. His finger trails over my fingers and the ring.

"You moved your ring." Damon's voice is soft.

I lift my left hand in front of my face. Not that I can see it in the dark, but I imagine the weak light casting shadows glints off it. "My right hand was swelling. Seemed like the thing to do at the time. I could move it back now, probably."

"You don't need to, little devil." He catches my hand and brings it to his lips, kissing my knuckle above the ring. "I like my claim on you."

My heart spins happy and warm as I burrow against him. "I like your claim on me too."

---

## Hawk

I walk into the kitchen unclear on what to expect. The last time both of my parents had been home at the same time, the house felt cold and hostile. The silence was like a presence hanging over all of us.

But Dad said they wanted to talk this morning. Part of me hopes this is it. When they stop everything and figure out their shit, divorce and find something happy in their lives. I'm not naive enough to believe they should continue being together just for me. If they don't love each other anymore, it's time to let go.

We'll figure it out, but avoiding each other isn't helping anything.

I don't normally seek my parents out when they're home. We text so they know what I'm up to, and I know where they are usually. It's not like they completely neglect me, but I'm self-sufficient.

Tonight, I'm exhausted from what happened with Annie, and I just want to crash. But I need to get this over with.

The sound of voices floats down the hallway from the family room. It's odd to hear both my father's and mother's voices interwoven. The split happened so gradually I barely noticed when I started to hear only one voice at a time.

When one of them was home, the other was almost always gone. As a child, they were around more. Both travelled for work, but they usually found time to spend together and with me. I can't say when things changed, just that I was independent enough and trustworthy enough to leave on my own at some point.

I stop and lean in the doorway. Mom has her hair pulled back into a loose bun. She's wearing loungewear pants and a drapey top, a glass of red wine lifted to her lips. Dad sits relaxed in a pair of jeans and a long-sleeved shirt. His lips are curved into a smug smile, and he dangles his lowball glass of scotch on the rocks in his fingertips.

Mom notices me first. Smiling, she sets down her glass on the end table. "Hawk!"

When she stands, she wobbles just a little. Dad casually puts his hand on her hip to stabilize her. She puts her hand over his and her smile softens as their eyes meet.

I go still as I watch. Because this doesn't look like a couple on the verge of divorce. There's a warmth I haven't seen between them in years right now. It's almost fucking... cozy. I swallow and wait.

Mom straightens and comes over to me, pulling me into her arms.

"My boy." She runs her hand over my hair and stares up into my eyes with a smile. "How are you, my love?"

I glance at my dad, who takes a sip of his drink and waits for my answer. "Good."

Mom steps back. "Your father said you had your girlfriend over last night."

It's not phrased as a question, but there's a lot of curiosity in her eyes. I blow out a breath, and she takes my arm to pull me into their circle. I'm not used to having to explain myself. She sits and picks up her wine glass as I sit on the edge of the couch.

The back of my neck prickles with nerves. My dad smiles like we do this all the time. Like somehow he's comfortable with this. I blow out a breath.

"EvanAnn Ward. She's the one who's beating me for valedictorian." I rub my hands together and study the shared look between my parents. It's fucking weird. This whole thing is weird, but I don't want to point it out.

"Has she stayed over a lot?" Mom asks, like the answer doesn't matter, and takes a sip of her wine. But her eyes twinkle with curiosity. She wants to know.

"Not a lot." Fuck, this isn't what I want to talk about. My life is mine. I shift my focus to my dad. "What did you want to talk about?"

He has green eyes like me, and they harden just slightly as he leans forward to set his glass down. Is this cozy little family moment all a lie? A build up just to let me down? To pretend like we're going to be fine once they divorce?

My shoulders tense as if waiting for a blow.

"We know things haven't been easy these past few years." Dad reaches his hand out to Mom and she takes it.

I stare at their joined hands, trying to figure out if this is a reconciliation or a parting of ways. My stomach churns, but I lift my gaze to my dad's and wait. I don't know which choice would be preferable.

"Work pulled us in opposite directions." Mom smiles at Dad with a touch of sadness. "We all drifted apart."

"We decided to figure out if this living arrangement worked for us." Dad looks at Mom. His gaze softens. "We met up and decided we didn't want this to end. We still love each other and you. We put our careers ahead of our relationship for so long we almost lost it."

I clench my fists. "So what does this mean?"

"Well, we've taken vacation from work to sort some things out." Dad rubs his thumb over Mom's wrist as she smiles like he's the most brilliant man alive.

"So, Cabo?" I raise an eyebrow. It makes sense they came home to tell me they're going to work things out together. Alone. Which suits me just fine.

Mom laughs. "No. We'll be staying here. You're part of our family. We're a little bit broken, but with time, we'll be able to strengthen our bond again."

I open my mouth, but what the fuck am I supposed to say to that? That's great? I'm so excited for you? But seriously, I'm good? You two can fuck off to wherever you vanish to, and I'll continue with my life the way it is, because it works for me.

"This is a good thing, Hawk." Dad lowers his head and meets my eyes, almost like he's daring me to back talk them.

I glance at Mom's hopeful eyes. "I have a lot going on with hockey and the play."

Mom grins and settles into her chair. "Oh, yes, the play. *Othello*, right? I can't wait to watch it. When are your shows?"

"In about a month." I expect her to fly in for one of the shows. This can't last that long, right? A few days, maybe a week. My parents are devoted to their careers.

Mom lights up. "Perfect. That's how long we took off."

## CHAPTER 4
### *Damon*

Monday at school, everything feels the same as last week. With the exception that I drove Evan to school this morning so she wouldn't have to try to hold on. I re-bandaged her hand and looked over all the little cuts.

Between classes in the hallway, we make sure we're with Evan. Not an issue because Cam has her in literature and I have her in calculus and history. We make sure to take notes for her since her hand still hurts.

She has a red paper flower tucked behind her ear after first period that remained there through third. As I carry her tray out into the courtyard, Hawk has his arm wrapped around her waist.

"My parents are here to stay for at least the next month." He shakes his head. He texted us the details last night while Evan and I slept. Evan told me about them this morning. "I don't know how much I'll be able to get away with."

Evan blows out her breath as she sits on the bench next to me. Her left hand braces on my shoulder to help her lower down. She holds her hand with the white gauze wrapped around it up a little. "This is like waving a red flag in front of my mom. She made me breakfast this morning."

"I doubt she actually *made* you breakfast," I say.

She smirks at me. "Probably not. The staff made me breakfast. She just gave it to me."

"Fuck, goody." Cam sits down on the other side of Hawk. "I love it when you wear things I give you. Can I buy you more things to wear?" He gives her a cocky grin. "I mean, Damon practically dresses you every chance he gets. I'm sure some lingerie isn't out of the question."

Some heads turn from the table next to ours. Curious assholes. I narrow my eyes on the students, and they turn back to their own food. Fuck, sometimes I hate this school.

We're at a table of our own, away from the other people out in the courtyard. It's not like we wouldn't let someone sit with us. We did last week with some teammates and even Mia. But I'm wary of letting anyone close to Evan today. Someone got to her when we were watching. Hurt her.

It's not happening again.

Evan makes a small hissing noise and her brow furrows as she sets her hand in her lap. I noticed it in history too. Her hand hurts.

I take her pain meds from her backpack where I put them this morning and shake out a pill for her. She doesn't want to take medicine all day, but she can take the edge off at least.

Her blue-gray eyes meet mine and she smiles softly. "Thanks."

The rest of the courtyard is normal. Well, as normal as it can be with Olivia gone. There are rumors she's being transferred to an elite boarding school, which means she was asked not to come back to Deimos. By making it sound like it's voluntary, her family saves face.

Couldn't happen to a nicer bitch. She may not get time for what she did to Keira, but at least we don't have to deal with her. Putting that video out on social media means no one can sweep it quietly under the rug.

No one has really stepped into the vacancy as top bitch. Her friends Megan and Gemma sneer at us and talk behind their hands, but they aren't Olivia. They're still popular, but they're not as conniving as Olivia was. And while they hold some power, they aren't as rich as Olivia either. They were always second best to her.

The apparent queen bees of Anteros sit a little taller, talk a little louder. Maybe they think they can fill the void. They also make sure to ignore Evan like it's their job. Not that we even stoop to pass their table on the way to ours.

Mia sits with those girls today. Evan doesn't seem to mind, but if it becomes a problem, if *Mia* becomes a problem, we'll handle it. I still don't trust her. If she stabs Evan in the back, Evan will have one less friend, and I'll make sure the whole school knows what we think of Mia.

At the end of lunch, Mia comes over to claim Evan and take her to her acting seminar. I let her go reluctantly. I'd sit beside her all day if I didn't need to keep my grades up in my other classes.

Besides, I have the tracking app open on both Evan's ring and her phone all afternoon. It's the next best thing to having her on a camera. Which I would prefer, but Evan insisted wireless cameras would interfere with the sound equipment in the theater room.

I don't like any of this. Jackson hurt her. It has to be him. And if it is him, it means he isn't working alone. We've been worried about him trapping her somewhere, but we never expected this. He punished her by inflicting pain.

Not knowing when and how the stalker's going to strike next drives me nuts. It would be easier if I knew why he's so focused on her, but I can't figure out his motive. Why hurt her? Because of us? Assuming it's Jackson, what's his goal? Scare her into being with him?

Or is it just to scare her period? What kind of fucked up game is he playing?

My mind keeps twisting the puzzle around to try to find the solution. The problem is, this could be revenge. It might not have been Jackson. Chase could have done it, because of what we did to him. Hawk said Chase looked genuinely concerned when he carried Evan out, but was that an act? He is an actor.

Fuck. I need eyes on her. Maybe I'll check with my tech guy to see if he can hack the cameras in the school.

Right now, though, I have practice. That means no phone. I hate not being able to check in on Evan, but I have to focus. The towel guy, Rich, should be around here somewhere.

I nudge Cam. "Give Rich your phone to watch Evan while we're playing."

Cam nods and opens the apps. "I think you're paranoid but fuck it. I'm not risking it. Not after yesterday."

Hawk glances toward us. His face is solemn. He was there for her again when she needed someone. I'm grateful this doesn't all fall on me, but part of me wishes I hadn't been tied up working out. That I could have been the one to protect her and hold her when she was hurt.

Not that I could have.

It might have been a fucking disaster when Heather showed up at the urgent care. I don't know if I would have been able to control myself. To pretend like Evan was like a sister to me. Fuck that shit.

During practice, all three of us will be on the ice. No one can protect Evan if she needs us. It's a prime opportunity for whoever is after her. I run a hand through my hair and lock up my phone. But Rich will let us know if she moves outside the Anteros hallway.

As I make my way to the ice, Coach stops me.

"Storm, talk to me." He pulls me aside and jerks his head across the ice where some guys sit in the stands. "There's a coach who's interested in talking to you after practice. Show them what you're made of today, yeah?"

He claps me on the shoulder.

"Yes, Coach." I take the ice for warm-ups and glance over at the men watching. He didn't say what school they're from, but Crowne Mawr isn't far away. The Yale coach was in town this weekend though, so maybe it's him. Either way, I'll do what I've trained for years to do. Impress the fuck out of them.

I turn off all the extra shit going on and concentrate on the ice, my stick, the skates, and the puck. This is my future and I'm going to play like it's for keeps.

---

MY HAIR IS STILL WET FROM MY SHOWER WHEN I PULL OUT my phone again and check on Evan. The ring and phone are still together in the black box theater room. Good.

"Don't worry. I'm heading there now." Cam grabs his backpack from his locker and claps me on the shoulder. "Let me know how it goes."

I nod and drop my phone into my pocket before grabbing my bags and heading to Coach's office. Laughter carries into the hallway from the office as I approach the open door.

Coach grins when he sees me and gestures me in. "There he is."

I walk in and drop my stuff beside the door before turning to greet the man sitting in what's affectionately known as Coach's hot seat. If you're sitting in it, you're usually in trouble. When he stands and meets my eyes, this man needs no introductions. He was a legend in the NHL before he retired. He's also the current coach at Crowne Mawr.

Andrew Mitchell offers me his hand. "Damon Storm."

"Coach Mitchell." I try not to go all fanboy on him, but it just slips out. "That goal in 2015 for the Cup runs on repeat in my brain when I'm trying to bring in the puck. Your career is what I aspire to."

He grins and releases my hand. "Good, because I know you've probably got recruiters coming out of your ass trying to get you to come play for them. I'll use whatever leverage I can get."

Before the accident and injury, I had plenty of interest in my career. I had a plan for my future. When I glance at Coach, he leans back in his chair and puts his hands over his stomach with a satisfied smile. Apparently, he's taking a backseat on this one.

If Andrew knows I don't have a lot of options, it wouldn't put me in a great negotiating position.

"Maybe." Part of me doesn't want to admit it will be a struggle now. I would have had more options if I'd attended the USHL like I was supposed to. Options that might have included a contract for an NHL team. Last year, Crowne Mawr never would have been a contender. We were talking with quite a few recruiters unofficially, but knowing I was in an accident and had injured my leg made them leery. If I'd still attended the USHL, I could have shown them I healed, but Dad didn't want me to go. Which made it seem like the leg was going to be more of an issue than it is.

"Let's talk." Andrew smiles and offers me the seat next to him.

I perch on its edge, too anxious to relax. My knee bounces a couple times before I force it to settle. Crowne Mawr is Cam's school.

Last year this wouldn't have been an option, but I also didn't have Evan, Cam, and Hawk to think about. If this is a real opportunity, it could work for all of us. It wasn't on Evan's list of places she'd already applied to, but she mentioned it to my dad as a potential. And it's not a party school, even though Cam claims it is. It's a well-known school with a rigorous curriculum for Hawk.

"I recently took over coaching the hockey team at Crowne Mawr." Andrew gives me a cocky grin. "I know we're fresh on the D1 scene, but we're doing our best to compete with the big dogs. We're building a team to get us trophies and impress the NHL with our talent."

I straighten and keep my expression pleasant. "My coach thought your scouts might come to some games this season."

But that he came to practice to see me, that's a fucking honor.

"And we will, but there are some players we want to look at first, before they make their commitments." Andrew gives me a look like I'm going to have multiple offers coming in.

Last year I would have. Now, I'm not so sure. Deimos isn't a boarding school that usually gets hockey recruiters to come to it. Other sports, yes. And while our team is good, I'm definitely an outlier when it comes to the sport. We get a lot of recruiters from D2 schools though.

But that's not what I want.

"We've set up an invitation week for a few players to come and try out for the team before the season begins. See how you interact with our current players and each other." Andrew leans forward. "I know this is last minute for you, but when I found out you hadn't committed anywhere, I came to invite you personally. I want to start next year right. I've got players who will help us make waves this year, but I need to continue to develop fresh talent if I want to stay at the top."

Before this year, I could have gone to any number of colleges to sit on their bench for a year before having an opportunity to really play. I would have gotten ice time, but during games, it would have been short and far between. I don't know if Crowne Mawr will be settling, but if it is, I want something from it.

"What kind of playing time do you offer your freshmen?" I have nothing to lose by asking.

He smirks. "Honestly, I don't play by the old rules. If you want to fight to start as a freshman, I'm all for it. I want to build a team that can crush the competition. I don't want seniors pulling rank on my new players. I want everyone to try their hardest to be the best."

Satisfied with the answer, I say, "What are we looking at?"

# CHAPTER 5
## *Damon*

I'M WAITING at the dinner table when Dad and Heather walk in. Dad's eyes widen in surprise to see me, but he doesn't say anything as he takes his seat. Heather sits on his other side. Monday night isn't our typical night for family dinner.

Evan walks in next. She freezes for a moment. After Sunday, she was supposed to take it easy, but I know she still pushed through rehearsal today. They cut it an hour short though, so I figured she'd be here too.

I'm here because I need to talk to my dad.

And even I can admit dinner with Heather usually puts him in a better mood.

Evan catches herself and walks over to sit next to her mom. I don't know which is worse. Sitting next to her and not being able to touch her or sitting across from her and not making it obvious I want her.

I don't know how much longer we'll be able to keep what's happening from our parents with these mandatory dinners. It's hard not to go too far in the other direction and ignore Evan, which would also make him suspicious. Normally, I'd just skip until Dad forced me to put in an appearance. If the plan was still to get rid of Heather, dinners would have been a perfect way to push on any sore spots.

But I'm not about to let her take Evan away from me.

"Good to see you, Damon." Dad leans back in his chair at the head of the table, and the server brings out our meals.

"Are you doing okay, Evan? Are you in pain?" Her mom reaches over and touches the back of her bandaged hand delicately. Her brow is furrowed in concern. "You could have stayed home today. I would have stayed with you. You don't have to push yourself so hard."

"I'm good, Mom." Evan's smile is a little tight, but her eyes are soft for her mother. "I'm only a little sore from the cuts, but the burning is gone. It really wasn't that big of a deal."

The adults frown, and I tighten my fist. No one at this table believes that. Of course, the parents don't realize it wasn't an accident. They think Evan hurt her hand on the rose, and something irritated the wounds. They don't realize it was intentional.

They weren't there when it happened. They didn't hear her scream of pain. When Hawk described what happened, I don't know how he remained calm in that moment. But we're trained to handle stressful situations. To think on our feet. And he got her the medical attention she needed.

Whoever did that to her needs to pay.

"That's good." Heather blows out a breath and glances at my dad, who smiles at her. She relaxes and reaches out for his hand. When he takes it, it's a stark reminder that my dad is letting go of my mom. Or maybe Evan is right. Maybe they aren't letting them go but moving on the best they can.

When I look away, Evan watches me. Something settles in my chest. My future sits across from me. I just have to make it so we can stay together after we figure out who's stalking Evan.

When my plate is put in front of me, I say, "The hockey coach from Crowne Mawr was at practice today."

Evan's eyes widen and her smile grows as she looks like she wants to ask a million questions. I can tell she's excited, but I keep my focus on Dad. Besides, I don't know if her interest in Crowne Mawr at dinner that one time was real or feigned to divert the conversation from me. I guess I'll find out. Later.

Dad's face is like stone at first. Heather draws her hand back and tucks it on her own lap.

"It's a good school." He leans forward in his chair, watching me warily. "What did they want to talk about?"

"He's recruiting early for next year. Wants me to come up next week and spend time on campus with some other promising players. Play with the team and see if I'd be a good fit." I don't dare glance at Evan. It was a risk telling her in front of our parents. I assumed she'd be excited and trying to hold it in, but I also didn't have a chance to talk to her before this, to give her a heads up.

"You'll miss a week of school?" Dad's tone is flat. He's not excited about this opportunity. But it's about the education and not hockey with him. And since I know this about him...

"I'm caught up in all my classes and will work with my teachers to make sure I stay on top of everything. We'll be going to classes with the players to get a feel for the school as well." I take a bite of my steak and swallow before saying, "They make sure their athletes maintain above a three-point-oh GPA. They also encourage their players to get a degree if they decide to pursue a career in the NHL. There are a few different degree options I could see pursuing while I'm there."

Dad's eyes brighten. "It sounds like a good opportunity."

Since Heather and Evan did a girls' night, we didn't have our Sunday dinner. So I have more to tell him, but I knew to start with Crowne Mawr. Yale still might be a pipe dream if Cam really has blown his chances of attending like he thinks he has.

I don't want to get my dad's hopes up and then have it fall through. Or for me to get in and then reject the offer because as a group we decided Crowne Mawr suits our needs better.

"At his birthday party, Tom introduced me to the hockey coach from Yale. Coach Farrell wants us to come up for an unofficial visit in a few weekends."

Dad's smile grows and his eyes light up like it's fucking Christmas. "Yale." He turns to Heather. "I got my law degree there. It's a beautiful campus. We should all go. Make a weekend of it. Visit the school. Evan-Ann, they have an excellent drama program. It would be a good school for you. You'll love it there."

Evan clears her throat. Our gazes catch before hers slides to my dad. "I can't miss rehearsal. After the play is over, maybe I can go and visit."

For a second, that throws my dad as he considers leaving her alone for the weekend. That's not happening. Not with everything going on. Evan can't be left alone. But maybe he just really wants to make this a *family* trip.

He smiles. "Maybe you can go stay with Chase's family while we're gone."

I narrow my eyes at Evan. She needs to come clean about Chase. Otherwise I'll do it. There's no way I'd let her stay anywhere near Chase, especially not under his roof.

"No, dear," Heather says, touching my dad's arm. "Evan and Chase broke up."

The tightness in my chest releases. Thank fuck she finally told her mom.

One less hold on Evan. But I'm still not going to leave her on her own. There's too much going on right now. I'm concerned about next week, but Hawk and Cam can take care of her. And our parents will be here. The weekend we go to Yale, she can stay with Hawk and Cam. We can tell her mom and my dad whatever they need to hear to feel good about themselves.

"There must be a friend she can stay with." Dad sits back, waiting for Evan to start listing her friends. His eyes are narrowed on Heather. Obviously, he's not willing to go without her. I ignore the twist in my gut.

"I can ask Mia or Keira." Evan pushes her food around on her plate, holding her fork with her left hand, obviously not wanting to have to ask her new friends. She's used to being on her own, but that's not an option right now.

Definitely not Mia. I don't know enough about Keira, but Hawk seems to think she's good for Evan. I can't say anything at the table. Besides, if I'm away, Hawk or Cam will take care of her. I don't give a shit what our parents think. They were obviously cool with the idea of her staying with Chase's family.

Tonight I'll need to talk to the guys about next week. After this rose situation, I'm not leaving anything to chance. Evan won't be left alone, and I can't count on our parents being here to protect her. I'd take her with me, but the program has me staying in the dorms with someone on the team.

Besides, Evan would never leave while she has her play.

Heather clears her throat and puts her hand on Evan's back.

"Why don't I stay home with Evan? You two go up to Yale. Evan and I will go later." Heather rubs Evan's back and smiles. "That way I'm here if an emergency happens. We're used to being on our own."

"It doesn't need to be decided tonight. We'll need to work out which weekend is best." Dad straightens and looks at me like I've made his day. "Yale."

Maybe Cam's dad isn't the only one wanting a Yale grad. Yale sours a little in my opinion. Suddenly Crowne Mawr looks like the better option, even though it's closer to home.

---

### EvanAnn

I sit on the counter in the bathroom as Damon unwraps my hand. The marble is cool against the backs of my thighs. He's in his boxers and I'm in panties with one of his Devil shirts on. He's intently focused on my fingers and each of the wounds. The swelling has gone down, and the wounds are no longer red and irritated. They ache a little, but nothing like the intensity of that burn.

"I can do this, Damon."

His gaze flicks up to mine and he frowns. "Let me take care of you."

My heart skips a little and I nod. No one has ever taken care of me the way he does.

He gently washes and dries my hand before applying the antibacterial gel and putting new bandages on. There are a few cuts that are larger, but the irritant of the oil made everything so much worse.

I clear my throat, and he lifts his gaze to mine.

"That was some big news at dinner tonight," I say softly.

The corner of his lip tips up slightly. "It's Cam's choice for college. You've said it would be good for film. And Hawk will do great wherever he lands. It's a reasonable choice for all of us."

"Do you really think Crowne Mawr will be enough for you?" I worry he's settling to be with us. It's in-state, and I didn't lie. It does have an excellent drama school for film. It's getting more recognition, and being part of a growing program might be perfect for me.

He smirks as he puts the last Band-Aid on. "I'll know better when I see the school and the team in action. Would it be settling for you?"

His blue eyes search mine like he's waiting for me to lie to him. I'm the one who insisted neither of us settle. It's important to hold that line. While we can both suffer a few bad decisions and still have good careers, why risk it?

"I've been researching the school for a while. I haven't applied yet, but that doesn't mean I don't want to go." Releasing my breath, I lift my hands to circle the back of his neck, careful not to actually use my injured hand and just rest my forearm on his shoulder. His hair is still damp from the shower he insisted we take before he worked on my hand. Where he lifted me and fucked me against the tile. He held my wrists with one hand while the other lifted my ass to hold me in place.

He claimed holding my wrists was to keep my hand from getting wet. But that helpless feeling makes an inferno roar inside me, and we both know it. I smile as I tangle my hand in his hair. His eyes darken, and my insides tighten in anticipation.

"If you could do anything next year, where would you go?" He lifts me up against him, and I wrap my legs around him and hold on as he carries me into his bedroom. "The ultimate dream. No restrictions."

He lowers me flat onto the bed, following me down. His lips tease the skin of my neck, and his cock presses against my pussy, making me ache for him again. I don't know how I'll survive a week without his touch. Without him in our bed.

"The ultimate dream?" Honestly, I'm living it. Him, Hawk, and Cam. Before them, the dream was much tighter, more defined, but I can't imagine a life without them in it. I'm not stupid. Our relationship could end. I know that, but there's this whisper of hope that keeps saying, but what if it doesn't? What if I can have it all?

He pushes up my shirt over my hips and drags his hand along the waistband of my panties. "Tell me, little devil."

His blue eyes are wicked as he trails kisses down the front of my shirt before reaching my belly, pressing wet kisses against my skin. I suck in a breath and tighten my fingers in his hair.

"I'd obviously get the internship. Either one. The showcase win with Alexis Bloom or the one I applied to with Sandra Cox. They would both work in the long run, but the showcase is only the summer, so I'll be able to attend college in the fall."

He drags my panties down as he kisses lower and lower. Each kiss brands me. He'll leave marks on my stomach from where he pauses and sucks and teases me with his teeth and tongue. My breath catches as the familiar heat roars into a blaze.

"Tell me more," he says as his heated gaze flicks up to mine.

I swallow as he strips my panties off and spreads my legs wide, settling between them. His hungry gaze drops to my pussy before him. I shift my gaze to the ceiling, trying to focus on what he wants to know and not what he's about to do to me. "Sandra Cox is amazing. The mentorship is a year with the potential to continue during college. I could take a lighter load of college work remotely while working for her, plus I have enough AP credits that would cover most of my freshman year anyway. But a lot of her work is on location."

Damon spreads my pussy open and slides his tongue over me. My breath catches. He sinks his fingers inside me, pressing forward as he latches on to my clit, sucking.

I gasp and tug on his hair, pulling him closer. He chuckles against me as he thrusts his fingers in and out. He's amazing at this. I'm addicted to having all three of them and what they can do to me.

"What college is your dream college?" he asks before getting back to work, driving me crazy. Lips, tongue, and teeth determined to drive me wild while he asks me about my dreams, about my future. A future that includes them now.

"I'd love to be in New York City even though most of the schools there are more theater-based." I pause and let out a breathy sigh. My hips rock against his face. I swallow and say, "I want to continue to grow as a director and actor." I cut off on a moan as he pushes me close to the edge. "Damon," I plead, needing my release.

"Actor?" He licks my clit before sucking on it again.

My lips part, maybe to tell him, maybe to moan, but I can't focus.

I can't answer him as everything bursts inside me. I cry out, and he keeps me in that moment, sucking and licking and biting. He shifts and suddenly he's over me. He thrusts his cock into my still pulsing pussy and pushes me right back over the edge again.

"Oh, fuck, Damon."

"You take me so well, little devil." He gives me a cocky smirk, grabs my hip and the headboard, and fucks me hard. My fingers clutch at his hair as he sucks on my neck. My brain is on full meltdown. I can't draw enough breath to say anything even if I could put together a cohesive thought. It's like riding a roller coaster that's all twists and steep drops, exhilarating, breathtaking.

He lifts my hip as he claims me. My legs shake as I wrap them around his waist. I never knew what sex would be like before these guys. I've read about it. Given myself orgasms. But nothing has been like this.

This wildness. The savageness with which Damon and Hawk claim me. The fun side Cam has shown me. The love that melts my heart when we come together. I want it all and I have it all with them.

Would I trade this for a future without them? If I could have my dream, would I choose it over them? Could my dream without them ever be enough?

I arch against him as my release spreads through me like slipping into a hot bathtub, submerged in his heat. He groans and the pulse of his cum fills me. When he collapses on me, I take his weight greedily. It's one of the best feelings having him inside me and weighing me down into the mattress. He never gives me his full weight, but I wouldn't complain if he did.

Our breathing eases together, our bodies still clinging to each other.

"You still want to act, little devil?" Damon kisses me and pulls out, rolling to the bed beside me and dragging me half over him. I set my bandaged hand over his heart.

There's so much I could say about that. Give him all the reasons why I chose directing over acting at Anteros. I take a moment because I want to explain this so he understands.

"Acting was my first love. Directing is great. I enjoy being behind the camera or in the audience and making sure everything goes to plan." His heartbeat slows beneath my touch. I kiss his chest and rest my cheek on his shoulder, snuggling in tight against him. He holds me close where I fit. "But there's something about bringing a character into being. I can control a lot of things being the director, but the actors are who make the characters. With the right direction, I can sometimes bring that performance out of them, but it's nothing like stepping into someone else's shoes and becoming them. As the director, I can bring the story to life. As an actor, I can bring my character to life."

Damon trails his hand down my back. "Would Crowne Mawr be settling for you?"

Hearing those words tossed back at me makes me really consider it. "The program is excellent. Surprisingly some of the best programs aren't in New York or California. Crowne Mawr is affordable. State tuition. Scholarships for academic performance."

"But will it be what you need?" He presses because I would do the same to him for any college we might attend. With four of us, it seems impossible one of us won't have to settle for something less than what we could achieve.

I blow out a breath across his chest. What I need is them. Can I really see a future without them in it? It used to be easy to see myself going away from all this. Even leaving my mom didn't really bother me because I knew she'd be okay without me.

"It can be what I need. They allow you to dual study in acting and directing. It's the first thing that caught my attention." I lift my head and meet his eyes. "As long as it's with you, Cam, and Hawk. I need you, and I don't think I can give this up."

He slides his hand into my hair and draws me higher so our lips meet. I settle back on his chest, and he turns out the light.

I'm almost asleep when he says in a low voice, "Dreams change, Evan."

## CHAPTER 6
## EvanAnn

Tuesday is more of the same. We go to class. Abby and her clique glare at me during lunch and watch my men like they should be on the menu. I try to ignore them the way they usually ignore me.

Hawk talks to me about the play and asks me questions about some of the directions I'm giving. We're off book now. Everyone has their lines memorized. We're working on the little things to tweak the performance. The things that will hopefully make it unforgettable.

Mia comes over at the end of lunch so she can walk with me to our class and sits down with a huff. "We need to discuss a joint custody arrangement."

Damon arches an eyebrow at her but shakes his head and looks back down at the book he's been studying for his test next period.

"What do you mean?" I ask and gather my things to head to class. "Who are we sharing custody of?"

"You. I get that you guys are new and need your space, but Abby can be such a bitch," she says in a low voice. "The way she pisses and moans, you'd think she actually had a shot with Damon, Hawk, or Cam, and you fucked that up for her."

I laugh. It's like Olivia was gatekeeping Damon before, and without her here, it's open season on him. I'm not blind. I've seen the way other girls look at them. Hawk and Cam have always been more accessible.

But Olivia allowed girls to be with Damon. Not that I want to think about any of them with other girls.

Hawk rolls his eyes. "I fucked Abby once years ago. It wasn't memorable."

My laughter stops as my chest burns and my stomach twists. We haven't really talked about all the girls they've slept with. After all, Hawk had a reputation for getting around. So did Cam. Damon was more particular, I guess.

I don't really know. I only know what I overheard shared in the girl's locker room. Or when someone desperately needed to pass on the latest gossip and decided to confide in me. And now that I think about it, Abby did say she fucked Hawk in the bathroom during auditions. But it didn't matter then. Does it matter now?

"She just wants to take Olivia's place as queen bee." Cam shakes his head. His dark eyes look over at their table. "It's sad when you think about it. She's probably just as wealthy and pretty as Olivia, but the hierarchy always divides along the schools first."

"She's just jealous you not only got the hottest guy in school." Mia smirks. "But you got the three hottest guys in school. I doubt any of those girls would be willing to try to please three guys at once though. They seem too selfish."

Damon rolls his eyes as he closes his book. He grabs the back of my neck and kisses me hard, possessive. "I'm not sharing Evan for lunch."

I inhale and glance at Mia's amused face. "Maybe you could eat over here with us more."

"Maybe." Mia stands and waits for me to join her. "It's no fun when I can't flirt."

"You could flirt with me," I offer with a cheeky grin.

She laughs and shakes her head. "Don't tempt me."

Hawk gives me a kiss before I stand. After I get up, Cam grabs me to kiss me before releasing me to Mia. He pats my ass. When I arch an eyebrow, he smirks and makes a kissy face.

"Behave, goody," Cam calls after us.

"You really are the luckiest girl in school." Mia leans into me as we walk to class.

"You have Liam and Fletcher," I point out. "It's not like they aren't hot. And hockey players. And two of them."

Mia smiles smugly. "Who knew I could be a two-guy type of girl? Usually I don't settle on even one guy, but those two definitely make it worth my while."

"Okay, change of topic." I smile as we reach the Anteros building. I'm trying to talk about more than boys with Mia. "What do you think of the new Taylor Swift album?"

Mia's eyes light up, and she bumps into my shoulder with hers. "So fucking good."

We walk into senior acting discussing the merits of each song and which ones are our favorites. Mr. Watson is already seated, so we grab chairs to drag out to the center of the stage.

He glances at Mia before he looks at me. "How's the hand?"

"It's healing," I say and set my bag on the floor beside me.

We haven't told anyone there was something on the rose. Mr. Watson emailed me the incident report he filed with the school. There's not much detail, just that I was cut and had to go to urgent care to have it looked at. The rumor mill believes I have an allergy to roses and that's what caused the emergency. It feeds into my dislike of actual roses.

We weren't able to find much more even after digging. We know someone planted it on the desk and that person couldn't have been Jackson.

There are cameras Damon accessed in the hallways and the parking lot. I try not to think about whether he had limited access to the recordings or if he's now stalking me at school too.

Jackson couldn't exactly sneak into our performance and leave the rose without someone seeing him. He stands out as much as Damon, Hawk, and Cam do. And if he'd tried to sneak in during rehearsal, the light from the hallway would have given him away. It's almost impossible to be sitting in the audience and not notice when the door opens and closes.

That means he's either working with someone from my school, or someone in my school knows more than they're letting on. How would they know about *pretty girl*? Someone could have overheard him call me that at the football game. Or even the hockey scrimmage.

It's not like the stands were completely empty. But how would they put the pieces together, even if Jackson called me that and they overheard? How would they know he had the potential to stalk me?

Even though it was a weekend, a lot of people were carrying backpacks to do homework during breaks or when they weren't on stage. Anyone could have brought the rose into the theater or left it there earlier.

We've tried to make a list of comings and goings. But we don't know if the rose was put there during rehearsal or the beginning of the break while I was talking to Mr. Watson.

"Today you'll be working with a scene partner." Mr. Watson stands and goes to shut the door after Crystal rushes in. I focus on class.

He passes out scripts. "Find a partner to work with."

I glance over the pages and see it's characters of opposite sexes. Mia gives me a sad smile before she turns to the guy on her other side. I blow out a breath and my eyes collide with Chase's. He smirks. Hell no, I'd do a one-woman show before doing anything with Chase Chadwick.

Mark steps between us. "How about it, director? Need a partner."

My hero. I sigh with relief and nod at Mark. I didn't want to get stuck with Chase, but Mark is an amazing actor who I haven't actually acted with. So I'm a little excited about this opportunity. We walk over to a section in the audience away from the others rehearsing their lines and sit down.

He glances at my hand but doesn't say anything about the bandages. I didn't miss much of Sunday's rehearsal, and even though we cut it short last night, things are going well with *Othello*. Obviously, what happened hasn't held me back.

He clears his throat and asks with a raised eyebrow, "So I'll be Rick and you'll be Cathy?"

I smile. "We could do it opposite just to throw everyone else off."

He chuckles. "We could, but I'm not sure how I'll look in a skirt." He leans in like he's telling me a secret and loudly whispers, "Knobby knees."

I shake my head and smother the little laugh that wants to erupt. I've always appreciated Mark's seriousness for the craft, but getting to know him through *Othello* has given me an appreciation for the guy he is. He's punctual and prepared. Smart and insightful when taking notes. He looks at his character through a lens not many can.

And when he's not on stage, he can be funny and inspiring despite his intensity with acting.

We run through the class scene a few times, each time tweaking our performances to match the other's. It's the easiest scene read I've had to do. Mr. Watson walks the room during class and stops at each set of partners to see how they're doing.

When it's our turn to perform for him, he nods. "You two are excellent. It's a shame we couldn't have capitalized on this pairing earlier."

"Thank you," I say. That's the best compliment I've heard during acting class.

"We all have different parts to play," Mark says. "EvanAnn chose to follow directing. I focused on acting. We didn't have as many opportunities before this year to work together."

Mr. Watson asks us to run the lines again with another tweak, and then satisfied, he moves on. I kind of wish Mark had been my scene partner last year instead of Chase.

Toward the end of class, we head back to our chairs. Everyone performs their scene and then we discuss how the exercise went for our groups. When I grab my bag at the end of class, Mark comes over.

"I do think you could have continued with acting if you wanted. Not that you aren't an amazing director, but..." He shrugs. "I wish they allowed you to do both here."

"Thank you." My cheeks heat at the praise I hadn't really expected. "I've always thought you were brilliant too."

He gives me a smile. "I'll see you at rehearsal tonight."

Mia stands and walks with me to the door. Keira waits in the hallway for me, looking at her phone. She doesn't look up when we stop next to her.

"Did you know Mark is gay?" Mia says to me in a hushed tone. "He's not out, but he told me last weekend when I tried to hit on him again."

My mouth opens and closes.

"Are you supposed to tell me that?" I can't help but ask because if he told her in confidence...

She chuckles. "I think he'd rather not have three hockey players breathing down his neck if Chase decides to poke your men with Mark." She pauses and seems to consider for a moment before she grins. "Actually, Mark might be into that."

I shake my head. "The guys wouldn't go that far. Hawk likes Mark. He's a good guy. And it wouldn't matter if he were straight. Me and my guys are good. We trust each other."

Keira smiles. "I couldn't imagine having more than one guy coming at me."

"You would if you knew what it was like." Mia winks. "I'm going to go find me a hockey player of my own."

She backs away down the hall with a sly smile and a quick wave.

Keira shakes her head. "Is the sex kitten thing an act?"

I release a breath. "Honestly, I don't know. She definitely comes off like sex is the only thing that holds her interest outside of acting. But if it's covering up something, I wouldn't be able to tell you what."

"Hmm." Keira turns and we head toward our directing classes. "I don't know if I trust anyone that's so one note. Take Chase. He plays the good guy, but he's a lying snake in the grass."

"I think Mia just hasn't really had the chance to be herself." We walk in and sit at our table for class. "She's been framed in a certain way by everyone around her for years. Maybe the sex kitten act was a disguise she wore at one point, but it became more comfortable than who she really is. She might not want anyone to see the real her."

It's easy to put on a mask when people think something of you. The guys thought I was a whore. How easy was it for me to fall into bed with three guys when I knew they thought that's who I was? They didn't even realize I didn't have any experience. I mean, they figured I wasn't very good at it, but I'm a quick learner.

"I'm just surprised she didn't try to reinvent herself for a new school. I know I would." Keira taps her pen on her tablet. "Isn't that the whole reason people go off to college? To escape who they became in high school?"

I turn her words over in my head as Brandt comes in. He stops at my desk while his assistant director goes to their table. I wait for whatever he needs to say. Neither of us do small talk.

"Heard about the accident on Sunday." He studies my hand like he can see the wounds through the bandages. "Shame you missed part of rehearsal for it. You don't think it might have been your angry ex-boyfriend who you fucked around on? After all, he would know you're allergic to roses, right? Or is this a recent allergy?"

For a moment, I'm stunned. We're not friends. We're barely classmates. Yes, it could have been Chase for a number of reasons, but why would Brandt point that out? What does he gain by throwing Chase under the bus? Damon's words about Brandt come back to me. Manipulative.

I school my features, prepared to improvise. I cock my head and study him like he's something I need to figure out. "Do you know something I don't?"

Brandt chuckles. "As a director, I'm constantly evaluating other people's life choices. Chase thought he had a good thing with you. After all, he could fuck around and no one let you know. His reputation with his parents soared. He even got asked by one of his dad's friends to audition for a film the friend is working on this summer."

I didn't know about the audition, but it doesn't surprise me. Chase will always end up on the right side of life. He has money and connections, and he can be charming when he wants to be. He has everything he needs. Damon can take away everything right now, but in the end, the universe will just give it right back to Chase.

"He sprained his knee recently." Brandt rubs his chin. "Funny thing that. No one really knows how. It wasn't during football practice. He's been pretty tight-lipped about it. Especially after the glitter incident. You wouldn't know anything about it, would you?"

"How would she? She's not his girlfriend anymore." Keira steps in to defend me, but I kind of like listening to Brandt's thinking.

Especially since he's pushing me to believe the lead in my play is trying to hurt me. Chase was in the hallway when I found the flower. Hawk said he was flirting with Sophie right before I screamed. Unless they just started flirting, he wouldn't have had time to drop the rose, hide the gloves or dispose of whatever he used to carry it in, and then race to the hallway to be found by Hawk.

Unless the rose was there earlier and we didn't notice it. We don't have a clear timeline of when the flower appeared.

Brandt gives Keira a fake smile. "Know your place, ant."

I furrow my brow at Brandt. "We're all ants."

Brandt smirks and shakes his head smugly. "Not really. We all know there are some who have what it takes to make it in this industry." He looks pointedly at Keira. "And those that won't."

"That's enough." I stand and get in Brandt's face.

He holds his hands up and laughs as he steps back. "Feeling powerful with the Devil's trio at your back." He lowers his hand. "Power is intoxicating, isn't it?"

He steps away and the instructor calls for our attention. What game is Brandt playing? And why does it feel like he's at least ten moves ahead of me?

I'll catch up though. I have to. I'm sick of not controlling my own narrative.

## CHAPTER 7
## *EvanAnn*

When I get out of my last class of the day, Keira walks with me to the black box theater for rehearsal. Mia leans beside the door waiting for us. It's getting a little frustrating being constantly babysat, but it's better than the guys following me around and missing their classes.

"Everything good?" she asks with a look at my hand.

"No more pain meds." I give her my audition smile. A year ago, I would have been happy with all this attention, so I let the smile sink in and soften. My friend is worried about me. "The pain is more manageable now. Just a little sore from all the cuts and unintentional bumping that happens during the day."

"Any word on who might have left the rose?" Mia cocks her head a little.

"No." Nothing new, unfortunately. We really don't expect anyone to own up to it.

"Mia!" Abby draws our attention as she walks over with a grin. "I didn't know you had rehearsal tonight too."

Abby tosses her long, dark hair over her shoulder and glances at me like she didn't notice me standing here. Her face goes blank as her dark eyes flick up and down me with disdain before dismissing me.

I release my breath, grateful, because I don't really want to play nice with her right now. And if she tried to include me in the conversation, I'd have to smile and be polite when I really want to start a catfight.

Hawk fucked her. I knew Chase obviously fucked her, but I was aware of it going into my relationship with him. But the guys and I didn't talk about exes or girls they slept with. I haven't really thought about all the girls they've been with until lunchtime. Now I can't help but wonder who else my guys have been with.

Which other girls know what they're like in bed? Or how it feels to have their attention focused solely on her pleasure? Is it possible to be jealous of the people they were with before me? Is that really the person I want to be?

"Anyway." Abby flicks her hair over her shoulder and focuses on Mia. "I wanted to see if you could come over to dinner at my house tonight. After rehearsal, of course."

Mia's gaze narrows slightly on Abby like she's aware Abby's trying to make me jealous. Well, congrats, it's working. I haven't even asked Mia over for dinner, but Mia hasn't offered either.

It was awkward when she didn't know I was living with Damon. But she knows now, so should I?

What about sleepovers? Damon's going to be gone next week. Maybe she could come and stay with me one night. Tomorrow night after dinner, the guys and I are supposed to talk about the plan for next week. I could mention that option.

"That's nice. I'll see what my aunt says." Mia doesn't sound thrilled, which gives me a little hope. It's hard to not be at least friendly with other people in our school. You never know who will make or break your career based on their experience with you in high school.

"I figured you'd have time since your *bestie* is busy with her men." Abby's gaze flicks to me with disgust. When I don't react, she adds, "You know they're just using you for sex."

I chuckle. "That's cute. Hate to tell you, but I'm using them for sex too."

Abby rolls her eyes. "Whatever. It's not like you guys are all going to get married. It's not even legal. They'll want girlfriends of their own someday."

"Okay." I shrug and turn to go into the theater room.

"You should enjoy it while it lasts," Abby calls after me.

I pause with the door open and turn back. I give her a gloating smile, because they're mine now. "I will."

---

Rehearsal is the normal length today. After a couple hours, we take a break. It's right around when hockey practice ends, so Hawk joins us. I nod at him from my desk as I look over the script and my notes, trying to make sure I'm not missing any important notes to give the actors tonight.

He sets his things down and comes over. It's not exactly easy to ignore him. I could, but I really don't want to. I blow out a breath, pull my focus from the script in front of me to meet his green eyes, and arch an eyebrow expectantly.

"Come on, Annie." He holds his hand out to me. He's got that determined look on his face, which means he thinks I need something. A little sizzle races through my veins, but I try to cool it. What I need to do is focus.

I glance at his hand, but don't move.

He smirks and crouches next to my chair. "How long is the break?"

I glance at my phone. Long enough to eat if the cast needs to. He grins when he catches my expression.

"A long one then. You've been working all day, Annie. Take a breather with me." He stands and offers again. "I promise not to take all your precious time."

With a reluctant sigh and a hot burst of anticipation, I scoot my chair back and take his hand. He leads me into the hallway where some of the cast stand around looking at their phones or eating. They glance up as the door opens to see who came out and then return to what they were doing.

Hawk draws me down the hallway and around the corner. No one is here.

Shivers curl around my spine as he leads me to a closet and opens the door. With a smile, he tugs me inside, turns on the light, and locks the door behind us.

I swallow and look up to meet his green eyes. He's studying me closely. When he slides his hand around the nape of my neck, I gasp in a breath at the rush of tingles sweeping through me.

Every fucking time.

Maybe I could use a little of what he's offering.

"You look stressed out, baby girl." He pulls me in tighter to him and strokes the corner of my jaw with his thumb. He tips my chin up so he can search my eyes, like he can see inside me. "What's wrong?"

I've put Abby out of my head for the most part to focus on rehearsal. But now, with Hawk looking at me, I can't help but wonder if he looked at her this way too. Did he ever care about her? How her day went? Or was it just a physical thing?

"I..." Fuck. I close my eyes.

"What is it, Annie?"

I open my eyes, and his are concerned. I put my hand over his heart and feel the steady beat against my palm, letting that warmth fill my cold veins. "It's stupid."

"If it's bothering you, it isn't stupid."

I look to the side. "I can't stop thinking about you fucking Abby."

He exhales and turns my chin so our eyes meet again. The green is soft. "You knew we weren't virgins."

My cheeks heat. "I didn't care when I was just using you to explore sex."

The words slip out, and my heart thumps hard against my breastbone. Now, I love them, and that makes me so much more vulnerable to them. If they leave me, it will cut me so fucking deep. If they cheated on me, I'd be crushed.

His chuckle is a little dark when he backs me up against the wall. His hand covers mine over his heart. He brings his forehead down to rest against mine. For a moment, he's quiet. His breath and mine are the only sounds in the closet. His heartbeat steady against my palm.

"Do you feel that, baby girl?" His voice is confident and soft. "Do you feel my heartbeat?"

"Yes," I whisper back, feeling him surround me. That hint of citrus and parchment fills my nose. His heart rate increases, and mine does the same.

"I've fucked other girls. The sex didn't mean anything to me. *They* didn't mean anything to me." Hawk cradles my head in his hands and his lips brush against mine. "You are my everything. My heart only beats for you, baby girl. It belongs to you. No one else has had it before. No one else will ever make me feel the way you do."

My heart warms.

"Hawk, I love you." Each word brushes my lips against his. I want to sink into him, give in to that need to be claimed by him, to prove that he's mine and I'm his.

"I've never loved anyone the way I love you." He kisses me, gentle, claiming.

I keep my hand on his heart, feeling the way it races against my palm as we explore each other's mouths like it's the first time. Like we have forever to be in this moment. Time ceases to exist as we just kiss.

His phone alarm goes off and he pulls back, taking it out of his pocket.

"Time's up, baby girl." He smiles and brushes his thumb against my lips. "Did you get what you needed?"

I nod and step into him, wrapping my arms around his waist. My ear rests against his beating heart, and I breathe this moment in. Warmth spreads through me at the thought of his love, knowing I'm theirs and they're mine.

That's all that matters now.

---

## CAM

Officially off house arrest, I stay at school after practice. Hawk went into rehearsal while I snuck into the back of the other theater room. Almost all of the cast is on stage. In the audience, Becca Anderson looks up from the magazine she's flipping through.

She arches a perfectly trimmed and shaded eyebrow at me. "You done with your little freak? Need a real woman to satisfy your urges?"

I sit a few chairs down from her and put my feet up on the seat in front of me. I smirk. "Nah. Checking out my girl's competition. For the play."

Becca lets out an undignified snort. "Whatever. Just be quiet or Brandt will yell at me again."

I glance toward the stage and then at Becca. "Are you in time-out?"

She laughs softly. "He didn't like my *energy* tonight." She glances toward him and flips off his back. "He's such a little nepo-baby."

"You're not wrong." I stretch out and watch as Brandt walks Abby through the scene step by step. She doesn't look impressed.

When his back is turned to her, she glances over at Becca and makes a face.

"So, no love for the director over here then?" I ask. Everyone in Evan's cast treats her with respect, because she treats them with respect.

"Hardly." Becca rolls her eyes. "But what are you going to do? He's got loads of contacts at his beck and call. EvanAnn is obviously the better director, but they just tote her around as the scholarship kid."

"They?" I keep my tone politely interested.

She waves her hand vaguely. "Them. They. Like, the people at the school who matter."

I nod. "So you're in here hoping to get in good with Brandt for the potential lift he may give to your career."

"Duh." She looks down at her magazine and flips the page. "At least we're past the point of having to do other stuff to get a role."

My lips tighten. I'm kind of grateful Evan is on this side of the camera. I don't know how I'd handle it if someone made her uncomfortable on a set. But I can guarantee it wouldn't end well.

"EvanAnn doesn't need to worry. She's got it made. This school is determined to make her something. To have her come back in twenty years and give some grand speech about how she couldn't have made it without this program. Some of us aren't so lucky." Becca frowns at the page in front of her. "We're just here to keep the lights on."

That's the biggest load of bullshit I've heard. "You've got a shot. It's not like your parents won't help you out."

Becca scoffs and lifts her blue eyes to mine. "I look like a thousand other wannabe actresses. I'm not even the lead in plays at school. I'll be lucky to be cast as an extra in the future. Hot girl at party number thirteen."

She flips the page, clearly dismissing me. Which is fine, because I'm here to find out what I can about Brandt. Damon doesn't like the guy. I don't know him well enough to have feelings about him. He definitely uses who his father is like a sharply honed weapon.

A few girls dated him because he said he'd introduce them to his father. I'm sure they did more than date him for that opportunity.

Brandt yells at the cast to reset and turns to Becca. "You too, Becca. Bring a better energy."

Becca sighs loudly, clearly put out, and drops her magazine on the chair next to her before walking over to the set with a practiced smile. The stage lights are on, and it's mostly dark over here, but Brandt squints at me.

I don't give a fuck if he knows who I am or that I'm here to watch him.

For all I know, he or one of these fuckers put the rose on Evan's desk Sunday. She may be doing better, but fuck them. It was meant to hurt her. I still haven't figured out why. It's bothering me.

If Brandt wanted to sabotage her, hurting her on Sunday didn't do that. It took her out of rehearsal for a few hours, but she has an assistant director who took over. They didn't lose any time. It didn't hurt her production, which might have been a motive for Brandt.

But it hurt her.

So who wants to hurt her? Abby? Chase's ex fuck buddy/girlfriend. Becca? She doesn't really have a motive, but anyone in this play might be bitter about not getting a part in Evan's play. Bitter enough to hurt the girl who made the decision to cast someone else?

Maybe, but then why wait so long? And what would be the point? The rose wasn't a great revenge plot for someone hoping to hurt the director. But the boy she ran from? The boy who took her first kiss? The boy who watched us get what he couldn't have?

That boy makes sense.

She hurt him because she didn't want him. So he hurt her to prove that he can get to her. That he can make her hurt physically while he hurts emotionally. Does Jackson think he's in love with Evan? Or is it just obsession? The one who got away? The one he's always wanted?

Damon, who gets everything, has her. I'm not blind to the way

Jackson hates Damon. Damon supposedly has everything. Money, a good school, hockey.

And Evan.

I'll stay and see what I can pick up about Brandt besides the fact he's a huge asshole. But the rose was a message. A message to us that as long as she's with us, he'll hurt her.

## CHAPTER 8
## *EvanAnn*

"How's school going, Evan?" Mom asks.

I look up at my name and meet Damon's eyes across the table. He looks bored. I look away quickly. Drawing in a breath, I refocus on the room. Wednesday night dinner with the family. My mind had wandered while Mom talked about her work.

There's this scene between Desdemona and Othello that's missing something. I've been struggling to figure out what it is. Running the scene over and over again in my head. Changing perspective to try to see what it is I'm missing. Is it something that Mark or Mia isn't doing?

Maybe I should call Keira. She might know what I'm talking about. Or I could call an emergency rehearsal with Mark and Mia.

"Evan?" Mom touches my hand and glances toward Adam with a rueful smile. "Sorry, she gets like this when she's got a production going. Head in the clouds is what Jason always said."

My heart clenches at the reminder of my dad. It may have been years, but sometimes his death and the grief feels as fresh as yesterday. Sometimes the memories will make me smile or sometimes they'll make me cry, but I love that I still remember him.

"Evan." Damon's voice is soft.

I lift my gaze, and his blue eyes center me, bringing me back here. Back to him.

"Sorry, Mom." I glance down at my half-eaten dinner, trying not to let how I feel about Damon come out. "School's going well. There's this problem with a scene that's using up most of my brain right now."

"*Othello* is a big production." Adam glances at Damon before focusing on me. His eyes narrow thoughtfully. "I'm surprised they let you take it on."

"The school likes to challenge the seniors. There will be a few other plays this year. Smaller casts. Shorter scripts. And then the spring showcase." I inhale because I'm comfortable talking about this. It's easier than trying to make small talk or just talking about my day.

Because my days and my nights are filled with the Devil's trio, but I'm not about to tell my mother about that. I can't tell her how I laughed with Cam at lunch when he told me a story about a party gone wrong. Or how Hawk can just touch my hand and settle my thoughts. Or how Damon holds me at night and makes sure I have something to eat during long rehearsals.

"The thing that's on my mind is how weird it was that you had a reaction to that rose." Mom cuts her chicken and takes a bite. "Maybe we should get you to an allergist. Make sure it isn't something that you'll come into contact with again."

My panicked gaze lifts to Damon before I bury the feeling. "I don't have time to go to a doctor right now, Mom. Maybe we can do it in late November or early December when things have calmed down."

I give my mom a smile and hope she lets it go.

"We should have had someone collect the rose." Mom shakes her head. "Maybe there was something on it."

"Unfortunately, someone must have thrown it away." I touch the back of her hand and smile when she meets my eyes. "I'm okay. It burned, but the rinsing and the antihistamines made it better. It's not like we have someone who could analyze it on speed dial."

Though my guys do.

"I might know someone." Adam smirks and, for a second, he looks so much like Damon my breath catches. "If something happens like this again, we should definitely take it to the police. Without the rose, we don't know if someone tampered with it or you just had a bad reaction."

Damon's foot presses against mine under the table, and I release the breath I was holding. The rose is safely with Cam. There's not more to it besides the oil. The note was written in block print, and Cam's guy did a test for fingerprints. We knew whoever put it down had to handle it with care or use gloves to make sure they didn't get pricked.

The guys and I talked about it, but right now, it just looks like a prank gone wrong to everyone else. I've gotten some mysterious texts, but that's it. There's no proof of the car in the parking lot—it was outside the range of the school cameras. The police have more important things to do than to analyze a rose when we already know what was on it. It wasn't anything illegal either.

"Hopefully nothing like that happens again." Mom shakes her head. "I don't know how I'd deal with another trip to the hospital."

Adam takes her hand, threading their fingers together, and smiles softly at her. "I'm sure you did fine."

"I'm sure I sounded like a maniac." Mom shakes her head with a wry smile. "I had no idea what happened. Just that Mr. Watson called and said they had taken Evan to urgent care. Pretty sure I broke a few traffic laws to get there."

"I also know a guy who can fix tickets." Adam brings her hand up to his lips and kisses her knuckles. My mom's cheeks turn pink. It's kind of sweet and also a little disturbing at the same time.

"I need to go..." Damon stands and gestures to our parents. "Anywhere else."

He walks away from the table, and Adam sighs.

"He'll get used to having you around." He picks up his wine glass and takes a sip. "His mother's death was devastating to both of us. I got him into therapy, but it doesn't help if you don't want help." Adam glances at me, and I swallow. "He seems calmer with you here. Maybe it's because he knows you went through the same thing. You're solid and thriving just like him. Thank you."

"Uh, sure." I blot my lips with my napkin. "I should go work on my homework. If you'll excuse me?"

"Of course, dear." Mom picks up her wine glass. "You remember we're going out for drinks tonight with some of Adam's colleagues."

I stand and nod. That's why we're meeting here tonight. "Have a good night."

## Hawk

Damon wanted to meet down in the rec room instead of his bedroom. Maybe to prevent us from fucking our girl before we have a chance to talk about him heading off to training next week. Honestly, I think we can accomplish both at the same time.

Cam walks in with me, and we head to the basement, grabbing a couple of drinks from the fridge before sitting on the couch. I'd hoped to at least make Annie come in the closet yesterday, but she had other things on her mind.

Important things that needed to be talked about. This relationship didn't start like a typical one, so we haven't discussed things besides that night she lost her virginity. Maybe we need another night like that. Where she can ask us what she wants to.

Annie comes down first. She smiles when she sees us, and my heart warms.

"Hey, goody." Cam rises and crosses the room to lift her into his arms. He kisses her and nuzzles her neck until she giggles. "I've missed spending the night with you."

"I've missed you too, Cam."

He sets her on her feet, and I reach out my hand to her. She comes to me and sits beside me on the couch, our thighs pressed against each other.

"Hawk," she breathes out.

"Annie." I draw her face to mine and kiss her softly. "How are you? Healing?"

I lift her bandaged hand and kiss her knuckles.

"Coming along nicely," Damon says as he walks in. "She'll be healed before you know it."

Annie presses into my side with a little exhale. Cam sits on her other side. Damon looks at the three of us and shakes his head with a smirk. He can fuck off. He gets her in his bed every night. We have to deal with the scraps of attention we can get. For now.

He leans against the wall and rubs the side of his lip. "We need a schedule for this weekend and next week."

The hockey week starts with him and his dad driving up Friday night.

"Mom's already mentioned a movie night for Friday night." Annie rests her head on my shoulder and tangles her fingers with Cam's. "I was thinking about asking Mia to spend the night."

Damon's mouth tightens. "No."

"I know she's not your favorite person, but she's my friend and I want to spend time with her." Annie straightens and glares at Damon. "I don't need you to control my whole life."

I smirk but try to hide it from Damon. That's exactly what he wants. He likes having full access to Annie. I imagine he'll have the whole house tripped out with video cameras while he's gone so he can watch her every move.

She's lucky he doesn't make her wear a body cam. Though it's not a bad idea, given someone's fucking with her. The ring will track her if she goes missing, but a body cam would tell us what happened.

Damon's gaze flicks to mine before he focuses on Annie. "Mia will probably sneak off to whatever party is happening, and you won't be sneaking with her. You don't go anywhere without one of us. Your girlfriends won't be able to protect you. It would be better if Hawk or Cam or both of them sleep with you. That way I know you're safe."

"I'm in the house with my mom and a security system that's top notch." She holds up her hand, showing her ring. "I'm tagged like a pet, so if I get lost you can find me. Not to mention the video surveillance you have set up to capture my every move. What exactly do you expect to happen while you're away?"

He turns his head to the side, looking away from us. His jaw is clenched. Both Cam and I go still.

"His mom got worse while he was at training camp for the summer," Cam says quietly. "He wanted to stay home with her, but she insisted he go."

Her blue eyes turn to silver, and she releases both of us to close the distance between her and Damon. She wraps her arms around him while he stands stiffly, not looking at her. Not really accepting her hug.

"I'll be fine, Damon."

"You forget to eat."

"I'll set a timer."

"You stay up too late working."

"I'll set so many timers I won't know whether I'm supposed to sleep or eat." She lifts her head and reaches up to tip his face to look down at her. "I kept myself alive for eighteen years, Damon. I think I can make it a week without you."

"What if I can't make it a week without you?" The words are soft, and it feels like we're intruding on this moment, but at the same time, we get it better than anyone else would. I'm hoping this week works out. I can't imagine being away from Annie for weeks at a time. Trying to make long distance work will be hell on all of us.

"We'll video chat, and you'll be watching me." She gives him this smile that tugs at something in my chest. Part of me still can't believe she loves us. That she loves him.

He's hard to love. Cam and I both know that. He's tried to shove us away over the years, but we don't let him. Everyone else can leave, but not us. He needs us as much as we need him.

We all need someone like Annie. Someone soft and gentle who lets us play rough with her but still comes back for more. I don't think I'll ever let her go. Maybe I'll join Damon in stalking her if she ever dares to leave us.

"Go back to the others, little devil." He rubs her back and then sets her away from him. "We need to talk before I have you on your knees."

She meets his gaze and wets her lips. His eyes darken, but she just smiles and returns to her place on the couch between me and Cam.

"Mom and Dad are being super weird," I admit.

Annie tips her head to look questioningly up at me.

"It's like they finally are in love again and want to share it with me." I shudder. "Which, while fascinating, watching it makes me nauseous. They kiss and giggle with each other like they're teenagers."

Annie's expression changes from concern to hiding a smile. "That's awesome."

"Maybe if I didn't have to witness it at the breakfast table." I touch her nose. "You know who bought all that art around our house? My parents. They are very direct about sex to the point I had to ask them to stop talking with me about it a few years ago because the last thing you want to think about when you have sex is your parents."

Annie makes a face.

"Yeah, not fun." I shake my head. "I'll see what days I can sneak out, but I'm sure Cam can figure something out too."

"I just got out of the corner, man." Cam chuckles. "My dad loves what my grades are doing and that I'm studying more, but he's not convinced I'm taking this seriously. I have to be home some nights."

"Then Evan can stay with you guys at your houses," Damon says like it's a done deal.

"I don't think my mom will go for that." Annie sighs. "You do know that me sleeping with you every night isn't normal, right?"

"Feels normal to me." Damon smirks.

"We'll work it out." I meet Damon's eyes. "She won't be left alone. You won't have to worry."

Cam claps his hands. "So that's done then? Because it's been a hot minute since I've had Evan alone."

Annie flushes and looks around the room. "Should we move upstairs?"

"Why, Annie?" I tip her chin my way. "I was thinking we should play another game."

"Then we should definitely move upstairs," she says.

"Our parents aren't home, little devil. Besides, games are more fun when there's an element of risk. Like getting caught." Damon moves to the chair and lounges in it.

Annie narrows her eyes on him. "If we get caught, you probably won't be able to have me in your bed and bathroom every night."

Damon's smirk is evil and relaxed. He leans forward and looks Annie up and down. "I'd like to see them try to keep me away from you."

She squirms between us.

"I vote fuck, marry, kill. If you don't want to sort the people you're given, you take a dare." Cam rubs his hands together. Guaranteed to make us take dares.

"I was thinking truth or dare." I brush my hand over Annie's back, and she shivers beneath my touch. "We could learn something about someone we want to know."

Damon leans back and steeples his fingers against his lips. "Person whose turn it is decides truth or fuck, marry, kill. They don't want to answer they do the dare."

Annie bites her lip and looks between us. "Who would choose truth?"

"You haven't heard the fuck, marry, kill choices yet, goody." Cam stands and walks over to the bar. "Besides, it's more about the dares anyway."

Grabbing a bottle of vodka and a few shot glasses, he brings them back to the couch and sets them on the table.

Annie's nose wrinkles. "Vodka?"

"Good vodka." Cam pours the drinks and passes them out. "One shot to start and loosen things up."

I clink my shot against Annie's and take the shot down my throat. Annie throws hers back and gasps. I capture the back of her neck and draw her in for a kiss. I don't know about the others, but I plan on winning this game.

## CHAPTER 9
## EvanAnn

WARMTH SETTLES throughout me after the shot, and I lean against Hawk. Cam caps the bottle of vodka and puts it on the coffee table on its side.

"Spin for us, goody."

I swallow nervously and lean forward to spin the bottle. When the bottle stops, it points to Damon. I lift my gaze to his, and he smirks.

"Evan."

I straighten.

"Truth or fuck."

My lips part and then I press them back together. "Interesting way to shorten it."

Damon shrugs and gives me a mischievous smile. "Pick, little devil."

I'm curious what sort of truth he'll ask me, but it might be easier to go with fuck, marry, kill. Either way, I'm not sure I want to take a dare from Damon. Not down here where our parents might return home at any time.

Normally I wouldn't worry, because Mom wouldn't come to check on me. Normally I'd be doing homework or studying or something else equally boring. But she's been concerned and focused since the rose incident. It's intense, but it can't last. It never does because usually my life is pretty monotonous and boring.

I'm sure I'll get back to the boring and monotonous from her point of view soon.

"Fuck, marry, kill." Seems like I'll be least likely to say no to.

Damon rubs his finger over his lip as those blue eyes study me carefully. "Cam, Hawk, and me."

What? "It's supposed to be celebrities, not real people. That's not—"

"It's my choice, Evan." Damon smirks. "So what's it going to be? Who do you want to fuck, marry, kill or do you want a dare?"

I should have known he wouldn't make it easy. I glare at him, but fuck him. "Fuck Hawk, marry Cam, and kill you."

Damon's chuckle is low and his eyes knowing. "You don't want to kill me, little devil."

"Right now?" I lift an eyebrow like *try me*.

Damon leans in and spins the bottle. "You'd fuck us all."

"Don't be so sure about that." I straighten like I wouldn't be one hundred percent on board with whatever they want me to do. But we all know I would be. My traitorous body hums with the thought of them fucking me tonight. All of them.

The bottle lands on Hawk.

"Truth or fuck, Damon." Hawk leans back and runs his hand down my spine. A shiver runs through me and I glance at him. He smirks but doesn't look away from Damon.

"I'm always down to fuck." Damon glances down at the juncture of my legs. I'm wearing jeans. I figured whatever we did would be in the privacy of his room, so it didn't matter what I wore. Eventually they'd just strip me naked. But if we decided to go for a ride, jeans wouldn't complicate matters.

Down here though, a skirt would have been more accessible for this game. But how was I supposed to know we'd be playing a game where our parents might wander down to find out what we're up to? My cheeks heat.

"Mia, Olivia, Evan." Hawk smirks.

"Not even a choice. Fuck Evan. Marry Evan. And kill Olivia and Mia."

"That's not how the game works," I say, crossing my arms over my chest.

Damon leans forward and his heated eyes meet mine. "Then dare me."

I glance at Hawk, and he's contemplating.

"Dress Evan how you wish she'd dress tonight." Hawk arches his eyebrow when I glare at him.

Damon stands and wipes his hands on his athletic pants. "Be right back."

He disappears up the stairs.

"This might take a minute." Cam grabs me and pulls me onto his lap. "So we have some time, goody. Or should I say wifey."

Laughing, I lean back against him and turn to ask. "What did you have in mind?"

"Something that would get you in trouble if your mother came home early." He undoes my jeans, and I suck in a breath.

"It's not fun if it's not dangerous, baby girl." Hawk grabs my legs and pulls them across his thighs, tipping me onto Cam's lap.

Cam lowers me so I'm laying across both of their legs. "Perfect."

He tugs my shirt up and draws the cup of my bra down before leaning over and sucking on my nipple. Heat floods me.

"Cam," I scold quietly, but my hand tangles in his hair to keep him there. His tongue is wicked, and the way he sucks on me makes my pussy throb.

Hawk tugs my jeans down over my hips. Making an indignant noise, I try to lift my head to tell him to stop. I don't really want to be naked in the basement.

"You have to change for the dare anyway, baby girl." Hawk's smile is mischievous, as he drops my jeans on the floor and shifts until my parted legs are around him. I bite my lip. I should really stop this before they get me in trouble.

But when Cam sucks harder, I stop fighting. Some rational part of my brain is still working. The likelihood of our parents coming home anytime soon is fairly low. It's probable Damon would intervene if necessary as he's upstairs.

Hawk tugs my panties to the side and lifts my hips. He latches on to my pussy with his mouth. I close my eyes and give into the overwhelming feeling of Cam and Hawk touching me. Sparks flood my system until I feel like I'm glowing from the inside out.

When Hawk thrusts his fingers into me, I moan. I love how they fuck me. Cam trails kisses up my neck before claiming my mouth. His fingers tweak my hardened nipples, sending a bolt of need through me. Hawk's tongue strokes my clit in time with his fingers stroking in and out, pushing me higher.

I'm a live wire ready to explode. Cam slides his tongue against mine as his fingers pinch my nipples. Hawk sucks on my clit and adds another finger to his thrusting. It's too much, and I moan my release into Cam's mouth as it buzzes through me. Hawk drags his fingers out and licks them off.

When Cam helps me sit up, Hawk grabs the back of my neck and kisses me. I can taste myself on his tongue and lips. I wrap my hand around the back of his neck to keep him from stopping.

I can't do much with my bandaged hand. It's difficult to remember where we are and what we're doing when all I want to do is take them in me and be what they need. To never stop this pleasure. When I start to straddle Hawk's lap more, Cam clears his throat.

"Stand, goody."

I pull away from Hawk's lips to focus on Cam, but he nods behind me. I turn and see Damon sitting on the chair, watching with a smirk on his face.

"Come here, little devil."

I stand and glance toward the staircase leading upstairs. Fuck, I didn't even hear him come down. He could have been anyone. I should be embarrassed, but I can't seem to care beyond what they can do to me.

I'm theirs to play with, and I love every minute of it.

"No one's here, and you need to change." Damon leans forward and grabs the elastic of my panties. "Get naked."

I finish taking my shirt off over my head and drop it on Cam's lap. He chuckles. My bra is practically already off. The cups are pulled to the side, exposing both my breasts. I reach behind me and watch Damon's hungry eyes take me in as I release the clasp and drop it to the floor.

The way they watch me. The way they want me. It's intoxicating and liberating.

I walk over to him in only my panties. As I slide them down my hips slowly, he tracks my every move. When they flutter to the floor, I lean over him and rest my good hand on his shoulder as I step out of them.

He wets his lips when I straighten, naked in front of him. My chest heaves with every breath. I need him to fuck me. My skin aches for their touch.

His smirk should have warned me, but he holds out my old uniform skirt, the too-short one he made me wear for him before. I take it from him and glance over at Hawk. I only have one good hand still.

"Can I get a little help?" I hold the skirt out to him.

Chuckling, he stands and takes it from me. When he steps behind me, his shirt brushes against my naked back. Sparks scatter through my system. I lean back against him as he puts his arms around me to hold the skirt for me to step into.

Their gazes are hot on me as Hawk buttons and zips my skirt once it's in place. Damon holds out the top, which is a white men's oxford, clearly one of Damon's. Hawk takes it and helps me slip it up my arms.

Damon stands, and I lift my hooded gaze to his. I want him to touch me, not just dress me. He smirks and begins to button the shirt. His knuckles brush my breasts through the material, making my nipples harden almost painfully. He stops buttoning under my breasts and ties the rest into a knot, leaving my midriff bare. I glance toward the chair to see if he brought panties for me.

He cups my jaw and tips my head back so it presses against Hawk's shoulder. Caught between the two of them, I'm so ready to move on to the next step.

"Did you want to ask something, little devil?" His eyes burn with heat.

I swallow. "Panties?"

This skirt is almost obscenely short. Without panties, I'm guaranteed to flash someone. I'm not worried about flashing the guys, but if my mom were to come down or worse, Adam...

"I don't see the problem." He rubs his thumb over my lips, and I breathe out at the hit of lust. "This is exactly how I would dress you."

He smirks and lowers himself into his chair. Hawk steps back, leaving me on fire but cold without their touch. I glance down at my modified uniform and put my hand on my cocked hip.

"This is how you'd dress me?" I arch an eyebrow.

"Absolutely." He leans forward and puts his hands on my thighs, drawing me to stand between his legs. "On your knees, little devil."

"It's not my turn to take a dare."

"Okay, truth or fuck, little devil."

"You didn't spin the bottle."

"But I choose you to ask, so what's it going to be?"

I narrow my eyes at him. "Truth."

"Whose cock feels the best in your pussy?"

My mouth opens. What a fucker. "That's not fair."

He smirks. "Then take the dare, little devil."

They might as well have called the game just Dare. I hate that he wins this one. I couldn't even decide who feels the best. They all feel fucking fantastic, and I want to feel them inside me now. "Fine. Dare me."

"Get my cock hard with your mouth and then sit with it buried in your cunt during the next turn."

I press my thighs together at the ache his words cause. I flick my gaze to the others who are watching this little production Damon's putting on. Fuck it. It's not like I don't want to do it.

The house above us is quiet. Our parents will be gone for a while. I lower to my knees between his legs and reach for his waistband, drawing it down, and find he's also not wearing any underwear.

When I lift my gaze to his, he shrugs. "I like to be prepared."

His cock is already hard, but it stiffens more beneath my touch. I stroke his cock while our eyes are locked. There's something sexy and heady about making him want me.

When I lower my mouth over him, taking him into my wet depths, he groans like he's been dying to get inside me anyway he can. Hands grab my hips, lifting them. I don't take my gaze from Damon's darkened blue eyes as someone strokes the head of their cock through my folds before notching at my entrance. Finally.

I'm soaking wet and ready to be fucked. I push back into him, taking his cock inside me, stretching me.

"Fuck, goody. I've missed this pussy." Cam pulls out and pumps back in.

I follow Cam's pace with my mouth on Damon's cock as Damon watches me with hooded eyes. His hands remain on the arms of the chair while mine rest on his thighs. Cam slides his fingers over my clit, winding me so much tighter. I moan as I come around his cock.

Damon slides his hand into my hair and holds me as he thrusts a few times into my mouth before he comes. I swallow as best as I can. Cam thrusts harder, pounding me so fucking good. I fall over the edge again as he groans his release.

"Keep sucking me hard again." Damon's words shouldn't turn me on, but they do. Cam pulls out and slides his fingers through the leaking cum before thrusting his fingers and his cum back inside me.

An aftershock ripples through me.

"I love the feel of your tight cunt on me." Cam slides his hand over my ass before he stands and returns to the couch. He sucks his fingers clean and winks at me.

Damon lifts my mouth off him. "Stand."

I do as he says, ready for more.

"Turn around and sit on my cock." He fists his cock to hold it in position.

I turn and Hawk is there, holding the elbow of my injured hand while I put my other hand on the arm of the chair. Damon helps guide me down until I'm slowly lowering myself onto his dick. Every inch sinking into me is like ecstasy.

Once I'm seated, he wraps his arm around my center and pulls me back against him. The urge to move is strong. His cock throbs like another heartbeat inside me.

"Damon," I whimper.

"Maybe if you're good, little devil, I'll let you ride it. But it's your turn to ask a question."

I squirm a little on his cock, and his hand tightens on my hip and he hisses. Good. We're both uncomfortably aroused, making this just prolonged torture.

I look at Cam and Hawk. Cam's already hard again, and Hawk slowly strokes his hard cock, as his gaze focuses on where I'm sitting on Damon. I spread my legs to the outside of Damon's and lean back so he can see better. I don't mind putting on a show for my guys.

"Fuck, baby girl." Hawk groans.

"Truth or fuck, Cam?" I turn to meet Cam's gaze.

He smirks. "I just finished fucking you, so how about truth."

I rest my head against Damon's shoulder, and he draws my skirt up. His finger rubs my clit in slow, steady circles. My breath comes out in almost pants. Both guys try to maintain eye contact with me, but their gazes keep slipping down between my legs to Damon's finger stroking me. Which is fair because that's where my attention is focused too.

I shift restlessly against Damon, needing him to quicken the pace. To fuck me. To push me over the edge again, but he just chuckles against my ear. My brain short-circuits at the electricity racing through me.

Cam clears his throat. I meet his gaze and push through the need, because Damon said I could ride his cock if I asked my question.

"How many girls have you fucked?" I ask. Unable to think of a better question and realizing this probably isn't the best time to ask since I've got another guy's dick buried inside me. Part of me doesn't even want to know, but the part that does is intensely curious.

Cam leans forward and thinks for a moment. "About thirty."

"About?" My voice is breathy as my hips begin to rock with Damon's fingers. He loosens his hold on my hip and lets me ride him. Fuck, that's what I need.

"There have been some nights I wasn't totally with it when a girl pulled me into a room." Cam shrugs and holds the bottle up. "I try not to get that drunk anymore. But a few years ago, I didn't care how drunk I got or who I fucked."

I press my lips together, but Damon leans forward with me, changing the angle of his cock inside me and thrusting up into me.

"Do you need to know how many girls we've been with, Annie?"

I glance at Hawk as everything inside me tightens around Damon's cock. There's no other thought going on but that I'm so fucking close. When I shatter with a moan, he fucks in and out of me in little moves until he groans his release. He holds me tight against him while he finishes shuddering.

"Damon," I whisper. Fuck, that feels so fucking good.

"Come here, baby girl." Hawk holds his hand out to me, and Damon helps me move over to Hawk's lap. I straddle his lap and slide my pussy down on his cock, taking him so fucking deep. When he's buried inside me, he tips my chin up and searches my eyes. "You know you're the only girl for us. The only one who has any hold over us. This is more than getting off."

I smile and cup his jaw. He's hard and solid inside me, and I can't resist rocking him in and out of me.

He hisses and then his hands are on the buttons of my shirt. He opens it and latches on to my breast while he guides my hips over him. I tip my head back, too turned on to care about anything but the way they feel inside me.

I never want this to end. Cam slides his finger over my clit, and I gasp out a breath. Before I can inhale, Damon's mouth is on mine, devouring me.

My insides combust at all their attention on me. I'm a burning phoenix as I ride Hawk through my orgasm. Damon lifts his mouth from mine but holds my face.

"Open your eyes, little devil."

I open them and meet his darkened gaze, filled with pleasure at watching Hawk fuck me.

"You're so fucking sexy when you're taking us. There's no one we want more. We just didn't know to look for you." He slides his thumb possessively over my lips. "Otherwise, the only girl we ever would have fucked would have been you."

My orgasm is hot and wet when I come. Hawk curses as he thrusts up into me until his release jets into me. He pulls back and looks me over as his cock continues to pulse his cum deep inside me.

Damon releases my head, and I turn to capture Cam's lips. He groans into my mouth as his tongue slides against mine, causing my cunt to clutch around Hawk's cock.

When I pull away, Cam's dark eyes are on mine. So focused on me.

His hand moves on his cock, and I watch him stroke himself. Desire curls hot and thick inside me even though I should be satiated.

"I want it, Cam." I wet my lips, and he stands as I part my lips for him. He thrusts into my mouth with a groan.

I take him as deep as I can and hum around him as I look up to meet his eyes. He slides his fingers around my lips stretched around him.

"You're it. The only one I want." Cam thrusts his hips a little, sliding his cock in and out of my mouth. "Always, goody."

He comes, flooding my mouth with him. After I swallow, Hawk holds me tight against him as Cam pulls out. I rest my head on Hawk's shoulder as he rubs his hands up and down my back. He's still hard inside me.

This could never end. I could spend forever fucking them.

Footsteps click on the tile floor above us. My breath catches and I freeze.

Without hesitating, Hawk stands with me attached to him and strides to the bathroom, holding his pants so he doesn't trip while I cling to him. I glance over my shoulder at the others gathering my discarded clothes.

My mom's voice rings through the space. "Evan? Are you down there?"

# CHAPTER 10
## EvanAnn

My heart clenches as Hawk closes the door to the bathroom and locks it. He doesn't turn on the light, just presses me against the door as we wait. I try to slow my breathing, but my heart is racing so hard it hurts.

Fuck, my mom almost caught us. Caught me with Hawk's dick in me and wearing... this. Fuck.

"Oh, hi, boys." Mom's voice sounds distracted, like she's looking around the room. Maybe she thinks I'm hiding? Because I am.

When Hawk's cock jerks inside me, I bite my lip to suppress my moan as I clench around him. He presses his forehead against the door next to my ear. "Sorry, baby girl. It's just difficult to be inside you and not fuck you." His words are barely loud enough for me to hear.

I'm tense, wondering if my mom saw us duck in here, but I'm still turned on.

"Evan went to her room after dinner." Damon must turn on the TV or radio because music fills the space. Hopefully, it hides the sound of my breathing because to me it's so loud. "Maybe you'll have better luck there."

I turn my ear to the door, releasing my breath against Hawk's cheek. I hoped to hear her leaving, but the music is too loud. Hawk turns his head and captures my lips. I sink into the feel of his hard cock filling me. He draws me off the door and presses me against the wall. Which I don't understand why until he begins to fuck me slowly, and it's all I can focus on.

The door rattling would have been noticeable even with the music playing. But against the wall, it doesn't matter, and I lose myself in his kiss. The thrust of his cock into me. The drag and slide. The way he tastes like mint and vodka and me. I try to be quiet, to not let any moans escape, but I'm already so sensitive and amped up from almost getting caught.

My cunt flutters around him before tightening into an explosion. White light bursts behind my eye lids. He groans softly as his thrusts become harder, faster.

"So fucking good, baby girl," he whispers against my lips. "Better than anything I've ever felt."

He thrusts in deep and fills me as best he can. I'm practically overflowing with cum as much as they've fucked me. I rest my head against the wall and look at the door. There's a back way up to our bedrooms, and I should really hurry to intercept my mother. I can make an excuse that I came down to get something from the kitchen, or I didn't hear her because I was in the bathroom. Which wouldn't be a lie, but it's not the bathroom she would assume I was in.

I'd also have to explain this outfit and the smell of sex.

Instead of hurrying, I pull Hawk's head back to mine and take his lips. Because he's mine. I'm going to have to figure out how to tell my mom about them someday. Not today. Maybe not this year.

But at some point, our relationship is going to be discovered. Maybe I can wait until Damon gets back from Crowne Mawr. Then we can all sit down and discuss this relationship with our parents like adults. No reason to do it before Damon heads off.

If I have to be uncomfortable with our parents knowing, he should have to be uncomfortable too. I don't want my mom to catch us fucking, but I should be able to relax with my guys in my house without worrying about her wandering in.

When I ease away from Hawk, he rests his head against my shoulder. "Do you think my mom will be okay with me dating you guys?"

Hawk chuckles. "Does it matter if she isn't?"

I shrug. It won't matter to them, but will it matter to me? When he pulls out of me and lowers me to stand on my own, I have to use the wall to hold me up. Fuck, I'm tired and my thighs are slick with their cum. Rushing upstairs wouldn't have done much good considering how I'm dressed.

Hawk brushes my hair away from my face and studies me the best he can in the dark. "It doesn't matter what our parents think, Annie. You're ours and we're yours. That's what counts."

"Except we live in our parents' houses. And they have control of us until we go off to college." I blow out a breath, frustrated that my mom might try to put an end to all this. She can't really though. But she can make it hard to see the guys except at school. I don't know if she'd be like that or not. I've never done anything like this. Ever.

She's never really tried to control my life before either.

"We'll deal with whatever they throw at us, Annie." Hawk touches his forehead to mine. "We always do."

---

DAMON HOLDS MY HAND AS WE CLIMB UP THE STAIRS. I cleaned up as best as I could in the bathroom, but we're not sure if my mom will linger or actively look for me. Our bedroom doors are closed and so are the bathroom doors.

When we reach the hallway, Damon releases me and sends me forward with a little push on the small of my back. I changed back into my jeans but put his white shirt on over my bra. I don't know what it is, but I love wearing his clothes. And from the heat in his eyes, he appreciates it.

I try to walk confidently to my room, but I'm also kind of creeping along the hallway. I have nothing to hide... at least not right now. The excuse that I went downstairs for a snack should work. Hopefully.

My room is empty, so I get out my phone and check to see if she texted. The door in Damon's room opens and closes. Which gives me the excuse to text...

> **ME:**
> Damon said you were looking for me?

> **MOM:**
> Just wanted to check on your hand
>
> See how you were doing

> **ME:**
> Oh, I was downstairs grabbing a snack

Fuck, was that too obvious since I don't know where she looked for me?

> **MOM:**
> I must have just missed you at your room
>
> This house is too big
>
> I'll be right there

This house is big, thankfully. I would have been caught in our house. I sigh and look up as the bathroom door opens. Damon leans against the doorframe and watches me.

"Mom's on her way to check on me." I put my phone down on my desk and meet his gaze.

A rush of heat flows through me. My pussy throbs at the promise in his eyes.

"Come to bed after." He steps back and closes the bathroom door.

I shake off the desire and open the hallway door. Sitting at my desk, I try to focus a little on homework while I wait for my mom. I don't have to wait long though.

Mom walks in and takes a seat on the edge of my bed. "I feel like I could walk all over this house looking for you and still miss you. How was your day?"

I smile. "The house is a lot bigger than we're used to. My day was good."

And I didn't get caught fucking the Devil's trio. So score.

Mom glances at the bathroom. "How is this working for you? Are you guys getting along? The bathroom hasn't been an issue?"

My cheeks heat when I think of how well we're sharing the space. "We're doing fine."

Mom nods and looks at my closet. "Do you need any more clothes? I wasn't sure what all you needed."

"I'm good. Honest, Mom. I don't need more clothes. My hand is doing much better." I walk over and sit next to her on the bed. "You don't have to worry about me. I'm taken care of."

She reaches over and takes my uninjured hand in hers. "I'm supposed to worry about you, Evan."

"Everything is good. The accident—" I hold up my hand, "was unfortunate, but it's healing. Just the same grind as last year. Classes, rehearsals, productions..."

Fucking my three boyfriends. I keep my face neutral as that thought floats into my head.

"Well, if you need me, I'm here." Mom smiles and squeezes my hand. "You might have to text me to find me though."

"I will."

---

## Cam

I meet Evan after her first period class to walk her to Mr. Ridgeway's classroom. I give her a small red paper flower, and her eyes light up. She twirls it between her fingers as we walk down the hallway.

"You don't have to keep doing this, Cam." She glances at me with soft eyes. "I really appreciate it."

"I like doing it, goody." I take her wrist to avoid hurting her bandaged hand. I don't tell her that as long as she continues to light up that way, I'll bring them to her every day for the rest of our lives. Maybe she'll grow tired of it in a few weeks or a year or maybe never. I'm willing to spend the rest of my life figuring out what makes her happy.

"I love them. So thank you." She smiles, so open and so in love with me that my heart nearly bursts.

When we walk into the classroom, I wrap my arm around her shoulders to keep her close as we head to our seats. This is the class we share with Chase. He's been quiet since the rose incident. Maybe he can tell we're on edge and it isn't a good time to push. Maybe he's not as stupid as we thought.

Or maybe he's actually worried Evan got hurt. I'd rather forget the fucker exists at all, but he's kind of present at school and in Evan's play. Makes him hard to ignore.

I guide her to her seat and set her backpack next to her. When I lean down, she lifts her face up to mine. My lips curve against hers at the brief kiss. I love having her for a girlfriend.

When I lift my head, her cheeks are flushed pink.

I take my seat and glance in Chase's direction. When I look at him, he looks away like I caught him watching her. Is he still planning on making a play to win her back? He can't be that stupid.

It's not like Evan would ever take him back. Even if we weren't in the picture. No matter how much he begged. He cheated and isn't the right guy for her. We are.

When Hawk walks in, Damon is right behind him. They come and sit down around Evan like we're her own personal guards.

"How's your hand?" Damon leans toward her to ask.

She blushes and looks away before saying, "Fine."

Damon smirks and straightens. He pulls his phone out and messes with it for a second before Evan's buzzes. She glances at the screen and shakes her head, but her face grows even redder.

"Are you going to share with the class, goody?" I ask softly.

Her blue eyes widen, but she hands me her phone with Snapchat open.

> SEX GOD:
>> You're always welcome to wake me up riding me, little devil
>
>> Just be more careful with your hand next time

I offer her the phone back and raise my eyebrow at her in question. She sighs and leans forward before glancing to make sure no one is paying attention to us. She wets her lips and says softly, "I accidentally grabbed the headboard with my bad hand. Needless to say, it hurt."

I give her a wicked grin. "Did Damon kiss it better?"

Her cheeks are bright red.

I catch her chin before she can pull away. Her blue-gray eyes meet mine.

"When we sleep together next week, I want you to wake me up fucking me, goody." I wiggle my eyebrows. I can't wait to wake to her riding me.

She rolls her eyes, but there's heat there. I'm sure she'll do it. This girl gets under my skin in the best way possible.

"I also want to fuck you while you sleep," I add. "Slow and gentle so you don't wake up."

Her breathing increases, and I lean closer.

"Tonight I want to fuck your ass while you fuck the others. I want you to sleep with us inside you, all of us." I search her eyes as she bites her lip.

"Cam." She glances around to make sure no one is listening in. "You can't even stay over tonight."

"I forgot." Fuck, my dad wants to talk to me about college next year. And in the morning, I have to come in early to school. It's part of the conditions of not getting anything on my permanent record for the drinking incident Dad worked out with the DA. I have to volunteer at the school. "Timing. We'll do it later. Or maybe I'll crawl into your bed and fuck you while you're sleeping so you wake up with my cum on your thighs."

Her eyes flare hot. I'm so doing that. Hopefully tonight. If not, I'll have her to myself next week. I can't wait to play naughty student and teacher with her. She can make me beg for it.

Mr. Ridgeway calls the class to attention. As I turn to the front, I catch Chase glaring at me before he looks toward the teacher. Can't really blame the guy. We did steal his girl after all. Glitter bomb his car. Freak him out in the woods.

Which fucked up his knee so he's missing out on football. We haven't yet distributed his epic fail in the woods.

Couldn't happen to a nicer dickhead. He fucked up Damon's

future and fucked around on Evan. I'd fuck her right now in front of him so he can see what he lost, but he doesn't get to see our girl like that. That's for us and only us.

I'm not sharing her with anyone else.

I just need to figure out how to unruin my chance at getting into Yale. So I can stay with my friends and our girl.

## CHAPTER 11
## EvanAnn

TODAY IS FLYING by and dragging at the same time. I want to spend all my time with Damon until he has to leave. It's barely over twenty-four hours before he heads off to Crowne Mawr.

This opportunity is everything. It's what he needs for his career. A chance at a D1 school. Not only would it work for him, but it would work for all of us. And his dad would be happy. It could be perfect.

Thursday afternoon has me waiting for rehearsal. And rehearsal has me waiting for the end of rehearsal.

I'm usually able to focus, but today there's a ticking clock. I haven't been separated from Damon since I moved in. I haven't really been alone in that house either. Next week is going to be strange. I'm excited to spend time with Cam and Hawk, but I'm so used to having Damon at night.

As soon as rehearsal ends, I can go home to him.

Crawl into bed with my men and have them take me to another plane of existence. Because I need them, and it's all I can think about. It's consuming my mind. But it wouldn't matter if I rushed home, because the guys have hockey. That keeps Damon as busy as rehearsal keeps me.

We just collide at night. He watches me study, brings me food, makes me shower with him, fucks me so deliciously good that I sleep like the dead. It's hard to imagine not sleeping with him in our bed.

I always slept on my own until I moved in with him, and now I'm not sure how I'll sleep without him. No warm body dragging me into dreamland. No arms holding me tight, protecting me from everything, keeping me safe.

Hopefully Cam, Hawk, and I can work out a schedule so I'm not really alone any night. I've gotten greedy. I can't help it. It's not my fault they spoiled me.

Besides, I've seen the envious looks of the girls around school. They want my men just as much as I do. It would be in bad taste if I didn't enjoy what I had and what those girls can't have. I'm going to hold on to it and refuse to let go.

I stretch my hand. The wounds are scabbed over, and it's probably okay to not bandage it every day, but Damon takes the time each morning and night to make sure I'm taken care of. And even though I don't need it, I love every second of it.

Being taken care of is a novelty that hasn't gotten old. Neither has being manhandled or fucked.

"EvanAnn." Keira clears her throat, and I look up from where I was supposedly taking notes. Or more like daydreaming about how much I want to be with my guys. I'm hopeless.

"Yes?" I straighten and try to focus. This isn't like me. I'm usually able to push everything into the background and focus on what's important.

Keira raises an eyebrow, and I glance down at my phone where I was typing notes. There's not much there. "Is it okay if I call a break?"

I glance at the clock and wince. I should have called a break ten minutes ago. "Yes, please."

She nods and turns to the cast. "Quick break. We're almost done for the night. Just another hour to go."

There's a couple of groans as everyone filters out of the little room. We've been at this for weeks. Earlier it was a thrill to be in here, but when you spend most of the afternoon in these rooms and then after school, eventually you want to be somewhere not so... black.

Keira sits next to me. "So, what's got you distracted?"

I blow out a breath. "Damon leaves for Crowne Mawr tomorrow, so tonight is our last night."

Keira smirks. "You know most couples don't get to sleep together every night until college."

I lean back in my chair and glance around the room. There are a few backstage people on the set resetting things. I should really tell them to take their break. Mia comes back in and joins us at our table.

"So, one of your men is abandoning you." Mia smiles and wiggles her eyebrows suggestively. "I guess the others will have to pick up the slack."

The heat in my cheeks is almost unbearable. I put my face in my hands as Keira and Mia chuckle.

"Maybe it's time to have a girl's night," Keira offers. "We could watch movies, eat pizza, wear sweats, and complain about boys."

Mia lights up. "Oh my god, I haven't done anything like that since middle school."

"I've never done anything like that," I admit.

"Then it's a date." Keira sits up straight with a pleased smile. "Or at least something we can schedule. I'm sure you both have things to do this weekend."

"I'm pretty sure you're not allowed to call boys *things*." Mia grins at Keira. "I'm all for objectifying them, but *things* is a little harsh."

I shake my head, but can't help the smile on my face. This is what I've been missing all these years. The love from the guys is good, but having friends is something I thought I might never have.

"Whatever. I've seen the way Liam and Fletcher follow you around," Keira teases with a smile. "They'd let you walk them around on leashes if you wanted."

Mia puts her finger to her lip like she's considering it. "Maybe the next party I will."

"The only one who would be wearing a leash in my relationship is me." I lean back in my chair as I consider how my guys might treat me as their pet. I wouldn't mind trying it out. My cheeks heat. "Though Cam might let me experiment."

"That's it, girlboss." Mia laughs. "Cam looks like he might be a happy little submissive with the right touch."

Flames must be coming out of my head. My face feels way too hot as I avoid their knowing looks.

"Okay, next week, what about Sunday or Wednesday?" Keira looks at her calendar on her phone.

"I think I can work that out." Mia flashes me a grin, and Keira turns to look at me expectantly.

"I'll find out which works better for the guys."

"Yay!" Keira practically wiggles in her chair in happiness.

Damon might not like the shift in plans, but he won't be here. It's only one week. The rest of the cast returns from the break, and it's time to focus again. I'm determined to concentrate on the play this time.

---

THE HOUR LEFT OF REHEARSAL FLIES BY AS WE DISCUSS HOW to fix the Othello/Desdemona problem I was having. Mark, Mia, and I sit down separately and really talk it through. Working with Mia and Mark to help me figure out the problem was Keira's idea while she works with the other cast members.

Neither Chase nor Hawk are here tonight. About fifteen minutes before the end of rehearsal, Hawk, Cam, and Damon walk into the space. They're quiet and take seats in the audience, trying not to be disruptive, but I don't think those three can go anywhere and not be a distraction.

The girls are the most easily distracted by them. Not Mia or Keira, but Sophie and Crystal act like they're auditioning to be the guys' girlfriends. Tits and ass pushed out. They're a little louder. A little poutier. A little more annoying.

The guys sit and watch me like the predators they are. The back of my neck tingles, and I can't wait to leave with them.

I need to start using my writing hand for notes. It's been frustrating just using my phone. Last break, I unwrapped my hand in the bathroom. It's time. The cuts are closed, and the air will be good for the wounds.

When Damon notices my hand, his eyes narrow on it like he's going to make me fix it. A little rush goes through me. What would he do if I didn't obey him? If I forced him to make me do it?

I like it when he holds me down and makes me take every inch of him.

"I never imagined a day I'd see EvanAnn distracted from her play by dick."

My cheeks heat at Mark's words as I turn to face him and Mia again. Mia struggles to keep from laughing, but then just releases it. Keira turns to check on us before rolling her eyes and returning to what she's doing with the others.

"I mean, it must be good quality dick to be that distracting," Mia says with a conspiratorial nudge to Mark.

"Unfortunately, I'll never know," Mark laments. "They seem to be focused on one girl in particular, and there's no competing for their attention."

I clear my throat, trying to take charge. "Are you two finished?"

"Probably." Mia chuckles.

Mark smiles. "Sorry, it's just nice to see your feathers finally ruffled. You're an amazing director and usually so focused and career-driven that I worried you'd be hard to work with."

My mouth opens and closes, but I don't know what to say.

Mia laughs again. "Please say you can come and hang out with us to watch movies at Evan's this week, Mark."

He arches an eyebrow at her. "What did I tell you about propositioning me?"

Mia rolls her eyes. "You'd be fun to hang out with. That's all I'm saying. Besides, I'll get plenty of dick this weekend. You'd be so jealous."

Mark chuckles. "I get my fair share of dick."

"Evan, Keira, and I are getting together to keep Evan company while her main dick goes to college." Mia glances over at the guys and gives them a little finger wave.

I look over my shoulder at them. Putting them behind me was the only way to keep my attention on what I'm working on. Not that it stops me from wanting to look or sneaking a glance. Damon rolls his eyes. Hawk leans back in his chair like he couldn't care less what Mia does. Cam notices me and sends me a kissy face.

I wink at Cam before turning back to face Mia and Mark. "You should come, Mark. It would be nice to hang out with you outside of all of this."

Mark takes a breath and gives me a nod that almost looks like a bow. "I'd be honored."

"You keep looking at her like that, and her boyfriends might get the wrong idea." Mia bumps Mark's shoulder with her own.

"I'm pretty sure they know where I stand."

I raise an eyebrow and refuse to turn back around and look at my guys.

"Full disclosure. I asked Hawk if he'd be interested in experimenting." Mark shrugs. "You never know. Some very straight guys say yes just to make sure or because they're curious. Some guys just can't turn down a blow job." Mark's grin grows. "Hawk was not interested, but he let me down gently."

I laugh. I can't help it. Mark asking Hawk to fuck him? I would have paid good money to be a fly on that wall. Mia grins, and Mark gets this wicked look in his eyes.

"If any of your guys feel like experimenting..." He gestures to himself as an offering.

"I think the only one they want to experiment with is me, but I'll definitely let them know they have options." I shake my head, but laughter still pulls my cheeks tight.

"Then I'm in on movie night to learn more about what that statement means," Mark says, and Mia claps her hands.

"We should focus." I glance over my shoulder quickly before returning all my attention to Othello and Desdemona.

# CHAPTER 12
## *Damon*

I STAND AS SOON as Evan ends rehearsal. I have her helmet and want nothing more than to take her riding with us. Obviously, I want more than that, but the key is to get her alone. We have tonight, school tomorrow, and then I'm gone for the week. Hopefully, I'll find out if Crowne Mawr could work as a future for at least me.

We'll have to visit the college together to figure out if it'll work for all of us, but this is a move in the right direction. A move toward our future.

Evan stands talking with Mark. She touches his arm, and he smiles down at her. Yeah, that's not happening.

"He's gay, Damon." Hawk grabs my arm before I can stalk toward them.

I glare at Hawk and then turn to look at Mark. He's a good-looking guy, obviously friendly with Evan. And she's mine, so I can go claim her.

I look at Hawk's hand and then meet his eyes. Whatever he sees in mine makes him hold his hands up in surrender. I cross the floor and wrap my arm around Evan's waist, drawing her back against me.

I meet Mark's eyes over her head, and he laughs softly, shaking his head.

"Damon, this is Mark. Mark, this is Damon." Evan leans her head back against my chest. "Mark wanted me to let you know if you ever want to experiment with a man, he's willing. I'm not sure where I stand on whether it's cheating or fair because I fuck other men, but we do keep it to a select few, so..."

She tilts her head so her wicked blue-gray eyes meet mine. She makes me crazy.

"Nice to meet you, Mark." I wrap both arms around Evan and rest my chin on her head. "I belong to Evan."

Mark nods. "Not trying to break anything up. And not into cheating."

"Good." I give him a nod like we've reached an understanding. I rub Evan's hip with my hand. "You ready, little devil?"

Her cheeks flush and she meets Mark's gaze. "I'll talk to you later about our movie night."

Mark waves and walks away. He shakes his head and glances back. His gaze lingers on my arms and hands with interest. Hawk seems to be right, but Mark could be bi.

"No offering me to others, Evan. That's not part of our deal." I loosen my grip so she can turn in my arms.

She touches my jaw. "I really wish I could have seen your face. But you're right, I don't share my men."

I smirk and lean down to kiss her.

"Kiss later." Cam puts his hand on my shoulder. "We need to ride."

I kiss Evan briefly before she slips away, and then we wait while she cleans up. Hawk grabs her stuff. We've been doing this for a while now. It goes smoothly. Keira and Mia help lock up and walk out with us. Cam walks them over to their cars while we get ready to ride.

Evan climbs on the back of my bike, still dressed for school in one of her new skirts and an old shirt. Besides the panties and bras I've given her, she still prefers her old clothes or my clothes to the ones her mother bought her. She's not what I expected at the beginning of this year.

Most girls would have taken advantage of the glow up, but not Evan. She's more impressed by the paper flowers Cam makes her than the expensive clothes in her closet. As soon as Cam joins us, we take off.

"So where are we going?" Evan asks.

"Our spot," I say.

"We have a spot?" She sounds surprised.

"The spot where we like to chase you," Hawk adds.

Evan's arms and knees tighten against me. Her voice is a little breathy and excited when she says, "Are you going to chase me tonight?"

I chuckle and speed up as we hit the edge of town and onto the highway. She clings to me, pressing every inch of herself against me. Watching Evan control her rehearsal makes me want to control her.

We're going to have to talk about what we want. How we want to play. We've played it fairly straightforward before, but tonight I don't want her to hold back.

Slowing down as we approach the wooded area, I turn in and park my bike. Evan slides off the back and removes her helmet. Before I can remove my helmet, she climbs on in front of me, straddling me.

Her hands reach between the two of us and grab my pants as I balance the bike.

"What are you doing, little devil?" I tilt my head with a cocky grin that she can't see behind the helmet.

She bites her lip. "If we're going to do this, I want you to make me wet." Her eyes lift to where mine are covered by the shield. "And I want you to wear your helmets."

"Like you aren't already wet?"

She arches her eyebrow. "Make me wetter."

"How do you propose I make you wetter?"

She takes out my hardened cock and strokes it. "Fuck me."

I chuckle low and don't take off my gloves. I press her back until she lies across my tank, dragging my hand down the center of her. She wraps her fingers around my handlebars. Her feet tuck around my hips as she arches up into my touch.

Pushing her skirt up, I look at her lacey panties, the ones I chose for her to wear today. Running my gloved finger along her groin, I tease the edge of her panties. She bites her lip as she watches me. The center of the fabric is visibly damp. Always so fucking wet for me.

"You going to miss me, little devil?" I stroke her pussy.

"Yes," she whispers.

When I fist her panties and rip them from her, she gasps.

But I don't stop there. I stand, straddling my bike, and thrust deep into her soaking cunt. I growl at the warm clutch of her around my cock.

"Harder," she says loud enough that something small rustles in the woods as it runs off.

I thrust into her hard, grabbing the handlebar between her hands and fucking into her until the bike rocks with every push.

"Tell me what you want to do to me." She opens her darkened eyes to search for mine. Her lips part and her tongue darts out to wet them.

"We're going to hunt you and fuck you like the animal you are." I strip off my glove and grab the lube from my pocket. "For when we fuck your ass."

She groans as her hips buck against mine.

"We're going to claim every inch of you tonight. Fill you up like the little cum slut you are." I grab the front of her shirt and rip it open. Buttons go everywhere, and she gasps.

"Damon!" Her tone is indignant, making me chuckle darkly.

"You're mine, little devil. The only way this stops is if you say *red*." I press her clit hard and feel her cunt flutter around my cock. "But you won't say it, will you, Evan? Because you want all the dick you can handle. You want to be my little cum slut, filled so full it drips from you."

"Yes," she whimpers as she arches her body. Her cunt chokes my cock as she comes. I pull out and flip her over on my bike. She pants and looks over her shoulder at me with those moonlit eyes. This girl drives me crazy in the best way. I cover my fingers with lube, drizzling it on her asshole.

When I thrust back into her still pulsing pussy, I ease my fingers into her puckered hole, fucking in and out of her ass with my fingers. She stretches out like a cat before me, panting and making little needy noises. I add another finger to her ass and she cries out her release. Her pussy milks my cock.

"Fuck her ass." Hawk fists his dick as he watches me fuck Evan. "Make sure she can take me."

Evan whimpers as I pull out before lining my cockhead up against her puckered hole. She gasps as I ease in steadily, pushing past the ring of muscles. Her knuckles are white on my handlebars. I lean down to kiss the nape of her neck and she turns her face toward me.

"Breathe, goody." Cam stands on the other side of us, stroking himself, watching her ass take every inch of me. "Such a good girl taking that cock. You're going to take us all tonight, aren't you?"

"Yes," she gasps out as I seat my dick fully in her warmth.

If it didn't feel so good fucking her, I would stay buried inside her forever. But it's not just us tonight and I can't wait to watch her take us all. I pull out and fuck into her. She lets out a harsh breath, but when I do it again, she pushes back into me. Right now isn't the time to be rough. She needs to adjust to having us inside her, let me stretch her out so that it won't hurt when we catch and fuck her.

"We're going to fuck you so hard when we catch you." I pull her ass cheeks apart so I can watch my cock disappear inch by inch into her welcoming hole.

She grips the handlebars and lets out a moan as her ass tightens on my cock. Her release drags me into mine.

"That's my little cum slut. Milk me for what you want." Groaning, I come inside her ass hard. I pull out and grab some moistened wipes to clean myself off before tucking my cock back in my athletic pants.

I use another wipe to clean her as she lays, breathing heavily, on my motorcycle. Fuck, I want a picture of her like this. Used and exhausted from pleasure, spread across my bike like a fucking offering.

I lean back as Cam grabs the lube and spreads more on her ass before pressing his fingers inside.

"What do you say if you want this to stop, Annie?" Hawk asks, still stroking his cock while watching Cam work her ass with his fingers.

"I say *red*," she pants. "I'm good. Don't fucking stop. Oh, fuck."

She keens as she comes, soaking my motorcycle. Fucking beautiful.

Hawk helps her climb off. Her shirt hangs open, showing her lacey bra that matches the ripped panties currently in my pocket. She staggers a little but looks more determined than ever.

I love this girl.

"Feel free to hit or kick us, baby girl." Hawk's face is hidden by his helmet, but I can hear the smirk in his voice. "You sure you want us to keep our helmets on? If not, no hitting our faces."

"I want the helmets." She wets her lips and nods, backing up slightly. She eyes me warily, knowing I'm coming for her. My cock is already hard for her again. My kinky little devil.

"You better hide well, little devil. We're going to ravage you tonight, but I'll take care of you when we get home."

---

### *EvanAnn*

I bite my lip and turn and run before they can start counting. Their laughter follows me into the woods. At least I'm a little familiar with these woods now, but I can't go to the same hiding spot as before.

I saw the packets of wipes and little bottles of lube in Damon's saddlebag. We're going to play rough, but they'll make sure not to hurt me in a way that will require medical attention. A few bruises and being fucked until I'm sore, I can deal with.

In fact, I'm looking forward to it.

I shiver with anticipation, and maybe a little chill with my shirt ripped open. At least it was one of my old uniform shirts. I ditched my tie at the beginning of rehearsal. This shirt is ruined, but I do have new ones I can wear.

We haven't publicized I'm living with Damon. It's not like the beginning of the year. Everything has already changed. I can wear the new uniforms and not give a shit if people think I'm a gold digger.

The forest is quiet. I can't hear if they're calling out numbers, but the helmets tend to muffle their words. For all I know they'll remain quiet and communicate only through Bluetooth. My wetness cools on my thighs. My pussy throbs with the need to be fucked again.

Do I want them to earn the right to fuck me? I lean back against a tree, trying to slow my breaths. I want to fight them. Not because I don't want them to have me. I want them to fuck me so badly. I'm hoping to fuck them all at the same time. Feeling them pulse deep inside me. Taking them all.

But first they have to find me and catch me.

The anticipation sizzles through my blood. Asking them to wear their helmets makes it scarier. Like a horror movie brought to life. I want to be the helpless heroine. I want them to overpower me.

It feels wrong to want it this way, but they don't judge me. And I don't judge them. It's why we're comfortable with each other. It's thrilling to hide and wait for them to find me. Even more thrilling to run from them, to make them catch me, knowing they'll cushion my fall as much as they can.

My heart is in my ears as I try to pay attention to the night, to the forest around me, to the sounds that don't fit. I draw in a breath and peek around the tree I'm behind. If they're out there, I can't see them. It must be close to a new moon tonight because there isn't as much light as the other nights.

I step out from the tree and look around, but I don't see the guys anywhere. The bikes are still in the parking lot, but I can't see the guys. I creep forward and wince when a branch breaks beneath my step. When no one charges me, I step forward again.

Apparently, instead of being the hunted, I'm the hunter. Or maybe I'm both. My skin tingles with awareness and unease.

I draw my shirt together in my fist and try to stay low and against trees while I figure out where they've gone. The back of my neck prickles, and I turn sharply to see if someone is behind me.

Nothing's there. The swell of anticipation falls. I could find a new hiding spot. Eventually they'll look for me, right? It wouldn't be much fun if we all just hid from each other tonight. I could call out *red* and find out what the deal is, but I don't want this to end.

My pussy and ass are cold as I walk forward trying to find at least one of the guys. Maybe we're circling each other. Of course, all they have to do to find me with this ring is open their tracking app. That shouldn't be allowed while we're playing, but we don't have a lot of rules for this game.

I pause when I think I hear footsteps behind me. I spin and find nothing, not even a shadow. The breath I was holding eases out of me. Staying in one place, I wait to see if they'll move again.

When I lose my nerve, I walk forward and the same echo follows me. I turn quickly and find no one. I swallow and release the fear building in me. No one knows about this place but us. I should have confirmed that with them.

I have a stalker. Or at least someone acting like a stalker. I stretch out my right hand. What if he shows up out here? What if he's hurt my guys? My heart thrums quickly in my ears. Maybe this is a bad idea. My breath catches, and I turn a full three hundred and sixty degrees to see all around me.

My guys wouldn't have gone down without a fight. They would have warned me. One guy couldn't take them all out. But what if it wasn't one guy? I shiver and press my thighs together.

This is so stupid.

I'm working myself up over probably nothing. But what if it's something?

Taking a breath, I move toward the bikes. If I can get there, I can get my phone out of my backpack. I'll call the police if the guys aren't on me by the time I get to it.

After a few steps, I hear the same footsteps and release the uneasy breath in my lungs. I force myself to walk a few more steps before spinning to catch them. Nothing.

When I turn back toward the bikes, a figure in black in a helmet stands about ten yards ahead of me.

## CHAPTER 13
## *EvanAnn*

I TAKE an involuntary step backward from the figure, and something in the corner of my eye catches my attention. Another figure shirtless, but wearing his helmet, stands in the open, not trying to hide or approach.

They both stand there motionless. My heart pounds in my ears. When I turn back the way I came, the third figure is there. These are my guys. I feel it in my soul, but the fear still clings to me. The fear I'm being hunted by someone I don't want hunting me.

Anyone could be behind those helmets. It's part of the fantasy, but also terrifying.

My breath stutters in my chest. I need to run. I need to get away.

They aren't moving. They just stand there, watching me, letting my panic build.

I narrow my eyes, but then focus, and run in the direction they aren't. It's away from the bikes like they're herding me back into the forest. I can't hear their feet over the pounding of my own and the frantic beat of my heart in my ears.

I release my shirt because running while clutching it is awkward and I don't want to fall. I duck behind a tree, knowing they'll be on me any minute. Expecting it, counting on it. I'm not going to be run to the ground this time.

No, I'm going to stand and fight. Not that I can take out athletes, but I have some combat training. Okay, stage combat training, but I just won't pull my blows and actually aim for the soft spots we're told not to hit.

I probably won't do much damage, but if I'm going to be bruised in the morning, so should they. I hold my breath, waiting for the sound of them arriving, but then there's nothing.

Fuck. I peek my head out and see nothing. The bikes are farther away, and I've done nothing but run myself out of breath. Where are they?

I squint into the darkness. There! That shadow moved. Didn't it? I turn to look the other way and again, nothing. My fingers shake. It didn't take them this long to get me either of the times before.

I inhale and step out into the open again. Turning around, I scan the entire woods surrounding me. How the hell are they hiding? Why are they hiding?

Is this like the final act of a horror movie where the fed up heroine goes to face the monster? But in this case, I'm going to fuck my monsters.

This is so stupid. Those heroines are so stupid. I don't have anything to defend myself with, but these are *my* monsters. They aren't the boy trying to frighten me because I rejected him years ago. They aren't my ex trying to make me want them.

These boys are mine. It doesn't matter if I hide from them because they'll find me. They always find me. So I walk in the direction I came from. Because my monsters won't hurt me, not really.

But they want me in a panic. They want me scared. But I've never been scared of them.

I can pretend, but I trust these boys with everything. My heart, my body, my desire.

They'll take care of me, and I'll take care of them. The guys off to the sides appear first, but I keep walking forward toward the one I saw first.

He comes out from behind a tree, stepping into my path. The others close in on me. Tilting their heads oddly in their helmets. I swallow, because it's still creepy.

"I don't want to run," I say. My voice is breathless, but audible.

"We'll take you then." Damon. A shiver runs down my spine as he closes the distance between us, but he leaves five feet. Enough room to dart away if I want to.

The fear continues to trickle along my spine, but desire swells with it. I wet my lips and turn to Cam. As they get closer, I can tell the difference in their stature, their build. I know every inch of their bodies. The helmets remain on and they don't say more.

"You were never monsters to me." I look at Hawk. "Maybe that's why I was so surprised you talked to me that first day. Who was I to draw the attention of the Devil's trio?"

They all stand a few feet away from me, waiting.

"I was afraid of what it meant. I had no idea what Chase had done to you. Had no idea what you would want from me. But it didn't matter. I needed you to shake up my life. To break down the walls I'd built to keep everyone out."

I let out a huff of breath. "I don't want to keep you out. You make me whole. You let me breathe. Even when you hunt me in a forest. Even when you fuck me roughly. Am I going to fight you tonight?"

Damon cocks his head. It's so odd in the helmet. Almost alien.

I straighten. "Yes, because I want you. I want you to make me into what you need. What you want. I want to be captured and forced into submission, because I love you and what it does for me."

Cam lifts his helmet off and tosses it to the side. Hawk follows. They're still a ways away from me. I stare at Damon. He slowly raises his hands and takes off his helmet.

The smile on his lips and the shake of his head should be a warning. Instead a little shiver of anticipation ripples through me.

"Little devil." He drops his helmet and lifts his gaze to mine. Even in the darkness, I feel his eyes on me. "I never wanted you submissive. You've always taken what we give you, but I'll always make you mine."

They all take a step toward me, and I shrink away instinctively.

"You sure you don't want to run, goody?" Cam laughs like he's entertained.

Fear forces my hand. That coiled up tension inside me waiting for something, anything to happen.

"You sure you aren't afraid, baby girl?" Hawk smiles, and he's so close I can see the white of his teeth. The tension ramps higher as they step closer.

Damon laughs, dark and menacing. "Run, Evan."

It's like my survival instinct was waiting to kick in. I run, but I don't turn my back on them. I aim for the space between Damon and Cam and take off.

Part of me expects Damon to capture me, so I don't go directly between them, which was a mistake as Cam grabs me and lifts me off my feet.

I let out a frustrated noise and kick my heels back at him. He holds my arms clinched to my chest.

"How's the hand, goody?" His breath moves the hair next to my ear. I soften a little at his worry.

"It's still a little sore."

He chuckles. "Guess you shouldn't ride Damon so hard in the morning then."

I try to wiggle out of his hold, knowing I'm only seconds from being surrounded. "Let me go."

"Never, goody." His words are a promise that sparks in my heart. I don't let it stop my flailing though.

"Grab her feet," Damon says.

I twist as Hawk reaches for my ankles. He gets ahold of one. But when I kick him with the other, he curses and grabs my other leg.

"Not so fast, baby girl."

Hawk has my ankles, and Cam holds me around my center. I try to use my elbows to make Cam release me. Even my deadweight wouldn't be enough to get them to let go. My struggle is nothing compared to what they put their bodies through for hockey.

Cam's arm is right there. Damon grabs my hair and pulls my head back from where I was trying to find a way to bite Cam. I let out a gasp at the pain.

"Now, now, Evan. That's not playing nice. Biting?" He clucks his tongue at me. "Cam had a good idea though."

I glance up at Cam and then at Hawk. They have me held tight. I'm not going anywhere, but I try to buck in their arms.

Damon tightens his hold on my hair.

"Ow, ow, ow." I freeze, but I don't say *red*. They all pause, waiting for me to say it. For me to end this game before the good part. Fuck that.

"You can ride me like the wildcat you are, while Cam fucks that pretty asshole." Damon gets up in my face. "You want us to fill your holes, fill you like the little cum slut you are."

So much so. "Fuck off."

"I need to get my dick wet." Hawk's words draw my attention to him. My breath catches even as my pussy grows wetter. "Hold her leg."

This is how I'll get away. He'll release my foot, and I'll kick... but he doesn't let go of my ankle. Damon grabs my knee and pulls it up to his chest, practically folding me in half and opening up my pussy.

Just being near them has me soaked. The idea that they'll take me. Force me. Makes me want it. Because in this twisted little game, I can't wait to be taken that way, like they can't help themselves.

Hawk pushes my other leg up and out. Cam holds me steady as Hawk uses his free hand to release his cock. Even as I try to struggle uselessly against them, I grow even wetter in anticipation. When he slides the head of his cock along my slit, I bite my lip at the sizzle in my blood. Fuck, that feels so good.

"You want it, don't you? You want me to take you? Feel how wet you are just waiting for me to fuck this tight, little pussy." Hawk notches his cock at my entrance and then slams inside me.

I cry out at the invasion, at the stretch, at how good it feels. He fucks me hard and fast. His pubic bone hitting my clit at the way I'm spread open for his use. I tip my head back against Cam's chest as I'm pushed over the edge. When I come, my moan fills the air, and my pussy squeezes around his cock, milking it, begging him for his cum.

He pulls out, and I almost whimper at the loss. "Lift her higher."

His fingers are slick as he finds my asshole and coats it. The head of his cock presses against my puckered hole and pushes in steadily.

"Oh, fuck," I grit out. He's so fucking thick.

"Don't worry, baby girl. I've got you. I'll fuck this ass real good, make sure you can take the others."

His breath is harsh against my lips as he pushes all the way inside. I gasp at the tight fit and how good he feels inside me.

"This would be better with you on the ground," he whispers against my lips. "The others holding you down while I fuck this ass hard. Do you want that, baby girl? Do you want me to wreck this ass for you?"

I flick my tongue out to touch his lips. He chuckles and slams forward. His lips on mine. His cock buried deep inside me. His abs press against my pussy.

Then he's gone, and I'm empty and throbbing with need. "On her knees."

I try to fight them maneuvering me into the new position, but I crave it too. Damon holds my head down, grabbing my wrists in his hand, as Cam keeps my hips where Hawk can fuck me. Cam must be facing my ass because he spreads my ass cheeks wide, holding me open.

And then Hawk slams into me.

"Oh, fuck," I whimper and clench my fingers, digging my nails into my palms slightly.

He doesn't ease me into it this time. He fucks my ass. Everything inside me wants this, craves it. I'm wound so fucking tight, so ready to explode. Damon's fingers drag across my cheekbone as I scream my release.

Hawk cries out as he unloads his warm cum inside me. When he pulls out, I force a gasp, trying to catch my breath. I'm limp. That last orgasm shattered me, but the guys aren't finished with me yet. They reposition me. Cam thrusts into my ass, pulling me back against him, holding my legs out to either side as Damon slams his cock into my pussy.

It's almost too much. I cry out, so full of them. Damon rubs my clit while he fucks me.

"When I finish, Hawk's going to fill this cunt with his cum too. Then I'll take Cam's place and fuck your ass again. Keep you so full of cock." Damon pushes my shirt open and pulls the cups of my bra down to reveal my breasts. "You'll like that, won't you, little devil? You'll leak on my bed all night, wrapped in my arms."

He teases my nipples with his fingers, and I ache with the need for release.

"Yes," I whisper, beyond fighting. Just needing what they can give to me.

# CHAPTER 14
## EvanAnn

I LOSE track of who's fucking me, who's kissing me, who's using me. It's rough and chaotic and all mine. Time loses all meaning beyond the tempo they each pump into me. The next climb. The next release. The next penetration. Damon locks eyes with me.

"You still with me?" He brushes his lips against mine gently while I'm being fucked.

My lips part as another release blazes through me. My throat clenches around a scream. It feels like my orgasms never end, like I'm being torn apart piece by piece.

"Little devil?"

I open my eyes and lose myself in his. Right now it's too dark to see the color, but the way he looks at me is everything. I reach out, surprised my hand is free, and trace my fingertips down the side of his face. The movement is tender in the roughness of our coupling.

"I'm yours," I whisper, needing him to hear it, needing to say it.

He smirks, and I run my hand through his pale hair. It's a quiet moment in the chaos, and I love this as much as I love being hunted. Hands explore me. Cocks penetrate me. I shiver a little even as hot bodies press into mine.

Cam groans against my ear. "I love your ass, goody."

"I love your ass too, Cam." My eyes pinch shut as another wave takes me under.

His warmth floods me. "No more. Fuck, I'm done."

Cam kisses my shoulder and falls away from me. Warmth steps into the space he left, and suddenly I'm full again.

I breathe out. Needing it, aching for it.

"One more, baby girl. I just want one more from you." Hawk's lips brush the side of my neck, his words glide over my bare shoulder.

"You can have them all." I want them to. To take everything from me.

Damon thrusts in time with Hawk, keeping me standing on the precipice of something amazing. I'm a live wire, and they're flooding me with electricity. I haven't come down and I don't think I can. But I know they'll take care of me. That when I fall, they'll catch me.

"Open your eyes, Evan."

I don't resist Damon's command. When I open my eyes, he leans in and takes my mouth. I cry out as I fall into freefall, dragging both of them with me into ecstasy.

I collapse against Damon, trying to catch my breath as Hawk kisses my neck and shoulder, sending tiny aftershocks through me, before he steps away. Damon holds me against him, and I can feel how wet everything is between my legs.

It's us, and I can't help wanting to keep it for myself.

Damon pulls out of me last and carries me through the woods back to reality. I tremble in his arms and watch Hawk and Cam following us. Their eyes on me like nothing else exists. It's powerful being what they need, what they want.

When we get to the bikes, Cam goes to his saddlebags. He comes back and gently wipes my bottom and pussy. Hawk brings over a duffle and pulls out one of Damon's hoodies and some of my leggings. Damon sets me down, and they all work on cleaning me up and dressing me.

I don't bother to help, just let my hand trail over their chests, arms, jaws. I'm in a daze, and I can't be bothered to care.

Loved. That's what I am. That's what these boys give me.

When I'm dressed, Damon straddles his bike and Hawk helps me climb on in front of Damon. I lean back into him as he holds me, staring into the dark woods. The others straddle their bikes too, but no one is in a hurry to leave this place as we come down.

Our place.

"Are you okay? Were we too rough?" Cam asks. He leans forward on his bike.

"No. It was all good," I say softly, like being too loud will dispel whatever peace we have. "Though I thought I could at least get a hit in before you subdued me."

Hawk chuckles at my pout. "You got me in the side before I caught your leg. If it bruises, I'll expect you to kiss it better."

I breathe in and release it. After all that, I just feel content, relaxed, and sleepy.

"We still need to talk." Damon rests his hand on my stomach.

I love how much larger he is than me, how I feel safe locked in his arms.

"She'll be safe." Cam winks at me, reassuring Damon. "We can handle this week so you can focus on proving you're the only choice they should make for their team."

"We won't leave her alone. We know what's at risk." Hawk rubs his hands on his thighs as he looks at me. "We're not idiots and are perfectly capable of keeping our woman satisfied and safe."

"I haven't been attacked, except the rose." I glance over my shoulder at Damon. "I'll be safe in the house. The alarm will be set, and I'll curl up in our bed where you can watch me with your surveillance equipment." I arch my eyebrow at him.

"My favorite time of the day is catching up on yours." He smirks and slides his hand around the front of my throat, drawing me gently to rest my back on his chest. "Whoever is watching you is going to know I'm gone. It's prime time for someone to try to attack you."

I let the rhythm of his chest rising and falling lull me. "For a second, I worried that someone knew about this place and the game we play. That's the only time I really felt afraid. That something might have happened to you."

Damon's hand tightens on my stomach for a moment. "No one

comes here. It's why we like to. The road doesn't get traffic, and no one can find us."

"We wouldn't put you at risk like that, goody."

I turn to look at Cam and Hawk. "I know that."

Hawk breathes out. "I'll slip out late if I have to, but I'm guessing my parents wouldn't be bothered if you came to stay with me."

My cheeks flush. "It's different sneaking around than being open about it."

Hawk smirks. "My parents are aware we're dating and likely fucking. They don't delude themselves with thoughts of me being innocent."

"I don't think any of your parents think you're innocent," I scoff. "But my mom doesn't worry about me like that. At least I don't think she does. I've never given her reason to worry about me." I don't add *until now*.

"We can wait and see how the week goes. If it's between you being left alone and you spending the night at my house, there's only one solution." Hawk's green eyes meet mine.

"I know." I rest my head back against Damon's chest and breathe out. "We should come out to our parents. It's going to happen eventually. We almost got caught last night. I'm surprised they haven't figured it out already."

"My dad is probably suspicious." Damon rubs my stomach. "Your mom might be too, but she's living in her delusion that this move was the best for her."

"It was the best for me too." I thread my fingers through his. "I want to wait until you get back to tell them though. If that's okay?"

I glance over my shoulder at him, and he cups my jaw. His eyes meet mine. "Anything you want, little devil."

The firestorm that had taken hold of me settles. He's not going to push this the way he pushed about Chase. Chase made sense. He would keep using the fact I hadn't told my mom about our breakup against me.

But this? I look at Damon's hand in mine. I wouldn't lose him, but it might make things uncomfortable in the house. And if Mom thinks the only way to protect me is to move, would she? I don't know if I want to test that.

Maybe she won't care, but if she does and still does nothing to stop it, what does that mean? That she doesn't love me enough? That she doesn't care what I do as long as she can have a life with Adam?

My heart aches. Have I been so easy she'll just figure I can take care of this too? That I'm mature enough to be in a relationship with three guys at eighteen? That I know what I'm doing?

Fuck. I don't want her to think she knows what's best for me. But I also worry she doesn't think about me at all sometimes.

"It will be okay, Evan." Damon rubs his thumb across mine. "Whatever our parents decide, they won't be able to keep us from each other. You're ours."

This is why I want him here when they find out. There's no way he'd let them take me from him. I want to be a united front.

We stay a little longer. None of us really wanting the night to end, knowing when we get back into town we'll be going our separate ways. Someday we won't have to. Someday we'll end the night together in the life we build with each other.

But right now, we're still beholden to our parents and their whims.

When Damon helps me off his bike to get ready to head out, I walk over to Hawk. He takes me into his arms, hugging me close to his body. "You okay, Annie?"

I sigh. "Just thinking about the future when we won't have to say goodnight."

He tips my chin up and kisses me like the world is ending. When he pulls away, he smirks and drags his thumb over my lower lip. "Dream of me, baby girl."

I nod and head over to Cam. He draws me onto his bike in front of him, facing him. I wrap my legs around his back and he kisses me, gently like I'm something precious. My heart thumps.

"I probably won't sneak in to fuck you tonight." His mischievous eyes meet mine.

My laughter breaks the silence of the night surrounding us.

"You need to rest, and I'm sure you'll be sore. Maybe I'll bring a cushion to school for you to sit on, goody."

My face turns red. "No one else needs to know I'm sore."

"But I'll make sure they know you're mine." He smirks and gives me another lingering kiss before helping me off his bike.

I walk to Damon, who holds my helmet out to me. I put it on, and even though I can do it myself, I tip my chin up for him to get the strap.

His chuckle is low and dark, but he helps me. I climb on behind him as he puts on his helmet.

"Everything is going to be fine." Damon's words send a shiver down my back.

"Fuck, man," Cam says. "You know that's what they say in movies right before everything gets blown up."

"This isn't a movie, asshole." Damon starts his motorcycle and pulls out onto the street.

"You might as well have said *I'll be right back* and go off to investigate the strange noise." Hawk pulls up alongside us on the empty road. "It's like you don't even know the rules."

"Not you too." Damon's voice is in my helmet.

"Just making sure I'm familiar with what my girl is interested in." Hawk's smirk comes across loud and clear. "And you never make bold statements in movies, or that's when everything bad happens."

"Nothing bad is going to happen," I say to make Damon feel better. "We're going to get through this week, and then we'll all be back together. We'll tell our parents about our relationship—without the fucking part. And then we won't have to hide anymore."

We ride the rest of the way with Cam and Hawk telling Damon how he doesn't know me as well as they do. He stays quiet for the most part, probably because he gets me to himself more than they do.

"Goodnight, goody." Cam turns to head off, leaving us to continue to our house.

"Night, Annie." Hawk keeps going down the street while Damon pulls into our driveway and the garage.

It's late, but at least the guys had the forethought to bring some of my clothes with them. I climb off Damon's bike and hand him the helmet before picking up my backpack.

"Do I have any sticks in my hair?" I turn my back to him, and he chuckles.

"Only the one I pulled out already." He brushes his hand over my hair. "You look fine, Evan. No one will suspect a thing."

I turn and put my hand on his chest, meeting his eyes. "I know I'm still putting off telling them. But I just want you to be here when we tell them and not heading off for a week. I'm happy to be yours."

Damon smirks and touches my jaw. "You don't want to face the firing squad alone. I get that."

"Pretty much." I go up on my toes, and he lowers his head to kiss me softly.

The house is quiet. If Mom and Adam are home, they're probably already in bed or at least in their bedroom. We go in the back way and walk to our rooms.

I go into my room to grab something to sleep in and meet Damon in the bathroom where the shower is running already. He's already stripped naked and hard for me, but he just helps me undress and guides me into the shower.

As we wash each other, I can't help yawning.

He smirks.

"What? I'm tired." I rest my forehead against his chest as the water cascades over us.

He cups the back of my head. "I'm not expecting to fuck you all night, little devil. You can sleep."

I blow out a breath and look up at him. "Today was long."

"This week will be brutal, but I'll be home before you know it." He kisses my temple and turns the shower off. He bundles me in a towel before grabbing his.

We go through our process of getting ready for bed like we always do. I glance at him as I brush my teeth.

He shakes his head. "Don't start something you can't finish, little devil."

I rinse my mouth and smile at him. If I had any energy, I'd be all over him, but I'm exhausted. I take his hand and lead him into our bedroom, climbing into our bed while he watches me. I love this time with him. It's something special just for me.

I just can't wait until I have all three of them with me all the time. When we all get to go to bed together.

"Take off the nightgown." Damon arches his eyebrow at me like I forgot to do it.

I strip it off, leaving on my panties.

"Better." He climbs in next to me and pulls me down onto his chest, covering us with the blankets. "I like the way your skin feels on mine. I love you, Evan."

I smile and brush my lips over his bare chest. "I love you."

# CHAPTER 15
## *Damon*

I'M BARELY awake when I hear something. I'm not even sure what. Evan is sprawled naked on top of me. Having her close to me, warm from our shower with her words hanging in the air, I stayed awake waiting for sleep to come. But all I could think about was her warm body against mine.

When she rocked her hips against mine, maybe in her sleep, I don't fucking know, but I stopped resisting. I rolled her onto her back and made sure she knew how much I loved her. She was definitely awake by then.

We clung to each other as we came, and I shifted her to sleep on top of me. Now, her hand curls into my side like she heard something too, or maybe she felt me move beneath her. It's dark out the window, and nothing stands out. I fade back into sleep.

"Damon!" My dad's voice. "We can't find—"

The lights turn on, blinding me.

"What?" Evan lifts her head.

"EvanAnn?" Dad's voice is questioning as realization floods him.

Fuck. I blink, but it's too late. I draw the covers up a little higher to cover Evan. There's no way to explain away any of this, except with the truth. I put my arm over my eyes and make sure Evan doesn't move. My dad does not need to see her breasts which are pressed up against my chest.

"Downstairs. Five minutes," Dad says sternly. The door closes, and his footsteps fade.

"Fuck." I drop my head on my pillow. Five minutes isn't long.

When I start to move, Evan clings to me. "Sleep," she mutters into my chest, oblivious to the shitshow awaiting us downstairs. It's Friday morning and way before we need to be up for school. We probably only got a few hours of sleep at best.

I scrub my hand over my face. "Little devil, the jig is up."

She rubs her nose against my bare chest and blows out her breath across my skin. "What jig?"

"Our parents know." I sit up, forcing her to sit up with me. She straddles my lap. "Or at least my dad knows."

"Shit." Evan pushes her hair out of her face and looks around like a shirt is going to magically appear.

I get out of bed, leaving her dazed and confused, and go into her bedroom, grabbing a pair of pajamas appropriate for being in front of our parents and some panties. I toss them to her as she's still sitting on the bed, frozen.

"I know you wanted to control the narrative, but we knew it would happen at some point." I pull on a pair of athletic pants and a t-shirt and then sit down next to her on the bed to help her dress.

Her eyes are wide as she tries to figure out how to fix this. I pull her top on over her head, and she finally pulls on the pants. I doubt she's ever been in trouble before. Always the good girl until we ruined her.

I run my hand over her hair brushing it away from her face.

"What are we going to do?" she asks in a small voice. Her eyes are wide.

I tip her chin up. "We're going to own up to it. We're eighteen years old. Yes, it's a little odd since our parents are dating, but teenagers have sex." I search her frightened eyes. "I'm not giving you up, little devil."

When I kiss her softly, she caves to the kiss like it's the last one she'll get. I pull away and reiterate, "You, Hawk, Cam, and me. I love you. You belong to us and with us. We'll get through this."

***EvanAnn***

When Damon offers me his hand, I look at it. Taking his hand means going downstairs to face whatever consequences are waiting. It's still dark outside. This just isn't my week. Dads finding me in compromising situations was not on my bingo card. I don't want to face this, but at least I have Damon to face it with me.

I take his hand and climb off the bed. He pulls me into his arms and hugs me tight against him. For a second, I cling to him, resting my head on his heart. Will this be my last opportunity to be with him this way? Will they try to separate us?

Before we head down, I go to the bathroom to clean up as best as I can. I hadn't planned on falling asleep right after sex, but that's what happened. We also hadn't planned on having sex though. Again. I wash my hands and meet my gaze in the mirror.

Fuck, this isn't going to go over well. Adam saw me in bed, naked on his son. My breath settles like a lump in my stomach. My face is pale. Damon leans against the doorframe.

"It'll be okay."

But he can't know that. I walk over to him and put my head on his chest. "I'm scared."

"I've got you, little devil." He takes my hand and leads me out of the room and down the stairs. The lights are on in the living room. My heart hurts and my fingers tremble in Damon's.

We pause when we hear voices.

"In bed? Together? Naked?" My mom's voice sounds near hysterics. "What—? How—? This can't—but..."

"Keep it down, love. They're on their way down here." Adam's voice is calm.

My heart slams in my chest as Damon pulls me to a stop so we can listen.

"This was a mistake. I shouldn't have moved in this year. We should have waited. I thought she'd be safer. This is my fault. I did this. We should have moved to the apartments." Mom sounds like she's pacing, but every word out of her mouth ratchets my anxiety higher. My heart is going to explode. "But the apartments—"

She cuts off.

"Heather." Adam's voice is soothing. "It'll be okay. You did what was best for your family. We don't know what this is yet. Maybe they found something in each other the way we did."

"But sleeping together? What kind of mother would I be if I just let them..." She drags in a breath. "I should stop this. Move out? We could live somewhere else." She doesn't seem sure, but it's all I can hear. It's why I hid this from her. "But go where?"

Damon slides his hand beneath my hair along my nape and tucks his head to kiss the top of mine.

"You're not leaving, Heather. Not an option. We need to talk about this. With them. They're eighteen. Nothing illegal is happening here. She didn't look like she was forced to be there. They were sleeping. She hasn't been acting strange, like she's being taken advantage of. We'll figure this out." Adam must have stood. "Would you go make some coffee for us please? I think this talk is going to take clear minds."

"But—"

"She's safe here, Heather. You're safe here."

What does that mean? That I'm safe with Damon?

"You're right. I just..."

"Coffee, love." The sound of a kiss precedes her footsteps walking away. Damon gives it a minute before leading me in. I don't want to do this, but there really isn't a choice, unless we want to get on his bike and just ride away. Not really an option. We have futures to work towards. School to finish.

Adam sits in a chair with his head in his hands. He looks up as we walk in. His face is resigned, but there's a little relief when he focuses on our hands.

Damon and I sit on the couch, our thighs touching, still holding each other's hand. I don't think I can release his. I'm probably crushing it, but he doesn't wince, just holds me.

What do I say? What can I say? We've been caught. All we can do is stick with the truth. Or you know, some version of it that doesn't make my mom move us out.

Adam sits up and puts his hand over his mouth. His hair sticks up oddly, like he just got out of bed himself. Apparently he doesn't know what to say either. He walked in on me in bed, obviously naked, on top of his son, also naked. So much worse than morning coffee with Hawk's dad when I was wearing a t-shirt and panties.

The only bright spot of this is that I'll truly understand humiliation. Helpful for acting and directing. I could list it on my resume. *Personal experience of mortification: check.*

Mom comes in from the kitchen with a tray of coffee cups. The tray shakes slightly, rattling the cups.

Her gaze locks on my hand in Damon's resting on his thigh. Her lips pinch, but she doesn't say anything. Her hair is up in a messy bun, like an afterthought. She has a robe on over her pajamas.

She thought about taking me away, but Adam talked her out of it. Would she have done it to protect me or because she doesn't want me with Damon? Why move us out at all?

She hands me a cup of coffee and then gives one to Damon. Her smile is tight. I take a sip, finding she's added a little creamer and sugar for me. The way I like it. She settles in the chair next to Adam and sighs.

It feels like no one wants to start this conversation. Everyone holds their coffee and sips at the hot beverage. I don't think there's enough caffeine to make this conversation any easier.

Adam and Mom don't make eye contact with us, but I'm not looking at them either. He knows I was naked on his son, and he told my mom.

"Was there a reason you came into my locked room?" Damon asks Adam casually, taking a sip of his coffee. Trying to be on the offensive, nice. But I don't think our privacy is going to get us out of this one.

Adam winces and runs a hand through his hair. He glances at Heather. "Heather got a text about EvanAnn. She went to her room and didn't find her. Her bed was made. I came to your room to get you to help look for her."

My cheeks burn, but I can't help being curious. "What text?"

"It was an unknown number." Mom is paler than normal. "It was an old advertisement from the eighties. *Do you know where your children are?*"

"Have you received a lot of texts from unknown numbers?" Damon asks. Maybe he's thinking the same thing I am. That maybe my stalker is reaching out to Mom too.

Mom's cheeks pinken, and she glances at Adam. "Not many."

I look at Damon. We should tell them about the texts I've been getting. Right? I never told Mom about Jackson. Maybe I didn't want her to worry. But after the thorns on Sunday, maybe it's time to bring her in. Especially with her getting texts too.

What if there's something she hasn't been able to make sense of? Some clue that would tell us for sure who my stalker is?

"We need to talk about where EvanAnn's been sleeping." Adam tries to bring it back around to *that*. I'd love to avoid talking about *that* for as long as possible. Maybe we could not talk about *that* at all.

"I know you're probably hurting from your breakup with Chase," Mom begins. "And it's common for girls to seek... comfort in the arms of someone else..."

Oh god. I look at the floor, trying to disappear. Maybe combust into flames. Anything would be better than my mom justifying me sleeping with Damon.

Mom falters and looks to Adam for help, but Adam looks just as uncomfortable. It's not like I'm his daughter. And it's made even more awkward because it's his son I'm apparently seeking comfort from.

I manage not to roll my eyes. Thankfully, we're past the just using each other to get off portion of our relationship. But I'm not going to let her assume this has anything to do with Chase.

"It's not like that," I say. Though it's kind of hard to deny we're fucking when his dad saw me naked sprawled over Damon. I really can't get over that. I'm just lucky Cam and Hawk weren't able to stay or I would be bursting into flames right now. Though it would have been amusing watching Mom and Adam flounder their way through that one.

Though Mom might have been more determined to move us out if she found me in bed with three guys.

I don't know how I would have told her next week, but maybe I would have eased her into it. Start with one guy and then maybe add on another after a week, see how that goes and then add the third.

"Chase was your first boyfriend." Mom tries again. "It's always hard when relationships end. Almost everyone goes through a rebound, and I'm sure Damon is a very nice boy."

Damon scoffs. Adam winces, and I resist rolling my eyes again. No one would call him a nice boy, let alone a very nice boy. My mom has blinders when it comes to Damon Storm. Or she just doesn't know him at all. Which is probably closer to the truth.

She plows on. "But rebounds usually don't work out. It's still possible you and Chase could get back together. You seemed so happy at the party, and that was just last week."

"What exactly did you tell your mom about your breakup, Evan?" Damon turns to me, and I want to shrink into myself.

Fuck, yeah, he probably thought I told her everything. Honestly, I want to climb onto his lap and hide, but that's definitely not going to happen. I'm already exposed, and he wants to push me into the spotlight harder.

It's not like my mom needs to know the truth about Chase. I meet his eyes stubbornly and keep my mouth closed.

"She said they broke up." Mom straightens, clearly trying to defend me. "I hope you aren't taking advantage of her when she's sad from the breakup."

"Evan," Damon scolds me. Yeah, I didn't figure I'd get away with silence. Fine.

"I told her we broke up. That's all she needed to know." I didn't tell her about everything else. Like how Damon blackmailed me into sleeping with him and his friends or that I'm in a relationship with three guys now. Or that I found out about my boyfriend cheating on me right before Damon gave me my first orgasm not from masturbation. Or how I didn't really resist falling into bed with three guys and let them do whatever they wanted to me.

In fact, I enjoy every minute of it.

Damon's sharp blue eyes meet mine. "So she didn't tell you he cheated on her their entire relationship?"

I narrow my eyes on him. He didn't have to tell her that.

"What? No. That's awful." Mom covers her mouth. "I'm so sorry, honey. No wonder you weren't crying. Guys can be very immature at this age."

Fuck it. I turn to look at my mom, watching her struggle to try to rationalize everything. There's nothing to rationalize.

"I'm not torn up about breaking up with Chase," I say. "He was just using me to make his father think he had a good girlfriend with excellent grades and a promising future."

"It's still hard after ending a relationship," Mom says, uncertain now.

Not when you have the attention of three hotter and much better guys. But I don't think she wants to hear that right now.

"Is this new?" Adam asks and gestures between the two of us.

Swallowing the lump in my throat, I don't think I can get any redder. At this point, I'm just going to burst into flames, which would be preferable. The thorns were less uncomfortable than this conversation. At least then I knew the pain would end.

"Is it, Evan?" Damon asks like he's not sure what the answer is in my reality. Fuck, why does he have to push me? This isn't going to help anything.

I'd snatch my hand back, but I don't want to let go. "Not exactly," I bite out.

"But you just broke up with Chase?" Mom asks.

"Not exactly." I close my eyes. Maybe this is just a horrible nightmare and I can wake up. Why does Damon have to make this worse? I hadn't planned to lead our conversation next week with Damon and I are having sex. I would have said we're together. Boyfriend and girlfriend.

If our parents inferred we were having sex that would be on them. I really didn't plan to lead with I'm fucking your son's brains out and his best friends too, but it's okay because we love each other. Not at first, but definitely now.

"But you didn't say anything until Sunday?" Now Mom sounds hurt. Great. I'm a disappointment, and I hurt her feelings.

I don't want to be having this conversation, so I take a sip of coffee. Unfortunately, they're all still waiting for me to spill the truth. And this torture won't end until I do. Fuck.

"Yes, I finally told you because Chase used the fact I hid our breakup and my relationship with Damon from you to make me pretend to still be his girlfriend. And since he didn't want to lose his new reputation with his parents, he didn't tell them we were broken up either." I don't want to spill the whole truth, but there is that. Apparently Damon has no issue with telling them everything about my relationship. But hopefully, he'll keep his mouth shut.

Because if Mom finds out he watched me and blackmailed me, I don't know that Adam will be able to convince her to stay. *Don't worry, Mom, he likes to watch me, and I get off on it, so it's all good.* Fuck my life.

"Is this why you got in a fight with Chase?" Adam asks Damon.

Mom covers her mouth like that thought is horrifying. I put my hand over my eyes.

"I punched Chase because he left Evan out in the middle of the woods. At night. Alone. Because she wouldn't put out." Damon squeezes my hand. "And then he came back to the party without her to get laid."

My mouth opens and closes, and I narrow my eyes on him. They didn't need to know that.

"That wasn't the only reason you punched him," I add snarkily. He doesn't get to air all my dirty laundry and get away scot-free.

He glares at me, like he's going to push me harder. "Evan hasn't slept in her own bed since the first night she moved in."

My heart pounds. What is he doing?

"What?" Mom squeaks out.

"She sleeps in my bed with me. What did you expect to happen?" Damon turns to my mother. "You left her alone. You always leave her alone. It's no wonder monsters like Chase found her. Like I found her."

I snatch my hand from Damon. I can't believe he told my mom that. My heart is racing. There's no way to undo what he just did. I want to put my hand over his mouth and make him be quiet, but this isn't the time I get my way.

"Maybe if you paid more attention to your daughter than your boyfriend of the moment—"

Fuck this. I stand up. "Chase is the one who hit Damon this summer. Chase was cheating on me at the time."

Damon glares at me. But I'm done. If he wants it all out there, everything should be out there.

"Stop using me to try to punish my mother or your father or whatever warped thing you're doing right now." I throw my hands up. "Yes, Damon and I are together and have been for a while. We're both eighteen, and there's nothing wrong with it. Maybe we started at the wrong place, but we're good now. Chase is a lying, manipulative bastard who used me and hurt Damon. He deserves any wrong coming his way. But neither of you gets a say in our relationship. That's between me and Damon. If we even have a relationship after this."

My heart squeezes and aches because his eyes have grown colder with each word out of my mouth.

"This would have all come out eventually." I sink back onto the couch with a little space between us. "It has nothing to do with your relationship, Mom. This isn't a way for the kids to get back at their parents. I'm never getting back with Chase. I don't even think I really liked him. He's just the only one who paid attention to me, and it was nice to have a boyfriend."

It hurts to think about how it's almost the same with Damon. He might never have paid attention to me if it hadn't been for Chase. If we hadn't moved in here.

I'm so tired. I just want to crawl back into bed and forget any of this ever happened. But I don't really have my own bed here. Tears choke my throat, but I swallow them down.

"You might want to tell the whole truth, Evan."

I lift my gaze to Damon's. His eyes are still cold, but I can see the hurt in them. I touch the ring on my finger and wonder if he'll want it back. If all this is out in the open for nothing. Because he won't want me anymore after this.

Fine, he wants everything out there.

"No more secrets?" I take a deep breath and turn to Mom. "I'm also dating Hawk and Cam."

"What?" Mom says. She looks like her head is spinning. Maybe I should have been honest from the beginning, but I was protecting her just as much as I was protecting myself.

I turn to meet her owl-like eyes. "I'm dating Damon, Cam, and Hawk. All of them. At the same time."

"Damon," Adam says, looking like he's chewing on glass. "Is that true? About Chase? He was the driver of your hit and run?"

The muscle tenses in Damon's jaw. "Yes."

"What do we do about this?" Mom turns to Adam.

For a moment, no one speaks. It's too early in the morning for any of this. There's this pit inside my stomach that pulses because I don't know if Damon's still mine. If I've lost them all because I gave away his secret, because he was giving mine away.

"Nothing. Damon leaves today for Crowne Mawr. It seems like you two could use the time away from each other." Adam stands and reaches his hand out to my mom. "We'll deal with it when he gets back."

## CHAPTER 16
## EvanAnn

It's too early to get ready for school, and I'm too energized to go back to sleep as we head upstairs. Damon hasn't said a word. I'm still mulling over what he did and how I responded. Overall, not good.

We walk into his bedroom. I follow out of habit. He heads to his dresser and pulls out workout clothes, ignoring me. My heart kicks up a notch. Instead of talking about this, he's just going to let it fester? Fuck that and fuck him.

"What the fuck was that?" I ask, crossing my arms.

He doesn't turn toward me as he strips off his shirt and pulls on a tank top.

"Damon, you fucking went nuclear on us and made that twenty times worse than it had to be." I grab the shorts he has in his hands and toss them on the bed.

He just grabs another pair out of the drawer. I do the same thing.

"Fuck, Evan! Don't you know when to leave well enough alone." He doesn't turn, but his words bite into me.

"Apparently not, but neither do you." I run my hands through my hair. I need to move, but I want to know what he was thinking down there. "You just couldn't stand being called my rebound, could you? Even though we both know that's not what this is. You've never been the side piece, but it grates on you."

He turns and those sharp blue eyes pierce me. "So you decided to rat me out to my father?"

"He needed to know. It's not like you could keep it a secret forever." I straighten. "But you're right. I can be mature enough to admit that wasn't the right time to say that. I said it because I wanted to shut you up before you admitted you blackmailed me into your bed."

His eyes grow menacing and he closes in on me. My breath catches, but I stand my ground. "I didn't really need to blackmail you at all, did I, Evan?"

He slides his fingers down my throat, sending a ripple of heat through me.

"You would have given in to me without it." He turns his hand around and holds my neck.

I swallow against the pressure of his fingers. "Tell me this wasn't just about you getting back at my mom for being with your dad. It was the perfect opportunity, wasn't it? Tell her it's her fault you fucked me? Because all this will ever be to you is a means for your revenge."

He squeezes slightly, taking my breath away ever so slightly. "You like me this way, Evan."

"I like when you aren't acting like a manchild who doesn't get his way."

He releases me and steps back, his eyes cold. He grabs a pair of shorts and heads into the bathroom. After a minute, I hear the door to my bedroom open and close.

A little shiver goes through me, but I shake it off and go through the bathroom to my room. Today is going to be rough. It was always going to be rough with Damon leaving, but now I don't know where we stand.

I should just stay home. Damon isn't talking to me. I don't feel like talking to him, but I want him to hold me and kiss me and tell me everything is going to be all right. Which sucks.

I'm exhausted and feel like my insides have been burned out. Tears press on the back of my eyes, just waiting to choke me. I can't tell if it's because I'm angry or sad or just fucking tired. But tears won't help anything.

I just want to curl up and die and burn the house down. Not literally, but fuck, emotions are hard.

It wasn't my place to tell his father about the hit and run. Not like that. But Adam needed to know. It won't fix anything, but how can Damon move forward without letting go of it?

It's the whole reason we're together. He wanted to take everything away from Chase. I was part of that everything. Mission accomplished.

After I get ready for school—way too early, I sit on the edge of the bed that isn't mine and stare at the floor. Because if I don't stare at the floor, I'll stare at the door to the bathroom and wait for him to come, to claim me.

He'll finish his workout and want a shower. And what good is a shower without me?

But he won't.

Because we fucked it up.

I left my door open so I'll see him when he comes back. I don't know if I want to yell at him more or plead with him to talk to me or just shove him against a wall. Mom knocks on my doorframe and wrings her hands.

"Are you doing okay, Evan? That was... a lot. I know I haven't been the best mother..." She pauses like she wants to attach a time frame to it but decides not to. "I don't really have an excuse. I didn't mean to leave you alone so much. I don't know what this is you have with Damon...and the others, but if it's something good, I'm not going to stand in your way. If you're open to it, I'd love to bring you to therapy with me. I think we could use some healing between us too."

My eyes burn, and the tears I've held back release on a choked sob.

"Oh, Evan." Mom comes to me and takes me into her arms. "I'm so sorry, honey. I didn't mean to leave you."

I crumple into her arms and cry because the boy I love is icing me out. And I should have known better. Everyone knows that's how Damon is with girls. Hot and cold.

But we were hot for so long, and I thought maybe, just maybe, I was different. It's like birds are ripping my heart apart inside my chest. I wanted to believe what we have could survive anything. But what if it can't? What if I fucked this up?

Because he was tearing apart my fragile world. He was speaking my truths to my mom. Because I didn't just lose my dad when he died, I lost both of them. I'm so mad and sad and don't know what to do with this tornado of emotions raging through me.

I want to hurt him the way he hurt me, but I don't want to lose him.

Mom strokes my back and grabs tissues for me while I cry about the boy in the room next to mine. About the secrets that never should have been spoken out loud. I don't know if he hears me or if he even cares anymore.

"I'm sure it will be fine, Evan." Mom strokes her hand over my hair. "Every relationship has bumps in them. Some are easy to get over and some take real work. I'm sorry I didn't see you were lonely. You were always so busy and seemed happy."

"I was happy." I keep my injured hand tucked against my chest but take her hand with my left. "It's not your job—"

"I'm your mother, Evan." Her voice is firm even if it shakes just a little. "Of course it's my job to notice when you're hiding things. I'm just sorry it took me so long to open my eyes. And that it took your boyfriend to force me to see you." She uses a tissue to clean the tears off my face. "You can stay home if you want. I can call the school."

I shake my head and blink back the tears. "Rehearsal, classes. I can't miss. But thank you."

She touches my jaw. "I love you, Evan. I just want us to be happy. This place makes me happy, but if you're not—"

"I'm happy here too." I blow out a breath. Even if Damon hates me, I don't want to leave. "If things don't work out, I'll be fine for the rest of the year, promise."

I'll be an emotional basket case, but I'll work it out. Because that's what I do.

---

WHEN I OPEN THE GARAGE TO DRIVE MY CAR, OR RATHER Damon's car, to school, he pulls up on his bike and holds out my helmet without a word. For a second, I consider not taking it, being stubborn and driving the car. It's not like he won't follow me to school anyway.

I don't know if he even turned on the Bluetooth headset in his helmet. I don't bother talking to him, and he doesn't say anything to me.

I hold on like this ride could fix us, but I know it won't. Nothing can wash away how we tore each other apart. Nothing will get us back to yesterday when he held me tight and called me his. My heart shatters into tiny pieces with every second I hold him. But I keep it all inside, lock it away, so I can get through this day.

When we get to school, his hand teases my back with just enough pressure to lead until we reach Hawk and Cam in the hallway. I keep my chin high. Then his touch fades, and I turn to watch him walk away from me. I swallow down the tears trying to strangle me. But they blur my vision and burn my eyes.

Fuck him.

I don't know what Hawk and Cam know. Did Damon talk to them? Are we over? Is he just protecting me because he feels obligated now?

Hawk kisses my temple and runs his hand down my back, but his hard gaze is on Damon.

"I've got you, goody." Cam wraps his arm around my shoulders and leads me to first period. I should have stayed home, slunk into our room, crawled into his bed, and slept, surrounded by his warmth and scent. Pretend none of this happened.

"Do you want to talk about it?" he asks when we sit down.

I shake my head and put my arms on top of my books, resting my head on them and staring out the window. I don't even know if I can fix this or if, after the anger burns off, if I'll want to fix this. I broke his trust, but he broke mine too. We hurt each other with the truth like it was a weapon. And for what? That's what I don't get. We were tired and caught and instead of staying quiet, instead of being a team, we just put everything out there.

We picked battles that weren't ours to fight. Damon went after my mother and I didn't think. I just wanted to hurt him the way he was hurting me.

Cam rubs my back until class starts. I'm so fucked. But I'm not going to let it fuck up my future.

When I straighten, he sets a red paper flower on my books. A tear escapes, and he catches it with his finger.

I choke down the rest of them and pay attention like nothing's changed. I shut off the waterworks and push Damon to the back of my mind where he can fester. After all, I still need to get into the colleges I applied to, and to do that I need to keep my grades up. Maybe I won't have to apply anywhere else.

After all, what's our relationship without all of us? Hawk and Cam won't betray their best friend to stay with me. I'll be all alone again.

My chest aches, hollow and empty.

Cam walks me to my next class, calculus. After I take my seat, Damon drops in the chair next to me. He doesn't flirt with me like he's done all week. Nope, he sits there like a sullen little bitch. He doesn't even text or Snapchat me.

I bite my lip to keep from crying more. Which just makes me angrier because I didn't push us to this. I'm better than this weepy mess.

When I found out about Chase, I didn't cry. It barely felt like a scratch. Yes, it wounded my pride, but it didn't hurt. Damon and I aren't even broken up. Not officially, at least. And I feel cut through to the bone. He's just icing me out, which is almost more painful.

I don't remember anything from calculus, but he follows me to history class. Part of him is still protecting me, even if he's angry at me. It doesn't help the turmoil of my insides. Because I just want to turn into his arms, have him hold me and tell me he'll take care of me.

"Cam's right." Hawk sits across from me and shifts his gaze from me to Damon. "You two need to get locked in a room until you either fuck or fight or both."

I glance toward Damon but look away when it looks like he's going to meet my eyes. I can't see that coldness again. I wince. It hurts too much. Mia comes in and sits next to me.

"No more bandages?" She looks at my hand with a smile. "Honestly, I was afraid you were going to make wearing Band-Aids cool and everyone would be doing it."

She notices the tension and narrows her eyes on me, really taking me in.

"We need to hit the girls' bathroom before lunch. You're nearly translucent." Mia pauses and looks at the guys and then me again. "What did Damon do?"

He's not paying attention to anything right now. His jaw is tight like he's chewing on rocks. He's definitely not listening to Mia.

I can't play this game, so fuck it. Acting got me here. I straighten and act like everything is just fine.

"Our parents found out about us, and I told his father about the accident after he told my mother about Chase cheating on me and leaving me in the woods. Oh, and basically calling her negligent." I pull out my history book and flip it open. "But he's going off to college today, so we won't have to argue about anything. And he can do whatever he wants to whoever he wants. I guess."

I sigh and blink back the tears trying to make an escape. Fuck. I'm done crying. I'm not crying anymore. A hand grabs my arm, startling me.

"Hey," I say, trying to pull my arm away.

I glance up and meet Damon's eyes, but they aren't cold. Far from it. I freeze, captured in those eyes. They're narrowed on me, but the blue is sharp, not soft. I narrow my eyes on his. If he wants another piece of my mind...

Hawk grabs Damon's arm. "Come on."

Damon releases me and lets Hawk lead him out of the classroom.

"How bad was it this morning?" Mia asks gently when the door shuts behind them.

I drag in a breath and shake my head. "I don't even know."

## CHAPTER 17
## *Hawk*

I PUSH Damon into the nearest men's bathroom and check the stalls for stragglers.

"What the fuck?" I glare at Damon. I've never seen Annie crumple before. No amount of pressure has broken her, but Damon seems to hold the fucking key to make her small. And she's struggling from what happened this morning.

Damon texted to let us know we'd be responsible for Annie today, that something happened.

Damon runs his hand through his hair. "I can't go to Crowne Mawr. I'm not going to leave. Heather's getting fucking texts from an anonymous texter. They fucking set us up."

I lean against the sink and watch him pace. If I'm going to have any chance to fix this, I need to know what I'm working with. "What happened?"

Damon stops and lifts his gaze to mine. "My dad walked in on Evan and me in bed."

My eyes widen. I knew they'd fought, but Annie wasn't saying anything. At least not to Cam. And Damon doesn't communicate. All we knew was Annie looked fucking miserable, and Damon was being a cold bastard.

"We were asleep," he adds.

"Okay. So the parents know. A bit earlier than Annie's timeline, but that doesn't explain why you look two seconds from dropping her, and she looks two seconds from crying or yelling at you." I run my hand down my face. "Seriously, I'm done watching Annie cry. Swear to god, I'll fucking deck you if you're the reason she cries."

His eyes narrow on me. "You think I like any of this?"

"Then what—"

"She fucking ratted me out to my dad." He balls his fists and looks for a target but decides against breaking his fucking hand. I was not looking forward to grabbing him before he did that. I'd likely become the target.

"I'm sure there's more to it than that. What happened?" I blow out a breath.

"I told Heather it was her fault Evan was mine." Damon turns and his eyes burn. "Evan didn't tell Heather that fucker left her out in the woods, alone. She didn't tell her mom Chase cheated on her. She only said they broke up. So Heather thinks I'm a fucking rebound and that Evan is looking for solace with the closest dick she can find—like her fucking mother does. It's like she doesn't know her own fucking daughter. Because she doesn't."

"Damon, you need to calm down."

"Fuck that. Evan told my dad Chase was my hit and run."

I cross my arms and look at my feet. "What did you expect?"

"That she'd keep her fucking mouth shut." Damon flings his hands down. "Fuck. I can't leave. Someone wanted us to get caught. They want her exposed. Alone."

I don't disagree with Annie. Maybe the method of delivery lacked finesse, but Adam Storm has always been on Damon's team, whether Damon chooses to acknowledge that or not.

"You have to go, Damon." I step away from the sinks and drop my arms. "This is your shot. You can't miss it again."

He runs his hand through his hair, and I can see the wheels turning in his brain. He'll only make her hurt more if he stays. Part of him will justify it. That she deserves it. She's strong, but she'll break under the weight.

"You and Annie are going to shatter each other if you don't get some space." I shake my head. "You'll only keep hurting each other if you don't fucking leave. Cam and I can take care of her while you go and do what you do best, prove that you're the right choice for their team."

Damon looks like he's going to argue, but fuck that. I'm right about this. And he's not going to break the best thing we've ever had. The girl and relationship we're willing to change our whole futures for to keep.

"You love her. What you do next could make or break the two of you. It could break all of us. Focus on hockey and let Annie focus on her play. Do what you two do best. Ignore the problem for a while. Watch your videos of her and tell us all what you're doing. Clear your head and figure out where we go from here." I clasp my hand on his shoulder and lower my head like a charging bull. "Don't fuck this up for us. We love her too, and I don't want to have to make a choice between you and her."

He takes in a deep breath and argues, "She's vulnerable."

"She's a survivor. And we're here. You aren't the only one looking out for her." I squeeze his shoulder. "You two are stronger together, but right now your emotions are too clouded with anger. She's still the girl you went to sleep with last night. The girl you love. Our future."

He runs his hand through his hair, and some of the wildness leaves his eyes. "We need to find out what texts Heather has been getting."

"Cam and I will get on that. Annie won't go anywhere without one of us at her side."

The tension drains from him. His voice is low and a little broken. "What if I can't forgive her?"

I smile because he's probably already halfway there. "You will. The real question is, how will you convince her to forgive you?"

---

## EvanAnn

Hawk and Damon come back in after history class starts. My heart aches, but I ignore Damon. I take notes even though my hand hurts. It's not that bad anymore. I looked it over this morning and decided not to rebandage it.

It's healing. I also had a few new bruises this morning from last night. It feels bittersweet right now and like it was so long ago. This morning gutted me.

I glance up at Hawk, and he smiles reassuringly. I avoid looking at Damon. Those cold eyes are like knives to my heart, and I don't know that I can take the bleeding without yelling at him more. He's determined to ruin what we have. Just like he does everything else.

When the bell rings for lunch, Hawk comes around the table and draws me against him, heading outside instead of toward the cafeteria. I don't glance behind me to see if Damon is following. I also don't ask where we're going. I don't want to deal with other people seeing the cracks in our foundation.

Hawk stops at his locker and takes my books from me. He grabs his spare helmet, but before I can take it, Damon holds mine out without a word. I take my helmet, but avoid looking at him.

"Come on, let's get some lunch and talk." Hawk takes my hand and leads me out to the bikes. Cam waits on his motorcycle for us.

I climb on behind Hawk and hold on. I close my eyes and try to remember last night. To hold on to that feeling because this morning sucked. Last night we were all together and it was fun and thrilling and everything I could ever want in a relationship. I didn't know how fragile the thing we were building was. How fragile Damon and I were.

We ride for about ten minutes and then pull into an Indian restaurant. Cam helps me with my helmet and wraps his arm around my shoulders to lead me inside. He puts me in the booth before he slides in next to me.

"Chin up, goody." Cam presses a kiss to my cheek. "I've got you."

Hawk sits across from me. Damon is next to him, looking away from me. Hawk and Cam seem determined to hold this together. Good, because I can't do it on my own.

Once our order is in, Hawk clears his throat. "We already know someone's out to get Annie, but Heather's getting texts too."

He tells Cam about the reason we got caught, and how Mom said she's getting anonymous texts.

Cam scrubs a hand over his face and shakes his head. "Jackson makes sense, but who does he know at our school who would deliver that rose? No one saw who put it there."

"Unless it was just a coincidence and someone else planted it." I fiddle with the straw in my water, trying to focus on the conversation and not the emotions swirling inside me. "Maybe someone knows about Jackson and wanted to prove a point. Maybe it's a girl who wants one or all of you."

It's not a ridiculous theory. There can be more than one thing happening at a time. And the rose could just be throwing us off. Whoever gave it to me may not even know about Jackson and just used the term *pretty girl* for whatever fucked up reason they thought of.

"Or he's not working on his own." Hawk studies me. "There might be a connection, and I just haven't figured it out yet. There's something we're missing."

"Evan can't be left alone." Damon's gaze darts between them, but not me. "I'm not leaving unless I know you two have her."

"For fuck's sake, you aren't the only one protecting me. You aren't leaving me alone. You have to go," I say. His gaze flicks to me, and for a moment our eyes lock and clash. "This is your opportunity. Don't use me as an excuse to fuck this up."

"Whoever is after you knows too much." Damon leans back in the booth and looks out over the restaurant. "They found out about Evan sleeping in my bed. That can't be common knowledge."

"There are still cameras in Annie's room?" Hawk asks. Of course there are.

"They're secure." Damon shakes his head. "No one else can access them."

"Are we sure?" Cam looks at Damon. "You don't think your nerd can be out-nerded? He build the wall around your server. Someone else could probably tear it down."

Damon chews on that for a moment. Even though he isn't paying attention to me, somehow I know he's aware of my gaze. That muscle ticking in his jaw gives him away.

"Or maybe your nerd found a higher bidder." Hawk drops it like a bomb ready to explode, because anyone can be bought. For the right price. That's the problem with outsourcing."

"It would explain how they knew I wasn't in bed last night," I say. "Not that I'm ever in that bed."

"What about your staff?" Cam asks.

"Someone could have noticed Annie's bed is always made," Hawk says. It would make sense. "I don't know how else someone would know about you two sharing a bed. The only proof is inside the house. So it's either your nerd or the staff."

"Or someone could have been guessing." Cam leans back and rubs his jaw. "It wouldn't take a rocket scientist to put together that if the two of you live together that you're probably fucking in the house and might share a bed."

"Lucky fucking guess," I mutter.

"I shouldn't leave." Damon looks off in the distance. Something stirs in the broken pieces inside me at him wanting to protect me, but that's not who we are. Maybe we aren't as broken as he's acting. We want to be more, and to do that, we have to make sacrifices.

"You're going." I have to say it. He's not blowing this over me. "We don't waste any opportunity."

"There will be other opportunities." Damon glares at me. But I'm not letting this go.

"We don't settle."

He looks at me with a fierceness that I love, but right now, it also hurts.

"She's right." Hawk runs a hand over his hair. "This isn't just any opportunity. You don't let it go. Right now, you have Yale and Crowne Mawr. Maybe in a few weeks, Coach will have a few other schools for you. But what other school is going to work for all of us? If I had a short list beyond Columbia, both Yale and Crowne Mawr would be on it."

I'm hurt and angry from Damon's coldness—that I don't deserve—and how he went after my mom, but I still love him and want what's best, so I don't drop my gaze from his. "You don't fuck your future up over this. Even if there might be another chance, there are no guarantees. We take what we're given and run with it. Go to the college. Find out if it will work for you, and then we'll figure out if it will work for us."

Damon presses his lips together and nods sharply before looking away. I draw a breath into my starved lungs. I won't be the reason he misses any opportunity. Even if I want him to stay with me and fix whatever is broken with us. I'll push him to leave, because he'd do the same for me.

"I think the space will be good for you two." Hawk reaches across the table and takes my hand. "This morning sounded like chaos and not the good kind."

"My mom knows I'm dating all three of you," I say it softly.

Damon scoffs, but this is what he wanted. He wanted everything about me out in the open. He wanted my mom to know the truth and wouldn't settle for less. He just didn't expect me to repay the favor with his dad.

The server comes over with our food and breaks the flow of our conversation.

Cam takes a bite of his curry chicken. "Tell me what you know about Jackson Riordan, goody."

I freeze and swallow the bite of my food. "I don't know what you want me to tell you."

"You hung out with him a little before he kissed you. So tell me what you know," he asks.

I sigh and set my fork down on my plate. "I was in awe of him. Half the time I didn't even really hear what he was saying because I was sixteen and a cute boy thought I was pretty and wanted to spend time with me."

"Not exactly loving this conversation." Damon glares at Cam. "We know Jackson is an asshole."

"But we don't know what Annie knows about him." Hawk takes a drink and sets it down. "Know thy enemy and all that."

I blow out a breath and think about that summer while I push around my food. "It was only a few weeks. He was nice and would bring me little treats. I could tell he liked me and wanted more, but I didn't know if I was ready for more than a flirtation. But you guys know that part of the story."

Cam rests his hand on my leg and gives me an encouraging squeeze.

"We went to the same elementary school. Back then he didn't really talk to anyone that I noticed."

"Anyone from your elementary school at Deimos or Anteros besides you?" Cam asks.

"I don't think so." It would make sense if there were. There are quite a few elementary schools in our district. But I haven't noticed anyone.

"What about neighborhood kids? Did he have a friend at the complex or someone who came over to hang with him?"

"I'm sorry. If he did, I didn't notice." I try to think, but it was just us that summer. "He paid attention to me. I didn't see him with anyone else. Not even at the community pool."

"You didn't think that was odd?" Cam sits back and takes another bite, chewing it and swallowing before saying. "People generally hang out with their friends."

"I didn't." Because that's who I was. I didn't have any friends to hang out with, just some boy who remembered me from grade school. "It wasn't unusual to me to not have friends. Maybe it should have been."

"What about kids from hockey?" Hawk looks at Damon and Cam. "He was in that PeeWee league with us. Anyone else from there go to our school or maybe knows someone from our school besides us?"

"It had to have been someone at rehearsal though, right?" I look at the others. "Anyone else would have been noticed."

"That or the other production," Cam says. "I can't imagine you would think twice if someone from the drama department came in during practice to *grab something* from that theater."

I bite my lip. He's right. I probably wouldn't have noticed.

"What about Brandt?" Damon asks. He's still cold, but he's participating. Maybe he just wants to solve this so he can really let me go. Is that where we're headed? Because I'm not ready for this to end, but what if he is?

"You just aren't going to give up on that guy." Cam shakes his head.

"You weren't there when he and his sister were saying shit about Olivia and Chase like it was a fucking game to them. Like that one movie with Buffy the Vampire Slayer." Damon arches an eyebrow like Cam should know what he's talking about.

"*Cruel Intentions*?" I offer, thinking about the movie. It's very much about manipulation similar to *Othello*.

He snaps his fingers. "Yes. They had that weird egging each other on. Fuck, Brandt offered me his sister to fuck at one point. And she was down with it."

I press my lips together and glare at him. For a moment, I forgot about this morning. Are we even still together? He's going off to a college campus. He's ridiculously hot. Someone will hit on him. Will he fuck her?

"How in the fuck would Jackson Riordan know Brandt Stanwell though?" Cam asks. His hand squeezes my thigh. "Brandt is fucking loaded and has famous parents. They didn't go to grade school together, and Brandt's never held a hockey stick in his life. They live nowhere near each other. There's no intersection of their lives."

"His sister goes to a boarding school." Damon rubs his temples. "I didn't ask which one, but Jackson is at Kentwood Prep."

It's possible that's a connection. How would we find out?

"You think Brandt's sister is the connection to Jackson?" Hawk asks.

Damon glances at me. "She knew both Olivia and Chase. She was at Tom's party. The way she talked she knew them. But it could have been her brother running his mouth to her."

"We'll look into your nerd, Heather's phone, and the connection to Brandt while you're gone." Hawk leans back and looks between Damon and me.

I sit back and look away from Damon. I should ask where we stand, but my chest aches. I don't know how we're going to fix this.

Hawk sighs. "What you two went through this morning was messed up. Some time away from each other might be what you guys need. So you can figure out how to make this right. Because I'm all in on Annie. No matter what happens."

"Same." Cam takes my hand and threads our fingers together. My heart beats a little harder. "It wouldn't be the same without all of us, but I'm not willing to give her up."

My heart softens. Fuck, I love these guys. When I lean against Cam's arm, I look up at Damon. If he decides he doesn't want me anymore, can we still do this? There would always be a piece missing in my heart. How would I be with them and not think of Damon?

Damon nods at the guys like he understands. "Let's head back to school."

## CHAPTER 18
## *Damon*

THE AFTERNOON SEEMS to fly by. I packed yesterday before we picked up Evan. Fuck. My brain is fucked up. Hawk might be right that I need space from her. Everything in me wants to turn to her and say everything will be okay. To make her smile instead of cry. To take that anger in her and turn it into passion.

At the same time, I'm so fucking angry. That wasn't for her to share.

But this morning was a trainwreck waiting to happen. It could have been avoided if she had been honest with her mom. I know I'm to blame for unloading all that shit, but her mom thought I was fucking Chase Chadwick's understudy.

Fuck that. Evan belongs to me.

I'm not going to hockey practice, so I say goodbye to Cam and Hawk after school.

"Take care of her." I swallow down the anger and pain. "Food, sleep. She's getting worse about both as the performance gets closer. She's worse when she's mulling over something."

"Maybe she'll sleep better without you keeping her up late at night. Don't worry, we'll have a strict bedtime." Cam smirks but then turns serious. "Honestly, we've got her. You're free to go and focus on hockey and getting on the team. No chicks."

I scoff. "Like I want anyone else."

And that's the rub. There's only Evan for me, but fuck, our trust is broken. We didn't have enough sleep and weren't fully awake. I'm just as much to blame for this whole thing. Maybe Chase's involvement would have come out eventually, but Dad doesn't understand my shit or why I didn't want to get the police involved.

"We'll make you some quality movies." Hawk holds his fist up for me.

I roll my eyes and bump his fist. "I need to know she's okay."

"You already watch her twenty-four-seven on video between the hallway cameras and the however many cameras you've got in your house." Cam shakes his head. "I'm just glad you aren't gay, man. I don't think I could handle that kind of focused attention."

I grab Cam's hand and pull him into me to give him a hug. "Make her smile."

"Not a problem. Focus on hockey this week." Cam grabs his bag and heads into the locker room.

"Are you going to tell her goodbye?" Hawk picks up his backpack.

I run my hand through my hair. But I don't have an answer. I need to see her, but I don't know if I can talk to her without making her even more angry at me. Especially without the guys with us.

"Text us. Text her. Maybe you can work out your shit when you can't fuck her." Hawk punches my arm before disappearing into the locker room.

I exhale and grab my backpack. I also grab Evan's helmet. Could I have given it to Hawk or Cam? Yeah. Did I? No.

It's an excuse. Because normally I wouldn't need one to see my girl, but today, after this morning, I do need an excuse. I'm not ready to talk it out. My feelings are a tangled snarl of emotions that I can't unwind.

But I need to see her. I need her to know… Fuck, that she's still mine. But…

I walk the halls of our school, mostly empty now. Anyone who's here is here for an after school activity and safely ensconced in a room.

The Anteros hallways are a little more active than Deimos. There's a flurry of activity around the visual arts studio, and a cacophony of music spills out into the hallway near the music rooms. I make my way to the black box theater. It's her short rehearsal night.

Most people will attend the football game this evening. It's where Evan would be if she were still with Chase. But she's not with him.

"Hi, Damon."

I ignore Abby and her friend by the door to the other theater room. I don't have time for her, and we don't need another Olivia situation. Encouraging any interaction is a no-go.

Knowing they're probably in rehearsal already because Evan runs a tight ship, I push through the door and walk in. Evan's focus was crumbling all day. Her anger seemed to be the only thing shoring her up. We didn't get much sleep last night. After staying up late, the drama of this morning, plus dealing with me being an asshole, I wasn't surprised to see her almost a shell of herself.

But in here, she's focused. She's electric. And nothing will take this from her. I'll make sure of that.

"What's up, asshole?" Mia steps up next to me as I stand and watch Evan work.

"I'm leaving." I don't like Mia, but she seems to care about Evan.

"Are you going to tell her goodbye?" Mia arches an eyebrow like I'm going to fuck this up.

Maybe I will fuck this up. On the ice, I'm golden, but off... with her? It feels so easy with her. Too easy. But right now it's hard.

Mia rolls her eyes and walks over to the desk to talk to Keira, who jerks her head up to look at me. Even her eyes narrow on me. No one likes me right now. Fuck, I don't like me right now.

Keira stands and goes over to where Evan is on stage with the actors. She waits until Evan steps back to let the actors run through it again. I've watched her work.

Evan glances over at me. Will she tell them to send me away? She's sad, but she's also angry. I don't blame her. But I want her to come over. To glare at me with those silver eyes. To fill my lungs with her woodsy scent.

I swallow.

My heart stops when I think she's going to send me away, but she turns to Keira and says something before heading my way. When she reaches me, she takes my arm and pulls me toward the sound booth.

I let her. When the door is closed, I'm tempted to back her into it and kiss her senseless. Fuck her against the door because that's where we connect, where we make sense.

She crosses her arms and glares at me. "You're heading out?"

"Yes." I hold out her helmet, and she takes it reluctantly.

"Hawk has a spare." She shrugs like I didn't need to bring it.

"This one is yours."

Her silver eyes lift to mine.

I reach into my backpack and pull out a little container. When I hold it out to her, she takes it with a raised eyebrow.

"A snack." I glance out at the cast working hard not to look over at us. At school, I've taken advantage of everyone knowing she's mine to kiss her whenever I want to. Which means people probably noticed the chill between us and Evan's red eyes.

"Thank you." She holds it against her heart.

"I'm not ready to apologize, Evan." I put my backpack on and put my hands in my pockets. "But this isn't over. I'm not going to go off and fuck anyone else. I'm still yours."

She opens her mouth and closes it. Her chin tips up stubbornly and she steps closer. "I was angry with you, but I shouldn't have told your father that way. I still think he should know."

Before she can step back, I catch her chin, close the physical distance between us, and kiss her softly. Her lips press against mine. I rest my forehead against hers for a moment, knowing tonight I won't sleep because I won't be next to her.

"Don't go anywhere alone. Don't take off the ring." I straighten.

Her eyes are pools of shimmering moonlight. She steps into me and wraps her arms around my waist. The container hits my low back while her helmet hits my ass. I wrap my arms around her and rest my chin against her head.

I don't know how we're going to fix this, but we will because I'm not giving her up. Ever.

"I'll miss you. Give them hell." She pulls away and wipes at her eye with the back of her hand before opening the door and heading out to her desk. She sets down the helmet and container and strides onto the stage like I'm already gone.

"I'll miss you. Give them hell," I say softly before heading out the door.

---

"Do you have everything?" Dad asks. He tosses his keys in his hand as I close the trunk.

"I can drive myself," I say for the hundredth time. This wasn't part of the plan. Hours in the car with my father. Joy.

"I'd like to look at the campus. Talk to the coach." Dad claps me on the shoulder and hands me the keys. "But you can drive on the way there."

I roll my eyes but get into the driver's seat. There's no way we won't be talking about this morning. Is this the divide and conquer method of parenting? He leaves so Heather can talk to Evan about this morning.

We get on the interstate, and Dad clears his throat. I roll my eyes and don't even bother turning up the music on the radio. He'd just turn it off.

"We should talk about Chase Chadwick." Dad seems relaxed in the seat next to me.

"His dad is your business partner."

"Did you think I would choose Tom over you?" Dad's voice is even.

I shrug. It's not unreasonable to think that way.

"Fuck, I'm going about this all wrong." Dad tries a different tack. "When did you realize Chase was the driver?"

"When I saw him getting head from a blond before he hit me." I keep my eyes on the road and my voice just as steady as his. I've taken a lot away from Chase Chadwick, but of everything I've taken, there's one thing he'll never get back. Evan.

Not that she was ever his.

Dad looks out the window at the landscape flying by the window. "EvanAnn?"

I chuckle. "I thought so, but no, some other girl. They weren't like that."

Dad lets that sit for a moment. "Why didn't you tell me? Or the police when it happened?"

"What? So you could invite Chase over for a playdate and make us hug it out?" I roll my eyes. "He didn't stick around. Besides, what proof did I have?"

"The damage to your bike and his car." Dad runs a hand through his hair and lifts his gaze to the ceiling. "There was proof, Damon."

"Okay, let's say they did file charges against Chase. What would he get for taking my future from me? How much would Tom Chadwick pay to keep his son from getting a record and doing time? It's not realistic to believe Chase would be punished at all."

Dad's quiet for a little while. I'm not wrong, and he knows it. The music plays in the background as the car eats the miles.

"I know how it works," I say quietly. "The rich get away with everything. Chase took away my chance at a future. Now I'm clawing and fighting to just find another way into the future that had been mine, while he would have gotten a slap on the wrist and a fine. His dad would have made some donation, and it all would have been swept under the rug."

"So what? You punched him to get your revenge?"

"Please." I laugh. "If I just wanted to punch him, I would have done it before school started. And I would have kicked his ass." I breathe out and say a little softer, "I really did deck him for leaving Evan out in the woods. It wasn't planned. Hawk was already on his way to go get her when Chase walked in like nothing was wrong."

Dad releases a breath. "You said it this morning, but I had other things on my mind. He really dumped her in the woods?"

"Outside of town, not knowing whether she had her phone or not. Yeah, he's a real class act. Probably wouldn't have gone back to get her until he fucked someone if he hadn't gotten arrested." I blow out my breath. "We're not stupid. We haven't done anything illegal, but we might have made his life a little extra uncomfortable for a while."

"I don't want to know." Dad shakes his head. "It's better if I don't know the details."

Probably, but we didn't do anything that was criminal, so it doesn't matter really.

"Is that why you're with EvanAnn?" Fuck, my dad pieced that together a little too easily.

I chuckle and glance in my mirrors. "First off, you moved her into the room next to mine without considering Evan is a gorgeous girl."

Dad opens his mouth and then closes it. He gives me a slight nod of acknowledgement. After all, Evan does take after her mother, and Dad fell for Heather.

"Second off, he was fucking around on her before we even made a move."

"We? Hawk and Cam?" Dad rubs his forehead. "EvanAnn said she was dating the three of you, and I really didn't want to ask how that works in front of her mother."

"We all love her," I say it softly, so he knows it's not me just being defensive.

"Again, I don't need the details."

I smirk. He probably doesn't want to think about what we do together. To the girl he basically gift wrapped and put in the room next to mine.

"And this had nothing to do with Heather moving in?" Dad gives me a skeptical look.

"I wasn't happy about you moving your gold-digging girlfriend in with us," I admit. Before he can defend her, I add, "But no, it had very little to do with your girlfriend at the beginning and not at all now."

He makes a noise that he realizes it had something to do with his girlfriend. He runs a hand through his hair and looks out the window before coming to a decision.

"Heather needed a safe place for her and EvanAnn this year. We started dating this spring, and I really didn't see a reason for her to move anywhere but with me. She already spent most of her time at our house. I didn't think she should leave Evan alone so much. I knew moving in wasn't ideal with two teenagers, but EvanAnn had a boyfriend."

"A shit boyfriend who used her as an excuse to continue being a manwhore," I grumble.

Dad gives me a nod. "Heather and I did talk it over, and it seemed like the best solution for all of us."

I'm tempted to ask Dad about Heather's texts, but then I might feel compelled to tell him about Evan's texts. It wouldn't hurt to have him know Evan might be in danger. Another set of eyes on her might make me worry less.

Maybe I'm overreacting. No one's come after her. Not really. The rose was weak and not meant to really take her out. Scare her? Yes. But it didn't do permanent damage. There hasn't been any new communication otherwise.

Do I think Jackson might be obsessed with her? But fuck, I'm obsessed with her. Do I only want to see him as dangerous because she's mine?

"Heather said EvanAnn was crying this morning." Dad's voice is soft, like he's not sure how to approach this. "You came at Heather pretty hard about EvanAnn."

"You don't think Heather deserved it?" I can't help but ask. My dad isn't blind. He has to know the way Heather treats Evan isn't right.

Dad sighs. "When her husband died, Heather was left with bills and a ten-year-old child who barely talked. They were both shadows of themselves."

I was older when Mom died, but I remember feeling unmoored, lost. I know how Evan is now. Focused, driven. Is that how she coped with her loss? Throwing herself into her work?

"EvanAnn is brilliant and talented." Dad blows out a breath. "And Heather was buried in grief, debt, and work. It wasn't right and we've talked about it, but EvanAnn was solid. She did her work and got good grades. She got into Anteros on her own. Heather did what she could to encourage her. But at the end of the day, she didn't have the energy to be there for EvanAnn."

"But she was there for her endless stream of boyfriends." She doesn't get a pass on this because she was grieving. Fuck that. She left Evan on her own.

"Grief is an ocean. Sometimes it can drag you under and you can't find the surface. Other times it gently laps at your ankles. It's always there, but sometimes you're in so deep you can't see the shoreline." Dad looks out the window and sighs. "We met at a grief support group I joined. Neither of us were looking for a partner there, but we got to talking. Every meeting we'd sit together and go out to coffee afterwards, just to talk. Eventually we realized there was more between us than just grief."

I press my lips together, because I know that meant Evan was left alone. It's possible she was busy with a production or school projects while they got to know each other.

"I know we should have said something earlier. Maybe gotten the family together sooner, so you and EvanAnn wouldn't have been in the dark, but it was all new, and fuck if I wasn't terrified, because what I feel with Heather is something I hadn't felt since your mother."

I glance at my dad as he stares out the window. Evan thought they might be with each other because they understood the other's sadness. Maybe that's why Evan and I are together. The revenge was just the tool to make us collide.

I focus on the road and what lies ahead.

# CHAPTER 19
## *Cam*

I sit in the back of the black box theater as Evan gives the actors notes from rehearsal. It's the same every night. There's something soothing about the way she pays them compliments while also giving them ways to be better. The sadness and anger from this morning doesn't seem to hang over her. At least not in here.

Everyone rises to their feet and heads out.

Evan glances my way with a smile before talking with Keira. Mia walks over to me.

"Guess you're not in the doghouse?" She smirks and drops into the chair one over from mine, leaving space between us.

"Nah, I couldn't fit with Damon shoved in there." I raise an eyebrow, and she laughs.

"He stopped by before he left." She watches Evan walk with Keira to close up the room. "Gave her a helmet and a snack."

"Did she throw it in his face?" I'm glad it's not me she's angry with.

"He kissed her, and she gave him a hug." Mia shrugged. "But it wasn't the way they usually are with each other."

"How so?" I cock my head.

"Those two give off second-degree burns with how hot they run normally." Mia grins. "The first time I saw them together, I told her she should suck his cock, but she's not that kind of girl."

I grunt. She totally is that kind of girl for us.

"I didn't know there was already something between them, but there's this intensity that's hard to miss." Mia shrugs. "Now, there's something more between the two of them. That fire is still there, but it's been dampened by the bullshit from this morning." She turns to me with a serious face. "You'll take care of her, won't you?"

I nod. "She's my girl too."

Mia breathes out. "I'm not good at the *being there for my friends* thing. I've fucked up too many times in the past. Hit on the guy they liked. Their boyfriend liked me better. That kind of shit. But I'm done playing those games."

I make a noise that she must assume means I think she's lying.

"I know how this looks." Mia rubs her hands together. "I would have fucked all three of you if you weren't with Evan, but I'm not doing that to her. Even if it was an option, which it's not. I know when I'm not wanted. Trust me."

"Why are you telling me this?" I can't help but ask.

"Because Abby's planning something. I don't know what it is, but I've been sticking closer to her to try to figure out what." Mia runs a hand over her hair. "She doesn't trust me enough to let me in, but I'm afraid it's something with Evan or one of you guys. If I figure out what it is, I'll let you know. But I'm warning you now to watch for her. Abby's a catty bitch and wasn't happy when Evan was with Chase. She's fucking furious Evan has you three."

I nod and lean forward. "We're watching Evan. What happened last weekend won't happen again. We'll make sure of it."

"Good." Mia stands and brushes her hands off on her skirt. She smiles as she watches Evan. "I like Evan. I think she's a good influence on me."

"You partying this weekend?" I ask out of habit more than anything else.

Mia's cheeks flush pink, but her smile is cocky. "I have a date."

"Who's next on your list?" I chuckle, thinking of our roster.

"Liam and Fletcher." For a moment, she seems like Evan. This soft, sweet look comes over her face. "I think I actually like them."

"Good." I stand and follow her over to Evan. Mia in an actual relationship is a good thing. And knowing it's Liam and Fletcher, I smirk. They'll have their hands full, but they're good guys.

Mia says goodbye to Evan and walks out with Keira, talking about a movie night. When Evan turns to me, her eyes are dry and she even has a smile on her lips.

"Hey," she says and picks up her backpack.

I take it out of her hands and swing it onto my shoulder. "Hey, goody."

She smiles and grabs her helmet. She doesn't even realize what that means. I doubt Damon told her.

"Do you know why Damon has that helmet?" I take her hand and pull her out into the hallway.

She stops and locks the door, looking over her shoulder at me with a questioning brow.

I smile and take her hand again. Feeling her small warm hand in mine is one of my favorite things about having her as my girlfriend. "When we started riding, Hawk thought it would be a great way to pick up chicks."

He wasn't wrong.

"That probably contributed to your numbers." She rolls her eyes, but there isn't any jealousy in her tone. No bite like earlier this week.

I smirk. "Probably."

She holds out the helmet. "So Damon bought this to get chicks?"

"Hawk said we should all get helmets for chicks, but he's the only one who did it." I shake my head. "Damon started riding when his mom was sick."

We push out into the evening air. The sun was making its way down, but there was still light everywhere.

She stops at my bike and looks at me with a question in her eyes.

"His mom always wanted to ride a motorcycle. He bought her that helmet so she could ride with him."

Evan looks at the helmet with tears gathering in her eyes. But they're different than the tears from this morning. She lifts her blue-gray eyes to mine. "Did she?"

I shake my head. "They talked about it a lot. About how they'd go out for a ride in the countryside, when she felt better..." I cough to clear the sudden lump in my throat. "He'd take video for her to watch when we got back from riding. We all loved her so much. She was our hockey mom. Every game, every practice, she'd be there cheering us on."

Evan wraps her arms around my waist and rests her head on my heart. "I'll be there when I can."

"I know, goody." I cradle her head against me and take in a deep breath. "No one wore that helmet until you. Damon wouldn't let anyone ride on his bike, because that's where she was supposed to be. But he gave it to you because it's his connection to his mom. Because you're important to him."

A soft sob comes out of her, and I hold her tighter.

"Everything's going to be okay, goody. I know it."

---

## EvanAnn

Cam brings me home and walks me inside.

"Cam, right?" My mom comes out of a room and holds her hand out to Cam. "I'm Heather, EvanAnn's mom."

Cam takes her hand and shakes it. "Nice to meet you, Heather."

Mom looks from me to Cam and back to me. "Would you two want to have dinner with me? Or are you going out? Do you only go out together? Will Hawk be joining you?"

I must look like a deer caught in headlights. Yeah, I told her about the guys, but I wasn't expecting her to be cool about it. In fact, I secretly thought she'd go in the opposite direction and forbid me from seeing any of them. Not that I'd let that happen.

"Adam took Damon to Crowne Mawr." Mom gestures for us to follow her to the dining room.

With a little chuckle, Cam practically pushes me to follow her.

"Have you planned your college trips, Cam?" Mom asks and gestures to the table that's been set for two. The server brings out another setting and sets it up. Still too weird.

Cam smiles. "Thanks, Adelaide."

My eyes widen when I look up at him. Of course, she has a name, but I just didn't think to ask, and no one introduced her.

Adelaide smiles and touches his arm in a friendly gesture before heading back to the kitchen. Huh. No one's really interacted with her before. Sure, there are discreet hand signals from Adam I picked up on, but I didn't know her name was Adelaide.

Cam holds my chair out for me, and I sit down. When he takes his seat, he pulls the napkin across his lap and looks up at my mom.

"Yes, I've got a few visits planned for the near future. Crowne Mawr is on my short list." Cam takes my hand on the table. Not hiding it below.

My cheeks flush with heat like he propositioned me in front of my mom.

"It's a good school, and with Deimos on your resume, I'm sure you'll get in."

Adelaide comes out with dishes and puts them in front of us. It's a vegetarian dish I'm not familiar with, but it smells delicious.

"Thank you," I say softly.

"Do you play hockey like Damon?" Mom cuts her food and arches an eyebrow at Cam. Playing the perfect host.

"No one plays hockey like Damon." Cam laughs. "But I do play hockey. I might even try out to sit on the bench in college."

"I'm sure you'll get some ice time." Mom sounds certain.

"It won't matter as long as I'm with my friends." Cam smiles and releases my hand to eat his food.

Mom clears her throat and looks at me. "How was your day, Evan?"

I swallow my bite and pat my lips with my napkin. "It was okay."

This morning was rough, but the day went by like any other day. Even afternoon rehearsal went fairly well. Hawk had pulled me into the hallway afterward and just held me for a few moments before he headed off to hockey practice.

"Is everything okay with you and Damon?" Mom asks. Her eyes watch me for any indication that I'm not okay.

I don't blame her really. I cried a lot this morning. But that moment when he came to say goodbye helped. He didn't explain the significance of the helmet. I wish he had, but I understand why he didn't.

"We think the time away from each other will help them figure out where to go next. Keep them from being too impulsive." Cam rubs my back and meets my mother's gaze. "But I don't see this being more than a blip."

Mom smiles and takes a sip of her wine. "That's what I told Evan. It's always hardest when you're in the middle of it though."

"She's got us to support her."

Mom dangles her wine in her fingers and cocks her head slightly. "But you're Damon's friends."

"Best friends. Practically brothers." Cam glances at me and his gaze softens. "But we all love Evan. This isn't some sort of game or phase for us. What we have is real and worth keeping. So we'll help them work through it."

My chest feels warm, and I can't look my mom in the eye right now. Yes, Damon and I are a little wrecked right now. But Hawk and Cam will hold us together, because we love each other.

## CHAPTER 20
## *Damon*

THE GPS DIRECTIONS take us to the arena on the edge of campus. This is where we'll meet the coach, the guys who will be going through this with me, and the guys who will be hosting us.

"I have a hotel room for the night if you'd prefer to stay with me." Dad opens his door and glances my way.

"Come in and meet the coach. We have a tour in the morning you can join us for." It's an olive branch. If Mom were alive, she would have been all over this. But if she were alive, none of this might have happened.

I'd probably be at the USHL impressing Boston colleges to pick me for their teams. What I wouldn't have is Evan. My gut clenches at the thought. I glance at my dad. He's been a lot more understanding about the whole Chase hit and run than I thought he would be.

There were more than a few moments in the past hours I thought about getting his take on the stalker texts. I'm certain whoever it is, they're waiting to escalate. Maybe they didn't give her the rose, but those texts were threatening. I'm worried about what will happen this week while I'm away, but I know Cam and Hawk have her.

Evan will be safe. They'll make sure of it.

Dad falls into step beside me as we enter the arena. It's empty of fans. Only a small cluster of guys sits in the bleachers. We move toward them.

Coach Mitchell stands with his back to the glass behind the players' benches, chatting with students and guests. Everyone turns to watch us approach. I recognize a couple of guys who went to hockey camps I attended.

Coach Mitchell grins and walks over to greet us. "Damon, so glad you could make it. And you must be Adam Storm."

Dad takes his hand. "You can call me Adam. We're excited to learn about the opportunity here."

"Not as excited as we are to have the option of getting your son on our team." Coach Mitchell puts his hand on my shoulder and leads me over to the group of guys. "Ivan will be your roommate for the week."

Ivan lifts his hand and smirks at me.

"Beside him is Axel, Spencer, Logan, and Ryan. You'll meet the rest of the team tomorrow." Coach Mitchell turns to me. "These are our freshman players who agreed to host you guys for the week."

I nod at them and look at the other two guys sitting there. They're the more familiar players.

"Caleb Brown and Landon Pierce are here to spend the week getting to know our program."

I'm familiar with their stats. Both of them might have made it into Juniors with a little push in the right direction. I've seen them at camps. They have some bad habits, which probably kept them from going that last step. Or maybe they've corrected those habits and just have parents who didn't want their kid gone for a year or two. It was a hard sell to my dad when I got in, so I imagine other parents might feel similarly. My dad is introducing himself to their parents, who sit a few rows back.

The guys return my nod of acknowledgement.

"I've said this before, but I want to reiterate. These guys aren't your competition. These are potential teammates." Coach Mitchell leans back against the protective glass and looks at us. "We're waiting for one more and then we'll be ready to talk a little about the program. I won't keep you too late since it's a Friday night and you'll want to get settled."

I take a seat next to Landon, and he glances at me with an assessing look. Yeah, we're too used to looking at each other as competition. But we're also used to being on teams for camp with people who the next day will be on the opposing team.

Coach Mitchell turns and smiles. "Ah, there he is. We have one more coming Monday."

We all turn to look at the newcomer. Jackson Riordan.

I should have guessed he'd be part of this program. He's almost as good as me, and as far as I can tell, he hasn't committed to any program yet. Fuck. I watch him as he smiles at the coach and gets the same song and dance I got, with the exception he doesn't have a parent with him.

At least with him here, Evan should be safe this week. Unless she's right, and it isn't just Jackson.

Jackson's eyes meet mine. He narrows his but maintains the smile on his face as Coach introduces everyone again. Jackson nods at the three of us, but none of us say anything. Jackson takes the seat next to me. I keep my face blank, but my gut twists.

If he's the one hunting my girl, we're going to have serious problems. If he's not hunting her now, he made her uncomfortable both in the past and present. Made her fearful. It doesn't matter if he's not the one stalking her. He made her afraid.

I focus on Coach as he tells us what our week will be like. Classes with our host, practices, scrimmages, the opportunity to play with the whole team and figure out if we'll fit in or stand out in a not good way. This is what I've been looking for. A chance to level up again. To continue to grow as a player.

But now I'll be able to find out more about who Jackson is as a person. He could be stalking my girl. Sending texts to her mother to out Evan in the middle of the night. This is my chance to pin down who Jackson is now.

---

WE GO AND GET OUR STUFF FROM OUR PARENTS' CARS AND say goodbye until tomorrow morning for the campus tour. Dad gives me a half hug before climbing into the car and heading to the hotel. With Jackson here, the urge to tell my dad about Evan's stalker has faded. He can't hurt her from here.

We leave our hockey gear in lockers at the arena and bring our suitcases with us to the freshman hockey housing.

"We find our freshman players do better living in a house together with some of the sophomores. Similar to a fraternity, but with fewer parties." Coach Mitchell leads us across campus to the dormitories.

This might be a problem if all freshmen are expected to live in the house. I'm not sure they'd let me have Evan live with me. But I keep my mind open. We can always pay for this house and an apartment for the four of us to actually stay in.

"There is a curfew, especially during the first year." Coach Mitchell stops in front of the door and turns to look at us. "It's a suggestion. You won't be punished if you stay out past curfew, but it's definitely frowned upon and might determine whether you get play time during games. We prioritize the game and your schooling. If either slips because of you being out past curfew too often, then there will be some sanctions placed on you."

Coach Mitchell nods to Axel, who steps up to the door and puts his ID on the reader. The door unlocks with a click. We all follow him inside.

"I'll expect to see you all after the campus tour tomorrow." Coach Mitchell looks at the four of us. "Axel will show you around the house. There's some basic gym equipment here. You'll get a pass for the athlete's gym for the week for extra workouts. Have a good night, and if you need anything, ask your host. If you need to speak to me, my number is in your email."

He claps Ivan on the shoulder and then leaves us alone with the freshmen players.

"I drew the short straw so..." Axel smiles and gestures to the living space we've entered. "I get to give the tour."

The house is three stories with a living area, a quiet room for studying, a kitchen, and dining room. The refrigerator is maintained by the campus food services. There's always food available and usually some premade foods to heat up. We'll see the other meal options on the tour tomorrow.

There are a couple rooms on the first floor. Both are upperclassmen who act as resident advisors for the house. When we head upstairs, Axel shows us his room that he usually shares with a sophomore.

"My roommate has a girlfriend who has an apartment off campus. He's going to stay with her this week." Axel glances at Jackson. "You'll be rooming with me, so you'll be getting a bed."

"Are there singles?" I ask. I'm not sure how I'll deal sharing a space with another player. Yes, I share Evan, but that's with my friends.

"Yeah, a few." Axel nods toward the third floor. "Every bedroom has its own bathroom. You're responsible for keeping it clean. There's a laundry on every floor. Use them. We don't need the house to smell like someone's feet."

There are a few chuckles as Axel leads us back to the living space that has multiple sets of seating areas kind of like a hotel lobby.

We take a seat and Axel discusses the sleeping arrangements. I'm with Ivan, who grins at me. He reminds me of Cam. A few times he interrupted with suggestions for parties, frats, and girls.

"Get your rest tonight. Tomorrow is going to be grueling. You're all professionals or you wouldn't be here, so act like it. Every step of this is an audition for a spot on the team. You've already made it to this part. You just have to prove you'll fit in with where Coach wants to take us next year." Axel stands, and so do the other players.

We grab our things and follow our host. Ivan glances over his shoulder at me as I follow him up the stairs to his room. He shows me where to drop my stuff and gestures to the made bed.

"They doubled up our roommates in a spare room so we could host and you wouldn't have to sleep on the floor." Ivan smirks and sits in his office chair.

"Nice." The bed is what I would expect in a dorm room. Extra-long twin. Basic mattress.

"Coach was surprised you were still an option." Ivan isn't at all subtle, which I can appreciate. "You got mental problems?"

I chuckle, not willing to give this guy anything. "Doesn't everyone?"

He smiles as he tosses a ball up and catches it. "No, really. Last we heard, you were off to the USHL."

"Yeah, got in an accident on my motorcycle." I rub my leg but it doesn't ache as bad as it did. "Dad realized I wasn't godlike and might actually be mortal and decided he wanted me to stay home."

He catches the ball and looks at me in horror. "Fuck, parents suck."

I consider how Dad hasn't made any changes to our living arrangement after finding out about me and Evan. Yet. He even talked Heather out of leaving. Though that might have been more for him. "He's not that bad."

I don't know if they'll decide to move Evan from the room next to mine. They have a whole week to fuck with my life while I'm gone. The guys will tell me if they do. I don't know if Evan will try to stay in touch. We left things so fucking broken.

My dad was okay about the Chase thing, but it doesn't make what she did any easier. The things I've told her were shared in confidentiality. She knew that. But I basically hung her out to dry, pushed her until she'd spilled everything.

"We're going out tomorrow night. There's a frat party. Some of the guys on the team are members. Delta Psi Lambda, you heard of them?" Ivan stretches and drops the ball on his desk before getting up.

I smirk, thinking of Cam's declarations at the end of summer. "My friend wants to join them."

"He into hockey?"

I nod. "He's my teammate."

Ivan smiles. "He should try out too."

"Maybe. I don't think he wants the stress of playing D1 sports in school."

"It's not all bad. The puck bunnies are worth it." Ivan looks me over. "The girls are going to love you."

"I have a girlfriend." I run my hand through my hair. What we are right now isn't up for debate. She's mine. We need to figure out our shit, but there's no way I'd let her move on to someone new.

"High school love never lasts, man."

## CHAPTER 21
## *Hawk*

Dinner with my parents was almost tolerable, but I have plans tonight. I ride over to Annie's house and slip in the back. While Heather might know about all of us dating, she might not be cool with us all sleeping together.

I don't really care what she thinks unless she tries to keep Annie from us. There's a party tonight, but Cam and I don't want to go. And I know it's not on Annie's priority list. The house is quiet as I walk to Damon's room. Sure, Annie has her own, but that's not her room. Not really.

When I walk in, Annie sits on the couch sideways with her laptop open, staring at the screen. Her back is against Cam's side as he flips a page in a textbook. They look up when I enter and close the door.

"Cozy Friday night study session?" I arch an eyebrow. Cam has our girl alone and this is what he chooses to do with her? I'd shake my head, but knowing Annie, it was likely her idea.

Annie shrugs. "I have a few things to catch up on since my hand wasn't useful most of the week."

I cross the room and sit near her feet. When I hold out my hand for hers, she gives me her injured hand. I'm careful with it and check her face as I gently touch the skin to make sure she isn't hurting. The cuts are all scabbed over and look to be healing. I bring her fingers to my lips and press a kiss to them.

Her cheeks flush a pretty shade of pink as she draws her hand back. Her eyes hold mine.

"How are you after last night? Were we too rough?"

Annie squirms, but her blue-gray eyes stay on mine. "No. I'm a little sore, but nothing hurts."

I nod, and she looks back down at her screen. Cam glances over at me as he turns the page. We've got shit we need to discuss, but we also need to know what happened between Damon and Annie.

"We should talk about Damon," I say.

Her eyes flick up to mine, but she doesn't say no. She closes her laptop slowly and sets it on the coffee table before wrapping her arms around her knees and glancing at the two of us. Cam sets his textbook down on the coffee table too. He slides his hand down her arm, and she shivers slightly and rests her head back on his shoulder.

"Damon told me what happened this morning, but I want your version, Annie." I sit back and wait for her. Both of them are angry and hurt. There are two sides of this story.

Her eyes haze over. "We woke up when Adam came into the room. Our parents were talking when we got downstairs, so we stopped and listened. Mom thought maybe she and I should move out. Adam talked her out of it."

She blows out a breath. "Damon asked why Adam had barged into his locked room. That's when Mom confessed to receiving a text of an old ad campaign from the eighties. When she looked in my room, my bed was made. Adam had come to wake Damon to help search for me."

"That's when Heather told you guys that wasn't the first text she received?" I ask.

Annie nods. "Then Adam brought us back on topic."

"So he knew about the texts." I lean back and let the puzzle pieces slip into place.

"I guess." Annie cocks her head a little. "Mom tried to rationalize my sleeping with Damon and said I was just hurting from my breakup and kept saying Damon was obviously a rebound and that I could go back to Chase."

"That's a touchy subject for Damon," Cam says and rubs his hand down Annie's arm. "He didn't like being your side piece."

Annie lets out a derisive huff. "He asked what I told my mom about the breakup. When I didn't say anything, he told her about Chase's cheating. Adam asked if what we had was new." Annie rubs her forehead. "I had to tell Mom it's been weeks since the breakup and that Chase used the fact I hadn't told her for Tom's party."

I glance at Cam. These are all things she could have told her mother, but I get it. Not wanting the attention, not wanting the focus. Maybe keeping us to herself felt safe.

"Then Adam asked if I was the reason Damon punched Chase." She curls in on herself. "He told them about the woods, about him dumping me out there and coming back to the party to get laid. It was so confusing and embarrassing, and it's like Damon just kept picking."

Her eyes fill with tears, and she tries to blink them back. But angry sparks flare behind them. "And then he blamed it all on my mom. That this only happened because she left me alone. I was so angry and so embarrassed. So fucking exposed that I told Adam about Chase being the hit and run. Everything came out after that. Damon looked at me so coldly like he did when we started. Like I meant nothing to him."

Tears roll down Annie's cheeks, and I draw her onto my lap to hold her.

"He hated me." She grabs on to my shirt and buries her face in my chest. "He hated me in that moment, and everything inside me wanted to disappear."

"He doesn't hate you, Annie." I rub her back and wish Damon was here so I could fuck him up.

Cam moves in closer and presses his head to hers. "He loves you, Evan. It takes a lot for him to love someone. Hate is easy, but he's fucking loyal to who he loves. It wasn't hate. He just shut down like he did after his mom died."

"I don't want to lose you." She reaches out and grabs his shirt, holding him to her too while she sobs softly into my mine.

"You won't." This is the last time Damon hurts her. The last time she'll cry over one of us. I'll make sure of it.

We lie in bed later. Annie has on one of Damon's shirts and rests on my chest. Her breathing is slow and steady. She had a long night followed by a long day. Cam is on her other side, his hand idly rubbing her back while he looks at his phone.

Our phones buzz at the same time. I look over at Cam.

"Text from Damon." Cam reads it and sighs. "Jackson is part of the program. He's one of the guys trying out for Crowne Mawr."

"At least we don't need to worry about him this week then." I lean down and kiss Annie's hair. She snuggles against me.

"Crowne Mawr apparently has their hockey freshmen live in a house together." Cam chuckles. "That's not going to fly with Damon unless Evan can live there too."

"Fuck him. He gets her our senior year. He can live with the hockey guys and visit Annie like we have to." I smirk at Cam. "Tell him we'll let him visit Annie from time to time."

Cam types with a smug grin. After another buzz, he chuckles. "Apparently that's *not happening*."

I chuckle.

"He asks how she is?" Cam says softly.

"Tired. Passed the fuck out. What does he expect after last night and then this morning?" I tighten my arm around her. Damon's right though. She'll run herself ragged if we don't make her stop. She protested going to bed even though her eyes were struggling to stay open and focused on her laptop.

"I told him I watched her eat and now I'm watching her sleep." Cam glances toward the corner we know the camera is in. We've both watched feed from it. Cam holds his middle finger to it with a smile.

"He'd be much worse if he couldn't watch her," I say.

"You're not wrong." Cam chuckles. "Damon says, fuck off."

"Good to know he can listen to us too." I roll my eyes. "You could just call, asshole."

Cam's phone buzzes, and he puts it on speakerphone. "How's college life?"

"I have a roommate. That's why I haven't called, but he stepped out to use the bathroom." Damon's voice fills the room.

Annie curls into me a little tighter. For a second, I just wish he was here with us, but it wouldn't make a difference. They're not really talking right now.

"What's the plan to find out about the texts Heather's been getting?" Damon asks, all business.

"I know a guy." Cam lies back and rests his phone on his chest. "I'm going to get someone to look into your nerd too. But we really shouldn't say much if your video is compromised."

Damon huffs out a breath. "Training starts tomorrow. I'll see what I can find out about Jackson. But this is a fucking interview, so he'll be on his best behavior. I doubt I'll learn much besides if he actually wants to go here or not."

"Whatever you can find out without getting into trouble." I brush Annie's hair out of her face. "I owe you a gut punch, man."

Damon sighs. "She cried."

"She thinks you hated her," Cam says.

He doesn't say anything, but that's gotta hurt to hear. "I don't."

"We know and she knows, but it's how she felt." I've never been more protective of anyone in my life, but how can I not with Annie?

"My roommate is back. Talk tomorrow." He hangs up.

It's not really fair that he can watch her, but Annie can't watch him. Maybe him watching her will bring its own comfort to her. That he still cares enough to stalk her.

---

### *EvanAnn*

I wake up too hot and needing to use the bathroom. I climb out of the bed that smells like Damon, from between Cam and Hawk. They don't stir as I pad across the wood floor to the bathroom.

After I finish, I wash my hands and get my phone from where I left it to charge. It lights up with a text message. I sit on the couch and pull on Cam's hoodie he left on the arm.

SEX GOD:

> Why are you up?

I glance around. I *knew* he had a fucking camera in here. For a while, I wondered, but now that I know, I want to see the feed. My heart pulses. It's just me and him. I'm too sleepy to argue or shut him out.

ME:

> You don't have a camera in the toilet?
>
> Amateur

SEX GOD:

> I do consider some things private

ME:

> Thankfully

I smile and glance over at the bed where Cam and Hawk are asleep. They made me climb into bed earlier. Now, I'm wide awake. Should I even be talking with Damon? Aren't we fighting? Should I bring up what happened so we can talk about that instead?

But I don't want to. I just want to go back to sleeping in his arms.

ME:

> Why are you up?

SEX GOD:

> Stalking you

ME:

> *eyeroll emoji* Go to sleep
>
> You have things tomorrow
>
> You barely got sleep last night too

SEX GOD:

> I'll be fine

Lifting my gaze, I try to glare at possible spots the camera might be.

**SEX GOD:**
Why are you squinting at the corners?

**ME:**
I'm trying to glare at you

**SEX GOD:**
Not very convincing

**ME:**
Not my finest performance, but I lack sufficient direction

**SEX GOD:**
Corner above the door

I hate night mode, but it's good to see your face

Even if you're glaring at me

**ME:**
Go to sleep

**SEX GOD:**
I can't without you

My heart feels too tight for my chest. I bite my lip. I have Hawk and Cam, but he's all alone. But I knew he'd miss me.

**ME:**
Check the pocket of your bag

I wait for a few minutes to see if he'll find it.

**SEX GOD:**
Fuck, little devil

I arch an eyebrow at the camera, imagining him holding a pair of my panties. Not the new ones that he buys me but the cotton ones I always used to wear. That I wore for him. I don't know where he keeps them, but I know he has a collection of my panties somewhere.

## DARK TANGLED TRUTHS

> **ME:**
> Full disclosure, I put those in your bag before we went to bed the other night

> **SEX GOD:**
> I'm glad you weren't mad at me then

> **ME:**
> I don't want to be mad at you

I can't help the confession. Curling into the corner of the couch, I try to imagine how we got to this place. Where the only way to fight was to blurt out truths?

> **SEX GOD:**
> I'm not mad at you, Evan

I rub my chest on my heart.

> **ME:**
> It feels like you are

His words from earlier echo in my head. He's not ready to apologize. That means he might be sorry for what he said.

> **SEX GOD:**
> Go curl up in bed, little devil
>
> You'll be asleep before you know it

> **ME:**
> Only if you sleep with me

> **SEX GOD:**
> Deal

---

I WAKE UP TO MY BODY ON FIRE AS HAWK TONGUE FUCKS MY pussy. Moaning, I come, and he crawls up my body to kiss me properly. The taste of me is on his tongue, but I don't care. I thread my fingers through his hair and wrap my legs around him.

I still buzz with need.

"Save it for tonight, baby girl." Hawk chuckles and kisses me again. "I need to get going or I'll be late for the scrimmage."

I reluctantly release him and drop back on the bed. Cam comes out of the bathroom, dressed and ready for the day. He shakes his head as Hawk stands and adjusts himself in his boxers.

"I was just going to pull you into the shower with me, but Hawk here was like, Annie needs her sleep." Cam rolls his eyes. "What he actually meant is he needed a morning snack."

I lean up on my elbows. "I'm cleared to come to your scrimmage, right?"

Hawk disappears into the bathroom, and Cam glances with a mischievous look over his shoulder before crawling over me on the bed.

"You're coming with Mia?" He bends down and kisses my neck, finding a spot and sucking on it.

I squirm, feeling needy again. "Yes. She's picking me up here and won't leave me the whole time."

Cam lifts his head and runs his thumb over what's likely a red mark on my neck that will bruise later. His dark eyes meet mine. "Good. Bring your helmet, and we'll go get some lunch after."

"Time to go." Hawk grabs his bag and smiles.

Heat swells in me. Cam kisses me before rolling off the bed and grabbing his things. "Sleep more, goody. We're going to keep you up all night tonight."

They head out and I try to sleep, but I can't. So I take a shower and head downstairs. Mom sits at a table by the pool, having breakfast. When she sees me, she gestures for me to join her.

I sigh and watch a different server head inside to grab me breakfast. "This is such a weird life."

Mom glances at the door the woman vanished into and smiles. "It's definitely different. I don't think your dad ever would have been comfortable being waited on."

I take a chair, and the server brings out some eggs and fruit with a croissant. Then she sets down a cup of coffee. I thank her and take a sip.

"Why didn't you tell me Chase left you in the woods, Evan?" Mom sits back and wipes her fingers on her napkin. "Were you worried I wouldn't believe you? Did he threaten you?"

Her blue eyes are focused on me with an intensity like she's hurt I didn't come to her.

I pick up a berry and eat it, trying to figure out how to not make this hurt her more.

"When I first started dating Chase, you seemed so... relieved." I take a breath. "Like I was finally normal."

"I never thought you weren't normal." She's offended, but I hold up my hand to stop her.

"I'm telling you how I felt, Mom. It's not necessarily how you felt, but you always had a worried edge to you when you talked to me. Like I wasn't behaving the way you thought I should. So, to me, Chase seemed to be moving on and seemed to let you breathe a little easier. I never thought he'd do what he did."

"Did he hurt you?" Mom looks fierce. "Did he force you to do something you didn't want to?"

I shake my head with a sad smile. "He was fine until Damon, Hawk, and Cam started paying attention to me. Because someone else wanted me, he suddenly started being more aggressive. He never hurt me physically." I rub my arm absently. "But that night he drove me out to look at the stars and then wanted to do more. When I said no and told him I knew he was cheating on me, he tried to talk me down, but then he scared me, so I took off into the woods."

I release my breath and meet Mom's gaze. Her hand twitches like she wants to reach for mine. So I take it and squeeze it.

"Instead of chasing me, he left me there. I called Hawk, and he came and picked me up."

I shrug like it isn't a big deal.

"I would have come for you, Evan. You could have called me," Mom tries.

"But you were out with Adam, and I didn't want to bother you."

Mom tears up. "He's right. I did this to you. Evan, you aren't a bother. You aren't some obligation I have because I'm the only one left. I wish I'd been stronger. I wish I could have told you how strong you were. But I was sleepwalking through life, trying to find that spark that always guided me home. But by the time I finally woke up, you were doing so much better without me. I should have tried harder. I'm going to try harder. I want a relationship with you so know I'll be there when you need me."

I don't know what to say to that.

"Please say you'll go to therapy with me." Mom clutches my hand like a lifeline. "I don't know how to fix this, but I want to."

"We can try, Mom."

## CHAPTER 22
## Damon

THE CAMPUS IS LARGE, with five schools under the university. As we follow the tour guide, I stay in the back with my dad and watch Jackson. If I do decide to go here, I'll be back with the others for a tour, so I can ignore the interesting tidbits about the campus.

I can't say it surprised me that Jackson is here. He's been one of the guys to watch since we were kids.

I am surprised he didn't go off to the USHL honestly. But maybe something here held him back. Maybe someone like Evan would have been enough to hold him back from chasing his dreams.

But even that doesn't make sense.

He was interested in her two years ago, and he only found her now? We live in a decent-sized city, but it wouldn't have been impossible to track her down. Fuck, he knew her name, which isn't common, and that she was interested in acting. All he had to do was look at high school plays if he was that obsessed.

If I wanted to find Evan, I would know how to go about it. I wouldn't just let her ghost me. So why did he really stay behind, and why did he all of a sudden redevelop an interest in Evan?

I clue in to the tour when my dad mentions something. I nod at how the law library is one of the biggest in the US. We continue through the campus. When the tour finishes, the parents are ready to leave.

"I'll see you in a week." Dad and I stand outside the rink.

I nod and give him a look. "Are you going to move Evan while I'm gone?"

Dad shakes his head and pinches the bridge of his nose like I'm giving him a headache. "What would be the point? If I thought it would stop you two, I might."

"It wouldn't stop me." I shrug because he has a point.

"I don't know how Heather feels about it, but I can see that being with EvanAnn makes you less angry. And before I caught you, EvanAnn looked happy at dinners. So no, I won't make any changes until after you come home and we have a chance to all talk together."

I nod and something loosens in my chest. "Thank you."

"If EvanAnn asks to be moved though..." He lets it hang there, but she won't.

"Make sure she's okay." I clutch my phone, feeling like it's a lifeline between me and her.

Dad studies me and almost seems to want to ask something, but instead he grabs my shoulder. "I will. It's only a week, Damon."

Even as I watch my dad's car pull away, I know it's going to be a long week. I turn and head into the rink to get ready to show them what I'm made of.

---

IT'S AFTER DINNER WHEN I FOLLOW IVAN DOWN THE STAIRS to the living room. Ivan walks over to Axel, who's talking to Riordan, and clasps his hand.

"Axeman!" Ivan hangs off Axel's shoulder and looks back at me. "Pretty sure my pre-frosh is going to bed lonely tonight. He's got a chick."

Axel shakes his head at Ivan. He's as tall as me, a little more filled out. He and Ivan have an interesting relationship on and off the ice. "Ignore Ivan. He's got a number to hit this year. I'd rather have quality than quantity any day, so keep your girl."

I smirk but notice Jackson watching me warily.

Axel nods to Jackson. "You two are from the same area, right?"

Jackson steps up. "Damon and I go way back. Played on the peewee league together."

His tone isn't great, but I don't like the guy anyway. It must show on my face.

Ivan laughs. "Keep the competition to the ice, boys."

Today was a bunch of drills. Putting us through the paces to see what we're made of. It was intense, but not competitive. Yet. Coach would mention corrections and show us new techniques to see if we could take instruction.

I'm sure tomorrow he'll have us run the same drills but watch us to see if we retained the training.

Axel looks between Jackson and me. "Just remember Coach is looking for guys who get along. So if you got beef with each other, get over it if you both want to play here."

"You two are hot shit, so don't be surprised to get offers." Ivan walks backwards toward the door. "Let's head out. The others will be along eventually. We can't stay out late tonight anyway. I need time before Wilder and his crew take all the girls."

"Sure." Axel leads the way, opening the door for us.

It's after dinner, so the sun has set. I glance over at Jackson, but he's checking out the buildings. Is he really considering this as an option? If so, can I get over our beef? Not if he's trying to intimidate or come after Evan. But I guess I can wait for him to be proven guilty before trying to ruin the guy's life.

"We got curfew most nights as freshmen," Ivan says. "Once you get past freshman year, they figure you've got your shit together, but the team will hold you accountable."

"Curfew on a Saturday night?" Jackson chuckles. "Do you have to be in bed by a certain time?"

Axel glances at him. "We're here to learn and to skate. If you have a problem with rules, this program ain't going to work for you. The rules are meant to help transition you from living at home. Too many freshmen blow it by going wild. Tanking their grades by partying too much. If your grades drop, you can't play."

"Any of your freshmen starting this year?" I fall into step with Axel. Ivan's fine, but not as serious as Axel.

"Wilder Bishop's starting this year. He came from Sherman High School. Him, Spencer, and Zane will be coming along with the others. They're already a tight crew." Axel rubs the back of his neck. "Even though Coach will let anyone move up, some of the seniors have been making life rough for Wilder. Once the old guard is out though, I think Coach Mitchell's leadership will make the team better."

"How long before the old guard is out? Three years?" I glance behind me at Ivan and Jackson. They're talking about girls. Maybe I can find out more about who Jackson knows this week. See if I can find the connection. But it's not like we're going to be best buds all of a sudden.

Especially if the fucker thinks he can take my girl.

"I think the juniors and sophomores this year will get with the new program. At least the sophomores will. They've got three more years, and Coach is willing to let them try for first string out the gate." Axel glances at me out of the corner of his eye. "You know Riordan?"

"We played on the same team as kids. He's in the same league now, so we play against his school." I don't need to spill all the dirt. Every moment is an interview. I'm sure these guys will sit down with Coach after this week to help him make his final decision.

Axel glances back again and gives me a piercing look. "You like him?"

"Not particularly, but I don't have to like a guy to play hockey with him." What I want to say is he's terrorizing my girl, but I don't have proof of that. What if we're focusing on the wrong guy? It can't help that none of us like the guy.

All I know is Evan's scared of him. That's all I need to keep him away from her.

I ask about the training program to shift topics. Axel tells me about the state of the art gym we'll work out in tomorrow.

As we hit frat row, the houses are lit up, and people have spilled onto the lawns. Bass pounds loud down the street, and every now and then some girl's shriek fills the air. This is exactly the type of place Cam would love.

"You sure you don't want a puck bunny, Damon?" Ivan wraps his arm around my shoulders. "What your girl doesn't know won't hurt her?"

"I'm good to just hang out this weekend." Even though I know my girl will probably get some tonight. At least she's not alone. "I don't cheat."

"How 'bout you, Jackson? Fancy a puck bunny or two?" Ivan turns to walk backwards as Jackson catches up with Axel and me. "Or do you have a missus to answer to at home too?"

Jackson chuckles. "Not anyone yet. I've got my eye on a girl though."

I narrow my eyes on him, but don't make it obvious. It's possible he means Mia, but he hasn't really reached out to her after getting her number. That we know of.

"Don't do it, man." Ivan walks in front of Jackson. "You come here, you'll be in pussy heaven. No girl is worth giving up that for."

"Again, you don't have to be friends to be on the team." Axel shakes his head at Ivan.

Ivan grins. "You love me, Axeman!"

Axel looks at me. "Just stick with me tonight. Ivan's going to get a piece of someone, but I'll make sure you get back to the house."

Ivan's already making his way through the crowd. Greeting people and flirting with girls. Once again, he reminds me of Cam, the life of the party. Or who Cam was before we fell for Evan. He may party occasionally now, but he's willing to work for his future with her.

As we walk into the frat house, the music is loud and a little overwhelming, but we follow Axel and find a spot to stand near some guys Axel knows playing pool.

A few girls are checking us out across the room. I make sure not to make eye contact. After the Olivia fiasco, I have no desire to even make another girl think I'm interested in her.

I could be in bed with Evan right now. I'm tempted to sext her, but I don't need to get a hard-on at a party. I'm not even sure she'd play. She's never responded to my Snapchat flirting before. And definitely not with Jackson hanging out beside me where he could see what we're typing.

I only send her dirty messages when I can watch her blush and roll her eyes at what I send. Or even better, watch her eyes darken. Fuck, I need to stop thinking about Evan.

I'm here to get to know the guys on the team. I need to focus on my objective. Though it's loud, and the only one currently near me is Jackson. I should get to know him, but I don't really want to.

"So you've got a girl?" Jackson asks when he notices my attention on him.

It's the first thing he said to me in the past twenty minutes. "Yeah."

He nods with the music. "Think she'll follow you to school here?"

Do I think he'll follow her if we don't deal with his ass this year? "We've talked about it."

He glances at me. "That Mia chick seeing anyone?"

"A couple guys on our team." I smirk.

"Is that how you guys all operate over at your fancy as fuck school?" There's anger in his voice that he can't quite disguise. Which is humorous coming from someone who goes to a boarding school more pretentious than Deimos.

"We do have an art school." I rub the side of my mouth. "If you want in on Mia, she might be willing to add a third."

"Seriously?" Jackson turns to look at me. His eyes are dark and a little wild. "Who wants a woman who everyone else has taken turns with?"

Does that mean he doesn't want Evan anymore?

I chuckle. "Look around us. There are puck bunnies galore at this school. Ivan's got two girls he's talking to right now. It's not exactly free love, but don't shame anyone else's game."

"Rumor has it you and two other guys are dating the same girl."

Good to know he knows.

I was wondering if he was working his way there. "So what if we are?"

Jackson glares. "You said you were in a relationship with a girl."

"I am."

"But so are two other guys?"

"For not going to our school, you certainly seem to know a lot of gossip." I turn to watch him, crossing my arms over my chest. "Who's spilling all our secrets?"

Jackson looks at the pool table. His lips are pressed tight together.

"Why do you ask?" I try another tact. "Do you want to find your own—what did Mia call it—reverse harem and want pointers? Or maybe there's a girl you wish didn't already have guys to worship her tight, little body."

Jackson's face grows red with anger, but he takes a breath and releases it. I almost want to keep pushing him to get him to react. To get him to admit that he wants Evan. To force his hand before he does something to her. Let him attack me instead.

I'm more than willing to fight this asshole to keep Evan safe.

Turning, I find Axel watching us interact. He's talking to a guy with dark hair. When he notices me, he gestures for the guy to follow him over.

"Hey, this is Wilder Bishop. Damon. Jackson." Axel glances over the pool room. The music is so loud he has to yell a little to be heard. "We can head out to the backyard. It should be a little quieter there. Easier to talk."

Jackson looks away from me, probably trying to maintain that tight control he has. But fuck, I want him to snap. Because if he does it on me, that means Evan is safe.

We follow Axel and Wilder through the winding halls of the frat and out the back door, down some steps into the backyard. The music spills out but isn't as loud. There's a fire pit and a bunch of chairs scattered around. Most of them are taken.

Wilder closes in on me. "That charity game last year. You were a junior, right?"

I meet his green eyes, recognizing him now that he's closer. He kept me on my toes that game. It was exciting to have someone of the same caliber playing against me. "Yeah."

"Fuck, I think this kid single-handedly beat us last year." He slaps Axel on the chest. "That charity game I was telling you about."

Axel looks me over. "From what I heard, he was supposed to be at the USHL this year."

"What the fuck are you doing here?" Wilder grins and shakes his head like it's inconceivable.

I shrug. How much am I going to hear that? "Shit changes."

"No fuck." Wilder leads us over to some chairs.

Jackson looks uncomfortable, but he takes a seat. "Why don't you have a pre-frosh?"

Wilder smirks. "I'm not fit for company. Also, I have a single."

"Zane doesn't either. Those two aren't exactly the ones you want rolling out the welcome wagon." Axel grabs some drinks from a cooler and passes them to us. "Sorry, Coach's order. Soda only. Otherwise, I'd offer you a beer."

The guys talk about the team and the training. It'll be interesting to get their opinions. These guys were recruited by the old coach, but this is Coach Mitchell's first year with the team.

My phone buzzes in my pocket. Snapchat message from Little Devil. Even though I've sent her plenty of messages, she usually only responds in text. I open it. It's a pic of her, Hawk, and Cam in Hawk's theater room with the caption *Watching a movie. You should watch one later. *winky face emoji**

Last night we just talked. We came to some sort of unspoken agreement when I left that we wouldn't press on the sore spots yet. It's better to wait until I'm home and we can have it out. Hopefully by the time I'm home, I've sorted through the mess that is my head.

"That your girl?" Axel asks. His gaze is on my phone before he meets my eyes.

"Yeah." I save the pic to the chat before closing it. "She's interested in directing."

"Movies or plays?" Axel asks, obviously making small talk.

"Movies." Part of me wants to share everything about Evan, and the other part wants to hoard her away from everyone.

Axel nods. "There's a guy on the team who's in the drama department. I'll hook you up with him so you can chat. He's a junior, so he'll be here next year if you accept."

"That'd be good." I sit back and just absorb this moment. It would be better with Cam and Hawk at my sides and Evan draped over my lap, her head resting on my shoulder. I could imagine a life here with them.

The only problem is if Jackson comes here too.

He needs to find out he can't have Evan no matter what. She's ours and is staying that way.

## CHAPTER 23
## *EvanAnn*

CAM AND HAWK sit on either side of me in the movie theater, where *Nightmare on Elm Street* plays on the screen. A giant bowl of popcorn sits on my lap so everyone can reach it. Hawk's parents are out for the night, so I didn't have to do the awkward, *yeah, I didn't have any pants on when we met* dance with his dad and didn't have to meet his mom. Yet. Thankfully.

I receive a text from Damon, and it sends chills down my back. I swallow and read it out loud. "Hanging at a frat party with Jackson Riordan."

Hawk hits pause on the creepy children singing. Cam lets out a sharp chuckle. The guys mentioned it this morning, but I needed to sit with it before processing. Now I'm ready to process that Jackson is with Damon this week.

"So does that mean I'm safe? At least this week?" I smooth out the wrinkles in my skirt, trying not to think about Jackson potentially going to the same college. "Not that I've been truly under threat. I don't think a rose with chili pepper oil really counts. It hurt, but it's not like he's trying to maim or kidnap me. But what can he do while he's out of town?"

"We stay the course." Hawk glances at Cam. "We don't know if he's in collusion with someone at our school. There may be plans in play."

I nod and rest back against the recliner. But I've been thinking. "What if we're scared for nothing?" I turn and look at Hawk. "Like obviously in this movie, they have a reason to be scared. Not that anyone believes them. The worst Jackson did to me was kiss me when I didn't want him to."

A little shiver goes through me. It might have been only a kiss, but the fear was there. I know how I felt. And every time he's close, there's a buzzing sensation like a warning alarm in my head.

"It doesn't matter what he was able to accomplish when you were younger." Cam reaches over and takes my hand. "It's what he hopes to finish now."

"A few threatening texts and a hot rose?" I blow out my breath. I don't want to live in fear, but that's what we're doing. "It's like he isn't even trying."

"It doesn't hurt for us to be with you, Annie." Hawk brushes my hair from my face. "We would want to be with you even if you weren't under threat."

I nod and gesture for him to continue the movie.

Even as we watch, I'm still unsettled by the thought we're preparing for nothing. That all of this is a huge mindfuck for no reason.

We talk about sleeping over at Hawk's, but knowing Damon's watching settles me somehow. So we end up back in Damon's room.

"Does being scared turn you on, Annie?" Hawk leans on the headboard in only his boxers. Cam is on his phone with a guy who might be able to access my mom's texts. I just finished getting ready for bed.

I pause on my way across the floor to consider it. "I like being chased by you and held down. The woods and waiting definitely gets my heart racing." I shrug and climb onto the bed, crawling up to him in only a t-shirt and panties. I braided my hair so it would be out of the way.

He watches me with hooded eyes and a cocky smile. I don't stop until I straddle his lap and put my hands around his neck.

He toys with the hem of my shirt, but doesn't do anything to guide me or take me.

"You like it when we're rough with you?" The tips of his fingers skate along the outside of my thighs, sending shivers through me.

"Yes." I meet his green eyes.

"Did you prefer it when it was a secret? A secret from everyone at school and then a secret from your mom? Did that get you off? Knowing they had no clue what you were doing?" Hawk teases the lace on the edge of my panties.

My breath catches. "It definitely added a heightened risk to everything we did, but I don't know if I prefer it. There's still a risk of us getting caught together. But that doesn't mean I don't want you now that everyone knows."

"Not everyone knows yet, goody." Cam tosses his phone on the nightstand and climbs in next to Hawk. Honestly, I can't get enough of seeing my guys' bodies. Hawk and Cam don't work out as much as Damon, but they're cut and sculpted and beautiful.

"Your parents don't?"

Cam shrugs. "I just got off the naughty list, so I'll play it safe before telling them my tutor is my girlfriend."

Hawk grabs my braid and tugs my head back suddenly. "Does it turn you on when we're rough with you, baby girl?"

"Yes, but I also like it when we're just all together or soft and sweet in the mornings." I grind my hips against his hardened cock between my legs.

"How do you want it tonight, goody?" Cam drags his finger along my jaw.

I swallow, thinking about what the three of us can do. What do I want? "I just want to be in this moment with you two."

Hawk releases my braid enough so that our eyes can lock. "Can we try something, baby girl?"

I wet my lips and glance at Cam before nodding. "What do you want to try?"

"Remember when we pleasured each other with our mouths."

I nod, remembering how I didn't quite know how to go about it. My panties are already soaked just talking about sex.

"I want Cam to fuck your pussy while I suck on your clit and you suck my cock." He strokes his fingers down my neck, sending shivers through me. "Then I want to switch places with Cam."

I smile and lean in to kiss him before turning and kissing Cam, ready to get lost in the pleasure of being with them.

LATER THAT NIGHT, TUCKED BETWEEN CAM AND HAWK, I can't get out of my head to sleep. The idea that this whole thing with the stalker is just a mindfuck.

It's like trying to dissect the villain's motivation in the film we watched. The first *Nightmare* was to get revenge on the parents who murdered Freddie by killing their children. But in real life, motivations get convoluted and aren't a straight line.

My phone buzzes, and a little rush goes through me, knowing it's Damon.

> SEX GOD:
> You're worse at this sleep thing than me

> ME:
> I'm contemplating the plot of Nightmare

> SEX GOD:
> I can see why you can't sleep
>
> Crazy dead pedophile goes into teens dreams to kill them
>
> Not a very deep premise

> ME:
> No, but it is a mindfuck for the people going through it

> SEX GOD:
> True

I turn and look up at where I know the camera is hidden. I don't want to get into it with him right now. Normally, I would tell him what I was considering for the stalker, but that might bring up my mom. I don't want to reopen any wounds tonight. They're still fresh and haven't even begun to heal. So I leave it.

> ME:
> How was the party?

> **SEX GOD:**
> Would have been better with you here

---

Sunday rehearsal is normal. Even Chase seems to be on point this afternoon. He has his lines down finally. Cam sits in the audience studying for another test this week. Mr. Watson walks around from time to time to make sure no one sneaks in. There are no gifts left on my desk. The whole thing is almost too normal.

When Cam and Hawk drop me off at home after, Mom's at the door and waves to the guys as I walk inside. Adam returned home yesterday. Dinner tonight is going to be awkward, and I wish Damon could be here to endure it with me.

"They could have stayed for dinner." Mom closes the door behind me.

"It's okay. I have homework to do, and they'll have dinner with their families." I glance back at the road.

That seems to settle Mom. I know she's still processing me having three boyfriends, including one who lives with me. She didn't really get the opportunity to interrogate Chase when we were dating. I don't know that she would have, but maybe she wants to be more aware going forward.

When I come down for dinner, I don't think I'll be able to eat anything. Seriously just thinking of walking in, sitting across from Mom and Adam without the buffer of Cam or Damon seems unbearable. But I know it's not an option.

I smile at Adelaide when I walk in and give her a little nod. Hopefully she doesn't think less of me for anything she overhears tonight. For all I know, the small staff who run the house probably already knows way more than any of us.

The table is set for three at one end. I take my seat and drink some water while I wait for the others to arrive. My pulse races as I check my phone for anything that might stall this from happening.

Mom walks in first and takes the seat opposite me. Adam walks in next and sits at the head of the table. With a signal from him, Adelaide brings out the food.

"How was your day, EvanAnn?" Adam asks politely as his wine glass is filled.

"Rehearsal went well. I'm mostly caught up on the work I couldn't do because of my hand." I lift my right hand as if to show him it's better, but I feel as stupid as the gesture looks.

"Crowne Mawr has an excellent campus. It's not Yale, but it's a good school." Adam takes a bite of his food.

I long to ask him about the drive with Damon. Yes, we text when we can't sleep, but it's not like everything is suddenly better. We don't ask about anything that might start a fight. Like our parents and what they talked about with us.

Adam clears his throat, and I stop pushing my food around my plate to look up into his kind eyes.

"I know I'm not your father…" He stops and looks at my mom, who reaches out and takes his hand. "And I would never assume you'll think of me like that. But I want you to know if you need anything, anything at all, I'll make sure you get it."

My breath catches and my brow furrows in confusion.

He blows out a breath. "Friday morning wasn't how I would normally approach what happened. But we were already panicked when you weren't in your room. And I love my son. But I'm not foolish enough to believe you were the one to instigate things between the two of you."

My cheeks heat, and I look down at my plate. Yup, Damon should definitely be here. Though none of this would probably embarrass him.

"What I'm trying to say and failing miserably is that if for some reason you don't feel safe or you want to change rooms or anything at all really, I hope you know that your mother and I are on your side. Damon doesn't want you to change bedrooms. And while part of me feels irresponsible for putting you that close to begin with, if it's not what you want either, there's no point in us upsetting your routine."

Mom smiles softly at Adam and squeezes his hand. She doesn't add to it but just looks at me. Dad used to take care of me when I was young. I know Mom loves me, but I don't know if I've ever been her priority. But Dad was my everything. I don't think he would have been as cool with all this as Mom is being. But Mom does care, just in her own way.

I set my fork to the side and take a sip of water before looking at them both. There's a part of me that wants to hand wave this away. But I know it will weigh on them if they somehow feel responsible and think this isn't what I wanted.

"I don't want to move rooms. Everything I have with the guys is consensual and it always has been. I haven't been coerced into this." I take a breath and lift my gaze to Adam's and Mom's. Maybe a little at first, but they never did anything I didn't want. "I knew it might make things difficult for you, which is why I chose to keep breaking up with Chase a secret. It was my decision to keep our relationship a secret because I was worried Mom would want to move us."

Mom opens her mouth and looks at Adam, who squeezes her hand. The look he gives her is reassuring. She doesn't say anything but returns her gaze to me.

I draw in a breath and steel myself. "I love Damon, Hawk, and Cam. There's no shame in that, and I don't feel shame that you know we're together. I'm ashamed at how you found out, and that was my fault. So I'm sorry for not being brave enough to tell you the truth."

Mom reaches across the table with her other hand and takes mine with a tight squeeze. "I'd rather know what's going on in your life than be kept in the dark to protect me. I know I haven't always acted as the parent, and that's on me, but I want to try to do better. Adam makes me want to try to do better."

I wish it would have been me who could have made her try harder, but Adam is focused on Damon in a way Mom never has been with me. Maybe it was the wake-up call she needed.

"I can tell you help Damon with his anger issues," Adam says softly. "And for that, I'm thankful. We should have considered you two more in our plans for the future. We'd like to do better going forward."

How long will the focus last this time? Maybe this time it will stick. I don't know how to feel about that.

After dinner, I head up to my room. For a few hours, I work at my desk before getting ready for sleep. I stand in the middle of my room and stare at my bed, but that's not really my bed. Like Damon said, I slept there once and have spent minimal time there since.

While our parents are trying to manage this development, they haven't said we need to change anything. Besides, Damon isn't here, and until someone else arrives, it would be nice to feel close to him.

Giving in to temptation, I head through the bedroom and climb into Damon's bed, still rich with his earthy scent.

Hawk is supposed to sleep here tonight, but I don't know what time he'll be able to get away. I pull up the group text. I bite my lip, thinking about last night with Cam and Hawk. I know Damon was watching later when I couldn't sleep.

ME:
> Did you like the movie we made for you?

CAM:
> Sorry if my ass was in the way
>
> Couldn't figure out where the cameras were

SEX GOD:
> No time yet
>
> Roommate hasn't left me alone

HAWK:
> Trying to get away

ME:
> If you put it in the cloud file, I could edit it for you
>
> But you risk me editing in more of Cam's ass

SEX GOD:
> Done
>
> I gave you access to everything
>
> Miss you

My heart beats a little harder. This wasn't our personal chat. It's not under cover of darkness where we make sense. This is the group chat.

Even being in his bed isn't close enough to him. Without him, I feel off kilter. We haven't slept apart really. This weekend was the first time I didn't spend the night wrapped in Damon's arms, but Hawk and Cam were here the past two nights.

It's different being alone in his bed.

I grab a Devil's t-shirt and change into it instead of my pajamas.

ME:
Miss you too

## CHAPTER 24
## *Hawk*

Sneaking into Damon's house is nothing new. We've snuck in and out for years. But as I head toward the back door to go in, I hear voices from the backyard behind the fence.

Curious, I creep to the side of the house. Normally no one is out here, but it's Sunday night, and Heather and Adam are both home. I'm surprised they didn't hear my bike, but as I get closer, I realize the music playing on the outdoor speakers probably drowned out the engine.

"Thank you for talking to her," Heather says softly.

"We're in this together now. You and me." Adam's voice is a little louder than hers. "We should talk about the situation. Are you comfortable with her staying in that bedroom? I know you hoped it would keep her safe."

Damon wouldn't allow them to move her. Annie would just move into Damon's room fully. They have to realize this isn't just two kids fucking around to get their rocks off.

Heather's quiet for a few seconds. "Does it really matter? They're sleeping together already. It's not like we're stopping them from doing something they haven't done yet. And interfering would just make it worse? More forbidden?"

"They are eighteen." Adam sounds disgruntled about that.

"I just want Evan to be happy." Heather releases a sigh. "She works so hard. She deserves someone who can love her. To be honest, I haven't seen her this happy in years. It's so subtle. The difference between her really being happy and just acting happy."

"I'm glad. You're taking this better than I would if she was my daughter."

"Jason would have gone crazy." There's a wistful smile in Heather's voice. "But she was always his little girl. He would have moved the world for her if it was in her way."

"I've always tried to help Damon. He's just so angry all the time. I don't know how to get through to him anymore. After Beth passed, it's like he shut me out entirely."

"Did you talk to Tom?"

Adam releases a sigh. "Went over there. Had it out with him. Apparently he figured out what Chase did. That's why he made sure the Yale hockey coach was at the party. Talked up Damon to give him his second chance at the NHL. Like that fixes everything I went through. What Damon went through."

"Your son is alive and healthy. You can't keep holding him back. You can't let your fear hold him back."

"Is that what your therapist tells you?" Adam's tone is lighter.

"No, she tells me I checked out of life a long time ago. Probably before Jason died. It was a protective reflex so I wouldn't feel any pain." Heather sighs. "The only other time I woke up, before you, was back before we moved into the house. The reason we moved into the house."

They're quiet for a long time, so I move away and head upstairs to Annie's room. Her bed is empty. I shake my head. She talked about sleeping in her own bed this week. Didn't even make it a day.

I relock the door and walk through to Damon's room. Little needy noises come through the mostly closed door. I open it quietly.

Annie lies naked from the waist down on the bed, her legs spread with her fingers buried in her cunt.

Quietly, I cross the floor and creep up on the bed. When I grab her hand to stop her from fucking herself, she opens her eyes and smiles.

"Such a naughty girl." I draw her fingers out of her and lick her slick from them. "You know you're not supposed to get off without permission."

"You took too long. I needed release." She arches her body and spreads her legs. Her pussy is wet and begging for release. Her gaze flicks to the corner where the camera is. I'll have to log in later to watch how she got herself to this point.

I shake my head. "That's not for you to decide, baby girl."

I take off my shirt and pants, glancing at the door to make sure it's locked. "Crawl across the bed to me."

She turns over and crawls over to me. Fucking powerful. I sit on the edge of the bed.

"Stand," I say.

She brushes against my arm as she climbs off the bed. She stands in front of me. Damon's shirt falls around her hips to cover her. Her gaze locks on my hard cock, straining against my abs, and she wets her lips.

"Lie down across my lap, baby girl. Ass up. You'll get five for not waiting for one of us to give you permission to touch yourself."

She arches her eyebrow like she's going to defy me.

"Do what you're told."

A little shiver rushes through her, but then she obeys me. It takes us a moment to make sure we're both settled and in the right position. I stroke my hand down her spine, and her body arches into my touch.

"So needy, baby girl."

"Yes, please, sir." The words slip out of her mouth like candy, so fucking sweet, making me want more.

"Be a good girl, and maybe I'll let you come after you take your punishment." I slide my hand over the curve of her ass cheek. "Tell me if it's too much and I'll stop."

She releases her breath and gives me her weight. "Red for stop? Yellow for pause?"

I rub her ass in a circle. "That will work. But if you say stop this time, I'll stop. Are you ready?"

"Yes, sir."

"Count them for me, baby girl." I lift my hand and bring it down on her ass cheek with a loud smack.

"Ow. One, sir." She wiggles on my lap a little.

Her ass cheek reddens from the slap. I run my fingers over the warm skin before bringing my hand down on her other cheek.

"Oof. Two, sir."

"Everything good?" I ask and rub my hand over the heated skin.

She moans softly, spreading her legs a little for me. "Good, sir."

I didn't tell her to call me *sir*, but I'm not hating it. It makes me feel powerful, like having her draped across my lap, waiting for me to punish her. I slide my hand between her legs.

She whimpers at my touch where she aches most. "Please, sir. I'll be good."

I smirk. "You need to take the rest of your punishment, baby girl."

I thrust my two fingers into her soaking wet pussy and fuck her with them hard and fast while she whimpers and quakes against my legs. I pull out before she can come on them.

"Fuck," she whines while I suck my fingers clean.

I shake my head before smacking her ass cheek.

"Three, sir."

Before she finishes saying sir, my hand comes down on her other cheek.

"Four, sir."

I rub her reddened skin, and she moans like it's the best thing ever. "Do you like when I rub at the hurt, baby girl?"

"Yes, sir." She pushes into my hand. "It feels so fucking good."

I chuckle and smack her ass cheek.

"Five, sir."

I thrust three fingers into her cunt. She gasps. But then I fuck her with them fast while I pinch at her tormented skin. She tries to move, but gravity holds her in place. Her hands grasp my calf as she cries out her release, gushing onto my fingers.

I don't let up though. She whimpers as I continue to fuck her.

"Who's pussy is this?"

"Yours, sir." She digs her nails into my calf.

"Who do you ask to get you off?"

"You, sir."

"Don't I keep you satisfied, baby girl?"

"Yes, sir. Oh, fuck." She whimpers. "I'm going to come."

I press my thumb to her clit, and she cries out again. My fingers are wet with her release. The sound of my fingers fucking her fills the room.

"Hawk, ah fuck."

"Do you need to tell me a color?" I don't slow down my fingers, but my cock aches with the need to bury myself in her tight little cunt.

"Green." She cuts herself off with a moan as she comes again. "I can't... No more..."

"That's not a color. I need to fuck you. Do you want me to stop?"

"No, sir, don't stop."

I lift her from me and lay her front half on the bed with her legs off the bed, feet on the floor. Grabbing her hips, I ease into her tight cunt. Fuck, she feels good.

I squeeze her ass cheeks, making her whimper as I fuck her. "Do you think you deserve to come again, baby girl?"

"Yes, sir. Please. Please make me come, sir. I'll be good for you if you make me come."

"Fuck, I love it when you beg." I reach around and stroke her clit.

She comes, clamping down hard on my cock, milking me. I spank her ass cheek and groan my release.

After I catch my breath, I pull out and rub her ass cheek. "Get into bed."

"Yes, sir." She turns and smirks at me as she crawls onto the bed and up toward the top.

"Clothes, Annie, or I'd fuck you all night. We need sleep." I head into the bathroom to the sound of her laugh. I clean up a little before bringing a washcloth back to take care of Annie.

With her panties and Damon's shirt on, she glances at the washcloth with curiosity.

"It's cold. To help with the sting of the spanking." I tug on my boxers and climb onto the bed, stopping next to her as she rolls over and tugs up Damon's t-shirt.

I pull down her panties and press the washcloth against her skin.

"Was that okay?"

She glances over her shoulder at me. "I mean, it's not very effective punishment if I like it, is it?"

I smile. "But you did?"

"I did," she admits. "Fair warning, I might be more inclined to misbehave in the future."

"I might encourage it." I take the washcloth into the bathroom and hang it up before returning and settling in under the covers with Annie and turning out the light.

"I love you," I say softly into her hair as she wiggles back against me.

"I love you."

## CHAPTER 25
## *EvanAnn*

As I leave Mia to head to second period, a girl pulls another girl closer to her and whispers behind their hands as I pass. This isn't anything new. Usually it happens when one of the guys is draped over me though.

Which, speaking of... usually Cam meets me to walk me to class, but he's not here. Odd, but with Jackson out of town and being watched, maybe the guys will be a little more lax in their focus.

I try not to notice the whispers following me down the hallway. I sweep my hand down the back of my skirt just to make sure and glance at my shoes, but Mia would have told me if something was out of place before she let me leave her.

The classroom is mostly empty, so I walk to our seats and glance at Damon's as I take mine. It will remain empty all week. My heart aches, but I turn and pull out my phone. There's something I wanted to look up in *Othello*.

I ignore the background noises around me as the other seats fill in. There's more chatter than usual though. I glance up to see if the guys are here yet, but it's still just me so far. Weird. Usually Hawk is here early.

Chase glances toward me briefly before facing front. It's strange but now that we're officially nothing, it feels like our relationship didn't really happen. Which it really didn't. After all, he wasn't really committed to me.

We went out once in a while, but nothing serious. He did try a little harder to get into my pants once we were back in school, but was that because of the Devil's trio's attention on me?

I release my breath and turn back to my phone and *Othello*.

"Annie," Hawk whispers as he takes his seat.

Cam drops into the chair ahead of me and turns with a small red paper flower to give me. Before I can ask where they were, the teacher calls for attention.

Class seems to take forever, but when we're released, Cam pulls me against him and kisses my temple.

"Morning, goody."

"Morning, Cam." I relax into him, feeling a little easier moving down the hallway with him at my side.

Hawk presses his hand against my ass before he peels off for his class.

"Did you have any trouble this morning?" Cam asks.

"Not really." We're moving quickly. Everything feels rushed. More rushed than normal, it sets off an alarm in my head. "Is everything okay, Cam?"

Cam releases a breath and glances at me. "Yeah, I just have to meet with someone before my next class."

I pull away and smile. "Go on, then. I'll be fine."

He steps into me and tips my chin up. "Goody," he chastises.

"We're at school with hundreds of other students. I'm good. Go on. Do what you have to, and I'll see you at lunch?" I push his chest. "Go. Class is right there."

I step away from him as he hovers for a second before giving me a quick grin and disappearing into the crowd. I shake my head and go to my classroom. Honestly, I forgot what it's like to have quiet time. Yes, I still get quiet time at home, but there's always this buzz of anticipation under my skin as I wait for Damon.

The class is fine. I notice a few girls talking and glancing my way, which is annoying, but whatever. A guy looks at me with a smile that's not exactly friendly, more suggestive or like he's seeing more than what I'm showing.

I smooth my skirt down, thankful once again that Mom got me new ones.

When class ends, it's a rush out to lunch. I go with the flow like I always used to. It's nice to just be a cog in the machine again. I don't even think about it as I walk to the salad bar to get my lunch and then outside to our table. We've done it every day for weeks.

As I step out, laughter bursts out from Abby's table. I glance up, but figure it's not about me. Mia isn't with them, but Abby and Becca watch me walk by with pleased grins on their faces.

That's a little alarming. They've mostly been ignoring me, but I push it out of my head and sit at the table to wait for Hawk and Cam. Mia comes out the doors without her lunch and zeroes in on me.

Abby laughs again as Mia ignores her and heads my way.

"Oh my god, Evan." She sits next to me and looks me over. "Are you okay?"

"I'm good?" I say but it comes out with a question.

"I'm sure the guys are on top of this." Mia nods her head and clicks something on her phone.

My phone buzzes, and I glance at the link she sent me. I don't do anything immediately because Mia sends me a lot of thirst trap links.

"Have you already seen it?" Mia looks me over again, like maybe I put my outfit on backwards. "No, you wouldn't be this calm if you had."

Mia shakes her head and unlocks her phone. She hands it to me with a somber expression.

I wipe my hands and take her phone. She's got a social media app open. The image posted is of me with Damon talking in the hallway. Obviously not from today.

I shrug and try to hand the phone back to Mia. "It's not that bad of a picture. A little grainy, but at least they got my good side."

"Evan, that's not..." She puts the phone down in front of me and scrolls. Photo after photo of me with the Devil's trio. Sometimes one of them. Other times two. A few capture all three.

"What is this?" I furrow my brow at the pictures.

She sighs. "Abby sent me the link. It's a social media page named *Hockey Wh*re*."

"Original," I scoff and turn back to my salad. "Okay, there are pics of me on the internet. I don't see what the big deal is."

Mia picks up her phone and holds it to her chest. "The pics are kind of stalkery, but they aren't the worst part."

I swallow and glance toward her phone. I take a breath and open the link she sent me. The posts with the photos are borderline pornographic. Okay, full on pornographic. They say how they want to use me like the Devil's trio. What exactly they would do to me and make the guys watch.

I put my hand over my mouth, but I can't stop reading.

"I figured you'd be happy with three hot guys, EvanAnn." Abby's voice pulls me back to the present. "I didn't figure you'd be so desperate to make up a whole other guy to be obsessed over you."

"What?" I can't even fathom what she's saying. "You think I wrote this?"

She chuckles like I'm beneath her. "Let me guess. You have a stalker?" She uses air quotes around *stalker*. "And he's so desperate to have you, he made a social media account all about you. Please," she scoffs. "I don't know how you're keeping the Devil's trio on the hook, but they'll grow bored of your innocent act soon."

My insides are numb.

"Did you do this?" Mia stands and gets in Abby's face.

Abby laughs and holds her hands up. "Why would I spend any amount of time on someone as trashy as EvanAnn?"

"Fuck off, Abby." Mia pushes her.

Abby straightens and glares at Mia. "Know your place."

"It's right here between you and Evan." Mia glares at Abby. "I tried to be your friend, but fuck, it's so much fucking work keeping your ego fed. It's a wonder you've ever had a boyfriend. They'd have to be a sycophant to please you."

"You know, I've been nice to you, Mia, but I don't have to be." Abby steps up into Mia's face. "I'm not like Olivia. I know how to bite."

Hawk strides over to where I am, and Abby turns to him. "Hey, Hawk."

He ignores her and sits down next to me. He glances at my phone screen and flinches. "We've been trying to get it shut down, Annie."

"Why didn't you tell me about it?" I ask softly.

"Maybe they thought you'd like it." Abby looks me over like I'm beneath her again.

Hawk stands and crowds Abby. "Go away, Baker. No one wants you here. If you talk to Annie about anything other than classwork, I'll make your life hell."

Abby smirks. "But I look so good in glitter."

"Go," his voice is quiet, but deadly.

She seems to take the hint this time and giving me an evil little smile, she walks back over to her table.

"I don't think she's behind this." Mia sits on the other side of me at the table. "As much as I hate her, this is too much work for her, and she's seriously allergic to work. But then again, she does have money and access to a lot of people who are really smart. She could be using one of them."

"Whoever is doing this has way too much information and access." Hawk runs a hand over his hair before sitting beside me and taking my hand. "I'm sorry we didn't tell you. With everything going on, we were hoping to let you know it was taken down."

"Is that what Cam's doing?"

Hawk nods. "Actually, he's talking to Damon's guy now, so hopefully we'll know whether or not he sold out. And we need to double check security. All the photos on the website are PG."

A shiver of fear runs through my center. If they had access to Damon's cameras, that would be a catastrophe.

"We have someone checking to make sure there aren't any videos out there," Hawk says quietly next to my ear. "If there are any, we'll take them down and clean up Damon's cameras."

"Have you told Damon?" I turn to Hawk.

He gives me a short nod.

"He can't come home." I grab Hawk's wrist. "He needs to stay there."

"And he will, Annie." Hawk kisses me softly. "He'll want eyes on Jackson, and he has them there."

I release the pressure that had been trying to suck me under. I won't be the reason he doesn't follow his dream. It won't be me that ruins his future.

---

## DAMON

There's a routine to this life that I like. It's similar to the routines I built for myself. Workout, eat, class, eat, class, practice, eat, workout. Our schedule is based on our roommate's, but mine had a bit too much to drink on Sunday night and decided to skip class.

Axel shakes his head when I show up at his door. "If Ivan keeps up this shit, he's going to be off the team. Coach is serious when it comes to class and practice."

I actually like Axel better than Ivan, but unfortunately, that means I'm also with Jackson most of the day. We're just leaving a freshman seminar when my phone dings. I glance at it and see a message from Cam.

"The cafeteria is where we take most of our meals, but there's also a special cafeteria for athletes. We'll go there for lunch today." Axel glances my way. "Everything okay?"

I open my phone. "I'll know in a minute."

The message from Cam includes a link to a social media account with the username Hockey Wh*re. I click on it.

"Fuck." Pictures of Evan with us in various places. Her on the back of Hawk's bike. Me kissing her that night after practice against my car. Cam dragging her into a closet at school. Private moments put online. As I scroll through them, heat burns through my veins.

> CAM:
> I've got someone working to take it down, but wanted to keep you informed
>
> It's stalker type pics if you don't have time to see it

> Don't read the captions

I won't read the captions right now, but I take a screenshot of a few to look at later. Hopefully, by then the guys will have the account down. I glance up at Jackson. If this was him...

"Hey," Axel touches my arm. "Whatever it is. You need to breathe."

The timing of this. I'm gone. Evan's mostly healed from the rose. But this might have been around for months just waiting for us to stumble on it. So why push it out now?

Axel glances around. Then nods toward a building. "Come on. You too, Riordan."

We follow him through the crowds of students into a building and head down into some tunnels beneath it. The walk is long and the tunnel is cool, but eventually it opens up to a larger open space.

"This isn't on the official tour." Axel grins back at us. "But if you need a place to blow off steam, this is it."

It's set up like a boxing gym with bags hanging from the ceiling and a few mats thrown on the floor.

"What is this place?" Jackson asks.

"The Devils wanted a place on campus to have fight nights and to work out."

For a second, I'm confused, but then I remember the fraternity Delta Psi Lambda are also called the Devils.

"Their house is packed, and there's always an adult monitor there. So they decided to use this space." Axel looks at me. "If you need to hit something, this is preferable to damaging a wall or some guy or shit and potentially hurting your hand. Fighting is frowned upon at Crowne Mawr. At least in public. Automatic suspension."

I look at my phone, and there's no signal.

"No reception down here. Most of the underground tunnels don't get reception." Axel drops his bag in the corner.

Jackson and I follow suit. Our bags have our workout clothes in them for later, in case we don't make it back to the dorms. The team has lockers to keep their workout gear in, but it's a different building than the rink lockers.

I want to text Evan to see if she's okay, but she may not even know about this. Cam didn't mention, but if it were me, I'd want to get it down and tell Evan when it's taken care of.

Is this an attack on her or us? Both?

I glance at Jackson. He's been with me all morning, but I wasn't watching him to see if he was on his phone. Besides, that shit could have been scheduled or Cam might have just become aware of it. I didn't look at the dates. But if Cam found it, it might be spreading around school now.

If those pics were put up as they happened, it will show Evan being with us before her actual breakup with Chase. Not that I care about it, but Evan might. Fuck, I should be there with her.

"Tape, chalk, extra gloves if you prefer." Axel takes the tape and starts to wrap his hands.

Jackson doesn't hesitate to do the same. Being here, I might be able to feel out Jackson more. See why he's targeting our girl and what his endgame is.

"Not a big deal if you don't want to. Some guys don't like to hit bags." Axel shrugs. "But I find it helps me relax for afternoon classes."

"Do a lot of people use this space?" Because right now, it's empty. I grab a roll of tape and begin to wrap my knuckles.

"It varies." Axel tosses his tape roll into the bin and moves to one of the hanging bags. "The place is packed on fight nights. But during class time, even during the week at night, it can be quiet and a good place to find your center."

"You do yoga or some meditation crap?" Jackson asks as he goes to a heavy bag and jabs into it.

"Coach has us doing a lot of different exercises." Axel starts fist rolling the speed bag, finding his rhythm. "Don't knock meditation until you try it, fucker."

His tone is light, like banter, but it's also a warning. Jackson makes a noncommittal noise. I step up to the body bag and work it a little to loosen my muscles.

"Problems at home?" Jackson asks, his interest a little more than casual.

If Axel had asked it, I probably would have answered without any hesitation, but this guy is after my girl.

"Some fucker started a social media account with my girl all over it."

"Fuck, man." Axel stops and looks at me. "Do you know who?"

"We have some ideas." I do a quick combo on the bag and step back. I glance at Jackson. "She's got someone stalking her."

Axel shakes his head before starting his fist roll again. "That's not shit you play around with. Have you gone to the police?"

"It might be time." I casually keep Jackson in my line of sight as I punch the bag. "This isn't his first move. Some creepy ass texts and then he left a rose for her at rehearsal."

"A rose?" Axel scoffs. "Weak."

"Maybe. If he'd bothered to de-thorn it. Instead, he smothered it in chili pepper oil and sent my girl to urgent care with blistering wounds." I punch the bag hard, and it swings away. I grab it when it swings back my way to center it.

"Definitely time to get the police involved." Axel hits the bag hard. "Don't play. Tell the police on that fucker."

Jackson has been quiet through this conversation. The problem is how much of this is him and how much is someone else? Brandt keeps circling my brain. He'd have something to gain if Evan is distracted. He may not have been interested in the director at the party, but what about the director who's offering an internship for the best of the showcase? What if he's like Chase and his parents aren't as forthcoming with their connections?

Jackson steps back from his boxing bag and unwraps his hands. "Maybe it's someone worried about her since she's dating three guys."

Axel stops and stares at Jackson. "What?"

"Damon and his friends are fucking the same girl." Jackson throws away his tape and studies me for a reaction.

I laugh. "You just can't get over the fact that she's mine." I shake my head and lean against the concrete wall. "She told me about you."

"Ah, fuck." Axel straightens. "Maybe a boxing ring was the wrong place to bring you two."

He wipes his face with a towel and works on taking his tape off.

"Maybe Evan can decide for herself." Jackson goes over to our backpacks and grabs his. "I know where the cafeteria is. I'll be fine for lunch on my own."

He takes off down the corridor.

"Please tell me we don't think he's the stalker." Axel walks over and picks up both of our bags as I throw away the tape from my hands.

"We definitely think he's the stalker." I take my bag, and he claps me on the shoulder.

"Then I need the story. Let's go to lunch."

## CHAPTER 26
## *EvanAnn*

MIA SITS with us for lunch. When Cam finally joins us, he doesn't have good news. The account is still active, and while he has someone trying to crack the login, there's not much the company will do to take it down. Mia walks with me to senior acting.

"It's not that bad, Evan."

The page has pictures of me and the Devil's trio. If it were just that, it would be easy to laugh off. But I read a few of the actual posts, and they were terrifying. The guys will keep me safe, but the things the poster said they wanted to do to me were graphic and violent.

A shiver creeps down my spine.

"You should tell your mom about it." Mia walks into the classroom. "Someone's been following you, even here at school."

That's the worst part. It's not just outside pics. It's pics in this school. Jackson couldn't have gotten those pictures. Not on his own. Which means he either has someone here working with him, or it's always been someone at my school. Suddenly my safe space isn't safe at all.

When Mr. Watson walks into the room, he comes directly over to Mia and me.

"Hi, Mr. Watson." Mia looks him up and down like he's a snack she wants to gobble up.

"Mia," he acknowledges, before turning to me. "EvanAnn, the faculty are aware of the page, and it's been reported to the police since the majority of the pictures are on school property."

"Thank you." I'm trying not to let it get to me, but fuck. It's like I'm already dealing with paparazzi, and this is just high school.

Mr. Watson rests his hand on my shoulder before moving to get ready for class.

"I hate to say it," Mia says as we take our seats. "I know you think it's Jackson, but could this be Chase? He's been pretty fucking bitter since you dumped his ass."

At that moment, Chase walks in with a shit-eating grin on his face. He clocks Mr. Watson before he opens his mouth though. His smug smile remains. He takes a chair next to Abby and leans in to talk to her.

Abby plays with a strand of her hair and smiles while they flirt.

"That's so gross." Mia makes a retching noise. She turns her back on them and focuses on me. "Seriously, though. He had to know he was losing you. Putting that shit online. Even the rose, he was there at practice. It could have been him."

"He didn't know about Jackson though." No one knew about Jackson and the kiss. I kept it hidden away, trying to forget it ever happened. The first person I told was Damon.

"We should look back at the texts. Maybe they're vague enough it's possible you read into it what you wanted to believe." Mia leans back in her chair. "Maybe you've been blaming the wrong guy all along."

No, that's not possible. It lines up with when Jackson found me. That obsessive look in his eyes at the game and scrimmage. Unless he was really obsessing about Mia now.

Could I have been wrong? I don't pull out my phone. All morning I was inundated with texts. Some from people who were concerned and others who wanted to gloat and say they knew I wasn't as good as I pretended to be. At the first threatening text, I turned my phone off. I messaged the guys first so they wouldn't panic when they saw my phone go offline.

Senior acting flies by in a haze. I do the exercises with Mia and then leave to go to my directing block. Keira catches up with me outside the black box theater.

"Hey, boss." She knocks her shoulder against mine. "Shit day, right?"

I blow out a breath. "Not the best. Do you think Chase could be behind everything?"

A laugh bursts out of Keira until she looks at my face. "You're serious?"

I shrug. "Maybe."

"I mean, Chase is a good actor and decent looking, but he's not working with a lot of brain power. Not that it takes much to stalk someone." Keira bites her lip. "You know what? We're good on *Othello*, so let's murder board this."

"Murder board?" I look at her like she's lost a few screws.

"I'm serious. I do it for all my productions. It's actually quite cathartic." Keira opens the door to our classroom.

We find a table away from everyone else, which isn't unusual.

When we pass Brandt, he leans in to say something to his assistant director. She giggles and glances at me before covering her mouth. My back straightens and I lift my chin. I'll still be professional even if they aren't.

"Okay." Keira gets out some plain white paper we generally use for storyboarding and spreads it out on the table. She dumps a ton of different colored markers on it. Grabbing one, she makes a line across the top. "Timeline first. Starting with the most recent."

I don't have a better plan, so we begin with laying it out, starting with the social media attack and tracing it all the way back to when Chase *noticed* me in class. "We were acting partners."

Keira sits back. "That can't be a coincidence."

"I think he picked me or we were the last two left or something." I shrug. My brain already hurts. I just want to go home and snuggle with my guys and hide. But that's not happening anytime soon. School, rehearsal, study, then snuggles.

"When were the showcase announcements for fall done in relation to the acting class?" Keira taps the marker on the page.

"Before Chase and I partnered together. At the end of the spring production." I make a mark on the timeline as the first point, writing beneath it spring production: announcement of directors for fall.

"Right, so Chase sought you out once he knew you'd be directing. Which maybe the intent was to show you how good he was at acting." Keira looks over the timeline. We put the guys on it too. Damon's accident in June. Olivia being the girl in the car. "Let's focus on this school year. You found a list of the colleges you applied for in his room?"

"Yes, we never did figure out how he figured it out or why he had it." I pause. "Wait, at Tom's birthday party, there was faculty there from a few of the schools."

"It would make sense." Keira tapped her lip. "His dad wants you to stay with Chase, so he works to give you what you want. Make it seem like Chase is truly listening to you."

I shake my head, but it makes sense. "So what? Tom gets my list from the school and gives it to Chase to memorize for his part in winning me over?"

"It sounds diabolical, but yeah, I could see that happening." Keira shakes her head. "What did the texts say exactly?"

I sigh and get out my phone. "I turned it off."

"I would have too." She nods and gives me a sad smile.

It loads and turns on after a minute. Notifications are off, so I don't get a flood of them. But it's still an overwhelming number of unread messages.

Keira holds out her hand. "Here. Let me. I'll delete any that aren't something we should report to the police or that you need."

I give it to her, so done with this day already. She quickly goes through the most recent messages. She doesn't open the ones from my guys, which I appreciate.

"I left the unknown ones that definitely weren't from some asshat I know." Keira hands me back my phone.

I go to the first unknown text. "I thought I lost you. After I replied, they said, I'm never losing you again, Evan."

Keira adds the words below the timing of the first text. "So right after Chase left you in the woods and got taken into the police station. And after Jackson saw you at the football game."

I nod. Now that I read them again, they're very generic. "It could have just been coincidence with Jackson. There's really nothing that ties him to it except the last hockey scrimmage when he showed up. He said he thought he lost me then."

"Maybe. It's pretty generic though." Keira taps her lip.

"Honestly, I thought it was a cast member being dramatic." Though not many people call me Evan.

She nods like that's plausible. "And Chase texted you and didn't get a reply to his number. But the person replied to your text with the never losing you again and your name because you insinuated they had a wrong number. Chase probably would have been cockier. Maybe. It depends on his motivation."

I sigh. "Would I have even guessed it was Jackson if I hadn't run into him at the football game?"

"That could have affected your perception." She sighs and picks up a different color pen. "Okay, what did you receive next?"

"You can block my number, Evan, but I'll always find you. You're mine. I know where you live. I watch you get in your car. I can get to you. Don't think I can't. And next time I'll finish what I started." I blow out a breath. "That was before Jackson showed up at the scrimmage and said things that sounded a lot like that text."

"But it was the night after Chase found out you were living with Damon?" Keira points to the timeline. "I mean, it's a little odd with the blocking of the number. But you did block the first number. It's possible Chase sent it to scare you or so you would seek him out for protection. You guys were broken up. He could have hoped it would help you get back together."

I shake my head. "Chase didn't find out about the guys and me until later when Olivia told him at his party."

"Or he already knew or worried about Damon having access to you." Keira leans back in her chair. "I mean, we know he can act, so it's a possibility. He has motive to want to keep you close. Maybe he thought it would push you over the edge. Maybe he didn't think the guys would step up the way they did to protect you."

Fuck, this actually makes sense. "But Jackson—"

"Might have just really liked Mia and sucks at using his phone. Maybe he does like you, but doesn't know how to start anything." Keira blows out a breath. "It could fit either of them or be neither of them.

It's possible it's someone else who just wants to fuck with you or fuck with the guys." She glances at Brandt's table. "Or wants to fuck with your play."

"So we've gotten no closer to the truth than I was before?" I look over the timeline to see what I'm missing. There has to be something that makes one of these guys make sense.

"You have an awesome timeline, and we did prove it might be Chase." Keira looks at everything. "He had the access to leave the rose. It's possible he even let the air out of your tire on audition night, hoping you'd call him to save you. The pictures in the school. He knows your schedule."

I hate to admit she's right. Without all the information and just with circumstantial evidence, we don't know who the stalker is, and the evidence can fit more than just Jackson.

Keira stares at the timeline. "If I had to say who was the stalker based on the information we have now, I'd say it's Chase. But I also know he's not that smart, so someone else might be steering the ship."

"Yeah." I rub my temples. "I wish we didn't have rehearsal tonight."

"At least the photos weren't explicit. The writing is what's scary." Keira scrolls on her phone, and I see that the account is still active. "Could you imagine if they got a video of you?"

She shakes her head, but my breath catches. If someone knew I wasn't in my bed, that means they might have access to the videos. Or they just guessed that Damon and I were hot and heavy.

I need to find out how secure Damon's server really is. We need to make sure his setup hasn't been sold to the highest bidder.

## CHAPTER 27
## *Hawk*

It's late when we get on my bike to head home. Rehearsal ran long, and Annie seems completely exhausted, but she kept going. Fortunately no one said anything about the posts. She's got some respect from her cast.

Maybe not all the cast since Sophie kept trying to flirt with me backstage.

Evan curls against me as we cruise down the streets.

"Did I tell you how I lost that bet for *Shakespeare in the Park*?" I say over Bluetooth.

Her arms tighten around me a little. "You said you did it on a dare?"

"Yeah, there was this night we were all bored at a party. Really, the party was boring, so we rode out to the woods." I smirk, remembering.

"Our spot?" she asks.

"Yeah, our spot. We didn't want anyone to find us. It was hot for early summer, and we had beers with us. We figured we'd get wasted and then head back when the buzz wore off."

"How responsible of you." Her tone is flat.

I chuckle. "It's not like we did it every night."

I stop at a light and put my hand on her bare thigh. Her breath catches over the Bluetooth, and I smile. I love the effect I have on her.

"We were fucking around, daring each other to do shit. It was right before Damon was heading to camp for the summer. Cam and his parents were going on vacation in the Bahamas. And I was going to be left here on my own. Dad and Mom were in and out every now and then, but mostly it was just me." I roll the bike forward and turn toward Annie's house.

"So how did you end up with a dare to perform?" she asks, relaxing into me a little. I can hear the smile in her voice and really wish I could be facing her right now. She's been pale since she found out about the account. It'd be nice to see a genuine smile from her.

"There was a lot of the usual shit like run naked through the woods, shouting I am a hockey god, and finishing a bottle of beer and then running in a circle. Stupid shit."

"I wish someone had taken video of that." Annie chuckles.

"I'm glad no one thought to." That would be embarrassing. "But it was getting late, and we were practically sober when Cam asked what I was going to do over the summer while they were gone."

I pull into the driveway and park in the garage, because it's habit from years of being friends with Damon. Long before Annie became part of us, binding us together even tighter, we were brothers.

Annie slides from the bike and takes off her helmet. She sets it on Damon's bike like it belongs there, like *she* belongs there. "Okay, that's the setup, but what happened that caused you to take on the dare? And whose idea was it?"

I get off my motorcycle and put my helmet on the handlebar before scrubbing my hand over my hair. I give Annie a smug smirk, and she raises an eyebrow.

"No guesses?" I ask.

"I don't think either of them would go for *Shakespeare in the Park* as a way to dare you to do something." She leans against the wall of the garage and folds her arms over her chest. At least I've got her mind on something else for a little while.

"You're mostly correct. From what I remember, and I wouldn't trust my memory of that night, we were saying things we never got to do because of school or hockey or just because we were too lazy to add anything to our schedule." I close in on Annie and lean my hands on either side of her head.

She smirks up at me. "And you've never had a chance to act?"

I loom over her, but she doesn't cower, and I wouldn't expect her to. If anything, her body almost aligns itself to mine, like we're meant to be two parts of one whole. "Someone said they always wanted to bungee jump. I think Cam said he always wanted to go to a Renaissance Fair."

Annie perks up like she wants to go too. "Ohh—"

"Because of the bodices that show off women's breasts." I smirk.

She shakes her head. "Yeah, now I don't want to go."

"Damon had read about a theater company doing *Shakespeare in the Park* this summer, which was the closest to the Renaissance Fair he thought Cam would get. Cam thought he'd be excellent with a codpiece and long-winded poetry about Juliet. Damon said he bet I'd be better at it than Cam. Cam said I'd never do it. That I would never wear tights. Damon thought I could definitely..." I pause before I say fuck Juliet.

Annie laughs and arches an eyebrow. "Let me guess, fuck one of your costars?"

I lean down and kiss her softly as an apology. "At least you're the first director I've banged."

"Yay for me," Annie deadpans.

"Anyway, one thing led to another and they dared me to do it. To get the part and to spend my summer doing Shakespeare while fucking costars." I shrug.

"This was a lot less exciting than it could have been." Annie grabs my loosened tie and tugs me down so our faces are level. "We need to work on your delivery and figure out a way to really sell this story. Maybe amp it up with a sordid tale of bed hopping."

"You want to help me grow into a better actor?" I pull her into me and kiss her.

When she wraps her arms around my neck, I deepen the kiss and lift her against the wall so I can straighten. Her legs wrap around my waist. I can't stay tonight, which sucks. As soon as I know someone is home with Annie, I should really leave.

But I don't want to stop kissing her, tasting her lips, sliding my tongue against hers.

Cam will be over later, but I don't want to leave Annie. I want to bring her upstairs and take my time with her. Show her how much I love her. Make her laugh and smile and sigh with pleasure. Keep away the thoughts of what's closing in on us.

When I pry myself away, Annie's stormy blue eyes are dark with desire. Her lips fuller from our kiss. It would be so easy to just be inside her and forget about going home for a night of talking with my parents over everything they feel they've done wrong to each other and me over the years.

"Are you sure you can't stay too?" Annie asks. Her fingers skate down my tie. Fuck, do I want to. She bites her lip, making me groan.

I press my forehead to hers. "Not tonight. We're rebalancing our chakras."

She chuckles, but releases me. I step away and pick up her backpack to bring into the house for her. She takes my hand and we walk up to the house. The lights are on. I didn't pay attention to what cars were here.

When we walk in, Heather is on the couch with Adam. She stands up and crosses over to Annie and pulls her into her arms.

"The school called. Are you okay? Do you want to talk about it? You can stay home if you want. I'll stay with you. We can make it a pajama and movie day." Heather pulls back and tucks Annie's hair behind her ears. "What do you think?"

Annie glances at me before stepping away from Heather. "I'm good, Mom. It's not anything truly embarrassing. And yes, it's awkward and mean, but I'm fine."

"The school wanted to report it to the police." Adam stands behind Heather. "We went in to make sure the police knew what was going on."

Annie swallows and looks at me before asking, "Do I need to talk to the police?"

"Not unless you have anything you want to add to the report. Right now they're trying to track down the user if possible," Adam says and looks at me. "You guys are making sure no one's messing with her at school?"

"Yes, sir," I say automatically. But I mean it. "No one's going to get near her at school."

"Good." Adam frowns. "Maybe we should move your bedroom closer to ours until Damon gets back."

"No," Annie says quickly, and then clears her throat. "I'm fine where I am, and this house is really secure. As long as I'm here, I feel safe."

And as long as she's in their rooms, Damon can see her and it's easy for us to sneak in and out.

"It's an option if you want to." Adam backs down and Heather squeezes his hand.

"Are you staying for a while, Hawk?" Heather asks.

"No, I have to get home." I step closer to Annie and draw her into my arms for a hug. "I'll pick you up for school."

She hugs me, and when she pulls away, her cheeks are scarlet. "See you in the morning."

Adam looks like he wants to say more, but doesn't. What do they know that we don't? Maybe there's more going on to this game than we're aware of. Cam's guy hasn't been able to get to Heather's texts yet. Apparently he has a big project he's working on. We could just ask, but with the way things are with Damon and Evan and their parents, I don't want to stir up anything more.

---

## DAMON

"You're sure?" I ask Cam for the seventh time.

"If we could get in, we'd be in." Cam sighs over the phone. "Your server is secure. Your nerd is content and verified no one can get in, including him. I need to head over to your house soon. Evan's expecting me."

"She's still working on homework." I'm glad to know no one has gotten into my camera feed. That shit's just for us.

"You know that's creepy, dude." Cam chuckles.

"Maybe, but she's into it." I pull up the live feed and she's still working at my desk. Her bare legs pulled up with her toes dangling off the edge of the chair. She has on my Devil's t-shirt and not much else.

"How's the situation there?" Cam asks. He's asking about Jackson who, because of this program, seems to be everywhere I am.

I blow out my breath and look up from where I sit on a bench outside the athletic complex. There are a few students walking around, but I left the gym to take the call from Cam. "It's hard to get a read on him, honestly. He's trying out for the team too, so he's got a lot riding on this. It's not like he's going to admit to stalking my girl in front of everyone here."

"Do you think this is him?"

By this, he's talking about the account and the creepy ass messages, basically telling us how he wants to fuck my girl. "I don't know. Do we know how this became public knowledge?"

"Some girls shared it, and it spread. For a while, they kept it to a small faction. But then Fletcher caught wind of it. He told me and Hawk this morning and we've been scrambling ever since." Cam breathes in. "Hawk said the school turned it over to the police. Your dad and Heather went up to make sure everything was properly filed."

I stare across the green space in front of the complex unseeing. "We need to figure out who's doing this and soon. I don't like that we're just finding out about this account. It seems like we should have known about it a lot earlier."

"I guess no one wanted to tell us and possibly get punched for the effort." Cam rustles something in the background. "But maybe they figured we deserved it or she deserved it."

"When has Evan ever deserved what this fucker's done to her?" It's not a question, and I'm done playing. "We need to close this loop, start pressing in hard on the people we suspect."

"Should we schedule a call?" Cam shuts a door.

"Not yet. We don't have any real information." I rub the back of my neck.

"You could talk to Evan." Cam dangles that out there.

"I can't tonight. When we have more information, we can talk."

"Fine." Cam sounds smug when he says, "I'll go tell our girl you're not in the mood tonight."

I roll my eyes. "Keep me updated."

We end the call, and I return to the gym. My headphones are still in as I get on the treadmill next to Axel. He's already at a fast pace, so I don't say anything as I set my speed and program.

I flick my screen over to where Evan's studying. She glances over her shoulder toward the camera almost like she can feel me watching. Something that's been twisted all day unravels inside me.

She's safe, waiting for Cam to come over to sleep with her. She's not alone.

While I warm up, I watch her and listen. There's not much sound. The rustle of movement, the click of the keyboard. It's soothing. The door to the bedroom opens, and Cam walks in. Evan swivels in her chair and grins.

I cut the connection, just in case things go the direction I'd take them in. I don't mind someone catching a glimpse of my girl studying, but no one but us gets to see her fucked. I click through the files and skip the ones in the bathroom for now.

I scroll back to when she walked into my room and follow her walking over to my desk and deciding whether to work there or go back to her own room. She glances guiltily at the camera I told her about, but then makes herself at home in my chair.

Pushing my books gently to the corner and using my space like it's her own. I smile as sweat drips down into my eyes. My heart rate is up and my legs strain at the pace, but it all feels good. Normal.

Axel is still walking when I slow my pace to cool down. Jackson's on the other side of the gym, but he's been watching me. Fuck him.

"Is your girl all settled?" Axel asks, nodding to the phone. He can probably tell I'm watching her, but he doesn't say anything. "The media thing?"

Jackson doesn't appear to be listening to us, but I'm betting he is. We stop our treadmills at the same time.

"Yeah, the school took it to the police because of the threats and pictures are being taken inside the school." I grab my towel. Dad texted earlier about it. I'm glad he thought to loop me in.

"I'm glad the police are involved." Axel grabs my shoulder. "You need anything, let me know."

I nod and wipe my face with my towel. Jackson walks over to the free weights, and I move to an arm machine near him. He works as hard as I do at this, which I would expect given where we are and what we're going for.

How can I find out if he's still interested in Evan? Besides using her for bait, which I'm not going to do. I doubt he has anything like a lock of her hair in his gym bag. But there might be proof on his phone.

"You know the girls go nuts for the brooding look." Wilder asks as he takes the machine next to mine. "But this almost looks like you're contemplating something. What's up?"

"Espionage." I set the weights to what I usually work out on.

Wilder chuckles. "What kind?"

"Wondering if a nerd I know can get into someone's phone."

Wilder leans back on the machine and looks me over. "There's this guy at my old high school who knows fuck all about everyone. There's not a machine you can keep him out of. I know, I tried."

"Is he trustworthy?" I hadn't thought to look outside our school, but maybe that's the answer.

"I mean, he usually is for a price, but Jack usually barters with information rather than money. I don't know if you'd have anything that would interest him." Wilder shrugs. "I can give you his information. He's the best I've ever seen."

I nod and glance at Jackson. It couldn't hurt to get an outsider. Maybe he can check my system for leaks too. "Text it to me."

## CHAPTER 28
## *EvanAnn*

When my alarm goes off, I draw the covers over my head.

"You want to stay in bed all day, goody?"

"Yes." It's not even a question. All the pictures and "love notes" are still up and may never come down.

Cam chuckles. "If I want to get into Yale, I have to go to school."

I flop the covers down. "You're right."

He leans over me and kisses me softly. "I can see why Damon likes sleeping with you. You clung to me and only me all night. It was the best."

I sigh. "Are you staying again tonight?"

Cam runs his hand through his hair. "Yeah, Hawk's parents are being very needy, and mine have decided I must be doing something right. The world is upside down."

We get ready for school and head down the back way. When we climb on his bike, Cam rolls it out and down the drive. He kicks the engine on and we pull out. Hawk comes alongside us.

"Morning, baby girl." Hawk's voice echoes in my helmet.

"Morning."

"Still not feeling it?" he asks.

I blow out a breath but don't answer. When we arrive at school, I stick with Cam until calculus. I miss Damon, but he texts me. Mostly in the middle of the night when everyone else is asleep. Almost every second of his day at Crowne Mawr is scheduled, which makes sense.

History is weird with just Mia and Hawk. For lunch, Hawk leads me toward the parking lot instead of the cafeteria.

And I don't protest. Too many looks from girls and guys today like they know all my business. I've kept my head up, but it's wearing on me.

"Tell me what you want to eat, Annie." He leads me out to their bikes, and Cam is waiting for us.

We go to a little hole in the wall sushi place. For an hour, I don't have to think about someone trying to capture a picture of me and posting it to a social media account that shouldn't exist.

Instead of stalkers, we discuss how the horror genre has changed over the years. Cam wants to download some current movies that reflect the movies we've been watching from my dad's list.

"There are some slasher films that would give Freddie a run for his money." Cam leans back in his chair and puts his napkin on the table. "Like *It Follows*."

"I'd love to compare the haunting genre. *The Conjuring* universe versus *Poltergeist*." Hawk brushes my hair behind my ear. "We could do a marathon."

I smile. "That would be awesome. Do you have time for a marathon? Because I don't. I have a production and homework and college admissions coming out of my ears."

Hawk leans in and kisses me. "Don't worry, we've got you, Annie. It can wait until the show is over."

"Isn't that when hockey season starts?" I steal the last California roll and pop it in my mouth.

"Close." Cam smirks. "We'll have some time before it really gears up."

There's always going to be more work to do until we graduate. It's weird to think about being with them in college when we've barely even begun to date. But I also can't imagine not being with them. We don't have to make any concrete decisions until spring, but that doesn't take the stress off.

When we return to school, I ignore the looks and whispers. The link has made its rounds, so most of the school has seen it. If I didn't know better, this would have been a great way to destroy my good girl reputation without showing Chase videos of them fucking me. Because those pics show how easy it was for the Devil's trio to insert themselves into my life and take it over.

It doesn't show me resisting them at all. At the beginning, I did.

Mia meets us where Anteros and Deimos split. "Boys."

Hawk pulls me in for a hug. "See you in rehearsal this afternoon."

When he releases me, Cam draws me into him and tips my chin up. His dark eyes search mine. "Something else will come out soon, and this will fade to the background."

"I can only hope." I lean in as Cam kisses me.

They leave me with Mia, who links her arm with mine. "Where'd you go for lunch?"

I slip into an easy conversation about lunch and classes with Mia. She avoids any talk about the social media stuff. But she does tell me way too much about her lunch with Liam and Fletcher. When we sit down in our acting studio class, I get a notification.

Dread floods me. I can't leave my phone off, but some of the anonymous texts have been almost as awful as that page.

When I check, there's a new post to the page. My heartbeat is loud in my ears, but it's better to know. The picture is Cam kissing me from a few minutes ago. Fuck. How did I not notice that?

I show the pic to Mia. "Who was around us?"

"What the fuck." Mia takes my phone and glares at it. Her eyes narrow and she turns it like she's noticing something. "We should go back and figure out the angle because I'm not sure anyone could have gotten that shot."

When she hands back my phone, I look at the picture. It's from a fairly high angle, and it probably would have been obvious to Mia or Hawk if someone held their phone up while passing us to take it.

"You think it's a planted camera?" I ask. I scroll through the pictures to see if I can find another pic in that hallway. My heart races because that would explain how Jackson could be there and still have access here.

"Possibly. Or someone doesn't care if they get caught and we just happened to be looking the wrong direction when they took the picture." Mia blows out a breath. "This is so weird. Posting this looks like a full-time job. Who the fuck has time to do that and be at this school?"

Before I can respond, someone sits in the chair next to me.

I turn and am surprised to find Chase. He smirks like he's caught me.

"EvanAnn." His tone is gloating, and I don't think I like this.

"What are you doing, Chase?" Mia snarls.

"It's class. There aren't assigned seats." Chase shrugs and leans back, making himself comfortable.

For a moment I consider moving. There are open chairs in the auditorium, but fuck that. I'm not being chased out of my seat by this asshole.

"Do you enjoy being their whore, babe?" Chase says soft enough that Mia probably can't hear, but he emphasizes *babe*.

"Better than your girlfriend." My phone is still in my hand so I set it to record whatever he has to say.

"You know my dad's the one who first pointed you out." Chase continues to face front. The seminar is starting, so he keeps his voice low. "The spring showcase when you and Brandt were announced as directors for fall."

I glance his way, but his face is expressionless like none of this matters.

"My dad said you were the one to watch. The one going places because you had drive and ambition." Chase chuckles. "I didn't tell him you were an uptight nerd who didn't have any friends."

I shake my head. "So you decided to date the nerd to appease your dad?"

"It worked beautifully. You've got all the trappings of a pretty girl. Tits. Ass. A decent face. It wasn't really a struggle to kiss you." Chase leans back like he doesn't have a care in the world. "Besides we both got something out of it. You got to say you had a boyfriend and go to parties, while I got to do whatever the fuck I wanted, knowing you'd be exactly where I left you. At home. Alone. Because that's who you are."

We already figured out this part, so I don't respond. It doesn't stop my anger from flaring though. He used me because I was easy to use.

He leans into me, his shoulder touching mine. "I did try to get into your pants at first. Thought, why not? She's got a cunt. Then you told me you were a virgin, like I didn't already know." He scoffs, and I draw away from him. "I spun a future, figuring that's what you wanted. The fucking fairy tale. You and me, riding off into the sunset."

He chuckles like I was in on the joke. "I didn't have to wait for you to be ready for sex though. I already had plenty of girls willing to ride my cock when my parents thought I was with you. The golden little scholarship girl from Anteros. You were the best cover."

"You think I didn't figure that shit out?" I laugh. Not willing to tell him the only reason I knew was because Damon, Cam, and Hawk told me. Fuck, Damon even showed me proof. I let an easy smile grace my lips. "You remember Fletcher's party, when you came into a room to get Abby to suck you off and Cam interrupted?"

He turns and his eyes narrow on mine. Yeah, fucker, how would I know about that. Maybe he thinks Cam told me. That won't do.

I give him a smug little smile. "I was there, in the closet with Damon. My pants unzipped, pressed tight against him with his mouth on mine, coming down from the best fucking orgasm of my life."

Chase's face flushes with anger, but he can't do anything here. That's why he approached me, because I wouldn't make a scene during class. Fucker, it goes both ways.

"See, if I'd been attracted to you the way I'm attracted to them, I would have gladly sucked your cock. But it turns out I just liked you because you noticed me. Why not date the attractive boy who asked me out?" I shrug like it's not a big deal and face forward. "You don't know how good they kiss or eat pussy, but I do. That night while you were getting your blowjob from Abby, Damon took me home and I sucked all their cocks and swallowed their cum while they took turns getting me off over and over again."

Chase practically radiates in the seat next to me. It's a dangerous game, but fuck him for thinking I would ever be an easy target. Fuck him for choosing me to be his good girl, the trophy for his shelf.

I lean into him and whisper, "You know why they like me? Because I'm always their good girl."

I settle back in my seat and leave the audio recording going just in case he wants to confess anything else. Like the rose or the texts. But even though it's possible Chase is doing all this shit, I don't think it's him.

He's too petty. He'd want the recognition. He'd want me to know it's him. Narcissist asshole.

The fact he went so long without telling me he was fucking other girls is a testament to his acting ability. Because I'm sure he wanted to tell me every time. Gloat in my face when I wouldn't go down on him that five other girls would be lining up to give him what he needed.

In the end, he's just the asshole I considered giving my virginity to.

When class ends, he bolts from his seat like it's on fire. I turn off the recording and smirk.

"Are you okay?" Mia touches my arm and searches my eyes. "I could tell he was saying shit, but I couldn't hear. Let me know if you want me to knee him accidentally during rehearsal."

I send the recording to the group chat with the Devil's trio. "He just thought he could slut shame me. So I told him they like me because I'm their good girl."

Mia laughs. "Nice."

We head to the black box theater room for rehearsal. Hawk waits next to the door for me. He's got his cocky smile on. Did he get to see how angry Chase was?

"Want to take a break, Annie?" Hawk's smug, and I love it on him.

"Maybe later. I need to focus." I put my hand on his chest and press in close. His heat engulfs me and I'm so fucking grateful he kissed me that night in my living room. That they stormed into my world and took over.

"I can help you focus." His green eyes search mine with barely banked heat.

Mia gestures away from us. "I'm going to the bathroom. Don't do anything I wouldn't do."

When she's gone, I go up on my toes to whisper in his ear. "Did you like my recording, sir?"

"Such a good girl." He grabs my hips and pulls me against him fully. His hard cock presses against my stomach, making me calculate if we have enough time for me to drag him to a closet before class. "We're playing tonight, baby girl."

Sadly, not enough time, but tonight... I breathe in the scent of leather and Hawk. That rush of anticipation zips through my veins. "I can't wait."

---

### DAMON'S PHONE

HAWK:
You heard the recording?

CAM:
Such a fucker

ME:
Post it

HAWK:
What if he comes after her?

ME:
Then we make sure he knows what happens when he fucks with our girl

CAM:
Done

## CHAPTER 29
## *EvanAnn*

WEDNESDAY, when I walk into second period, Chase isn't there. I don't think I've even seen him in the hallways this morning. Not that I care, but it's like this little niggle in the back of my mind, because if he isn't here for rehearsal, Jason will have to step in again. We're getting to the point where I need my actors present at every rehearsal.

Cam and I walk back to our desks. I've been texting with Keira, Mia, and Mark about finding a good day or night to get together for a movie or just to hang out, but with all this crap going on, I'm still on lockdown. It wouldn't be the same if Hawk or Cam had to hang out with us.

And while this weekend sounds good for everyone, Damon comes back, which fills me with equal parts excitement and dread. There's a lot we need to talk about, but I just want to feel his arms around me. I want them all to be with me so I can breathe again.

The usual buzz of people gossiping fills the room. I haven't looked to see what the latest post is on the social media account, but it's apparently all anyone can talk about this week. I wish it would just die, because there's no getting it down. Cam convinced me to shut off notifications, but it feels wrong not to know what to expect.

Hawk comes in with a smirk on his lips as he zeroes in on me.

He pauses next to my desk and leans over to give me a kiss. When he lifts his head, he gives me a grin before taking his seat. He's definitely up to something. I turn in my chair and give him a questioning look.

What's he all smiley about? When he doesn't say anything, I let out a huff.

Clearly gloating, he nods toward the door. I turn and watch Chase walk in. A few guys stand and clap. Girls giggle behind their hands. Chase stops, and the pleasant mask he wears falls.

"Fuck off," he grumbles before taking his seat.

My phone vibrates, and I look at the link Hawk sent me. It's a video. I click on it and see Chase out in the woods captioned *When he thinks he's meeting a girl...*

I watch it without sound. Chase walks into the woods and gets surrounded by guys. Then he waits there, crying, alone, until he runs to his truck in the same place he abandoned me. His truck lists to the side. Clearly one of his tires is flat.

My heart pounds. He's left there alone in the woods exactly like he left me. I lift my gaze to Hawk's. He touches my jaw, lifting my chin slightly.

"It's better with sound." He winks, but his eyes are dead serious. "No one fucks with you, Annie, and comes away unscathed."

---

"Isn't there a way to get this down, Adam?" Mom sits next to him, glaring at her phone. It's been a rough week so far, and it's only Wednesday. New pictures keep appearing, along with the deranged things the poster wants to do to me.

It's also family mealtime. Without Damon.

It's hard to stay mad at him when I miss my quiet time with him. How he scoops me up and makes me shower with him after his workout. How he brings me dinner in his room while we work on homework. How when I lie down on his chest I can hear the steady rhythm of his heart lulling me into sleep.

It's hard missing Damon because it's sullied with what he did. My chest squeezes thinking of how he bared my soul to my mom without even a thought. Was I lonely before him? Yes. Did he need to tear into my mom about it? Not at all. Mom didn't deserve that. I didn't deserve that.

I love being with Cam and Hawk. How they make sure I'm taken care of. Cam gives me flowers during the day and runs his fingers along my spine until I fall asleep. Hawk talks with me about Shakespeare until I drift off. I swear we could stay up all night talking.

And honestly, sleeping with just Cam or Hawk is a whole new experience that I'm loving. I wish I had more opportunities to be with them individually.

Adam clears his throat, bringing me back to the conversation.

"If EvanAnn were younger, maybe." Adam shakes his head and turns his blue eyes to me. "I'm sorry you're going through this."

I nod. It's all most adults have been able to say. At this point I'm resigned to my pictures being on this Hockey Wh*re page. It's not harmful—they don't have my name and address and phone number on it—just disturbing words and an invasion of privacy. At least I already told my mom about the guys, or there would have been a lot of questions to answer.

We're over that awkward moment of me sleeping naked on top of Damon. Okay, maybe not over, but we're dealing. Honestly, these posts might have been a much easier and less embarrassing way to find out than how she actually found out about my relationship.

And Damon and I wouldn't be fighting. I push my food around on my plate. Damon and I still talk, but under the cover of darkness, when it's just him and me. Those conversations give me hope that we can get through this. He said he wasn't ready to apologize. That means he will, right? And what will I do when he does? Will I be able to accept that he tried to blow us up because Mom thought he was my rebound?

When he gets back, we'll talk and see how it goes.

Until then, maybe I can figure out some things we haven't been able to get a handle on. I push my food around, trying to figure out a way to bring up the texts Mom got. There are ways to ease into a conversation like this, but I just need to know.

"You said the text that night wasn't the first anonymous text you received?" I ask with an arched brow. "What did the other ones say?"

Mom glances at Adam and then down at her plate. She releases her breath. "It was just little texts at first. Like *do you know where your child is*? It reminded me of a horror movie Jason made me watch. So I'd check in on you with either a text or find you in the house. Most of the time nothing was happening."

My cheeks flare with heat remembering the three times she interrupted me and Damon in the beginning. When he showed me his blackmail. After that first kiss. In the bathroom when he showed me his after he'd seen mine. Those were just coincidences, right?

"When?" I ask, feeling a little choked because if they happened at those times that means someone has been watching us in this house.

"After we moved here." Mom shrugs like it doesn't matter. "I blocked most of the texts."

"It doesn't bother you that someone texted you that I needed to be checked on? That the last time they did, you found me missing?"

What if I can't stay here? What if we have to disconnect Damon's cameras?

"They didn't happen often, and came from different numbers. I didn't always check on you, Evan." Mom reaches across the table for my hand. "Are you okay? Why are you so pale?"

I set my fork on my plate and give up all pretense of eating. My mind spins with all the possibilities. I need to know everything. "Why did we move from the apartments, and why didn't you want to go back there?"

Something happened. I know it did. I never questioned it because I wanted away from Jackson.

Mom puts her hand to her throat and sits back in her chair.

"You should tell her," Adam says.

It hurts to know she trusted Adam with this and not me.

"The apartment building was inexpensive. It was what I needed to be able to get ahead on some debts." Mom clutches her neck like she doesn't want to tell me any of this. Her gaze remains on her plate. "I figured if we could make it a year we'd be able to save up for somewhere better. Somewhere safer."

I lean back in my chair and watch her as if she's a movie.

She sighs and lifts her gaze to mine. "Our next door neighbor was a cop, and I thought that would make us safer, but his wife seemed to think he had a thing for me." Mom shakes her head. "She'd bitch at me about the simplest things. Like you left your wet shoes out in the hallway once. Or how you slammed the doors in the apartment, which you didn't. I could have lived with that, with her nitpicking."

"What made you move out?" I lean forward, expecting something like the husband finally made a move.

She reaches for Adam and he takes her hand. "Someone was breaking into our apartment when we weren't there. At first I didn't notice, but things would be moved or something little would be missing. I figured you moved it."

My breath catches. It's reasonable to believe it was me. "What made you realize someone else was doing it?"

"I noticed I was missing some panties." Mom stops and covers her mouth for a second, and then she meets my eyes. "I didn't want you to worry. When I realized what was happening, I rented the house the next day after staying up all night with a baseball bat and my cellphone next to me."

It's hard to think. I wouldn't know if I was missing anything while we lived there. What if it was Jackson breaking in? What if it was some other monster?

Mom looks down at her plate before lifting her gaze to mine. Her eyes shimmer with unshed tears, and distress lingers in the depths. "I did what I thought would make it all go away. I rented the house, changed our phones, and got us out of there. I bought that security system and used it faithfully for months. Fuck, I was tempted to change our names and move towns, but I couldn't take you from your program at school. Jason would have never forgiven me, and it wouldn't be fair to you."

She wanted to take me from here? Someone had been in our apartment, and I didn't know? Energy flows through me with no outlet, releasing me from fear's hold.

"Why did you keep this from me?" I jerk to my feet.

"I didn't want to scare you. To have you looking over your shoulder every moment. I wanted us to feel safe. You were sixteen, and I was supposed to be the parent. This was what I could do." Mom looks down at the table before looking up at me. "I thought it was someone trying to make me move. Maybe our neighbor. Maybe someone else. That apartment building wasn't good. So as soon as I could, I got us out, but then the house cost so much more. I worked overtime to try to make it work, but they wanted to raise our rent this year. I couldn't tell you we were practically broke. I didn't want you to worry. You seemed so happy, like everything was going your way. Adam—" She cuts herself off.

My heartbeat is erratic. Was that the real reason someone did that? To get us to move? Is that threat gone or has it just taken a new shape? How safe am I? Did they break in while I was there? How would I have known? Damon was in my house when I was asleep, and I never knew. Could this person have done the same, and I never would have known?

I struggle to work through the problem.

This doesn't make sense. I was alone a lot in our house. If it was Jackson, why stop? Maybe what happened at the apartment wasn't related to Jackson. Maybe they accomplished their goal—to scare my mom into moving. Otherwise, what were they waiting for? Why not strike when I was alone in our old house?

While this house is far more secure than that apartment, I'm glad Damon kept me to himself in his room. That he hoarded me in his bed like treasured gold while calling me his.

There were all those nights she left me alone in our old house. When I was unaware of any danger. Damon snuck in. What if he wasn't the first? What if whoever broke in was more careful about what they took? What if they'd taken me?

I'm cold all over. I can't settle on a single thought. My voice is stuck in my throat with so many questions tangled around it.

Mom takes a breath and meets my eyes. "Adam and I were dating when they gave me the new lease agreement. When I showed it to him, he asked me to move in with him. Even though I already knew I loved him, I figured it was too soon. I thought I'd be able to find something else for us, but the only apartments available were back at that apartment building, and I couldn't bring you back there."

Between here and there, here was definitely the only option. What would I have done if we'd had to move to the apartments? I knew about Jackson, but I didn't know about the other parts. Is it possible Jackson was the one who broke in? Could he have felt the same way Damon did about my mom? That my mom wasn't there for me and was trying to force her hand? Or did he want her to be afraid that I could slip out of her life in a moment?

I glance at my phone. I never told her about Jackson. Never told her about the boy I was secretly seeing while she was working. Was he my stalker? Was he the person creeping in our house? Would things be different if I had?

Mom clears her throat, and I lift my gaze to hers.

"I finally accepted this would be the safest place for us. I don't know if what's happening now is related to anything that happened at the apartment complex. But when Adam showed me the room next to Damon, I figured it would be safer to have someone nearby in such a big house." Mom plays with her fork on her plate. "I believed we left it behind when we left that apartment building."

"And Adam knew about all this?" It hurts that she treats him more like family than she treats me. But he's supposed to be her equal, her partner.

She nods and smiles this soft, loving smile at Adam. "He really is the best thing that's happened to me since your father died. Beth died two years ago, and it's taken him this long to really love someone."

"When did the new texts start?" I try to remain calm, try to think rationally, but all I want is my guys here with me, to hold me, to love me, to make me feel safe, to help me breathe. I want Damon here, but I'm not going to get that.

Mom glances at her phone, and the light goes out in her eyes. "It was an anonymous texter, and I figured they had the wrong number at first. I didn't think whoever was after us at the apartment complex was back." She shivers. "I thought that was over."

"Was it before or after we moved in here?" I need to add this to the timeline. Even though fear still clouds my mind, I need to figure this out.

"After." She sinks in her seat a little. "By about a week."

A week after meant that was after the times she almost caught me with Damon.

I take my seat and lean back in the chair, letting it support me. "I need to tell you both about everything."

"I'm sorry I didn't tell you before. I just didn't want to scare you." Mom squeezes Adam's hand so hard her knuckles are white.

I draw in a breath. Fuck. I don't know what to think, but I do know it's time to talk this through with the guys. I release my breath. All these threads feel random, but maybe there's a thread that makes it all make sense. I just need to find it.

---

ME:

We need to talk tonight.

What time works for you?

DAMON:

I'll be back at the dorms at nine

CAM:

I'll grab Hawk and we'll be there

## CHAPTER 30
## *Damon*

I KNOCK on Wilder's door. Ivan is playing Xbox in the room, and I just need to find somewhere I can talk to Evan and the guys alone. Evan insisted.

Wilder opens the door and looks me up and down. "What's up?"

"I need somewhere to talk to my girl." I glance down the hallway, hoping Jackson isn't anywhere nearby. He's been quiet since the boxing room. Basically ignoring me, which suits me fine. It would be easier to find out more about him if I pretended to like him, but everything inside me curdles at the thought. So we've just been avoiding talking.

Unlike Ivan, Wilder seems like a guy with his priorities straight. Hopefully, he understands.

Wilder nods. "If this is a conjugal visit, I'd say no, but Axel says she's got a stalker."

"Yeah, she needs to talk." We're not in the right place for a conjugal visit. But when I get home, I might have to fuck her before we talk. Prove to her and me that she's still mine.

Wilder steps back into his room and opens the door wider for me to come in. "Give me a minute, and I'll go fuck off somewhere else. Take as long as you need."

"I'll be done before curfew." I'm not going to take up his room for too long.

He slaps his hand against my back. "I've got something to prepare for this weekend, so I'm going to be a while anyway. Take your time. Don't nut in my room."

He takes off out the door and closes it behind him. When Axel realized me being with Jackson probably wasn't the best for anyone involved, he passed me off to Wilder since Ivan isn't exactly school-oriented.

Wilder is focused on classes and hockey. It's a much better fit. And he seems like a good guy. The guy he knows at his old school is apparently going through some shit with his girl right now too, so he's not really available to help me out. Which sucks, but I understand.

I run my hand through my hair and sit at Wilder's desk in front of the window. I prop up my phone on the desk and start the video call.

Evan picks up on the first ring. Her pretty face fills the screen. Her blond hair hangs around her. Her blue eyes lift when she smiles softly and something loosens in my chest. Fuck, I've missed her.

"Hey," she says. That sadness still lurks in her eyes, but it's tempered by determination.

"Hey." Fuck, I don't want to be miles away from her. I want her on my lap, threading her fingers into my hair. Her body warm against mine as we sleep curled into each other. I miss fucking her, but not having her sleep beside me feels like an open wound bleeding.

"Fuck, I miss you." She shakes her head. "We really need to figure our shit out and college too. I don't think I'll survive long distance."

"I'm working on it, little devil." I smirk. "Crowne Mawr is a good option."

"Good." She sets the phone down and Hawk and Cam come into view. Fuck, I miss all of them. How did we ever consider going our separate ways? It would have been torture not having these guys at my side.

"What's going on?" I ask.

Cam glances at the others. "The social media account isn't down."

"I get alerts when something new posts," I say. It's not frequent, but there were two new posts from this week and Cam confirmed those were new photos. I had to stop reading the comments because people suck.

"My mom talked to me tonight." Evan folds her hands on her lap and meets my eyes. "We knew she had received some texts. They started about the same time I received my first text."

I swallow. We knew about the texts but we weren't able to get into Heather's phone. I was hoping to find someone outside of Deimos to hack into both Jackson's and Heather's phones.

"She also told me why she was in a hurry to move us out of the apartment complex." Evan takes a deep breath, and Cam rubs her back. She leans against Hawk, but her eyes meet mine.

"Just spit it out, little devil. Whatever it is, we'll deal with it."

"She wanted to wait until you were with us to tell us," Hawk says as he takes Evan's hand.

"Mom was being harassed by the neighbor whose husband was a cop, but that's not why we moved." Evan shivers. "Someone was breaking into our apartment and taking things. Little things. Mom noticed some of her panties went missing, and that's when we moved."

My insides boil. Jackson. It has to be him. He was at the complex, and he found her again. He's fucking right here. I could take him out and the problem would be gone forever. Getting away with murder is hard. While everything points to him, it's possible I'm letting my dislike for the guy push us in that direction.

"She never reported anything, and she's not sure who it was." Evan bites her lip. "I told our parents about my texts and Jackson."

I don't say anything. I don't know what good it will do to tell them. But having my dad know there's danger isn't a bad thing.

"Your dad wants to take everything to the police. But without a name, there's not really anyone they can file a restraining order against." She blows out a breath. "And I'm not comfortable accusing someone when it might not be them."

I'm glad it's not just me in this. I'd be going nuts if she was alone. I wouldn't be able to sleep. Even if our house is harder to get into than their apartment, it's not impossible.

"Do you still think it's Jackson?" I ask, wanting her read on it. She's always thought it was him.

"Maybe." She blows out a breath. "I told Mom and Adam about Jackson at the apartment complex. It might have been coincidence he kissed me and we moved shortly after, since someone had been in our apartment."

"But there's a good case for some of the recent shit to be Chase Chadwick." Hawk runs his hand over his hair. "Annie and Keira worked out a timeline."

"If we disregard the apartment complex as maybe someone just wanting us to move, then yeah, it could be anyone." Evan looks down at her hands in concentration. "Chase really didn't start paying attention to my existence until his dad pointed me out at the spring showcase."

Yeah, I listened to the recording she sent of him bragging in class. I'm going to punch him in the balls next time he dares to talk to Evan.

"How do we untangle this?" Evan looks up at me. "Obviously Jackson isn't taking pictures in our school. He's hours away with you, but someone is still taking pictures. Maybe the account isn't him at all. Someone at the school could be doing some of it. Like the rose and the social media account."

I press my lips together. Bringing up Brandt again won't help anything. No one else heard what he said to me. Maybe Brandt isn't directly involved, but I bet he's whispering in someone's ear. Telling them exactly what they need to know to fuck with Evan.

"It's possible. We need to keep digging." I blow out a breath. "Maybe I can lean into Jackson a little more in the last two days we're here."

"Don't fuck up your shot for that asshole." Hawk leans forward. "There's something wrong with him. If you corner him, he might lash out, but it may not be you who takes the hit."

Hawk looks at Evan, and she swallows. Implying Jackson might go harder on our girl. I figured that out. Especially if he loses his shot here because of me. Maybe his attention before was all about Evan, but now knowing she's mine could be tipping him over the edge.

How much more can Evan take? She's strong, and she's put up with a lot from us. But what's her breaking point? What happens when she reaches it?

"The phone numbers on the texts are a dead end." Cam leans back on the couch. "We can't trace the social media user id, but I've got a guy trying to dig into the metadata on the photos."

"Mia thought the angle of the picture today was off," Evan says. "Like the person would have to be super tall or holding the camera up, which would have been super obvious, or—"

"Or there's a camera in the hallway someone accessed," I finish. Fuck. "There aren't many cameras around the school. Mostly just security ones. The pictures on the account seem to be too good of quality to come from the security footage."

"Unless they run them through AI to make them appear like photos and not security." Hawk shakes his head. "It's possible. They could also be using AI for the content."

"We've got that footage of the hallway from the rose incident." I glance at Evan. "Who do we give it to to see if that works?"

Cam's already typing on his phone. "On it."

"Two more days," I say, drinking in Evan.

Evan's smile is a little too bright. We still have things to talk about. "Can we talk about something normal? How's the visit going?"

"Honestly," I clear my throat and look around the dorm room, "the guys on the team are great. The facilities are top of the line. Apparently, a donor really went nuts when the team became D1. The house is a house and could be an issue. I'm in Wilder's room right now. He's got a single. I'd be surprised if Ivan is here next year, but the rest of the team have been awesome. It's an excellent opportunity."

"But..." Cam knows me too well.

"But if it doesn't work for all of us, it doesn't work for any of us. There isn't another college close by. I have no doubt we can all get in, but it's just if the programs they have are good enough."

Cam chuckles. "I'm all in, but you know that."

"We'll dig a little deeper into the programs and make a decision," Hawk says. "In a few months, we can take a weekend and ride up to visit."

"I'm ready to be home," I admit.

Evan gives me a soft smile. "We're ready for you to come home."

THE ICE IS SMOOTH AND FRESH FOR PRACTICE. IT'S ALMOST A shame to cut it up with our skates. But that's what it's there for. I glide out on the slick ice to begin my warm ups. This week hasn't been easy. Coach Mitchell has been putting us through our paces—drills, scrimmages, the works—to find out if we're good enough to play on his team.

Axel bumps his glove against mine as we pass. There's a lot Crowne Mawr has going for it. The team is good and a challenge, which I love. Coach has worked with each of us one-on-one to perfect skills. To see if we can learn still or if we'll always keep going back to bad habits.

This is what I wanted for this year. I love playing with my friends and our teammates at Deimos, but I've been missing this challenge. Our coach does his best to push me, but my skill set is already surpassing what he's able to train.

Yale is an unofficial visit, but I hope I get some ice time with their team to better make a decision.

When we head to the bench, Wilder gives me a nod. I talked with Evan and the guys for way too long last night, but Wilder still hadn't come back by the time I left. His door auto-locked behind me.

"Scrimmage today." The assistant coach, Matt Goods, separates us into two teams. Only the freshman players and the two goalies are here today. They're splitting the five of us into two teams. The other guys trying out are nice enough. We've had dinners together and chatted about shit. Jackson isn't on my team today.

If he gets an offer too, I don't know what we'll do. Maybe that will make the decision for us, and we'll all go off to Yale. It's possible Jackson returning to Evan's life is a huge ass coincidence, but too many little things line up a little too well.

Jackson definitely brings what he needs to the ice, but his obsession with my girl might be the tipping point. I'd do anything to keep her safe. Ivan and Zane are on Jackson's team while Axel, Wilder, and Spencer are on mine.

Since they want to see us play, they start all five of us on the ice. The puck drops, and we're off. I've worked with this team all week and gotten a feel for their plays and their weaknesses.

It's a fast game. At one point I'm skating trying to get open from someone on the other team when Axel yells. I turn and see he's shot me the puck as he's pushed into the boards by Ivan. I move to get the flying puck and someone rams into me, body checking me into the boards.

Fuck. Someone else grabs the puck, and Jackson skates away from me. Asshole.

I'm called out, and so is Jackson.

"That would have been a penalty in a game," Coach says to Jackson.

He nods, but doesn't look at all remorseful. I need to calm down and remember what's important. Getting into this program is a step toward the NHL. The first positive step I've taken since the accident.

I ignore Jackson on the bench. Shit talking him isn't going to win me any favors, so I just keep it to myself.

We keep going round and round until Coach calls it. The score is tied, each team getting in two shots.

"Head to the locker room and clean up."

We make our way down to the locker room and get changed. I'm trying to keep my head in the right space and not picturing Jackson holding my girl while he takes her first kiss. I definitely don't need to think about him standing over Evan while she sleeps like I did that first week.

Her covers kicked down to the bottom of the bed. Nightgown tucked up around her waist. Those plain white cotton panties covering her. Did he do the same thing I did? Creep into her room and watch her sleep?

Fuck, how am I any better than her stalker? When I did the same things? Worse, I recorded her and blackmailed her into my bed.

I stand in the shower and let the water pour over me, trying to wash away that part of me.

Is it all right because I love her now? Because she didn't fight falling into a relationship with me? Because she wanted me as much as I wanted her?

Fuck.

"Good game," Axel says as he leaves the shower.

I raise my hand to him and shut off the water, grabbing a towel to dry off. I can't tell if I hate Jackson or if I hate myself. She's mine. I've already warned her if she goes somewhere else, I'll still be there. That I won't let her move on.

What if that's what Jackson is doing? Except with me, Evan loves me. He scares her, which is a major difference. But how easy would it be for Evan's love to turn to fear?

I get dressed and let the locker room talk turn into background noise. I'm not giving Evan up. She's mine, but did she ever have a choice in it? And would I be willing to let her have a choice if it meant she might not choose me?

"Hey, man," Ivan says to someone. I glance up, but no one is near me.

"What's up?" Jackson says.

The voices are coming from the other side of the lockers. They either don't know I can hear them, or they don't care who overhears. Either way, I'm curious about what Ivan has to say.

"I saw what you did today." Ivan sounds a little pissed.

"Played a damn good game?" Jackson sounds cocky.

"That boarding would have been a penalty." Ivan's talking about the one on me.

"He went for the suicide pass. It's his own damned fault."

"Yeah, it's also our teammate so we don't need anyone getting hurt." Ivan picks up something. "Know which side you're playing for, and don't injure your own player in practice."

"But he's not my teammate yet." Jackson closes the locker. "Why are you defending him? Why does everyone think his shit don't stink?"

"You think I care if you hurt *him*? This is a fucking interview. Every step of it. A chance at something more than our crappy home lives. Everything from talking to us, staying with us, how you perform, and how you treat your fellow teammates. It's all a fucking test. I know where you come from because I grew up in that shitshow of a life too. But you don't have to let it define you. This is your opportunity. Don't fuck it up."

"Maybe you should get your own act together before calling me out on mine." Jackson walks away.

"Prick," Ivan says under his breath.

I couldn't agree more.

## CHAPTER 31
### *Cam*

I WALK DOWN the hallway after hockey practice toward the black box theater. I ran out and got Evan something to eat since Thursday is her late practice. As I draw close, there are voices in the hallway.

I stop to listen before rounding the corner.

"You know there's always a part for you in my show." I'm confident that's Brandt's voice. "Leaving EvanAnn's production will show her how much she actually needs you."

"I've got Iago, why would I give that up?" Chase, fucker. "You wouldn't be able to offer me something like that this late in the game. As an actor, I'd be a fool to give this role up."

"Like she hasn't already made you into a fool. EvanAnn sits there lording over you that she's fucking three guys, and you just let her." Brandt makes a *tsking* noise. "You look weak."

"Weren't you the one telling me she's the perfect good girl? That I could have it all, a girlfriend my parents approved of and my social life because EvanAnn doesn't have one? It's not like anyone would tell her I'm cheating on her?" Chase laughs bitterly. "I should have just fucked her and then she would have stayed with me."

"The Devil's trio was never part of the plan." Brandt lowers his voice. "That's your own fault. Did you think Damon would let you get away with the hit and run? That there wouldn't be consequences? I had to convince Olivia to make a play for him to distract him from coming after you. I didn't count on EvanAnn moving in with Damon."

"I should have just taken the hit and gone to the police."

"What good would that have done?" Brandt laughs. "You would have been fined and everyone would have hated you for taking out their king. You did the right thing."

"He never would have taken EvanAnn from me if I'd gone to the police."

"Do you honestly believe she would have moved in with Damon Storm and stayed with you? She was always a lost cause. You just couldn't see it. Now you want to stay in her play, which is also a lost cause. Suit yourself. Just don't come crying to me when it fails." Brandt moves away, his voice growing distant.

"Asshole." Chase mutters before his footsteps move away.

Damon might be right about Brandt playing sides. But that doesn't mean he has anything to do with the stalking. Though he could be planning to ruin Evan's show. Stealing her lead would definitely cripple her production at this point.

I wait a few minutes before heading into the theater room, careful to do so quietly because their rehearsal is in full swing. I walk over to sit behind the desk where Keira works. She waves at me as I pass her.

My seat is behind Evan's. She doesn't always talk to me during rehearsal, but she knows I'm here, and it gives me time to do my homework. Turns out I just needed a good plan, not really a tutor, but I still like it when Evan tells me what to do.

Chase takes the stage with Hawk. Their dynamic plays well. Chase's jealousy of Hawk bleeds through in his performance. He truly hates Hawk for taking Evan away from him. Brandt can blame Damon all day for Evan falling for us. But when it comes down to it, I think Hawk is who pushed Evan over the edge.

None of us could have won her on our own. Not when she thought she had a loyal boyfriend. But Hawk seduced, I flirted, and Damon came through with lust. We work well as a set. At least for Evan.

She finishes giving direction and comes back to the desk. Her eyes light up when she sees me. I got her a cheese quesadilla from a restaurant she loves. I'm going for brownie points tonight since I'm taking her home.

It's Mom and Dad's date night, so they won't notice if I'm not in, and since they took tracking off my phone, I'm free to do what I want.

The actors take the stage again and run through their lines. Fuck, if I keep coming to this, *I'll* know their lines. I get out my English Literature book and focus on the paper that's due.

"Cam?" Evan sits down next to me. Hawk walks our way, but everyone else is gone.

"Maybe I am a good student." I grin at her.

"Or maybe our play is really boring after the fifth time of the same scene, and you zoned us out." Evan brushes my hair out of my face. "We're good to go. Thank you for my quesadilla."

I turn and press a kiss to the palm of her hand. "Anything for you."

"Hey, I gotta head home." Hawk looks between me and Evan. "Do you need anything else, Annie?"

"No, I think we've got it." Evan stands and gives Hawk a hug and kiss.

I gather up my notes and stuff them into my backpack. Hawk hesitates.

"I've got her. We're good." I stand and put my backpack on before taking Evan's and tossing it over my shoulder too. "But if you want to ride with us to her house…"

The tension leaves Hawk's shoulders, and he wraps his arm around Evan's waist to walk her outside.

She's riding with me, so he can have this. She locks up, and I notice Brandt's room is dark. I need to remember to dig a little deeper into Brandt.

We get to the bikes, and I get Evan settled on mine before we ride toward her house. I love riding with Evan on the back of my motorcycle. I'm sure Damon will take over once he's home again, but maybe I can talk Evan into going on rides with me.

Hawk continues to his house as we stop at Damon's. We pull up to the garage, and I open the door. She gets off and drops her backpack, and then takes mine and sets it on the floor beside hers.

"Remember when you promised to take me for a ride whenever I needed it?" she asks with her helmet on, so her voice is in my helmet.

"Yeah." I also remember the last solo ride we took and how amazing she was spread out on my bike as I fucked her.

She comes back to me and climbs on my bike. "Now, please."

I close the garage door and back up before heading out to the road. "Any place in particular you want to go?"

"I just want to enjoy a night ride with you," she says softly. "It's been a rough week."

It has. I've enjoyed spending more time with Evan since Damon was out of town. The social media thing sucks. But it doesn't seem to have spread farther, and the pictures are still PG, so they don't have access to Damon's stash.

Thankfully.

Even though Damon and Evan talk in the night on text, they still aren't over what happened before he left.

I take it easy through town, but when I get to the highway, Evan holds me tighter.

"Let's fly, Cam."

I shift gears, and we take off down the deserted road. Her arms hold me tight. Ten minutes in I see the little pull off we were at before. I slow down and ease into the parking area. There are no other cars around. When I turn off the engine and the light, the darkness and subtle sounds of the night surrounds us.

I take off my helmet, and she slips off the bike behind me. She hands me her helmet and I hook it on my handlebars. I set the kickstand, but don't get off the bike. She walks over to take in the view. Her arms wrapped around her. Her skirt rippling in the breeze.

"Do you think they'll photograph us out here?" She looks over her shoulder at me.

"Nah, goody. They'd have to find us first. I think we're safe." I lean back on my bike and watch her.

Her gaze is on the city sprawling down below us, a blanket of light in the darkness. This has always been our favorite place to ride to and just hang out. It's where we came when we decided to fuck Evan all together.

She turns to me and comes closer. "If you had the opportunity, would you really fuck me in front of Chase?"

I give her a slow, easy smile. "As long as he didn't get to see an inch of you. He could see my dick coated in you and be jealous I have your perfect pussy wrapped around me. See what he could have had if he'd been a better guy. His loss is my gain."

She glances at the area in front of me and then down at her skirt. "Will you help me on?"

I sit up and help her climb onto the bike in front of me, facing me, her legs over mine. She cups my face. Her thumbs follow the curves of my cheeks and lips and eyebrows.

"I don't know that I want to do that, but I like imagining the look on his face." She smirks.

"Yeah, goody? You want revenge? I'd help you get it."

"Maybe. But no one else gets to have me the way you do. No one but us gets to watch the way you fuck me." Her blue eyes are hard to see in the dark, but her look is wicked.

"No, they don't. You like the idea of us getting caught though."

"The idea of it, but not actually getting caught. I'm just glad we were asleep in Damon's bed when his dad walked in." She leans in and presses her lips against mine. A soft kiss with a sigh. "Do you think this will all work out? A future with the four of us."

"I want it to." I slide my hand up her thigh beneath her uniform skirt. "I think if we want it to work out, we can make it happen."

"Are you still lonely, Cam?" Her eyes study me.

Back at the beginning, I told her I was lonely at that party because she wasn't there. But it wasn't just that. I felt disconnected.

"No. I don't feel lonely now that I have you, Hawk, and Damon." I grab her hips and shift her closer so she can feel how much I want her, pressing my cock against her pussy. "My future doesn't feel as lonely. I don't have to walk through this world by myself. With you, I don't think I'll ever be lonely again."

"Cam?" she says softly, coming in close and wrapping her arms around my neck. There's only a breath between us.

"Yes, goody." Our lips are close enough to touch, but neither of us closes the distance. She rocks a little against me, making me groan.

"Fuck me please." She wets her lips, and her tongue flicks out to touch mine.

I groan before I take her mouth, tasting her tongue with my own. She whimpers into our kiss, and it's the sexiest noise I've ever heard. She's the sexiest girl I've ever fucked.

I slip my hands under her skirt and cup her ass cheeks, rocking her against my cock in the athletic pants I put on after practice. She gasps against my mouth but keeps kissing me.

We've fucked this week, but even though it's been just us, it felt like a performance for Damon. A way to include him this week, since he's gone and we know he'll check the video feed.

But tonight is about us. This craving we have for each other that's separate from the need to all be together. Tonight, it's about me and her.

I slide my hand lower and under her panties, finding her wet and hot for me.

"Fuck, goody," I say into her mouth, as I thrust a finger into her tight pussy. "I don't know how I'll keep myself from sneaking into your room every night. I've gotten used to having all your time."

She moans, and her pussy clutches at my finger.

I fuck her slowly with my finger as she pants against my lips. I press my thumb to her clit, making her gasp. Every noise she makes is all mine.

"We'll never get enough of you. You won't get enough of us either," I say.

"Never." She shakes her head. "I need you, Cam."

"Next time I fuck you on this bike, I want you stripped naked, spread out before me. Tits bouncing and pussy clenching me in all the right ways." I push my pants down and slide her panties to the side before lifting her against me. When I slide my cock against her clit, her lips part and she bathes my face in her sweet breath.

I lift her before lowering her onto me. She slides down my cock, taking me with a gasp against my lips. There's never been anyone like her before, and I know I'll never find anyone else like her. Everything in me insists I keep this girl, and that's what I'm going to do.

Bind her to me so tightly no one else will ever pry us apart. I press my forehead against hers, enjoying the feeling of being buried deep inside her.

"I love being inside you so fucking much." I open my eyes to meet hers.

She blinks at me, her eyes pools of silver in the low light. My cock jerks inside her. I lift her against me and lower her gently. Her eyes flutter shut and her lips part. So in tune with each other as we slowly fuck.

It's not a show tonight. This is just for me and her. Soft and subtle movements. She presses on my shoulders to help me move her. I sit back a little to take her in.

She tips her head back as she rides me, and I run my hand up her back to sink into her hair to support her, to tangle in that beautiful blond hair. My lips find her jaw and I nibble on the delicate bone. Her breath comes out in waves.

There's no rush to our movements. No hurry to get to the end. Though the tension is winding tighter around us, I keep the same pace. No one is ready to take her away from me. Aching just as much to get into her. Distract her. Overwhelm her.

She's all mine in this moment, and she's beautiful.

She strains against me, so close her cunt trembles around me. I reach between us and stroke her clit.

"Is this what you need, goody?"

"Cam." She whimpers as her forehead presses against mine.

"You need me to push you over the edge?" I capture her lips, and she wraps around me as I fuck into her harder, rubbing her little clit in circles. I'm the one doing this to her. Fucking her with the others is amazing, but knowing I can take her there all on my own is fucking powerful. That she needs me just as much as the others.

"I like having you to myself, goody. Almost as much as I love sharing you."

She bites my lip and cries out as she pulses around me, drawing me into my release. I thrust a few more times and groan as my cum floods her. Wrapping my arms around her, I hold her close to me. She's wrapped just as tight around me as our breathing slows.

Like we never want to let go.

A little sob comes from her, and she buries her face in my neck. She's been so strong.

"What's wrong, Evan?" I can only guess, with the number of things currently wrong in our world.

She shakes her head as she cries in my arms with us still connected.

I drag a breath of her woodsy scent in and release it. "This week has been a lot. I know, goody. But Damon comes home tomorrow night, and everything will be better."

"Will it?" She pulls away and her eyes glisten with her tears. "He'll never trust me again."

I hold her chin and search her eyes. "He trusts you, goody. He just wasn't ready to tell his dad about the accident. I'm sure he would have gotten around to it."

"What if I can't forgive him?" Her voice is soft and miserable. "He was terrible to my mom. He was terrible to me."

"I wasn't there. I don't know how bad it got, but there's something between you and him that's undeniable." Wiping my thumb across her cheek, I brush away her tears. "You guys may need to work on what's between you, but we aren't willing to let go. We're going to keep you, Evan. Forever. That means we'll find our way through this. You guys don't have to figure it out on your own. Hawk and I are here to help however we can."

"I don't want to lose you." Her eyes shimmer.

I chuckle softly. "You couldn't lose us if you tried, goody."

## CHAPTER 32
## *EvanAnn*

CAM'S STUDYING for a test and I don't want to disturb him. I need to think about something else besides the inevitability of having to talk to Damon tomorrow and sort out our shit. I'm caught up on all of my schoolwork, and I need a break from the play.

Damon did give me access to his video files and permission to edit them. Fuck it. Seeing what Damon sees might be inspiring or at least give me something to do.

When I open up the cloud account, there are so many videos. Each camera seems to have its own folder. I glance at the camera in the corner and glare at it. There are multiple files of cameras.

I figured he had a couple here and there, but this is a lot. It's going to take time to figure out which camera goes with which room. Curious, I go into a file and click on a random video.

The video I chose shows me walking across my bedroom and sitting at the desk. Okay, so this is my bedroom cam.

The next file is the living room camera from our old house. I get out paper to make notes about what camera file goes where. I'd rename them, but it's probably best not to mess too much with his filing system. I've gotten through about half of them. It's a little alarming how much Damon watches me.

But I doubt he watches all of these files.

When I click into the next file, it's an angle looking over Chase's shoulder in his bedroom. I check the time stamp on the file, and I'm surprised it's after Olivia's blowup. I figured after we released the video of Olivia, Chase would have found them and taken them down. Or that Damon took them before he left. Maybe we never used this angle.

I focus on the screen, and Chase is on social media. I click the unmute and there's some music playing in my headphones.

"You can't just post pictures." That's Abby's voice. "Unless you know a way to get nudes."

"Even if I did, those would get taken down so fast." Chase turns to look over his shoulder towards the bed. "So what else do you want me to post?"

Abby strides over and straddles Chase's lap. Ew, so not the porn I wanted to watch.

"What are you watching, goody?" Cam's voice makes me jump.

I hit pause and turn to see him standing behind me. I disconnect the headphones. "Maybe proof that Chase and Abby set up the hockey whore account. Or my ex and his ex having sex."

Cam's eyes widen and then he lifts me out of the desk chair and puts me on his lap. He gestures for me to continue. I hit play because I'm too curious about what they're talking about to stop watching just yet. But I do hover my mouse over the pause button just in case.

"What would you do to her if you knew she was a filthy whore you could use?" Abby rakes her hands through his dark hair. "If you could do anything to her."

I swallow down the urge to vomit.

"You want this to become homework? Fuck that." Chase runs his hands up to her breasts.

"Fine, we'll get something started and feed it into AI to make it work." Abby smirks and stands before settling back on his lap with her hands on the keyboard.

I pause the video and turn to look at Cam. "What do we do with this?"

Cam's smile is wicked. "If we expose them, you'll lose your lead. So what do you want to do with this?"

I bite my lip and really think about it. "What they did wasn't as terrible as the rose unless they did that too, but I really think Chase would have gloated about it more. Both Abby and Chase approached me once they knew the account had been *discovered*. Even if it's just to rub shit in, they're too narcissistic to let something go. And as much as I hate to admit it, Chase is perfect for Iago."

"One, this is obviously a violation of his privacy. Two, if we took it in to the principal, Chase would get suspended. Three, Chase's dad would definitely sue about the invasion of privacy." Cam leans back in the chair and rubs the back of his neck.

"Let's shut it down then." I glance at the screen and wonder how we can get back into his bedroom.

"You might not like what I'm about to suggest." Cam arches his eyebrow warily at me.

---

## Damon

I sit in the locker room before our final practice and really look around. The whole team is here for this practice, and the guys are all at ease with each other. They joke around. Some listen to their headphones. Others are on their phones.

But it's just like practice at home. But more. So much more.

These guys are following their dreams. Not all of them will continue with a career in hockey, but they'll always have this time in college. It's awe-inspiring to be a part of this.

Axel sits down next to me on the bench. "You ready for today?"

I smile. "This is what I've been waiting for my whole life."

"Don't tell Coach that. Gotta make him work for it a little." Axel bumps my arm to show me he's just teasing.

"That accident fucked up my life, and I didn't think I'd get another chance at this." I breathe in, holding this feeling inside.

"You would have. Hockey is in your blood. Not everyone can make a future in it, but you..." He makes a dismissive noise. "Of course, you're going to make it. You just need the right people around you to make you shine."

"Thank you," I say and mean it. "This week's been good because of you, Wilder, and the team. I wasn't sure I'd want to come here. But now, I'm not sure I want to go anywhere else."

Axel smiles and knocks my arm with his glove. "At least make Coach buy you dinner first."

He gets up and heads into practice. I stand and follow him. When we hit the ice, it's like a coordinated dance as we move through warm ups. There's nothing better than this moment, being so close to my dream.

Except Evan.

Everything about Evan is worth having to go through this. Being forced to stay home and reevaluate my plans for the future. Knowing Hawk and Cam will be with us too. I'm ready to go home to them. To her.

I'm not sorry for what I said to Heather. Though I do regret doing it the way I did. Evan can't always tiptoe around her mother's feelings and expect her to finally pay attention, but I didn't mean to make Evan think I hated her or didn't want her. Nothing could be farther from the truth. I need Evan. More than I've needed anyone.

I need Evan, Hawk, and Cam. They're my team for everything. Which means I need to make things right with Evan. I need her to know I'll think of her first before I let my anger get carried away. That she, Cam, and Hawk are my priority now.

We run through practice with the rest of the team, included as if we're already part of it and not just trying out for a place. I don't know if all five of us will be here when the school year begins in the fall, but I can see me being here. Evan working on her next film. Cam going to his frat. Hawk burying himself in schoolwork.

It's a fantasy that feels like it could come true. And it exists because of Evan. I owe her everything, and it's time I make sure she knows that.

Coach pulls us all in at the end of practice. "We've had a good week, and I hope you five take away something from your time on the ice with us. We're working to build something new on the foundations that the previous coach built. We won't tear down that foundation, but rise from it, better, sharper, ready to take championships and prove to the rest of the league that we're ready to become great."

"I THINK YOU SHOULD TALK TO JACKSON." AXEL SITS ACROSS the table from me. The dining room isn't crowded yet, but students are arriving for lunch. "I know you don't need to be friends to be on a team together, but our team works because we respect each other. Jackson has a good chance of getting an offer, and I'd hate for you not to come because he does."

I blow out a breath. "He attacked my girl when she was sixteen. It was only a kiss, but he had her trapped and she was afraid he wanted more and would have pushed for more. As soon as he realized she was at Anteros, Evan started receiving texts from an anonymous number."

"And you think it's him?" Axel leans back in the chair and watches me.

"She does." I lean forward on the table. "It would fit with who we know him to be. He's a loner and doesn't play well with others."

"Has anything happened to her?" Axel asks. "Besides the texts?"

"Nothing that can't be explained away. A rose sent her to urgent care, but he would have to be working with someone at her school." I run my hand through my hair. "I thought I might figure him out better while we're here, but time's almost up."

Axel nods. "Fuck, man. I know stalkers can be dangerous, but what if you're wrong about Jackson? There's no one else in your girl's life who could be doing this?"

"If it is, they aren't making themselves known." I press my lips together. "This is why we haven't gone to the police or accused him."

"But you think Jackson wants your girl?" Axel asks.

"The way he acts. The texts. The things he says sometimes." I shrug.

"Just talk to him. If you have to, ask him outright if he has a thing for your girl." Axel pushes to stand. "Chances like these don't happen every day. And I don't want you to lose out because you *think* he's after her."

Axel taps the table and walks away. Maybe I should confront Jackson. I don't trust he wouldn't lie to me, but it can't hurt. I can get some sort of read on him. It's worse going back and not knowing. Fuck.

I take my tray over to the trash.

"I overheard you talking to Axel." Jackson stops beside me. "I don't know why you think I want your girl. I was interested in Mia. Well, until I found out she had two boyfriends."

I narrow my eyes at him and try to remember every interaction. Mia was always with Evan when Jackson sought them out. But it also gave him a plausible reason to talk to Evan.

"Here, you can look at the texts Mia sent me. She's got some crazy idea that Evan is in her way at her new school. When we talked at the football game, she wanted to know what I knew about Evan as a kid." Jackson pulls out his phone and taps on the screen.

He holds it out for me to see the text conversation.

MIA:
This is Mia's number

ME:
I hope you don't delete my number

MIA:
Why would I?

Are you coming to the party?

ME:
Can't get away

Though I'd love to see you

How about Sunday night?

MIA:
Sounds good

I just have rehearsal and then I'm free

"Mia said she hasn't heard from you." We saw her phone and there was no back and forth, but she handed over her phone with no problem at all. From Evan, I would expect that, but from Mia, she might hesitate to give her phone to someone. That always bothered me.

Fuck, Evan and Mia being friends always bothered me.

But texts can be deleted or faked. What Jackson showed me only has

Mia at the top not a number. So which is it? Did Mia delete the evidence or did Jackson create it?

Jackson smirks and puts away his phone. "She's been texting me since I got her number at the football game. We've met up a few times even. But she doesn't want to be tied down. Well, not in a relationship."

I try to think of everything we asked Mia. The things we told her. She's been close to Evan this whole time. She knew Jackson called her *pretty girl*, and that we thought he was stalking Evan. But why?

I don't buy that Evan is in Mia's way at school. Evan made her fucking lead in her first play. That's not in the way. And if something goes wrong with Evan's play, that's Mia's bread and butter. But Evan also has us, and Mia did say she wanted to fuck us. She even warned us away from Evan.

"Do you still want Evan?" I ask, because fuck it. I study him closely.

Jackson's dark eyes meet mine, and I can almost see the calculation in them. "Why would you think that?"

"You've shown up to games and sought her out." I'm not going to mention the texts. Hopefully he'll slip up if he sent them.

"I came to see Mia." He shakes his head and shoves his hands in his pockets. He releases a slow breath before saying, "Evan and I were together for a couple weeks when we were sixteen before she ghosted me. I took the fucking hint. The girl didn't want me, but that doesn't mean I'm going to pretend not to know her. We were friends."

He runs a hand through his hair. "Look, I didn't want to say anything because it isn't any of my business..."

I wait, letting him talk.

"If someone's after your girl, it's probably Mia."

## CHAPTER 33
## *Cam*

*I TRUST you* is what Evan said to me when I explained what we'd need to shut it down and who I thought would work best for this operation. Because there are multiple parts needed to get into a social media account.

Mia stands waiting for us when we get to the school. I nod toward an empty classroom, and Evan, Hawk, and Mia follow me in. Once the door is shut, I turn to Mia.

"You thought Abby was up to something?" I ask.

"She's a fucking bitter bitch, so yeah." Mia glances toward Evan.

Evan steps forward. "We want to close that social media account."

"Okay, what can I do to help?"

We ran through videos to find when they logged into the account. Chase isn't very good at typing, and Abby had to tell him the password multiple times, so we have the password.

"We need Abby's phone or at least the access number that pops up on it." I lean against a desk and cross my arms. "Do you think you can get close enough to get it, and give us the code, then wipe all evidence of us accessing it from her phone?"

Mia smiles. "You mean you want me to help you shut her down. It would be my fucking pleasure. And yeah, I'm an actor. I can be whoever you need me to be."

Getting the website down over lunch went smoothly. It was a relief for all of us and knowing it was Abby and Chase means they'll be too lazy to recreate it. Thanks to Abby's phone we deleted all the images they stored on her cloud account.

My phone buzzes with a text. I'm in afternoon lecture and while I'm sure the history of the Vikings would be fascinating on the first read through, this isn't my first time hearing about them. And Mr. Carter doesn't add anything new to what I already know.

> DAMON:
> Need to talk
> Gotta moment?

> ME:
> Yeah
> I'll call

I raise my hand and Mr. Carter stops his monologue to call on me.

"Can I take the bathroom pass?" I ask.

He glances at it.

"Yes." The word has never come out more depressed than when Mr. Carter uses it.

I take the pass before heading out of the room. His class is toward the end of a hallway with an exit. There's a vestibule between the hallway and the outside. If the outside doors are opened, a warning alarm will go off, but not the doors to the vestibule. It's the perfect phone box.

I lean against the wall and call Damon.

"Had an interesting conversation today," Damon says.

"Anything has to be better than history class," I glance down the empty hallway.

"Mr. Carter?" Damon's wince can be heard through the phone.

"Indeed. I got shit to share too. You're coming home tonight, right?" I can't think of another reason he would call. "I didn't tell Hawk because he would punch you twice, but Evan cried about you last night."

After we went to bed, I woke once to her on the couch with the light of her phone making her face glow, so I know he talked to her. She always sleeps better after they message each other.

"Yeah, I'm coming home." He blows out a breath. "Jackson says he's been in contact with Mia. That all the times he was talking to them, he was talking to Mia. He thinks that Mia might be Evan's stalker. I need some fucking clarity, so I called you."

"Did you check the number?"

"It's not like he handed over his phone. It's possible it was a dummy text."

I glance out the doors and think about what I know about the timeline. "Okay, Evan received her first texts after the football game where Jackson sat with them. Mia was there. Mia had access to Evan's desk for the rose and knew we thought Jackson was stalking her and his nickname for her."

"So what doesn't fit? Because I'm not about to blow up Evan's friendship unless we're fucking sure."

"There are the texts Heather received. Mia might have known you two slept together, but she wouldn't know Heather's phone number." I try to think through everything that's happened. "The social media account isn't Mia."

"Why wouldn't it be? All she'd have to do is suck off a nerd to get him to do it." Damon blows out a breath. "Mia's warned us off Evan before."

"Evan found a video of Chase's room last night. The social media account was created by Abby and Chase. We took it down at lunch. It doesn't exist anymore. Mia helped us get Abby's phone for it. We also took pics of her text conversations with the guy she got to help with the photos. That part we at least know what happened. But we don't think they did the rest of it."

Damon lets out a huff. "It could be Mia doing the rest. Jackson said she was jealous of Evan."

"You really think she'd do this to Evan just to get in our pants?" I have my doubts. We're hot, but not go *illegal to get us* hot. "Yes, Evan gets a lot of attention at the school, but Mia's new, but she's not doing bad for herself. Besides, Mia seems to genuinely care about Evan. She was waiting at the urgent care, just as worried as I was."

"Maybe the rose was more effective than she thought it would be. Maybe she was worried about getting into trouble." Damon growls. "Fuck, I don't want to think it's her, but what if it is? She showed us her phone with no messages from him, and he just showed me messages he received from her. Even said he thought she was jealous of Evan."

"Why? Because she has us?" I scoff. "Come on. The girl can get any guy she wants. She's not like Olivia looking for a relationship. She just wants a fuck. And she's got Liam and Fletcher for that. I think Jackson might be trying to set her up."

"Or she's trying to set Jackson up. Maybe they're in it together? I need you to make sure Evan isn't left alone with Mia." Damon blocks the receiver for a moment, and I hear him talking to someone else. "I have to go. I'll be home tonight."

"I'll work the puzzle to see if Mia fits."

---

I WALK INTO THE SMALLER BLACK BOX THEATER ONCE hockey practice is over. Chase is on stage with Mark. I spent the rest of my afternoon classes outlining what we know. There's some really damning evidence to say Mia did it.

Jackson could have given Mia all that information just in conversation. Or they may be in it together, and Jackson is pushing the blame onto Mia.

There's one thing I haven't checked, and it kept slipping my mind. With the social media account, we didn't look into Brandt's sister. Hawk knows some guys on Jackson's team, but they may not run in the same circles as he does. I pull up Kentwood Prep where Jackson goes to school. Elizabeth Stanwell should be easy to find if she goes there. A search of their website doesn't give me much, but then I try her social media.

Because, if she's anything like Damon described, she'll be on all of them. And at some point, she might have a pic in her school uniform.

That would be the hope. Of course, with a famous father, she has her social media set to private, but it's easy to pinpoint her with Brandt, who definitely doesn't mind riding his father's coattails.

I pull up one of my accounts I use to slide into DMs, before I was with Evan, of course.

I ignore the multiple DMs waiting for responses they'll never get and friend request Elizabeth's account. I also friend some of her friends. Can't hurt.

It's a Friday night, so I post about going to a party, hoping to hook up with new people. My account is not private, so when she looks it will be the first post.

I lean back in my chair and watch Evan give stage direction. Her tone is gentle, but her voice carries. I can't imagine anyone being mean to this girl.

When I consider Mia's meet cute with Evan, it seems like it could have been a set up. It was easy to slot herself into friendship when Evan didn't have any close friends. Mia's an actor. It doesn't mean she's lying, but if she is, we might not be able to tell.

Evan's done everything to help Mia. Mia is the lead in Evan's play. Why would she want to throw Evan off her game? The only one who really benefits from Evan's play not doing well is Brandt. And if Damon is right and Brandt was the one who made Chase look twice at Evan, then he had to know Chase would fucking break her heart.

He's a manwhore with a horrible reputation. If he'd been a little more attentive to Evan, she probably could have fallen for him. I shake that out of my head because now I want to kick Chase's ass even more.

Jackson has a lot to gain by blaming Mia. It gets us off his scent. And if we bring Evan to Crowne Mawr, he can try to woo her away from us. It won't work, but he doesn't know that.

Fuck.

Hawk comes in and sits in the chair beside me. "What's Chase done now?"

"What?" I turn to look at him.

"You're glaring at the asshole like he kicked your puppy." Hawk leans back in the chair and puts one foot on the seat in front of him.

"Damon talk to you today?" I ask.

"Not yet." Hawk arches an eyebrow at me. "Why?"

"Jackson thinks Mia is behind the texts and the stalking," I say it quietly, but no one is around us.

Hawk sits with it for a moment, and I can see him going through all the evidence in his mind to see if it adds up for Mia.

"What would Mia's motive be?" Hawk doesn't look disturbed by the thought of it being Mia.

"Maybe she's working with Brandt? Or Chase? Or Jackson? Maybe she's mad Evan got us." I shrug. I don't like the idea of girls fighting over us. Before Evan, I thought it was hilarious. But now, fuck that. There's only one girl for me.

"Collusion makes it harder to figure out who's responsible." Hawk leans his head back and rests his eyes.

"Didn't you get enough sleep?" I noticed he was dragging on the ice too.

"My parents. Them finding their family again is going to fucking kill me. I'm considering running away." He opens his eyes and turns to me. "Can I come and live with you? Your parents are normal."

"Man, if you're going to run away, go to Damon's." I scoff. "You must be tired if you think of me before climbing into Evan's bed."

He chuckles half-heartedly. "Wake me when it's time to fuck Annie."

I shake my head and glance down to see my friend request hasn't been answered yet. I need to get to the bottom of this.

Rehearsal ends, and Evan packs up her things. Keira left practice earlier. Mark leaves with Chase, leaving just Hawk, Evan, and I.

"Do we know when he's supposed to be back?" Evan bites her lip when she glances my way.

"Eager to see your stepbrother, goody?" I tease.

She sticks her tongue out at me and zips up her backpack. "I'm just ready to deal with the consequences. I hate putting things off. This week has sucked for so many reasons, but having this unresolved thing hanging between us is the worst."

"Worse than the social media account?" I arch an eyebrow as I pick up my bag and kick Hawk's foot off the chair.

He wakes up swinging before he realizes where he's at. "What the fuck, man?"

"You said to wake you."

He looks around the black box theater room. "We doing this here?"

He starts unbuttoning his shirt.

"Hawk!" Evan chastises and has the audacity to look around like she's a fucking nun.

"What, baby girl?" He smirks. "Feeling shy? Don't want to put on a performance they won't forget? I know I won't."

She rolls her eyes, but she smiles. "Let's go get something to eat."

# CHAPTER 34
## *EvanAnn*

NERVES SKITTER along my spine as my eyes keep being drawn to the door. Damon's due back any minute. We're down in the rec room waiting. His dad is driving him back, so it's not like I can jump him the minute he comes through the door, but I kind of want to.

Even though I'm still mad as hell about him risking everything to just get even with my mom and to punish his dad. None of that was about me. It was all about his ego and his revenge.

Hawk draws me to lean against him. "If you want, track his phone. Fuck knows he tracks yours."

"How?" I hold my phone out to Hawk.

He chuckles and opens the app. When he hands it back to me, I wait for it to update with his current location. He's not far. Like a few blocks away. Fuck. I stand and pace.

"What do I say? What do I do?" It's so easy to chat over text in the middle of the night, but the last time I saw him, that kiss, that hug. Both were bittersweet and felt like the end of something and the beginning at the same time.

What if it really was the end? It doesn't make sense. We've talked since and everything was good. But there's this pit in my stomach that fears the worst.

Cam grabs my hand and pulls me down to sit across his lap.

"Goody, you don't have to worry. It's Damon. He'll take one look at you and take you into the bathroom to bang you."

"If he makes it that far." Hawk chuckles. "I'm guessing he just grabs her and fucks her."

My cheeks heat because that wouldn't be so bad. It won't solve anything, but it's one of the parts of us that's always made sense. I swallow. I didn't change after rehearsal when we got home. I'm still in my uniform. Maybe I should have changed into something he'd like.

Not that he doesn't like my uniform, but a short skirt and crop top would provide better access. He can't resist a short skirt. Fuck, I'm an idiot. It doesn't matter what I wear. We need to have a discussion. He needs to know I'm not just a pawn in his fucking game.

I need to find that anger again.

Cam kisses me, and it's like a shock to my system. He threads his fingers into my hair and holds me while he kisses the hell out of me. The firestorm raging inside me swirls hotter. Until I forget what we were talking about and sink into the feel of his lips, the slide of his tongue, the hint of mint, and something darker that's all Cam.

Liquid heat flows through my veins. I could drown in him.

He pulls away, and I meet his darkened eyes. "How'd I do?"

I cock my head in confusion, but he glances at Hawk with a smirk.

"About three minutes." Hawk leans back on the sofa, still looking tired. "I mean, if you want a distraction, I can tell you about the therapy my mom and dad made me attend last night, which is why I didn't get much sleep. At least it wasn't sex therapy. Apparently that's on the schedule for tonight so I don't care what's happening later, but I'm sleeping here. Damon can deal."

My mouth opens and closes. Sex therapy? I really don't know what to say to that, but it does keep my mind off other things. Things like Damon and that he's been gone for a week. It's like an overdose of anticipation mixed with dread because of how we left things.

Cam runs his thumb across my cheek and rests his forehead against mine. "Listen, goody. We know you and Damon need to get through what happened. If you want us to stay, we can. We're on your side. We want to help make this better."

I cup his jaw and just breathe him in. He's the glue for us. The heart.

Hawk reaches out and takes my hand, weaving our fingers together. "You have us, Annie. If Damon is still being an ass, let us know, and we'll take him out back and beat some sense into him."

I laugh at the thought and turn and kiss Hawk. "I love you both so much."

Voices come from upstairs. My heart clenches, and I scramble off Cam's lap. I check my skirt, my shirt, my hair, and then there are footsteps on the stairs. Heartbreakingly familiar footsteps. My stomach ties in knots.

He stops at the bottom of the stairs when he sees me. My breath catches. His gaze roams over me, but I can't be bothered to notice as I look him over. It's been a week, but it feels like forever. Fuck, this is so stupid.

I couldn't tell you who moves first. All I know is neither of us stops until he has one hand on my hip and the other in my hair, tipping my head back. And then his lips are on mine and nothing else matters.

I wrap my arms around his neck and he lifts me off the ground. My back hits the wall as we rediscover each other's mouths. There's nothing that could tear me away from him.

Someone clears their throat, loudly. Okay, maybe something. Damon lifts his mouth from mine with a growl that makes my already soaked panties wetter.

"Public space," Cam hisses from where he stands near the stairs. "Maybe keep it a little more PG than PG-13, heading toward R?"

"Any longer and it would have definitely been X-rated." Hawk smirks. "I'm here for it."

My cheeks heat. Without looking at either of them, Damon studies my face. "Hello, little devil."

I melt, fucking melt for this guy. "We should..."

Disengage, but I really don't want to.

He lowers his head and brushes his lips against my ear. "Fuck until we can't fuck anymore?"

Yup, that sounds much better than my idea.

My mouth is poised to say *yes* when Cam says, loudly, "Mr. Storm, how was the trip?"

Damon groans softly but lowers my feet to the ground. I quickly adjust all my clothes and he shifts me to stand in front of him when we turn to face the room. His hard cock brushes against me, sending warmth skittering through me.

"It's a good drive," Adam says. "Damon said you were planning on going to check out Crowne Mawr. Beautiful campus. It's not Yale, but it's a hell of a school." Adam steps into the rec room and scans it quickly before his gaze lands on me with Damon behind me. "I see you've found EvanAnn."

Damon ducks his head, but not before I see the grin on it.

"It doesn't take long for those two to collide," Cam says, and my face feels like it's on fire.

Damon walks me forward, probably to hide how thrilled he was to see me. "I was just going to tell the guys about the team. You were heading out? Dinner plans?"

Subtle. Real fucking subtle.

"Yeah." Adam runs a hand over his hair. "This is going to be weird for a while. I've never seen you with a girl before. And EvanAnn's been living with us."

"If you want, Mr. Storm, I can make sure to occupy Evan with PDA when you're around." Cam smirks and gives me a wink.

Yeah, that's not happening either. Damon steps a little closer to me, and a shiver ripples through me.

"Thank you for the offer, Cam, but I think I'll just go." Adam glances over the four of us and then meets my eyes. "If you need anything..."

He leaves it open-ended. He's in my corner and so is my mother if I need them. It's hard to describe what I'm feeling because while my mom supported me, it felt like I was alone for so long.

"I'm good. Thank you." I glance down at the ground, unable to meet his eyes.

He looks just as uncomfortable as I feel and lifts his gaze to Damon's over my head. "Think about what we talked about."

"I will."

Adam sighs and moves to the stairs. "Stay close to each other until we figure out this mess."

"We've got her, Mr. Storm." Hawk rises from the couch to stand with Cam.

Damon touches my hip, pulling me back against him. The move is subtle, and I don't know if Adam caught it, but it reignites the flames burning under my skin.

Adam gives a small nod and heads up the stairs.

"Breathe, little devil." Damon's words are soft and for my ears only.

I draw a breath into my starving lungs. My mom's voice meets Adam at the top of the stairs, and I wait to see if she's going to come down, but their voices move away. I rest my head back against Damon's chest and breathe him in.

The past few nights it felt like his scent had faded on the sheets, but now with him here, I'm intoxicated by his dark, earthy scent. The feel of his warmth pressed against me. His presence.

Fuck, I missed him. I missed this. I missed having them all here.

"If you want us to stay, we can. But I have the feeling you two need some time to be alone." Cam gestures to Hawk. "Come on, there's a party I want to see if a girl will show up to."

"I mean, I could just watch," Hawk says, and his eyes darken.

My gaze jerks to Cam at the mention of a girl.

He chuckles and closes the distance between us. "Just following up on a lead, goody. The only girl I want is right here. We'll be back later." He lifts his gaze to Damon's. "After you two have had some time to get reacquainted and talk."

Cam tips my chin up and kisses me. I grab onto his shirt as Damon grabs my hips. I groan into his kiss, needing more from all of them.

Hawk pulls Cam away, and I look up to meet his green eyes. "I'm going to down some energy drinks and be back to make you scream, baby girl."

I bite my lip. Spending time with each of them alone has been the highlight of this week. Hawk and Cam together always make me overwhelmed in a good way. But just holding on to them at night, knowing they're there for me... I'm glad we got to take this time with each other.

"Try not to make her too sore." Hawk hits Damon's arm before he swoops down to kiss me breathless.

"No promises." Damon's voice runs down my spine like a caress. "You know how she likes it."

"Talk. Fix your shit so we can get back to everything else. We need to be solid again." Cam looks at both of us.

Damon gives a small nod before Cam and Hawk head out, leaving Damon and me alone. For a second, we just stand there, pressed together. His front to my back. Just breathing in the moment of finally reconnecting.

Damon steps away, and I turn to see what he's doing. He lifts me against him, and my legs automatically wrap around his waist. My fingers tangle in his hair. His smile is cocky.

"I need a shower." His blue eyes are soft for me and only me. So different from last Friday. My heart soars.

He carries me up the stairs and into our bedroom. Once we're in the bathroom, he sets me down on the counter. When I reach for my tie, he grabs my hands.

"Not yet."

I search his eyes, but nod. Are we going to talk first? Something dark lingers in my stomach, waiting for the gut punch, but I don't think it's going to happen. Not really. I just don't trust that everything will go my way.

He steps away and turns the shower on. When he returns, he grabs my hips and pulls me to the edge of the counter before resting his forehead against mine. His eyes close, and I reach out to wrap my hands in his t-shirt.

"Damon, I—"

"Shh, I just want to hold you." He slides his hands beneath my skirt. "I missed you so fucking much, Evan. With the way we left things, I felt so distant from you."

I touch his jaw. "I'm always yours."

He releases his breath against my lips and some of the weight falls off him. He leans in and takes my mouth, tentatively, softly, exploring me. My lips part beneath his and I let him in, because I'll always let Damon in.

It's as easy as breathing. He pulls away and toys with my tie.

"Good because I'm not letting you go." He slips the tie off me and kisses my neck while he works on the buttons of my blouse.

When I tug at his t-shirt, he stops to take it off with one hand and then he's back at my neck, working on leaving his mark because the last one he left faded. I explore his chest, reacquainting myself with the dips and swells of his muscles.

He undresses me slowly, kissing every inch of bared skin. My collarbones, the tops of my breasts, my stomach. After he tugs my skirt and panties off, he lowers himself to his knees between my legs, pushing my knees out wide. I flatten my hands on the counter behind me to stabilize myself.

My breathing is fast and unsteady. He lifts his darkened gaze to mine before his mouth closes over me. I cry out at the first touch of his tongue against my clit. When I try to close my legs around his head, he holds them firmly open as he rediscovers me.

When he slips his fingers inside me and fucks me, I arch back, caught up in the feeling. He pushes me closer to the edge with every stroke until my release takes me. My toes curl as he keeps fucking me and sucking on my clit. It's too much.

"Damon, I can't—" I cut off on a cry as I tip into another release. He kisses my inner thigh, making me tremble. Boneless, I watch him with hooded eyes as he rises and strips off his pants.

He presses his cock against my entrance and grabs my hair to tip back my head. "Look at me, Evan."

Our eyes lock, and he thrusts into me. A wave takes me under at the feel of him stretching me open.

"Fuck, little devil." He lifts me against him. His warm skin collides with mine as I wrap myself around him. "I've missed the feel of your cunt taking all of me."

Water falls on us as he steps into the shower and pins me against the tile wall. He holds my hips against it as he fucks me hard. I clench my fingers in his hair. I can't breathe, can't think. All I can do is feel what he does to me.

Every thrust lifts me higher and pushes me closer to the edge. He brings his mouth down to my neck and sucks on my pulse until I shatter all around him, drowning in the feel of him, milking his cock for every ounce of cum he can give me.

Crying out, I tumble through ecstasy with every thrust. He groans his release as he fucks into me a few more times. My pussy throbs around him as his cock pulses his release deep inside me.

I open my eyes and he's watching me, waiting for me to open them. I feather my fingers through his hair. "I've missed you. I'm still mad at you."

"I know," he says softly, and leans into my hand, closing his eyes. This moment is worth fighting for.

He kisses me, and I groan into his mouth as need rushes through me again. He pulls out and moves us under the shower. I let my legs drop and he lowers me to stand on my own. I don't want to break this feeling by talking about what happened or how our parents know or the social media fiasco.

The only thing I want to do is bask in having him here with me.

He seems to be on the same page as we wash each other, like we've done for weeks. I'm gentle on his hip where he's bruised from hockey. I mentally catalogue every bruise. Once he's rinsed off, I don't resist leaning in to kiss his chest. To explore the ridges and dips of his muscles with my mouth as I grab hold of his hard cock.

He pushes my hair back and runs his hands over my body until I drop to my knees and take him into my mouth with a moan. There's this part of me that's desperate to have all of him. To make him remember how good we are together before we get to the tough part.

He threads his fingers into my hair and fucks my mouth gently as I look up at his hooded eyes.

"Touch yourself, little devil. Sink your fingers into that needy little pussy of yours."

I groan around him as I do what he says, pressing my fingers into my slick heat.

"Fuck, I thought about you every night. This body, this mouth, your eyes. Everything about you. You're part of me. I'm never letting you go." He watches me before he takes over, thrusting a little faster, a little deeper. I match his pace and fuck myself in time with him until his cum floods my mouth and my pussy clutches around my fingers. My release shudders through me.

"That's it. Take it all." His words, his cock inside my mouth, his hand in my hair. A pulse of rightness flows through me.

I swallow as he lifts me to my feet. He takes my fingers and sucks them into his mouth, tasting me, tasting him, tasting us.

My lips part as I watch. He turns off the shower and wraps me in a towel before running one quickly over his body. Then he's lifting me, carrying me into the bedroom, our bedroom. He drops me on the bed and follows me down.

He thrusts into me like he can't bear to be away and hovers over me, our eyes locked while he fucks into me slower. He runs his hand over my body as he holds himself up with the other. I can't look away from his eyes. Fuck, I love when he sees me.

When I reach up to touch his jaw, he leans into the touch briefly before turning my palm over. He scans my hand, noticing the healing of the little scars before he kisses each one. Then he takes my hands and pulls them over my head, stretching me beneath him, holding my wrists captive as he fucks me harder.

"Mine," he growls and everything inside me melts. Accepting his ownership. Knowing no matter what, he's mine and I'm his.

## CHAPTER 35
### *Cam*

"Why are we here again?" Hawk downs his energy drink like it's gold.

The here is a party. It's not as big as Fletcher's parties, but it's decent. Most girls give us once-overs as we pass. The guys size us up and decide not to fuck with us. I don't give a shit about anyone else here. I'm just looking for one person.

"Elizabeth Stanwell," I tell him as we move through the rooms of the party. She didn't accept my friend request. Probably saw I was from Deimos. Maybe even asked her brother about me. But one of her friends did, and that friend was happy to post about the party they were attending tonight.

"I don't know what it will prove if Elizabeth goes to the same school as Jackson. It doesn't mean they know each other." Hawk's still grumbly, even with the caffeine. Probably because we both know Damon is fucking Evan, and Hawk wanted to watch— maybe even join in.

Those two need some time together before we descend and help fuck our girl into the weekend. As I look around the party, I'm not seeing anyone I know. Every now and then Hawk will nod at some guy.

"He plays hockey." And then he'll list off a school, but not Kentwood Prep. I just nod because I know most of the guys who play hockey.

I glance at the girl's feed and see a picture from out by the pool. Signaling Hawk, I make my way out back where the party is a little more quiet but not any less boisterous. As Hawk steps outside, the girls zero in on him like flies to shit. Then they notice others noticing him and eye each other up and down like they're daring each other to make the first move.

He doesn't even look at the girls, but I expected that. He hasn't seen anyone else but his Annie for a while.

We walk over to a cooler and grab a couple of beers.

Hawk lifts his brow, but I just shake my head. It's easier to talk to others with something in your hand. It makes them more comfortable approaching you. I casually tip some out into a nearby potted plant—sorry plant—and hand one to Hawk. He lifts it to his mouth like he's going to drink and then lowers it.

"Enemy territory." I glance around. I haven't seen anyone from either of our schools here. I'm not surprised. It was a drive, and there's a small party in town tonight.

"You brought us here. Do you see your target?" He leans back against the exterior of the house and looks around lazily, but he's scanning.

"It would help if I knew what she looked like." I found an old news article. Even Brandt doesn't have pictures of his sister on his social media. And she sticks to pictures without her face in them. Damon gave me a description. Well, height, hair, maybe color of eye. Hoity-toity, stuck up, rich girl.

Unfortunately, that description applies to most of these girls.

Hawk glances at the picture of the friend on my phone and then looks around again. He bumps my arm and heads toward a group of girls in some chairs.

"Raven," he says as we approach.

A dark-haired girl looks up at him and the confusion on her face clears as she checks him out. "Do I know you?"

Hawk smirks. "I've been sliding into your DMs for weeks now. I hope so."

Raven smiles. She doesn't know who he is, but she doesn't want to admit it. "That's right. How are you?"

The other girls drink their pink cocktails slowly, eating up every minute of this interaction. I take them all in. I don't think any of them are Elizabeth.

Hawk keeps up a conversation with Raven that's just this side of not talking about anything specific. Poor Raven. A few of the other girls are glassy-eyed and stare at the two of them like a tennis match.

One girl looks me over and nods for me to come closer. Her makeup is dark around her eyes. Fuck it. I need a break.

She leans into me, making sure her mouth isn't in the direction of her friends. "He doesn't know her, does he?"

Her pale blue eyes lift to mine. I smile cockily and shake my head just slightly.

She smirks and looks me over again. "What's your deal?"

"Looking for a chick to ask her something."

"I'm a chick." She takes a drink of her beer. She's the only one in this group drinking a beer instead of a pink cocktail.

"Are you Elizabeth Stanwell?"

The girl chokes on a laugh. "No, not even close."

"You know her?"

She snorts and takes a long pull of her beer. "Yeah, everyone here does. She's got a famous as fuck father. Everyone wants to be her friend. Is that why you're looking for her?"

Her eyes narrow on me.

"Nah." I take a sip of my beer and glance at Hawk. He's still chatting with Raven while the others continue to be mesmerized.

"What do you need her for then?" the girl asks.

"I got this theory I want to find out."

"You a stalker?" The girl arches her eyebrow.

"Would I tell you if I were?"

She snorts. "Probably not. Tell me your theory."

"I know this guy who goes to a school, and I want to see if they know each other."

"Hmm." She looks thoughtful before saying, "She's not here tonight."

Fuck.

"But I tell you what. I'm bored, and this party is lame. What if I answer your questions? For a price." She smirks and finishes her beer.

I narrow my eyes. "What price?"

"There are rooms—"

"I have a girlfriend. I don't cheat." I make sure to use a tone that she understands this is non-negotiable.

"Shame." She shrugs and turns to look at Raven and Hawk.

After thinking about it for a moment, I say, "You didn't really want to fuck me, did you?"

"Just seeing how desperately you want the information." She glances my way with a cocky grin. "What do you need to know?"

"How do I know you'll actually tell me the truth?"

"You won't." She shrugs. "But I'm guessing a guy like you could probably track me down."

"Again, I've got a girl." I run a hand through my hair.

"Not offering. But you never know when having an acquaintance at another school might pay off." She gives me a shrewd look.

That I can agree with. "Fine."

"What's so important about Elizabeth if you have a girlfriend?"

"Not sharing that."

"And we're sure we aren't a stalker?" She arches an eyebrow.

"Not a stalker. Where does she go to school?"

"Hmm. A stalker would be able to find that out, probably." She taps her finger on her lips like she's thinking.

"Probably." I shrug.

"Fine. She goes to Barrington Academy." She must notice the disappointment on my face. "Not the answer you were looking for?"

"No, but thank you..." I don't know her name.

"Morgan."

"Thank you, Morgan." I glance at Hawk and see he's running out of things to say to Raven. "You've been helpful."

"From the looks of it, I haven't." Morgan smirks. She pulls out a small card with a name and number on it. "You need anything else, text me."

You never know. I take her card. "Cam."

She smiles. "Nice to meet you, Cam."

I jerk my head to Hawk, and he disengages. We walk away.

"Find out anything?" he asks.

"Nothing good, but made a new friend." I pocket the card, ready to get back to my girl and see if they've finally made up.

---

## DAMON

I toss a pair of jeans and my t-shirt at Evan. She's stretched out on our bed, practically boneless. She sets them to the side and props herself on her elbows. Her stormy eyes are suggestive, and with her naked, I'm tempted to sink back into her.

We could spend hours reconnecting physically, but this needs to be dealt with before the guys rejoin us. Those eyes of hers make me want to say fuck it and fuck her.

I shake my head and put on my own jeans. "We need to leave this room or we'll just fuck all night."

"And that's a problem?" She gives me this cheeky grin that makes my heart do funny things and my cock get even more ideas.

I chuckle darkly. "No, but we won't have a chance to work out our issues if I'm buried deep inside you."

She releases her breath and grabs the shirt, not bothering with a bra. I toss her a pair of panties. She arches her eyebrow as she pulls them on.

Standing, she shimmies into her jeans as I put on a shirt. I grab the front of her jeans and draw her into me. She slides her hands under my shirt, touching my abs, my sides, my back. Fuck.

When I lower my face to hers, she tips her head expecting a kiss.

"Be a good girl and get your shoes on."

She pouts when I don't kiss her. But when she turns to go find her shoes, I smack her ass.

She shakes her head and glances over her shoulder at me. "Hawk does that better."

I laugh. She smiles before disappearing into her room to get her shoes. Fuck, I love this girl and need to do everything in my power to make this right.

I sink down onto the edge of the bed to put on my own shoes. I haven't taken the time to watch all the videos from this week. Mostly because I didn't want to have a hard-on and not be able to do anything about it in Ivan's room.

I'll probably watch them with Evan sitting on my dick or her sucking my cock. Either will work.

Not watching them just made me want her more. Watching her do her homework. Talking to her over text when everyone else was asleep. I could see her, but not hear or feel her. Even a little broken, we're bound tight together.

She comes back in and leans in the doorway to the bathroom. "Your dad asked if I wanted to move rooms."

I lean back on my hands on the bed and arch an eyebrow. "What made you stay?"

She glances toward her bedroom. "That's not my bedroom."

She pushes off the doorframe and walks over to me stopping between my knees. "This is my bedroom. It has been since I moved in."

I grab her and pin her down on the bed. She laughs, and I lean down and kiss her.

---

## *EvanAnn*

The night is a little chilly, so Damon added his sweatshirt to my look before we headed out. I snuggle into his back as he shifts gears and drives us out of town. He doesn't go to our spot, but the pull-off where Cam and I parked.

When he rests his bike on the kickstand, I slide off. I hook my helmet next to his on the handlebars and have him help me climb on in front of him. As much as I want to see his face, I sit with my back to his front, resting against him.

It'll be easier to focus and feel more like our late night chats. Except he can hold me, and I can feel his warmth.

He wraps an arm around my middle and rests his chin on my head. I tangle my fingers with his and give him my weight.

"Last Friday was fucked up," he says, opening up the conversation.

"It was bound to happen. We've been sharing a bed for weeks, and they just caught on to it." I blow out a breath. "I'm not upset they know, but it's made it awkward a few times."

He chuckles before growing solemn. "I know you care about your mom—"

"Damon." I focus on the city lights sparkling below us as I gather my thoughts. It's not the best view, but it's not awful. "I know you think my mom checked out a long time ago, and maybe she did because I let her. She could have done more to protect me, but when it really comes down to it, she does. She moved us and tried to keep me safe without disrupting my life. Not telling me about Adam is probably my fault as much as it was hers.

"When I was eleven, she tried to bring around a guy she was getting serious with, but I wasn't having it. I was a brat and went on a hunger strike. I couldn't understand how she could be with someone who wasn't my dad. That young I felt like she was betraying my father's memory. Probably a lot like when you would run off your father's girlfriends."

"They were all gold-diggers," Damon mutters.

I chuckle. "Sure. I'm sure every one of them was only after his money. Your dad is attractive and fit."

He rubs his chin against my hair, but he doesn't deny it. I blow out a breath, trying to gather my thoughts. Because this is important. I've told him before that she doesn't neglect me. Not the way he assumes.

"I didn't want to know who she was dating. I wanted to pretend it wasn't happening." I tip my head to the side to look up at him. "I didn't even realize how hard she was working to keep us in the house. She admitted she liked having a home again and saw that I was happy. So even though it was expensive, she tried to make it work. For us. She was trying to give us a life, but she had to work more to achieve it."

I settle into his arms. "We've agreed to have more open conversations with each other so we don't feel like we have to hide things from the other. Things like being in love with the three of you."

I swallow and look out at the city lights. "I know you don't like that my mom is with your dad, but they really do work well together. And I understand why you went on the defensive with her that morning, but you were hurting me by doing it. You were using me as an excuse for what you did to Chase when that was always about you."

"Leaving him out in the woods, scared and alone, was all for you." He softly squeezes my hand. "Punching him was about you. I watched him kiss you like he had every right. And what stung was he did. He was the guy who was your boyfriend. Sure, he sucked at it, and I forced you to stay with him, but he could kiss you, claim you. So it wasn't all about taking his future away, little devil. Not entirely."

I take in a breath. "I'm sorry I told your dad about the hit and run. If I had a dad like Adam, I would have gone to him from the start. Your dad cares about you. I get why you were angry with him after your mom died. You know that was her decision, but it doesn't make it hurt less, and I'm sorry for that."

Damon rests his chin on my head for a moment. The city lights twinkle, and I feel this weight lift off my chest. We're both figuring our way in this relationship. But now it's his turn. I hope he's ready to apologize because this won't work if I'm the only one caving.

"Turn around. I want to look into your eyes." He helps me turn on his bike to face him. He tips up my chin, and the soft worry in his eyes almost undoes me. "Have I ever told you how beautiful your eyes are?"

I blink. "No."

"They are and you are. You're the most beautiful girl, and I'm grateful to be yours. I need you to know I've never hated you, Evan." He brushes a strand of my hair that escaped my bun behind my ear and refocuses on my eyes. "Not even at the beginning. The anger was never about you. I hated being called your rebound and got defensive. You were right to call me out. When you told my dad, I was angry and didn't know how to deal with that because I love you. I'm sorry I wanted to punish your mom the way I punished my dad. I know they both care in their own ways, but it's hard to see that sometimes."

He slides his hand to the back of my neck, and I put my hand over his heart, focusing on the steady beat against my palm.

"I can't promise I won't shut down again. That I won't go cold, but know that under that anger, my heart still only beats for you. That when push comes to shove, I'll choose you and us and Hawk and Cam over whatever petty revenge stirs my heart, I don't want you to think I can hate you. It's not possible."

"You can't just ice me out when things don't go your way." I grip his shirt. "We skipped a lot of actual dating with the way we got together. I don't regret it, but I don't want to lose what we have. And I'm so afraid I'm going to fuck this up."

"Fuck, Evan, if anyone's going to fuck this up, it will be me." He rests his forehead on mine. "But at least we're not in this with just us. Hawk and Cam won't let us fuck up."

I smile and cup his jaw, feeling the rough stubble of the day forming there. "No, they won't. I guess it works better for us to be a foursome instead of a twosome."

"Probably." He breathes in and exhales. "I shouldn't have pushed you in that conversation. I should have let you lead more, trusted you to tell the truth when it would be needed. The most frustrating thing about all this is I feel like I need to thank Chase Chadwick."

I lean back and search his eyes. "Why?"

"Because if he hadn't been an asshole, I wouldn't have you. I'd still be friends with Hawk and Cam, but we would have grown apart. I'd still be angry at my dad for my mom. And I never would have known you. I love you. I can't stand having you mad at me. I hate that I made you cry. That isn't who I want to be.

"I want to be the person who holds you when you cry and helps destroy the people who make you angry. I want to be there for all of your big moments and all of the small ones. You make me into someone better. I thought I was ready to move on before this year. I thought I was ready to get on with my life, but without you, that would have been a mess."

My heart feels like it's going to burst out of my chest.

His blue eyes are soft as he studies me like he wants to memorize me. It's intense and breathtaking.

"I love you. You've made me into a better person and I don't ever want to lose you by being a dick to you. I need you to tell me when I've gone too far. To have you by my side."

He reaches into his pocket and pulls out a small jewelry box.

My eyes widen. "What are you—"

"It's not really from me." He smirks and opens the box. Inside lies the pendant my dad gave me. "The guys and I took it to get it fixed. They finished today, so I swung by to pick it up."

My eyes well with tears as I cover my mouth.

"It's still the same chain, but they made it stronger, so it won't break again." He lifts it out of the box and undoes the clasp. "May I?"

I nod, too overwhelmed to speak. He fastens it on my neck and straightens the heart on my chest. I reach for it and then lean forward and hug Damon to me.

"Cam, Hawk, and I are like that chain. We need each other to hold you together when the world tries to tear us apart, little devil."

"Damon." I rest my head over his heart. "I love you."

"I love you too, Evan." He breathes out against my hair and holds me tight against him. "We should probably let the others know we've talked, and the orgy can begin."

I smile and look around the deserted parking. Biting my lip, I reach for his belt. "We don't have to hurry, do we? Didn't you promise to fuck me so hard on your motorcycle? Something about making me scream?"

He smirks and takes my mouth, saying into it, "I fucking love you."

## CHAPTER 36
## *EvanAnn*

SATURDAY MORNING, I'm huddled in the stands of the ice rink with a hot chocolate. Keira, Mia, and Mark have all joined me to watch the guys in action. The guys told me what Jackson said about Mia. How he pointed to her as the stalker, to which I laughed in their faces.

There's no way. But they pointed out the possibility, just like with Chase, she could fit the circumstantial evidence. I don't point out that it's just as likely them doing all this to get closer to me. To make me need them.

I don't think they would have taken that well. But I did agree to think about it.

Uncomfortable on the hard plastic, I shift in my seat again. Mia laughs.

"Was someone grateful to be home last night?" She nudges me with her elbow.

Mark chuckles and looks at his phone.

Keira smirks. "She's practically glowing."

I press my lips together, refusing to say anything, but they curve into a smug smile. When Damon and I finally got home, Cam and Hawk joined us. Damon was far from done fucking me, and the others happily participated. I woke in a tangle of limbs and very messy, but Damon just lifted me in his arms and took me into the shower with him.

"Everything good in married life?" Mia leans back in the chairs. "I mean you guys live together and fuck together and eat together."

"No more forbidden romance. No sneaking around anymore because the parents don't know," Keira adds on.

I blow out a breath. "We'll see how comfortable with us they really are at dinner tomorrow night."

"Keeping it in the family." Mark puts his phone away and grins at me. "So how about you get us a backstage pass to the locker room? I'm sure one of these guys can be convinced to try something new."

I shake my head at him.

"When's Fletcher going to have another party?" Keira asks. "Mia, you guys are seeing each other. What do you know?"

"I would have thought you'd be wary of parties after the last one," I say, a little concerned.

Keira shrugs. "Olivia is gone, and I learned a valuable life lesson about getting my own drinks. I just never thought a girl would give me a spiked drink."

"Any offering from Olivia should have been met with a heavy dose of skepticism." Mia rolls her eyes. "That girl was crazy. Fletcher tends to prefer a private party these days. Less likely to get him into trouble."

"I just think it would be fun to party together. We're just going to have to name a time for getting together and commit to it, aren't we?" Keira straightens. "Something else can always come up, but maybe Sunday after rehearsal? It would get you out of family dinner, EvanAnn."

"Don't tempt me." I smirk. "It would serve Damon right. I had to field our parents on my own since he was gone last week."

"How was his trip to Crowne Mawr?" Mia asks.

I glance her way to see if her question has any hidden meaning. "Besides Jackson being there too, the whole experience was good for Damon. I'm working on my application to their drama school. We're already planning on going down to visit after the play ends and before hockey season begins."

"Was Damon able to learn anything more about Jackson?" Mia asks.

I glance over at her and sigh. "No, they didn't really get any new information. With the social media account, all our focus was on that."

I wish that were the truth. What Jackson said about Mia doesn't make a lot of sense. Like the motivation is the Devil's trio? To fuck them? Because they're mine?

At least Olivia thought she could make Damon hers. Mia didn't have any grand plans with the guys besides fucking one or all of them at the same time. And I don't see that same gleam in her eye when she looks at them.

Even jealousy of me doesn't make any sense. I cast her as the lead in my play. She's not here for directing. If anything, Keira would have more motivation to steal my show, but she has her senior year to dominate. If I couldn't finish the show for whatever reason, they'd have another senior step in to work over her, not give her the show.

The problem is, I can't let Mia know what Jackson said about her. The texts haven't come in a while. The rose? Did I do something to make her mad that week? Or did she just think I was too comfortable in my love nest with my guys?

Maybe she's actually been working with Chase this whole time. She did ask if I thought it could be Chase. Was that a misdirect? Or is this a misdirect?

The scrimmage draws my attention. Damon skates circles around the competition. He talked about the program a lot with the guys and me, while we lay in our bed, sated. He liked the guys who are on the team as well. It seems like the perfect fit for him.

I just need to figure out if it's the perfect fit for me. And what happens if I get an internship? The year-long one will push my admission to college by a year, but I can probably work with the program chair to get it to count for some of my credits.

They do encourage internships in their program. But I don't know how we'll deal with me on location and them at school. We barely made it a week, and yes, it was a stressful week, but it was only a week. I'd be separated from all of them.

"Does Sophie always come to games?" Keira asks and gestures toward Sophie across the ice rink. "Maybe she's got a boyfriend on the team?"

"I don't think I've seen her here before." Mia squints.

"You sure you weren't distracted with other sights at previous games?" Mark asks.

"Maybe." Mia shrugs like it doesn't matter. "Abby and her lot showed up to one scrimmage. I think they've finally given up on the guys, but now that Damon's back, who knows?"

Mia also helped us take down the social media account. I don't know if Abby even realized Mia took her phone at lunch. We also found out who was helping her with the pictures at the school. Hawk had a talk with the guy, and he agreed to wipe everything he had.

Maybe it's not the guys Mia wants, but to monopolize my time? They do take a lot of my time, and Mia is new in town. If we broke up, I wouldn't be with anyone for a while. Actually, probably ever. But the guys aren't going to break up with me over a stalker. It just makes them more protective. Mia knows that.

"Without an outright confession or stunning evidence, I doubt we'll find out who's behind the social media account." Mark leans back in his chair.

Mia and I look at each other, but until *Othello* is finished, we're not going to say anything.

"It got taken down yesterday. Probably some bot finally got around to the content." Mia flicks her hair. Both Keira and Mark are happy to hear it.

After we focus on the game again for a while, Mark sighs. "Two weeks before tech week and then one week until performance. It's creeping up on us."

"We're ready for it," Keira says.

"We are," I agree.

---

## Hawk

Annie rides on the back of my bike over to my house. My parents asked if she'd join us for dinner on Saturday, and when I told Annie, she unexpectedly said yes. So we're heading there now. I asked to include the guys, which isn't normally a big deal.

Here's the thing. My parents know about me dating Annie, but they don't know about her dating Cam and Damon too. Of all our parents, I think my mom will be the most accepting of our relationship. But I don't know if she ever considered it a possibility.

I'm not sure how Dad will react.

I pull into the driveway, and Annie gets off. Damon and Cam pull in next. If Annie can be out with all of us, I guess I can too. The thing I'm not looking forward to is explaining that the sex is between Annie and us, and not between me and the other guys. I'd rather not explain the sex at all if I can help it.

I take Annie's helmet and hang it on my bike before taking her hand. She put on a white dress with little blue flowers on it. She shakes out her hair after having the helmet on. When she straightens, I pull her in close and kiss her.

She goes up on her toes to kiss me back. I'm tempted to say fuck it, and just go off somewhere to have sex. Seems like the easier thing to do.

"Come on." Cam gestures to the door. "I'm not looking forward to telling my parents I'm fucking my tutor and so are my best friends. I might get grounded. But you telling your folks?" Cam grins like a kid in a candy store. "I can't fucking wait."

Damon brushes his fingers against Annie's and she looks up at him. They seem to be good again. Thankfully. She also showed her gratitude to both Cam and I for repairing the necklace.

I hold open the door for her, and she walks into my house. The guys follow us as I lead them down the hallway to the sitting room where my parents are expecting us. I swallow and push open the door. Lately it's been a crap shoot of what I'll find behind any door in the house. My parents are definitely in the honeymoon phase again.

Fortunately, they're clothed and waiting with drinks in hand. When we walk in, they rise.

"You must be EvanAnn." Mom practically beams. "I'm so glad to meet you."

"Pleased to meet you too, Mrs. Wilker." Annie holds out her hand, but Mom grabs her and pulls her into a full body hug. I probably should have warned Annie about that. After an uncomfortably long hug, Mom holds Annie's shoulders and pushes her out to arm's length to look her over.

"You can call me Naomi." Mom touches Annie's hair. Mom's blue eyes sparkle when she looks at me. "She's so pretty, Hawk."

"Thank you," Annie says. Her face is flushed.

"And so polite. I love her already." Mom pulls her back in for a hug, and Annie glances at me. "Can we keep her? I've always wanted a daughter."

"I'm not planning on giving her away, Mom."

When Mom releases her, I draw Annie in against me so Mom can't keep hugging her. She's known to be a clinger.

"Dad, you remember EvanAnn."

Dad holds his hand out, and Annie takes it with a small smile. Her cheeks flush even redder.

"Mr. Wilker, it's nice to see you again."

"Paul," he says as he releases her hand and looks at Cam and Damon. His face changes into an honest smile. "How have you two been? It's been a while since I've seen you at the house."

Probably because my parents are rarely here to see anyone including me.

Both Damon and Cam get a handshake from Dad and a hug from Mom. Mom touches their hair and their arms and comments on how tall they've gotten like we're still little boys growing up before her eyes.

When we all take a seat, Dad leans forward. "How's hockey looking this year?"

"I think we're in for a good season," Damon says. He's still riding the high of last week and probably from fucking Annie last night.

I hold Annie's hand as Cam, Damon, and I tell my dad about the team's prospects this year as well as the other teams we've played in scrimmages.

"I hear you're directing the play Hawk is in." Mom finds a break in the conversation to say, trying to draw Annie into the conversation.

Annie clears her throat. "Yes, I'm directing *Othello*."

"Lovely." Mom looks at me knowingly. "Top grades too. Talented and smart."

Annie smiles and her hand tightens on mine. Probably worried my mom will offer to adopt her again.

"We should go in for dinner," Dad says.

Damon glances at me with a raised eyebrow. My parents obviously don't think there's anything unusual about me having my best friends here when they meet my girlfriend for the first time. When we sit at the table, Cam takes the chair on the other side of Annie.

She smiles at him and then looks at me. Her look asks if we're going to do this or not.

After the first dish is set in front of us, I clear my throat. My parents look at me expectantly.

"EvanAnn is very special to all of us." I clear the lump that seems permanently stuck in my throat. There's no easy way to say this. "We aren't in a typical relationship."

Dad sits back and steeples his fingers against his lips as he waits for me to say I'm just fucking the girl or that we're friends with benefits or some such bullshit.

Mom raises her wine glass and looks at us with curiosity.

Fuck it. "EvanAnn is in a relationship with me, Cam, and Damon."

Annie keeps her smile locked in place and doesn't look at all nervous or uncomfortable, but her fingers twitch against mine. I move our hands to my leg.

"Do her parents know?" Dad asks.

"Yes," Annie answers. "My mother is aware of our relationship."

"Well, I think it's amazing." Mom grins and holds her glass up. "To young love."

She takes a drink and looks at my dad. He's still trying to wrap his head around it. I don't know what he's thinking. It's not like anyone is taking advantage in this situation.

"We can talk about this later, Hawk." Dad's voice is a little rough, and I can tell he's uncomfortable. That's the difference between my mom and my dad. I don't think if they met today, they would have made it.

He's let her have her way with chakra alignments and soul readings, but only with the compromise of seeing certified therapists. They've worked to balance their relationship, but my dad is a very by the book type of guy.

Mom evens him out. Mostly.

"There's not really anything to talk about." I lean back in my chair.

"It's my relationship, and it's not going to affect my grades or anything else about my life. So, it's not really up for discussion. I'm informing you of my choice to be with the girl I love and to be with her with my friends."

"I think it's lovely," Mom says and takes Dad's hand on the table. "Paul, Hawk is right. This is his life, and he can do what he wants with who he wants. As long as he's being safe and responsible, there's not a lot more we can ask for."

Dad takes in a breath and looks at Damon and Cam. "Have you two talked with your parents about this?"

"My father knows," Damon says.

"My parents have met Evan, but they don't know about our relationship yet," Cam admits. "I guess they're next on the tour though."

"Let's talk about something else." Mom claps her hands. "I can see that your father needs a little time to digest this new information. So why don't we talk about colleges? Damon, Hawk said you just got back from a week at Crowne Mawr. That must have been exciting."

Damon answers my mom's questions while my dad and I have a silent battle of wills. It would be easier if they just left me to my own devices again. But they've determined that in order to function as a couple, we need to function as a family.

Annie, Damon, and Cam are my family though. And they aren't going away. My dad nods slightly to me before answering my mother. The rest of dinner is spent talking about colleges, plays, and hockey.

## CHAPTER 37
*EvanAnn*

My phone buzzes in the dark like someone is calling. I push myself up from between Damon and Cam and look at the nightstand. It stops and then starts again. Damon reaches across Hawk and grabs my phone, handing it to me blindly.

I glance at the time. Four a.m.

It's Mia calling. I sit up in bed in only a t-shirt, letting the covers pool at my waist, and answer the phone.

"Evan?" Mia's voice is shaky.

"Are you okay?" I breathe out. A flashback to being alone out in the woods races through my mind. She could be hurt or stranded. I wake up more fully, ready in case she needs me.

She takes a steadying breath, but the words still come out shaky. "I don't know what's happening. My brother's been hurt. He's in the hospital, and they're worried he won't make it. I have to go. My aunt is getting dressed right now."

"Oh my god. What do you need from me? What can I do for you?" I grip the blanket.

"I don't know. I'll let you know when I know more about what's happening. But I'm going to miss play rehearsal today."

"Of course, you have to do what's best for your family. We'll figure it out. I hope he's okay."

Damon's hand touches my back through my t-shirt.

"I just..." she pauses. "I'm scared, Evan. My parents won't tell us much. Just that he's in the hospital and will be going into emergency surgery."

I take a breath. Not every visit to the hospital is a bad thing. Not every illness ends in death. It's hard not to feel that way though. "I'm here if you need to talk. Anytime, Mia. You can call me."

"Thank you, Evan. Thank you for being my friend. I've got to go." She hangs up.

I lower the phone, and the screen goes dark.

"Evan?" Damon asks. He wants to know what's going on.

When I shake my head, water splashes on my hand.

"Hey," he says softly and sits up, drawing me into his arms. I turn and press my face to his chest. "What happened?"

I laugh as I sob. "I don't know why I'm crying."

"That was Mia?"

I nod as he gently runs his hand over my back. "Her brother's in the hospital. He's been in some sort of accident and needs surgery."

He takes my phone and returns it to the charger and pulls me back down to lie on his chest. He doesn't say anything, just holds me. Cam wraps around me from behind. Hawk takes my hand and holds it.

I'm not crying for the guy I barely know, but for my friend for having to deal with this.

In the morning, I'll have to figure out what to do with this information as the director. But right now, I just cling to the boys I love and am grateful none of them are in the hospital.

---

KEIRA AND I MEET IN THE BLACK BOX THEATER AN HOUR before rehearsal.

"Mia doesn't know when she'll be able to return. Apparently it's complicated. I told her she could let me know when she's ready. But that means we need someone for Desdemona." I blow out a breath. We have a list of the entire cast in front of us.

"Are we sure she'll be back for the show, or should we recast assuming she won't?" Keira taps her pen.

"Okay, if we just let Jason stand in and deliver her lines, that holds the spot for when she's back. But if we do that and she doesn't come back, we've lost a week that someone could be learning Desdemona's lines and staging." I stare at the stage, wondering who would even be available to pick up my lead. Everyone I would have considered is already cast in one of the two shows.

"Okay, so both Crystal and Sophie have been around enough to know some of the lines and some of the staging."

"But then we'd be training two people their roles." I push to stand.

Cam glances up from his homework, but seeing it's nothing, he returns to his laptop.

"The people who could pick up the role quickly already have a part in *Othello* or *The Crucible*. Unless you go with one of the underclassmen." Keira runs her hand over the back of her neck.

"I know. I don't think an underclassman can carry this lead." I pace to the stage and try to envision anyone else in the role. The underclassmen are strong, but they haven't gone through as much training as we have.

Then there's all the work I've done with Mark and Mia to make this convincing. The chemistry isn't something I can just recreate. "We would have to hold auditions and have Mark there. It would take away from our rehearsal time."

Keira stands and comes around the desk to lean on it, her gaze on the stage. I imagine she's doing the same thing I'm doing, trying to sort through all the possibilities.

"Okay, hear me out." Keira comes up next to me and crosses her arms. "We need someone who can step seamlessly into this role, and if Mia comes back, she can take over. But if she doesn't, this person would be able to carry this role on show night."

"I'm not hearing anything that we don't know yet." I turn to Keira.

"There's one person who knows every bit of this by heart and has been with Mia and Mark this entire journey." Keira smiles and looks at me like I'll put together the puzzle she's presented.

"I just don't think Jason—"

"You, Evan," Cam calls out from his chair. "She's talking about you, goody."

My heart stops. "Me?"

"You're perfect for it." Keira's eyes light up as she looks me over like she's envisioning me in the role. "There's a lot of time Desdemona's off stage, enough that you can still direct. And when Mia comes back, she'll be able to take over her role. And if she doesn't, you're a performer."

"I don't—" I cut myself off. I need to think this through. Not just dismiss it because it doesn't fit what I was thinking.

Of course I know all the words and staging. I know what we've tried to do with every step of her characterization, but would that translate into how I would do this role? How would I direct myself differently?

But in this case, I would have play the character Mia and I created for her. Because if she does come back, the transition has to be flawless. So seamless no one could tell the difference.

"You can do this, EvanAnn." Keira steps back. "When you need to make notes on a scene, we'll have Jason step in, but he can't perform on stage as Desdemona."

"What are you afraid of, Evan?" Cam's voice carries.

I turn to look at him. Still trying to wrap my head around it. Could I do it? Yes. But, should I?

"It's a valid option. You're an actor. You know this thing inside and out. No one would do justice to the role like you would." Cam grins.

"We'll know better if Mia will be back by tech week." Keira touches my arm. "We make the big decision then."

The big decision, meaning who will perform. The actor who missed two to three weeks of rehearsal or the one who just stepped into the role two weeks prior.

"This may not be necessary," I say. "Mia could be back at school this week."

"But we should give our play the best shot, and why waste two or three rehearsals waiting to hear when we could have you learning the part better?"

Keira's right.

I take a deep breath and glance at Cam. "I'm not going to have time to tutor you anymore."

Cam holds up his books. "Doing fine, goody. Make your production shine. You've got us in your corner. We'll support you how you need us to."

I release my breath and get to work.

---

I HAVE THE SCRIPT OUT ON THE DINING ROOM TABLE, verifying the places I need to make any changes when Damon sits in the chair next to mine. He takes my left hand and kisses my knuckle above their ring.

I glance up at him, and he smirks.

We haven't done the PDA thing in front of our parents before and apparently, Damon wants to. I don't know how I feel about it. How comfortable I'll be with it.

"Why are we working at the dining room table?" he asks, releasing my hand. He cocks an eyebrow at my script.

I straighten and meet his eyes. "With Mia gone, I'm down a lead. My understudy was for Hawk, which is Jason, and while he does a fine Desdemona, it's not really the look I was going for."

Damon chuckles. "I imagine not."

"So for the time being, I'm stepping into the role."

He touches my cheek and sparks light beneath his fingers. "You'll be amazing."

I blush. "I hope so, but I have to make sure there's nothing that needs to be shifted. And I won't be able to give notes as well for the scenes I'm in."

"Evan, you can do this. There are directors who act in their own films."

"Yes, but they have replays to watch. I usually watch as it's happening. I guess Keira could give me notes."

"Film it."

My mouth opens and then closes because he has a point. I can do dailies. I could watch while we go onto the next scene or during breaks.

"You're a genius." I lean in and kiss him, barely a peck, but it warms me.

A throat clears, and Damon smiles against my lips as I pull back. Oops. A different warm nervousness floods me.

Adam stands in the doorway with my mom. Mom smiles knowingly at me. My cheeks heat. Especially since I'm the one who kissed Damon. I guess I'm okay with PDA. Of course, I worried about doing it inadvertently before our parents knew about us.

I got used to kissing them at school. Kissing Damon whenever the mood struck. Or him kissing me. It was bound to happen sometime.

"Sorry to interrupt." Adam walks in and pulls a chair out for my mom.

"You weren't interrupting." I gather my pages and put them on the chair next to mine. Being the first one here, I didn't want to just sit and play on my phone. I'm going to need every spare minute to make this work and to make sure I have the lines down.

At rehearsal, I used the script to make sure I have everything, but I need to be off script by tomorrow. I didn't need to look as often as I worried I'd have to. But it's different knowing the lines and performing the lines.

"You usually don't work during dinners." Mom nods to the pages. "Everything okay?"

I lift my gaze to hers. "My lead had to go out of town. Her brother is in the hospital. We don't know when she'll be back."

"Oh, honey. Is that your friend Mia? Is she doing okay?" Mom looks like she wants to give me a hug across the table.

"She said he's out of surgery, but everything is still up in the air. She can't say much about what happened though." I received a few update texts throughout the day. I can't help but worry. It sounds serious, whatever is going on.

"How's that going to affect your play?" Mom sits back and studies me. This is the side of my mom Damon's never seen. The part that's willing to be my support when something fails.

"My assistant director and I talked it over, and I'll step into the part. If for some reason she can't come back in time, I can perform for the showcase. But we're weeks into rehearsal, and bringing someone else in would make everything more complicated. Especially if Mia returns and that person doesn't have a part anymore."

"I think that's an amazing decision." Mom lets the server place her plate in front of her and then leans back in. "You'll be amazing. I haven't seen you perform in years."

"You don't act?" Adam asks as he cuts his food.

"I do, but for Anteros as you get higher in the program the tracks split. I chose the director path." I take a bite of my food. For a second, I savor the rich sauce on the vegetables. How I got by on frozen pizza and grilled cheeses eludes me. I don't know that I can go back to frozen mac and cheese.

The staff have definitely spoiled me.

"So what do you want to go to college for?" Adam asks. He's being careful not to talk about Damon's and my relationship, which I appreciate, but it feels like the elephant in the room we're all pretending doesn't exist.

"Film mainly, but I'd love to be able to direct and act." I take a drink. "There are programs that allow you to do both, and some that it's almost impossible to do both at the same time."

Damon slides his hand against my thigh. I nearly jump out of my skin as my attention shifts to him. My eyes widen, and I'm not sure if our parents know he's touching me. Or if they didn't and my reaction told them.

"I talked to a guy on the team who's in the drama program at Crowne Mawr," he says.

"Yeah?" I ask, unable to hide my excitement.

"He gave me his number so you could call him and ask him your questions. He's a junior." Damon searches my eyes. I want to lean in and kiss him again. He smirks knowingly.

"Fantastic." I drop my gaze before lifting it to our parents.

Mom's smile is soft. Adam looks utterly amazed.

I clear my throat. "Anyway, so I'm going to be extra busy for the next few weeks. Normally, production picks up a couple weeks before the first performance anyway, but I've made sure to stay ahead in all my classes. So I should be fine."

"As long as you remember to eat," Damon says pointedly and nods to my plate.

I take a bite and drink some water. After chewing and swallowing, I give him a look like *see*. "It's going to be intense, but it was always going to get more intense from here on out. This is when my actors need reassurances, when the crew needs to figure out the exact timing of scene changes, when I need to stop making changes and make sure what we have works."

Adam looks impressed, but I'm used to that from adults. Damon hasn't removed his hand from my thigh and his thumb rubs slow circles. I'd tell him to stop, but I doubt he would, and it would only draw attention to what he's doing.

"I was a little worried about giving scene notes, but Damon mentioned taking video and reviewing it to give feedback." I smile at Damon and he squeezes my thigh.

"Has there been any new texts or anything unusual?" Adam asks.

I shake my head and glance at Damon. Will he tell them about Mia being a potential suspect? I don't want my mom to think she's bad news if it's not true. Trusting Jackson is telling the truth might be as bad as trusting Mia at this point.

But will things stop now that Mia is preoccupied? I guess this is the litmus test to find out. I doubt Jackson knows Mia is out. So if the threats continue, then can we assume it isn't Mia?

"What do we need to do to help protect you?" Mom asks.

Adam clears his throat. "It might make sense to hire someone to make sure she's secure."

"No, thank you. I don't want someone following me around all day." I can't even think about some hired man hanging around me. It would be intrusive on a level I'm just not willing to accept. "The rose was the only time someone's actually hurt me. It was barely anything."

My hand tingles where the wounds are still healing.

"We plan on being there for her." Damon squeezes my thigh. "Between the three of us, we'll keep her protected."

Adam looks between the two of us and releases his breath. "This is going to take getting used to."

Mom takes Adam's hand on the table. "But we will. And it would be nice if you had your boyfriends over for dinner some night. I know it might be a while since the play will keep you busy, but I'd like to get to know them better."

"Okay." I don't know what to say to that, but I'm appreciative she's being supportive.

---

"What do you need from us to help?" Mr. Watson sits across his desk from me. He wanted to make sure everything was under control after I emailed him on Sunday.

It's Monday morning before classes.

"Besides the camera set up for rehearsals, I think I'm good. I figured I'd bring in my own equipment, if that's okay." I sit with my hands in my lap and my legs crossed.

"That'll work. You're welcome to any equipment in the AV department as well." Mr. Watson rubs his chin. "What about costuming? Are you going to have two sets of clothes made for Desdemona?"

"It wouldn't hurt, and it would still be within my budget for costumes." I look at the list in front of me. "Mia might not be gone that long, but it's always good to have a backup in case she gets hurt and can't do the production."

"Unfortunately, with two productions, we can't cast understudies for all the parts." Mr. Watson leans on his desk. "If you need anything additional to support your production, let us know. We really want you to be successful."

"I appreciate that." I tuck my hair behind my ear. "Damon and Cam will be coming to rehearsals until the production. With the rose prank, they want to make sure nothing else happens during rehearsals."

"It's your rehearsal, EvanAnn. If you don't want someone there, you can kick them out. But if you want someone there, you're welcome to have anyone there. If you need any help, I can also resume coming to observe."

"I don't think that will be necessary." I gather my things and stand. "I do think Mia will be back and everything will go smoothly, but I want to be prepared for any contingency."

"That's understandable. And the sign of a good director. You can't always plan for everything though. So if something comes up you can't handle, let me know."

## Cam

Monday night rehearsal is mine. I walk in during their break after I get out of hockey. Evan sits at her desk watching her laptop with headphones on. She's focused, so I drop off a red paper flower on her desk and head to my seat in the audience.

Tonight I'm working on my college applications. Evan agreed to look at my essays for me before all this stuff with Mia happened. I'm tempted to just ask Hawk and not even tell her about them.

She's going to have every minute of her day filled at this point. Even at lunch she sat with us and worked. Homework or the play. Pretty sure the only time I'm going to be able to do anything with her is while she sleeps. Maybe I can lure her into a closet for a quickie.

She reaches over and picks up the flower, twirling it in between her fingers a moment before turning and giving me a smile. I love the way her eyes light up. I give her a wink and return to my laptop.

As the cast returns, Keira sits next to Evan and they talk. I've been considering whether the stalker was just trying to throw Evan off her game. Anyone who knows Evan knows the play comes first, school comes second, and then her social life, which is now us. Of course, prior to this year, she didn't really have a social life.

When Evan gets on stage with the cast to fill in for Desdemona, I'm fucking mesmerized. I've never seen her act before, but I've seen this part a few times now. Mia is good, but Evan is fucking golden.

There's this subtle way she makes me buy into her being Desdemona. She even mimics some of Mia's performance, but makes the part even better. I'm in awe. It's like watching Damon on the ice.

You know you're seeing something that transcends the ordinary. That this isn't just someone going through the motions, but someone who is doing exactly what they were meant to do.

If I didn't know she was already exceptional at directing, I would wonder why anyone wouldn't have forced her to pursue acting. Of course, I'm not exactly impartial, but I can see how everyone knows she's the one to watch.

And how that could make some people jealous. Jealousy makes

people do crazy shit. Jealousy over her career choices. Jealousy over her having us. Jealousy over the attention she receives. We need a way to make sure she's safe.

No more reacting to the shit that's thrown her way. It's time to draw this motherfucker and his friends out into the open.

ME:
Need to chat tonight

DAMON:
Our spot

HAWK:
What about Annie?

ME:
She'll be working after this

I'll drop her at home

Adam and Heather are there

I want to talk about the stalker

## CHAPTER 38
### *Cam*

WE RIDE our bikes out to the spot. Sure, we could have done this in Damon's house or his room, but Evan is a distraction. And right now, she needs us not to be *her* distraction. Damon made sure she had food in front of her before we left, but she was already buried in her books.

When we park, we take off our helmets.

"We need to stop letting this fucker control the narrative," I start off with.

"Do we really believe it's Mia?" Hawk asks, running his hand over his hair.

Damon shakes his head. "She might be part of it, but she's not the person pulling the strings."

"The texts. Clearly personal to Evan." I lean forward on my bike, trying to think through everything that's happened since the beginning. "But they haven't continued. Why? All it did was put Evan on notice that someone was watching her."

"It freaked her out." Damon gazes off into the distance. "Scared her, put her on edge."

"But it wouldn't have worked if Jackson hadn't reentered her life." I breathe out. "It can't be a coincidence. So either it was him or someone who knew about him."

"Her flat tire was the first thing. Audition night." Hawk meets my gaze. "That could have been coincidence, but with everything else, it becomes suspicious. She didn't have a spare. She would have been stranded and had to call her mom or ask Mr. Watson to take her home. If I hadn't waited for her, she would have been alone in that parking lot. Brandt left before her. Maybe he didn't look at her car, but there would have only been their two cars left in the student lot."

"That was before the scrimmage where Jackson saw her?" I ask, trying to imagine the timeline.

Damon gives a sharp nod. "It could have been a bad tire and not part of the stalking. The thing that bothers me is, if Jackson was so obsessed with Evan when she was sixteen, he could have easily found her again. I wouldn't have given up on her that easily. She's all over the Anteros website. Even a YouTube search would give you where she goes to school. She's not difficult to find."

"She doesn't have a rich daddy who keeps her protected," I add. "Elizabeth Stanwell is practically a ghost on the internet. You'd have to do a deep dive to find out anything about her."

"So, if Jackson really was stalking her, why wait until now to come after her? Opportunity? Because we were interested in her? Is there little stuff Evan wrote off that shows he's been after her this whole time? When she was alone and vulnerable?" Damon looks like he could break something right now.

"Maybe he was being honest when he said he took the hint," I offer.

Damon glares at me, and I raise my hands in surrender. But he's right, a stalker doesn't always make their presence known. It could be that he watched her for years.

"It's not impossible. Maybe seeing her again resparked his interest," I say. "Or maybe someone else noticed that Jackson seemed keen on Evan."

"You mean like Mia?" Hawk asks.

I nod. "Which puts her back on the playing field. The thing that stops me is, I don't believe Mia wants to hurt Evan, but she's friendly with Abby, so maybe she let something slip."

"Mia seems too savvy to let something slip inadvertently," Hawk says.

"You want to add Abby to the list?" Damon scoffs.

"Why not?" I ask. "Honestly there are a lot of girls jealous as fuck of our girl right now. It's not like we keep our attention quiet. Girls notice and talk. Add to that, the attention Evan is getting for being director. It's a perfect fucking storm."

"None of these girls scream mastermind of the operation though." Hawk smirks. "Annie would be able to do this, maybe Keira. They think similarly, but I wouldn't think Keira had it in her."

"Why not? She has just as much ambition as Evan." I have to point out. "While I'd love to eliminate people, I think we've narrowed our focus too much. Olivia isn't the only crazy bitch at our school. And she isn't the only one who wanted us."

Damon presses his lips together but doesn't say anything. Olivia was a misjudgment on his part. He thought he could control her, but there's no controlling crazy.

"I looked into Elizabeth's school. It isn't Kentwood Prep, but that doesn't mean much." I think back to my search into her school and Kentwood. "They cross with sports and some of their parties. It wouldn't be unheard of that she and Jackson know each other. It's just not something I can pin down."

"I'd love to have something concrete." Damon smooths his hand over his handlebar. "It would make this easier."

"Okay, timeline, then." I rub my hands together. "The tire, the texts, the car." I pause.

"More texts. Olivia outs us to the school. The rose. Social media account," Hawk adds. "Though the social media account turned out to be revenge by Chase and Abby."

"You forgot the text to Heather. Someone wanted us to get caught." Damon shakes his head. "Only the rose physically hurt her."

"The car could have." Hawk breathes out harshly. "If I'd been any slower, they could have clipped us before speeding off."

"We do need to make Chase and Abby pay for that account." I run my hand through my hair. "Both of them gloated to Evan about it. Mia said that Abby was planning something. Hopefully, that was it. I don't see them doing the texts, but possibly the rose."

"I did enjoy leaving Chase in the woods the first time..." Hawk rubs his chin thoughtfully. Then he grins evilly. "Maybe after the play we can revisit it. We can't fuck with any of Annie's actors right now. She's stressed enough as it is."

Both Damon and I nod. It's like Evan has shut down to everything except the play. She's got a lot on her plate since she lost her lead.

"She's going to be brilliant," I say. When I meet Hawk's gaze, he nods.

"She's amazing as a director, but acting with her on stage is something else entirely." Hawk lies back on his bike and stares up at the stars. "Wherever we go for college, Annie needs to act as well as direct."

"She was saying the program at Crowne Mawr allows that." Damon smiles, and then he gets serious. "Brandt has his fingers in this somewhere. You won't convince me otherwise. Especially since he was the last to leave before Evan found her tire flat."

"From what I've heard and seen, I agree about Brandt." I straighten. "He was trying to convince Chase to quit and come to his production to show Evan. But even Chase isn't that gullible to leave a leading role to be an extra."

"Chase actually has his priorities straight." Hawk chuckles. "Brandt should have offered him pussy, and then maybe he would have changed his mind."

"Is the internship really what Brandt's after?" Damon asks.

"He's got industry connections through his father, but maybe, like Chase's dad, daddy isn't willing to help his son be a little nepo-baby." There might be a way for me to find out. I just have to ask the right ants.

"Do we know how they decided on the showcase directors? Evan obviously deserves to be in the showcase, but how did Brandt get in?" Damon asks.

There's always the obvious way. Buy in.

"There were a couple of donations in the spring. One for additional lab equipment in the science wing. Another for some of the classrooms that need to be renovated. I can't remember the other one, but I'll look into it this week. It wouldn't be the first time a parent bought someone their future," I say.

"It's worth exploring, but we need to be careful so we don't kick the hornets' nest and cause trouble for Annie," Hawk straightens. "It's less than a month until the performance. We can keep looking into this, but we can't really confront anyone, especially if they are in the play."

We all sit with that a moment. As much as I want to confront the asshole or assholes fucking with our girl, if it is someone in her cast, then we can't push and end up hurting her play.

"I don't mind the overkill of tracking Evan, but do we really think someone is going to take it that far?" I have to ask because I'm ready to do whatever it takes to keep her safe. With what's happened, I just don't see someone escalating to that level.

"If she wasn't mine, I would take her." Damon's words are cold and dark. If Evan had continued to reject him, I don't know how this would have gone. Damon locked into her pretty quickly, but Evan didn't really resist.

But it's also a wakeup call, because what someone is willing to do is determined by their obsession. It depends on the motivation again. If it's Brandt, he's trying to win. It's not about Evan. He wants to ruin her chances to make sure he wins. Losing Mia a month before the performance should have hurt her production. So maybe things will calm down now.

But if it's someone obsessed with Evan, what happens when they decide they want her no matter what?

The thought sends chills through my body.

"If it's someone truly stalking her, then it's not unreasonable that they might see us as threats and come after us." Hawk sits up and looks over at Damon. "It depends on the motivation, right? Do they want to own her, or do they just want to fuck up her life? We wanted to fuck up Chase's life. We never would have kidnapped him. But if this person feels like Annie owes them something more..."

He lets that hang over us. I'd prefer them to come after us. We can take it. Evan is strong and smart and could probably take mental torture, but she's also soft. I can't even think about someone violating her without my stomach turning and rage pumping through my veins.

"We keep our eyes open and keep digging." Damon shakes his head. "She belongs to us."

### *EvanAnn*

Every moment of every day seems full. The days slide into each other. I'm fully immersed in the play, in my character. Mark's and my chemistry rivals his chemistry with Mia, for which I'm grateful. If things fell flat between us, I would have been tempted to bring in someone else.

Mia hasn't reached out in a few days, but from the little she's said, something is horribly wrong. Her brother made it through surgery, but there's still some risks involved. Apparently she can't talk about what happened with anyone.

I wish she could. Talking with a friend would have made it easier to deal with my father's impending death. But I also respect that if she needs to talk to me, she'll let me know. I just need to make sure she knows I'm here for her.

"Goody?"

I turn and look at Cam. He gives me a small smile.

"You ready to go?"

When I glance at my phone, it's almost ten o'clock. Everyone else left about an hour ago, but I wanted to go through the recordings to see if I missed anything. Time passed, and I didn't even realize it.

"I'm so sorry, Cam." I stand and start gathering my stuff.

He gets up and drops his bag next to my chair before helping me. "It's okay. I'm at your service."

"No, I should have just done this at home." I shake my head.

Cam chuckles. "Like Damon would have given you an uninterrupted hour."

"He's not that bad," I argue and look at Cam. "I just can't focus as well in our bedroom."

Cam touches my face, and I lean into his warmth as sparks drift through me. "You need to take more breaks."

"Thank you." I step into him and wrap my arms around his waist, resting my head against his beating heart. "You guys keep me tethered. And make sure all my needs are met."

Cam laughs as he kisses the top of my head. "Come on. We should get out of here."

I release him and turn back to the table. I pick up my laptop and find one of his red paper flowers crushed. "Oh, no."

I put my laptop in the bag and turn back to the squished flower. "Oh, Cam, I didn't even see when I did this."

"It's not a big deal, goody."

The paper is coming undone and there's ink toward the center. I spread it open a little more, and it unfurls completely. Inside is this little cartoon drawing. It's the group of us on the bikes. It's small but so detailed I can tell who is who.

"Cam?" I hold it up to him with questioning eyes.

He shrugs and smirks. "I like to doodle."

"Doodle?" I inspect the drawing, which could compete with any of the drawings I've seen from the visual arts department. "This is better than a doodle. Are there pictures in all of the flowers?"

I keep every one of the flowers he's given me on my desk. When I'm working, I love to glance over at them. They fill me with warmth every time.

"Of course." Cam rubs my back.

My mouth opens and closes. "But to see them, I'd have to undo the flowers."

"You could, or I can send you the pictures I took of the drawings before I made them into flowers." Cam smiles down at me.

I grab his collar and drag him down to kiss him. He groans into my mouth and lifts me. I automatically wrap my legs around his waist, not thinking about where we are.

"Unless you want to give the janitor an eyeful, you really should lock the door."

I jerk away from Cam at Damon's voice. He stands near the door with his keys in his hands.

"You're running late," he says. "But don't let me stop you."

I lower my legs and back away from Cam. He releases me reluctantly with a cocky grin. "Sorry. Cam just made me realize the time."

"We would have been there shortly." Cam brushes his hand over my hip, and heat swells inside me. "Evan just wanted to go over her notes again."

Damon presses his lips together. Probably wants to chastise me for not stopping, but I know the amount of time he spends working out and training. We're probably on par for how much we put into our future careers. And he hasn't even started hockey season yet.

They help me lock up, and Cam rides with us on the way to our house before heading to his. I can't wait until we don't have to say goodbye at the end of the day.

## CHAPTER 39
### *Hawk*

It's a full read through this Sunday. Mia still isn't back, so Evan is on stage opposite Mark. Cassio isn't in this scene so I'm in the audience watching. There are a lot of talented actors here, but Mark and Evan? Together they make the rest of us look like students play acting. They truly are stars already.

"Hey, Hawk," Sophie says as she sits in the chair next to mine.

I don't say anything. She's been a little bit more attentive since Chase went back to dating Abby. I haven't been friendly, but I'm trying not to be mean since we perform together.

"Do you want to go into the hallway and run lines with me?" She twirls her hair around her finger and must have put on fresh lipstick.

"No, thank you." Normally, I would, but she knows her lines, and after a few minutes, she'll want to chat with me like we're friends. We're not friends. I've learned from Damon's mistake that you don't encourage a girl you don't want.

"It's just the one scene where I feel like I trip over my tongue," Sophie tries again with a little hint of whine in her voice. "I just don't want to do anything to damage the play since Mia isn't here to carry it anymore."

My brow furrows, and I turn to look at her. She smiles now that she has my full attention, like that's all she's been wanting. When I don't say anything, she takes it as her cue I want more information.

"I mean, EvanAnn is good, but she's a much better director than actor." Sophie settles in the chair, content to stay here. "Obviously. Otherwise, she wouldn't have gone into directing."

"You know Annie's my girlfriend, right?" Have I not been obvious about it? Fuck, what do I need to do? Wear a *Property of EvanAnn* shirt to practice? Because if that's what I need to do, I'll fucking do it.

"Oh." Sophie giggles a little. "Yeah, I know, but it's not like you guys are exclusive."

Fuck. This. Girl.

"What makes you say that?" My voice conveys my anger. I narrow my eyes at her, and she shrinks a little in her chair.

"She... You..." Her face flushes red, and she stands abruptly. "I need to—"

She walks away quickly. There's no way I'm letting someone tell me what my relationship is or isn't. Annie is mine. She's ours.

I don't need to explain it to anyone, and there are no openings for extra people in this.

Annie finishes on stage and walks over to the desk to watch the others perform. I wish I could go join her, or sweep her into my arms and kiss her. But I won't, because I respect my girl and what she's doing. Enough to know not to make it about me.

This is her rehearsal. Her stage. And she owns every inch of it.

From what I can tell, she's burning the candle at both ends to make this work. To be both a principal actor and director. I won't put my needs above hers. Especially when it's just to show some other girl that Annie is mine. She needs to focus, and we need to take care of her.

This isn't forever. Yes, she'll always have something she's working on or working in, but that doesn't mean we won't get time. She'll take care of us too. She does take care of us. Maybe it isn't an all-night marathon, but more stolen moments here and there for now.

She turns, and when she sees me, she smiles softly. Because this morning, she woke to me sucking on her pussy before I fucked her hard while she sucked on Cam's cock. Damon watched before rolling her onto her back and fucking into her.

I'm not sure how many times she came, but she definitely had a smile on her face this morning for breakfast. This week flew by. Mom has been breathing down my neck, wanting to have another dinner with Annie, but I had to tell her she's busy for the next few weeks.

My parents seem to have settled into a rhythm. It's still not safe to enter rooms without knocking or making loud noises as approaching, but they're less affectionate than they were. Which is good, but it's still odd to have my parents around all the time.

The rest of rehearsal goes off without a hitch. Cam and Damon were busy today, so I get to wait with Annie. She's already at her desk, scribbling notes, as some cast members are hanging around, talking. I walk over and take Keira's empty seat next to Annie, but I don't say anything to disrupt her train of thought.

"Chase!"

Abby hurries into the black box theater. She walks over and kisses Chase, like he's returning home from war. I can't wait to fuck with their little relationship. Guarantee he hasn't stopped fucking around just because he's with Abby.

"I missed you, babe," she says, loud enough that even the people in the hallway probably heard her.

He might just be more sneaky about it.

"I think I've lost my appetite," Annie says softly to me.

I chuckle.

But it must not have been soft enough, because Abby turns to glare at Annie.

"What did you say to me?" Abby projects to the whole theater.

Annie sighs and looks up. "I'm sorry, but I didn't say anything to you."

Abby braces her hands on her hips and gets a snotty look on her face. "You couldn't even keep your man satisfied enough to stay with you. And now, you're whoring yourself out to the Devil's trio." Abby laughs coldly. "Everyone thinks you're pathetic."

Annie leans back in her chair with a smile. "Really?"

Her nonchalance enrages Abby. "Everyone knows they're only with you because you put out."

"So which is it? Am I a prude or a whore?" Annie taps her chin with her finger like she's thinking it over.

I could step in, but she's got this, so I sit back and enjoy the show.

"Whatever. No one likes you." Abby turns to put her hand on Chase's chest. Chase has the decency to look uncomfortable with all this. He's probably remembering everything we did to him and doesn't want a repeat.

"I like her," Mark says. "Honestly, I'm pretty sure if you asked anyone in here to pick you or EvanAnn, I bet they'd pick EvanAnn."

"You don't even count." She waves her hand dismissively.

"Why?" Mark straightens. "Because I'm not from wealthy parents who bought my way into this school? Or is it because I didn't have to bribe the guy whose parents bought him a spot in the showcase? I mean, you've got some talent, Abby, but you'll never reach the caliber of performance EvanAnn will. So tell me again how I don't count?"

Abby's mouth opens and closes, but she's not wordless for long. "I bet EvanAnn set up that social media account herself to get attention. And how do we know Mia actually went home? Maybe EvanAnn hurt her somehow."

"Are you that threatened by me?" Annie hasn't moved at all. She's still relaxed in her chair. "Are you so worried everyone would choose me over you? Even your boyfriend? Sure, he was an asshole, but he needed someone like me to clean up his image after you ruined it. Do his parents even know you two are dating again? Or is he still keeping our breakup a secret?"

While Abby tries to figure out what to say to that, Annie stands.

"Rehearsal is over. I need to lock up." She looks directly at Abby. "You don't belong in here."

Abby huffs and grabs Chase's hand, tugging him toward the doors.

Annie watches them go before gathering her stuff like nothing happened.

"You amaze me," I say. She remained completely cold during that whole interaction. Nothing fucking fazed her.

She smiles and nods to the camera she uses during rehearsal. "You want to stop the recording so I can take it home?"

"Nice." I chuckle and do what she asks. "You going to use it?"

Annie shrugs. "You never know when a little blackmail might come in handy, and I do owe her for that social media account."

I chuckle. "Damon would be so proud."

Mark comes over. "Sorry, I got carried away. Those girls have been catty since freshman year, like they fucking own the program."

"You didn't say anything I hadn't thought before." Annie touches his arm and smiles. "Thank you for defending me."

"Anytime." Mark nods to me.

"What did you mean by Brandt's parents bought his way into the showcase?" I ask. We've been looking into it, but it's hard to find the paper trail.

Mark steps in closer and lowers his voice. "Brandt wants to be a lot of things, but he doesn't really have the talent to act or direct. But his mother is his biggest fan. Daddy, not so much, because he's had to clean up his son's messes."

"Messes?" Annie asks.

Mark smirks and glances around, but no one else Is close to us. "Brandt uses his dad's fame like a calling card. It gets him into clubs, free stuff, and girls he otherwise wouldn't have a shot with. That leaves behind a trail of really fucking bitter people who are willing to expose their stories to the media."

"How do you know this?" I ask because this isn't something we've been able to find out.

Mark smirks. "Guys talk. Especially when you give excellent head. I also listen when they think I'm not. Apparently Daddy Stanwell has been threatening to cut off Brandt. Thinks Brandt needs to pay his dues and figure out his own success without relying so heavily on him."

"So he needs the win for the internship to prove to his father he can be something because his dad isn't going to give him anything else?" I ask and some of the shit that's been happening falls into place. We didn't have a motivation before, but if Brandt really is the one pulling the strings, it would make sense. But what we don't know is how many people he has under his thumb.

"Thank you, Mark." Annie steps in and gives him a quick hug. "I really do appreciate everything you've done for me."

"I'm just happy to be part of your production." He smiles. "You're an amazing director and actor."

He gives me a nod before heading out. I touch Annie's cheek because I can't believe this girl is mine.

"I love when you stand up for yourself, baby girl." I brush her hair behind her ear.

Annie steps up to me and puts her hand on my chest. "I'm done trying to fit what people think I should be."

I tip up her chin and search her blue-gray eyes, seeing my future in them. "Good, because I like you this way."

---

### EvanAnn

Damon beats me to the dining room table this time. I take the seat next to him and lean my head against his shoulder. I just want to go to sleep. It's been a grueling week, and next week doesn't seem like it's going to get better.

"I'm going to have to make a decision about Mia soon," I say softly. It's weighing on me, but I know it's coming.

"And you don't want to?" he asks, taking my hand and threading our fingers together.

I shake my head against his shoulder before I straighten and look at him. "She's my friend, and I really think she's the best actor for the role. But we're almost to tech week. I'll have to decide when's the last day she can come back in and still be in the play. She's missed a week of rehearsal. We have one more week before tech week."

"If I missed two weeks of practice, I wouldn't expect Coach to put me in the game. Even if I was ready for it." Damon brushes my hair behind my ear. "You'll make the call you need to make when the time comes. I'm sorry you have to make this decision, but I know you'll do what's best for your production."

He's right about missing rehearsal and still expecting to slot in. Maybe she's practicing, or maybe she's so distraught she isn't even thinking about the play. It makes sense to tell her she's out, but I'm all tangled up inside over it. Just like when Jackson accused Mia of being the stalker. It doesn't feel right because she's my friend, but if it's true, I'll have to do something about it.

I look down at our hands and then up into his blue eyes. "I don't know how I would have made it through this year so far without you."

He smirks. "I think things would have gone differently without me in your life."

"Probably." I lean in and kiss him after verifying our parents aren't in the doorway. "But it wouldn't have been half as fun."

His eyes darken, but he just leans in and kisses my temple. "I'm glad I was here for this."

My eyes widen in surprise because the alternative would have been going off to fulfill his lifelong dream of playing hockey. There's this resolve in his eyes that floods me with warmth. That maybe, given the choice, he'd choose me.

"How's the play going?" Mom walks into the room and sits opposite me. Her gaze flicks to our joined hands, but she doesn't mention it.

"Recording the rehearsals is a game changer. There are things I miss when we're doing run throughs, but now that I have playbacks..." I take a breath. "And I forgot how much I enjoy acting. I love directing too, but it's nice to step into someone else's shoes for a while. Even if my character is killed in the end."

"Spoilers," Mom says, pretending to be horrified.

"You've had your whole life to figure out the end of *Othello*." I roll my eyes but smile at her.

"Fair." Mom glances to the door as Adam walks in. Her tone softens when she says, "Hey you."

He sits next to her and kisses her softly before turning to us. "Did Damon tell you?"

"I hadn't gotten around to it yet." Damon leans back in his chair and turns to me. "The Yale coach wants us to come up this weekend. We'll fly out after Saturday's scrimmage. It's going to be quick, but we'll get back late Sunday night."

"That sounds exciting." I squeeze his hand. Yale could be an option for me. It's not ideal though, but there are a lot of colleges within train or driving distance that could work better for undergrad. It would mean a little long distance, but better than flying across the country to see each other.

"I really wish you two could go with us." Adam brings my mom's hand to his lips. "But I understand. It's just not the right time for EvanAnn."

"Maybe Mom could go with you," I say. "It's only one night. I could stay with Cam or Hawk if their parents would be okay with it."

I can't meet my mom's eyes. It took a lot for me to even offer that. But it's not like I'll be left alone, and I can tell Adam really wants to take my mom with. I wish I could go with Damon and experience campus with him.

"We could have them over for dinner on Wednesday night to discuss it. It would be good to get everyone on the same page." Adam smiles. "But I don't see why not."

Mom opens her mouth and closes it, but what can she really say? Is she worried about me sleeping with my boyfriends? Because that ship sailed when they found me in Damon's bed.

Besides, she was willing to let me stay with Chase's parents. Or would she have said no to that? Adam offered, but she already knew Chase and I had broken up at that point.

"Nothing new happened this week," I say.

This week meant a lot more rehearsals for both plays, and homework and tests are ramping up. No one has the time to mess with anyone else.

"Okay, that's settled then," Adam says. "EvanAnn can spend the night with one of her other boyfriends, and we'll all go up to Yale for a night."

Damon's hand squeezes mine. He and the others worry about me, but it's not like they won't know where I am. Besides, either Hawk or Cam would have stayed with me while he was gone anyway. We're just going to stay at their house instead of ours.

# CHAPTER 40
## *Cam*

IT'S BEEN QUIET. Almost too fucking quiet. No threats. No new social media posts. No unwanted gifts.

Is it because Mia is gone and she really was the stalker? Or is Mia's absence enough damage to Evan's play? Or is the stalker using her absence to lull us into a false sense of security? It weighs on my mind because it feels like the quiet before the storm. But it's not the biggest thing on my mind.

My parents and I have been invited to dinner on Wednesday with Evan's mother, Adam, Evan, and Damon. It's Tuesday when I sit down with them and explain how Evan is my girlfriend, but also Hawk's and Damon's.

Mom's mouth opens and closes, and she gets this look like she's trying to figure it out, and then her mouth opens again like she really wants to ask questions, but then she closes it like the questions aren't appropriate. Dad watches her for a few minutes, letting her stew.

Finally he says, "At least your grades are much better, so she must be a good influence on you."

"She is," I admit. There's a lot less partying when I could be with her instead.

"All three of you?" Mom finally bursts out.

I nod, but it's not comfortable talking about this part with my parents. Because she's not talking about the *dating* part. "Yes, Mom."

Mom thinks about it for another minute and shakes her head. "That poor girl."

Dad laughs. I think of how much we love Evan and how much she loves us and just shake my head at my mom's drama.

On Wednesday night, I stand at the front door of Damon's house with my parents. This feels all sorts of wrong. When Adam opens the door, he smiles.

"It's great to see you again. Alex. Lisa. Cam. It's been a while. Come in." He backs up so we can walk in. Voices come from the living room as we follow Adam.

Hawk's parents sit snuggled up on the couch with Hawk sitting a little apart from them. Evan sits between Heather and Damon.

"Please have a seat. Can I get you something to drink?" Adam asks like this is completely normal.

Mom and Dad let Adam know what they'd like. I ask for a soda and walk over to the other chair in the room. Evan looks at me like she wants out of here. Normally, I'd just catch her hand and drag her out to my bike, and we'd be gone. But this is important.

We're not only reading our parents in on what's happening. We're deciding whose house she's staying at on Saturday. It doesn't really matter to Hawk or me, because we'll both be with Evan wherever she ends up. But we're doing this on the up and up. Which means our parents will be fully aware our girlfriend is staying at our house. Preferably in our beds.

My parents introduce themselves to Heather, and then Adam returns with their cocktails and a soda for me. He sits beside Heather, and we all take a sip of our drinks. So fucking awkward, but I guess someone will have to break the ice.

"Have you heard from Mia?" I ask Evan.

She inhales and shakes her head. "Whatever happened, she's not allowed to talk about it, so she texts now and then. She's not even sure if she's going to be able to come back to Anteros at all. Security issues might be a problem."

Damon meets my eyes. That means if Mia is part of the whole plan to do whatever to Evan, she's a missing piece on the board. Maybe that's why it's been so quiet since she's been gone.

"Is Mia a friend?" my mom asks, gently.

Heather reaches over to squeeze Evan's hand.

"Yes." Evan smiles. "She's the lead in my play, and we've become friends. Her brother got injured about a week and a half ago, and she had to go home for a while."

"Injured?" Mom takes a sip and looks thoughtful. "Wasn't there something that happened to that one school..." She snaps her fingers like it will magically come to her.

My dad just shakes his head like he has no idea what she's talking about. Mom reads a lot of news, but tends to forget pertinent details.

She touches his arm. "You know, that high school. Something went wrong at their homecoming."

"I don't remember, Lisa." Dad's voice is quiet.

Mom shakes her head. "Maybe I'll remember later." She turns her attention back to Evan. "I hope your friend is okay. Did you have to recast her part?"

"We weren't sure how long she'd be gone. Or even if she'd be back in time to perform. We were down to the wire. Since I knew the staging and lines, I stepped into the role." Evan glances down at her hands. "It looks like she probably won't be back, which is a shame because she truly is a brilliant actor."

Mom nods, and Heather squeezes Evan's hand reassuringly. There's a brief pause while everyone takes an awkward silence drink.

"So, Yale?" Dad says a little too brightly. "That must be exciting, Damon. Honestly, I've been trying to convince Cam to go up and visit. So he can see what it's all about."

"You should come with us." Adam smiles.

My eyes widen, and I look at the slight panic on Evan's face. "I don't—"

"That's a great idea. It's after hockey, and you don't have anything on Sunday." Dad glances at Hawk and his parents. "The problem we're here to solve is where EvanAnn will stay while her mom is out of town, right? So she can stay with Hawk, and we can go to Yale with Damon."

"Of course, EvanAnn can stay with us." Naomi takes Paul's hand

and looks at him. "It's only one night, and it's not like she hasn't slept over before."

Given Heather's wide-eyed expression, that wasn't universally known. Evan turns red and looks down at her hands in her lap.

Adam clears his throat.

"We do think you should be aware EvanAnn has received some threats and someone had a social media account with threatening language on it about her. That's down now thankfully." Adam leans forward and clasps his hands. "We're taking it seriously, and the police have been informed, but we want to make sure she'll be safe while we're gone."

"Threats?" Mom touches her necklace pendant and looks worriedly at Evan. "Are you going to be okay staying with Hawk? Because if not, we can stay home and you can stay with us. We just updated our security system."

"She'll be fine with us," Paul says. "It's only one night, and if you can visit Yale, you really should. Hawk's been looking into Yale as well. As an option. His first choice has always been Columbia."

Hawk glances my way. Fuck, this conversation is getting out of control. But I guess I'm going with Damon to Yale, and Evan is staying with Hawk until we get back.

"Crowne Mawr has already made Damon an offer to be on the team next year." Adam glows with pride. "We wanted to check out Yale and what they have to offer before we commit."

There's a possibility we all won't get into Yale even if that's Damon's decision. I hate to think about commuting to each other, but long distance will be worth it to stay together. Just harder to find time to be together.

"Cam's been looking at Crowne Mawr too." Dad glances my way. "I think it would be an easy decision between Yale and Crowne Mawr. Yale has an established D1 hockey team and excellent degree programs."

"But," Mom says before Dad can get on a rant. "Crowne Mawr is closer to home. It's established academically and rivals Yale in programs. You get so caught up on having a legacy sometimes you forget it's not you who gets to go back to college." Mom smiles at me and winks.

"Cam will do what's right for Cam, but I agree we should tour the campus because it will give you a feel for the school."

I love my mom. Dad nods, and the conversation turns to hockey and how the college teams are stacking up this year. When we walk into dinner, I linger behind to walk in beside Evan.

"Is that all right with you, goody?" I can't help asking, because I'd prefer to stay cuddled in bed with her and Hawk than tour Yale.

She catches my hand. "It's a great idea for you to go visit Yale. You've never really given it a chance before."

She's right. I was so determined to not be like my dad that I dismissed his school choice. But now it is a real option with the four of us. If I want to give it a shot, I should really explore it as an option.

I walk with her to her spot at the dining room table and hold her chair out for her. I take her other side since Damon is already seated beside her. Hawk sits on the other side of Damon. Our parents sit across from us with Adam at the head of the table and Heather beside him.

I pause for a moment to remember this. Because this is our extended family if we get through this. This could be Christmases, weddings, birthdays, celebrating any kids we have. Fuck, this could actually work.

---

## Damon

"I don't like this." It's Saturday and we're getting ready to leave.

Evan sits cross-legged on my bed behind my suitcase. If I could pack her in my bag and take her with me, I would. But she has rehearsal tomorrow, and it's tech week. According to her, this is when it all comes together, and sleeping becomes an option.

"You have the opportunity to see what it'll be like if we go to Yale." She smiles softly at me. "It's just like the week you were gone to Crown Mawr, but shorter."

"Jackson will still be here," I say, which means it isn't exactly the same.

"And it's been weeks since anything really happened." She climbs off the bed and comes over to hug me. Her suitcase is already packed and waiting in her room. Hawk's supposed to be on his way to pick her up. As well as Cam and his family to join us at Yale.

I put my arms around Evan, and the temptation to fuck her one more time before I go crosses my mind, but everyone should be here shortly. I don't think they'll be cool with waiting for me to finish. Besides, sometimes it's just nice to just hold Evan.

"I'm going to be fine. Hawk can take care of me for one night." She blushes as I pull away.

"He's going to try bondage tonight?" I arch an eyebrow.

Her eyes flare hot. He's been talking about it nonstop all week. I kind of wish we could be there, or that they'd do it here in my room where I can watch.

"I packed the camera you gave me," she says as she lifts her stormy eyes to mine.

I smirk. "I love you."

"I love you, too. Now finish packing." She gestures for me to hurry up and sits on the edge of the bed.

"You don't go anywhere without Hawk." I put the last of my things in my bag and zip it up. "Promise me?"

"Where would I go?" She shakes her head. "Honestly, I'll be fine. You'll have an awesome trip and you'll be able to decide between two colleges as to where you want to spend the next four to five years with us."

I inhale, letting that sink in. She stands and presses her hand against my heart.

"You didn't lose your future with that accident," she says softly.

"No, I didn't. I gained my future." I slide my hand across the nape of her neck. "Fuck, does this mean I should thank Chase Chadwick?"

She laughs, and it fills my room and my heart. "No. No one has to thank that asshole. I can't wait for the show to end so I can go back to pretending he doesn't exist."

I draw Evan in and kiss her. My door is open. The only reasonable way to ensure I won't fuck Evan and make us all late.

But also makes it easy for someone to come in. Like Hawk.

"I'm here to collect my prize." He grins. "Best idea ever. I should have suggested it myself. Can you thank Cam's dad for leaving me with Annie all to myself?"

"You can thank him yourself." I glance at my clock and grab my bag. "They should be here any minute."

"My bag is in my room," she says.

Hawk goes through the bathroom to grab it and bring it with us as we head downstairs. Voices rise up the stairs. It sounds like Cam and his parents have already made it. We meet Cam on the steps and Evan stops a stair above him.

"I expect an excellent movie to watch when we return, goody." Cam grabs her chin and kisses her softly. When he pulls away, he holds out a red paper flower.

Evan has to work at my desk because she has so many of those on her desk she doesn't have any writing surface left. When I mentioned throwing any of them out, she hit my arm and told me off.

She smiles and kisses Cam again. He gives me a cocky smile before leading her down to the entryway where our parents are waiting.

Heather steps over to Evan, away from the others. "Are you sure you'll be okay? I can stay here and we can hang out tonight." She glances at the three of us behind Evan and shakes her head. "Though why you'd want to hang out with me when you've got them is beyond me."

Evan smiles and hugs her mom. "I'll always want to hang out with you, Mom."

Heather returns her hugs and then pulls away. "You haven't had any more texts, and nothing weird has happened, right?"

Evan shakes her head, but looks over her shoulder at me. "I've been a little busy, but the guys have been keeping an eye out."

Heather nods and turns to Hawk. "You'll keep her safe?"

"With my life," he says.

"Hopefully it won't come to that." Heather smiles.

Hawk takes Evan's hand and pulls her into his side. "We should head out while you guys get everything arranged."

Evan squeezes his hand before releasing it and walking over to Cam to give him a hug. When they pull apart, she turns to me and hugs me.

"No settling," she says softly. "We don't compromise on our futures."

I breathe in her woodsy scent and hold her for a moment longer than necessary.

"I'll see you tomorrow night," I say.

"Have a safe trip." She meets my eyes, and then Hawk leads her out of the house.

"All right," my dad says. "Let's load up."

## CHAPTER 41
## *Hawk*

My parents insist on having dinner with us Saturday night. And then we play a board game in the game room. Annie's gaze keeps going to the wall mural. There's a lot going on there. It's graphic, but with small characters similar to ancient wall art my mom found during her travels. Except it depicts the Kama Sutra.

I think Annie's face has been flushed all evening.

"Do you like the wall painting?" Mom asks like she's asking about a painting of a vase.

"It's interesting," Annie looks back at the tile game in front of us.

"I find it fascinating how repressed a country can be, but when you look at their art, it's filled with graphic depictions of sex and violence. There was this country house in England I visited that had the most interesting carvings in the woodwork. I didn't want to duplicate it, but Dante's Inferno inspired me to do something a little different with that empty wall."

Dad keeps his eyes on the board as he tries to determine what to pick next. "Naomi was an art major and is a buyer for several museums and private collectors. She loves finding unique pieces to add to our own collection."

Annie takes a drink of water and then picks up some tiles to add to her board. "I've enjoyed exploring the house and finding new pieces."

Mom beams. "I could show you the catalogues of what I've found for buyers. Some of the pieces range from ancient to a few years old. From a few hundred dollars to a few million. Art is fascinating. It's part of what makes us alive."

I take Annie's hand, and she gives me a smile. I figured she'd be anxious to get away from my parents, but I think she might actually be enjoying talking with them and playing board games.

It's a novelty to me now, but when I was younger, we used to play games every Friday night. I couldn't imagine ever getting back to this place, but it's comfortable. And the longer my parents are home, the less I want them to leave.

But I'm also not going to pretend they won't leave again. They didn't quit their jobs.

It's almost eleven when I finally call it, and tell my parents good night. Mom draws Annie in for a hug.

"Good night, sweet girl."

"Good night, Naomi." Annie raises her hand to wave good night to my dad, and I lead her up to my room. "They take this staying over thing seriously. I'm surprised they didn't offer me my own room."

"Did you want your own room?" I close the door and lock it.

Shaking her head, she gives me a flirty look over her shoulder. She walks to the bed and sits on the edge of it. Her loose, flowy blouse makes me want to slide it off her to reveal those curves I know she's hiding.

"Did you enjoy your evening, baby girl?" I unbutton my cuffs and roll my sleeve up to my elbow, before doing the same to the other side. Slowly, purposefully.

"Your parents are nice. I haven't played a board game in years." Her smile goes a little distant.

"Your father?" I don't let the moment pass because I know it's important to remember. To let the ones we lost into our everyday lives.

"Yeah." She focuses on me. "We used to play a game every weekend. He loved to try new games. At one point we had so many, Mom said he had to get rid of at least half."

"Did he?" I lean back against the door and cross my arms over my chest, letting her sit in the memory. Not pushing to bring the heat back. We'll get to it. I like learning about Annie.

She chuckles, and there's this wicked glint in her eyes. "We hid half of the games. I don't think she minded because at least she wasn't tripping over them. But she had to know. We weren't very sneaky about it. Under beds, in closets."

"We could play board games anytime you want." I want her to tell me what she wants. What she needs. So I can be that for her. I want to give her everything.

She arches an eyebrow and leans her hands behind her on the bed. "I'd rather play games with you."

When she unpacked, she set up one of Damon's cameras to focus on the bed. I'm going to play with her how I like, but my girl likes an audience, live or recorded.

I rub my fingers across my lips and look her over. "Take off your clothes, baby girl."

She straightens and lifts the shirt off over her head, letting it float to the ground next to my bed. She drops her bra next. Her breasts are tight peaks waiting for my mouth. My cock throbs, aching to be buried inside her.

Standing, she unbuttons her jeans. Over the course of the evening, she walked barefoot through my house, leaving her sandals next to the door. She shimmies her jeans over her hips and down her legs before stepping out of them. The only thing remaining is her panties.

She hooks her thumbs in the sides and meets my gaze. I don't say or do anything as she pushes them over her hips and down her legs. They join the rest of her clothes in a pile.

"Get on the bed and crawl to the headboard."

Her darkened eyes flash at me as she kneels on the bed and falls to her hands. Swaying her ass as she crawls to the top of my bed.

"Stay like that, baby girl." Fuck, I could spend all night jacking off to her like this, but I won't. I'm tempted to fuck her, so that initial need is out of the way, but I like the way it feels to sit in the ache, make her beg for it while my body strains with the need to fuck.

If I relieve my ache, I'll ease hers too. I want her begging for it. I verify the door is locked and walk around the bed to the nightstand. Not that my parents will check on us. She turns her head to see what

I'm doing. I open the top drawer and put what I need on the nightstand.

A bottle of lube, a butt plug, a vibrator with a clit stimulator, and a few condoms.

Annie's brow furrows. "Condoms?"

I smirk and take her in. "So I can fuck your ass and then fuck your pussy or mouth. They'll just make transitions cleaner. Fewer trips to the bathroom."

She swallows and her waist dips slightly as she pushes her hips back. She's already so fucking needy. Her pussy glistens for me. I reach in for the last things.

I pull the silk through my fingers. Three pieces of fabric, all broad.

Her gaze lifts to mine, and she wets her lips.

"There are other things I want to try with you, but this is a start to see how you like it." I sit on the edge of the bed next to her, but don't touch her. I show her the fabric. "I'm going to tie your wrists to the headboard and blindfold you. At some point I might spread your legs and tie them to the footboard as well."

She releases a little moan at the thought.

I smirk. "We'll see what's most comfortable for you before I share you with the guys this way."

She trembles but nods.

"Maybe I'll try tying your wrists to your ankles at some point." I drag the silk over her back down her ass cheek. "Leave you spread open for us to take."

"Hawk," she whimpers.

"You'll come when I tell you you can, baby girl. Otherwise, I'll punish you."

Her eyes flare hot, remembering the spanking.

"I could decide to punish you by going to sleep without letting you come again." I arch an eyebrow at her pout. "But you're going to be my good girl, aren't you?"

"Yes, sir."

There's something sexy about her giving herself to me, to let me use her how I want. I want to share her with my friends this way. Control how much and what she takes until she's completely satiated.

"Come here, baby girl." I put my feet up on the bed and rest against the headboard.

She crawls to me, uncertain what to do next.

"Undo my pants and take out my cock."

She sits back on her heels. I study her naked body while she does as she's told. She's so fucking wet she'd be able to sit on my cock and ride it if I wanted her to. But I want her to be almost mindless when I take her. To be so lost in desire she just needs to be fucked any way I give it to her.

When my cock is free, she strokes it with her hand and looks up to me to see what's next.

"Suck my cock."

She wets her lips and lowers her mouth over me. I let her toy and tease me with her lips and tongue. As she slides up and down over my cock, she rubs her thighs together, probably wishing I was deep inside her instead of making her suck on me. I know this gets her off too.

"Enough."

She lifts her head and sits on her heels. Her pupils are blown wide. Her nipples beg me to suck them.

"Straddle my lap, facing away from me. On your hands and knees." I help her shift into position so her pussy is open before me. Presenting herself to me. I slide my fingers over her pussy and she moans. So fucking sensitive.

When I take my fingers away, she whimpers. Chuckling, I pick up the lube and the plug, carefully spreading the lube over the entire surface while she waits to feel what I'm going to do next.

"Lower your head to the bed."

She does as I ask, and I spread her ass cheeks. I drizzle lube over her puckered hole and use the tip of the plug to spread it before pushing it in and pulling it out of her asshole. Just the tip. She lets out a little noise and tries to widen her legs.

"More, please, sir," she tries to look back at me, but the angle is wrong for that.

I ease the plug in farther, keeping pressure on it until the whole thing is seated in her ass. I twist it lazily, letting her adjust to the stretch.

"Put your hands on my legs."

She repositions her hands. I grab onto her hips and draw them down until my cock presses at her entrance. She gasps in a breath.

"Please, sir," she whispers. Her hips buck instinctually.

I pull her down on me. Her cunt is tight with the plug in her ass, but she's so wet and so eager, I slide in easily. She pushes down on me to get every inch inside her. When she tries to lift herself, I grab her hips and prevent her from moving.

"Sir?"

"What, baby girl? What do you need? What is it that you want from me? Do you want me to fuck you like this? You can ride my cock while I stroke your clit until you come all over me."

"Yes, please."

"Or," I pause. "I can tie you to the bed and decide how I'll fuck you in the moment. When I want to. When I need to come. I'll take your pussy or your ass or your mouth over and over again. Maybe I'll let you come."

She bites her lip, and her pussy clenches around my cock. I tighten my fingers on her hips, needing the friction, to fuck up into her. Even if she chooses this, I won't be done with her for the night, but she can think whatever she needs to so she makes the correct decision.

"Tie me, sir."

I release her hips and she pulls off me with a whimper of need. "Good girl."

When I lean forward and kiss her pussy, she trembles.

"Back to where you were. Hands and knees facing the headboard."

She slowly moves back into the position that doesn't have her touching me at all. She gazes over at me with stormy eyes. I lick the taste of her off my lips and grab the silk ties.

"Sit back on your heels." I wait for her to settle where I want her. "Lean down on the bed with your arms spread in a V above you. Keep your ass on your heels."

She does as she's told and turns her head to watch me. I grab the closest wrist and bind it to the nearest slat in my headboard. She watches patiently, not moving because I haven't told her to.

I stand up and undress before returning with the other tie. I straddle her waist and lean over her to reach her hand, tying it as far away from the other as I can get. My skin brushes against hers, and she releases needy little noises. Wanting more. Needing more.

I'll give it to her on my terms.

"Comfortable?" I leave the bindings a little loose to not cut off circulation.

"Yes, sir."

I take the remaining tie, and careful of her hair, I blindfold her with it. I move to sit next to her, studying how I have her positioned and determining what I want to do first. I slide my hand beneath her breast and cup the weight in my hand.

Her nipple grazes my palm and I slide my fingers over it before pinching it. She gasps and her hips spread as she tugs on the bindings.

"Eager to have a cock in you, baby girl?"

"Yes, sir." She pushes her hips back against the air.

I move behind her. "Show me."

"Sir?"

"How much you want my cock? Show me your pussy and how much it aches for me."

She lifts her hips hesitantly, opening her legs more. She doesn't know where I am. When I move to kneel between her legs, she can probably feel the dip of the mattress.

"What do you say when you want something to stop?" I don't touch her.

"*Red* for stop, *yellow* for pause. Please don't stop, sir." She keeps her ass lifted as much as she can.

I grab the vibrator and the condom off the nightstand and place a towel on the bed beside us. I push the vibrator against her entrance.

"We haven't played with toys yet." I push it in all the way.

She releases a huff of breath. "No, sir."

I fuck her with it a few times. "Does it feel different?"

"Yes, sir."

"Good?"

"Yes, sir."

I turn on the vibration on low and press the clit stimulator against her. She lets out a startled moan before she rocks with my thrusts of the vibrator.

"You like being stuffed full, don't you? A cock in all your holes. It's not the same with toys, is it?"

"No, sir." Her voice is breathless.

"Don't worry, baby girl, I'll fix it." I push the vibrator in, and leave it while I put a condom on and spread lube over it.

Her hips rock, but without the pressure of my hand the vibrator isn't hitting where she wants it to. She whimpers in frustration.

"It's okay. I've got you." I get on my knees and push the vibrator in holding it against her throbbing clit. She almost collapses in relief. I pull out the plug and set it on the towel. She whimpers like she does when she's close.

I reposition her and ease my cock into her asshole. I'm halfway in when she comes, tightening around my cock.

I smack her ass. "I didn't say to come."

"Sorry, sir," she doesn't sound sorry at all.

I thrust the rest of the way into her ass and she moans. Reaching below, I click the vibrator up a notch. Her already sensitive clit won't stand a chance.

"Sir, I need to come. Please let me come."

"Tell me how good it feels."

The words spill off her tongue in a cascade. "I love the way you feel inside my ass. You fill me so fucking full. I want your cum inside me. I need you to fuck me. Fuck me hard and let me come on your cock again. Please, sir. I need it. I'll die without it."

"So dramatic." I grab her hips and draw my cock out of her ass before thrusting back inside.

"I'm going to... I can't... please..." She cries as I begin to thrust in and out of her ass fucking her. The vibrator still presses inside her pussy, making her even tighter. Her body tenses, and I know she's going to come.

"Come for me, baby girl. Milk my cock."

She moans as her release swells over her. She tightens on my cock like a fist. I fuck her through it until I feel like I'm going to come. Pulling out, I strip the condom off. Removing the vibrator, I thrust deep into her pussy, and she groans with pleasure.

I fuck her hard and fast, feeling her tighten again. When she comes with a cry, I feel my release overwhelm me. I fuck into her a few more times before filling her with my cum.

For a minute, I stay there, connected with her while we breathe chaotically. I roll onto my back next to her. She pants and trembles, still in position.

"I'm not close to done playing with you. How do you feel?" I slide my hand over her breast, and she trembles beneath my touch.

"So good, sir." Her words are soft and breathy.

I smirk and slide my hand between her legs, sliding over her pussy. She whimpers.

"I promise to let you sleep a little, Annie."

## CHAPTER 42
## EvanAnn

EATING breakfast with Hawk's parents after he made me cum so hard I nearly screamed the house down is a whole new level of awkwardness for me. He did let me sleep, but he also fucked me so good. I'm a little sore, mostly from the ass play, but it was worth it.

"Did you sleep okay?" Naomi asks.

"Yes." My cheeks flush with heat, and I glance at Hawk. Last night was a lot and I'm used to three of them using me. He gives me a soft, loving smile.

"You have rehearsal this afternoon?" she asks while pouring milk into her tea.

"Yes, it's a long one." Hawk lifts his coffee cup and winks at me. "We're doing a complete run through and starting on the tech aspect. We'll be getting done about the time Cam and Damon get back into town."

"Well, that will be nice." Naomi takes a sip of her tea. "It was a pleasure having you at our house, EvanAnn."

"Thank you for having me." Even as the words leave my mouth, I try not to look at the smirk on Hawk's lips. He definitely had me last night. Over and over again.

"Anytime you need a place to crash. You can sleep here."

"Thank you." I really do mean it. It's weird that my mom finding someone to move on with also made it so I moved on and got my guys and their parents in my life as well. I glance at Paul, who still has a dour expression on his face. I'm pretty sure that's just who he is and less about me. Hopefully. Maybe not all the parents are all in, but it's nice they respect our decision to be together.

After breakfast, we go back up to Hawk's room to hang out. While he studies at his desk, I spread out my work on his bed. There's one thing I've been dreading having to do, but I know it's time.

I pick up my phone and open my text message thread with Mia.

ME:

> Hey, I know things are difficult right now and I don't want to add to that, but we have to move forward with the play. You would have made an amazing Desdemona and blown everyone away with your performance. With only a week until performance, we won't be able to work you back into the cast in time. I'm so sorry and I hope your brother is doing better. If you want to talk, I'm here for you. I wish I had better things to say, but the show must go on.

> I miss you.

I hit send and then fall back onto the bed. Hawk glances over at me, and I turn my face toward him.

"Why do I feel like I just broke up with my best friend?"

Hawk sets his pen down and comes over to sit beside me on the bed. I move up so my arms are around his waist, and he holds me close. "You did what you had to. She'll understand. This is part of the business. It has nothing to do with whether you like her or not."

"I know, but it still feels shitty." I release my breath and squeeze him.

"The guys will be home later after rehearsal. We should go out and get ice cream or something."

I pull back, confused and amused, and raise my gaze to his. "Ice cream? What are we, twelve?"

"You don't like ice cream?" he asks with a look that says he wouldn't believe me if I said no. "You don't have to be a kid to eat ice cream.

Besides, when we're in public, it's less likely someone will strip you naked and fuck you. I, for one, would like to hear about the Yale visit prior to the fuckery."

I can't help the giggle that slips out. "We need to get you away from Shakespeare for a while."

For a second, I just hold him and consider that maybe Mia won't be mad at me for taking her part.

"Do you want to talk about Mia?" he asks softly.

I sit up and look at my phone. It's been days since she's responded, but I can't imagine what she's going through. Actually, I can imagine, and what I imagine is hopefully worse than what she's dealing with. It would be nice to hear from her, but I'm not pushing it.

"No." I release my breath. "Maybe. I don't know. I mean, according to Jackson, she was my stalker all along. But if that was the case, why not gloat about it? Also, nothing has happened since she left which does point in her direction again. But maybe the stalker is just busy. And then there's Brandt. Where the fuck does he fit in this mess? And am I shooting myself in the foot by replacing Mia in the play? Mr. Watson seemed to think it was a brilliant plan, and I made sure to tell him it was Keira's idea, but what if it isn't smart? What if I choke?"

Hawk chuckles. "I'm not sure if you want me to answer any of that, but you aren't going to choke. I'm angry at Anteros for making you choose directing over acting."

"I was being typecast." I shrug. "It was a thing, and I really enjoy directing."

"Fuck that. You should have been working on both, and everyone in your cast knows it. The way you flawlessly stepped into Mia's shoes and took over that role without even missing a beat is..."

"Amazing?" I arch an eyebrow and smirk. "I've been told."

"You have what it takes, and anyone would have to be blind to not realize your potential. It's like Damon on the ice. I could maybe push myself to be as good as he is now, but I will never reach the same potential he has. You're both going to grow so much in the next four years, and I want to be with you every step of the way, reminding you both how amazing you are."

We're working through act four, but everyone is dragging a little. It's a lot of stop, fix this, wait, okay, let's keep going. Next week we'll take it act-by-act through tech and put it together a few times before performances begin.

I glance at Keira, and she nods.

"You're doing great, but let's take a fifteen minute break." I smile as everyone almost breathes a sigh of relief. I love that this school focuses on making us professional. No one's going to let their crabbiness shine through, or the next time they probably won't be cast.

Hawk stops and gives me a kiss. "I'll be right back."

"Okay." I'm a little surprised. I'm used to having a guy practically on top of me during breaks.

He holds my hand as he walks away and then lets it go. But I have stuff to do. I turn back to my desk and drag in a breath. This week is going to be hell week, but at least Damon and Cam will be back.

Wanting to check on something, I walk across the stage to behind the set. We have a lot of moving parts in this production, and I want to make sure the prop table is set up well. The backstage crew must have decided to take the break, which is good.

I know they have a lot more opportunity to sit during the performance, so I let them do what they want.

"EvanAnn."

I turn at Chase's voice. He looks nervous to be talking to me, rubbing the back of his neck and hunching his shoulders like he doesn't want to be doing this.

"What can I do for you?" Professional. I can stay professional.

"I want to apologize for being such an asshole." He looks over his shoulder, but then turns his blue eyes to mine. "You've been more than fair with me in this production."

"Okay?" I'm waiting for the other shoe to drop. A cold breeze wafts my way. Sometimes with the lights on, it gets stifling behind the stage, and someone will prop open the door. If they do, someone is supposed to stay close and shut it before leaving.

I move that way to close the door. Chase follows me.

"My dad says I need to make amends to you for how I treated you."

"You never apologized for real when you fucked around on me and thought I'd give you another chance. Everything out of your mouth was fake or a lie, so why do you think I'd believe you now?" As I turn the corner, something makes the hair on the back of my neck stand on end. Kind of like when you walk into somewhere you aren't supposed to be, but it's stupid because I'm supposed to be here.

Chase sighs. "What I did to you was shitty, but Brandt is by far the bigger asshole. I'm pretty sure he talked Mia into being your friend this year."

I turn to look at him. "What are you talking about, Chase?"

"You know how Iago doesn't do anything directly to anyone?"

I nod and gesture for him to get to the point.

"That's Brandt. He just whispers in people's ears or gets them into tight spots where they don't have a choice but to do what he tells them to." Chase runs his hand through his hair. "He convinced me you'd be perfect for me."

I cross my arms as the breeze wafts through again. "I need to close the door."

When I turn around, someone steps out of the shadows. For a second, I don't think anything about it. It must be one of the backstage hands or extras. Good, they were at least keeping a watch over it.

"Do you have the door open? Because we really should have it closed at night. It's a breach in protocol for the theater," I say in a nice tone, but firm. "It's a security risk."

The shadow comes closer and grows taller. It grabs my arm and jerks me toward it.

"What?" I stumble forward into what feels like a brick wall of a person.

"Hey!" Chase yells and moves forward.

The shadow shoves me away from Chase. Before I can catch myself, I fall to the ground. Something hits the side of my head, and blackness engulfs me.

## CHAPTER 43
### *Hawk*

I GO to the exterior doors to let Damon and Cam in. Because we're the only ones in the building, it's locked up.

"You didn't tell her we caught an earlier flight?" Cam asks. He strides in and looks down the empty hallway like I'm hiding Annie behind my back.

"And ruin the surprise?" I run a hand over my hair. "Honestly, she's a hot mess today, and I didn't want her watching the clock, knowing you guys would be here. But we're on break now."

"Did she text Mia?" Damon asks.

I nod. "She's worried she lost her best friend. And also worried her best friend was fucking with her life, since we haven't been able to clear Mia."

Cam leads the way to the theater room. "How's the play going?"

"Good. Everyone's doing well." When I open the doors, I'm surprised Annie isn't where I left her. She was ready to do notes just like she always does, but maybe she had to use the bathroom.

Damon looks around like Annie might be hiding from him. "Bathroom?"

"Maybe?" I really didn't expect her to disappear in the few minutes it took to go get the guys.

Keira walks in, looking at her tablet.

"Hey, did you see Annie?" I ask.

Keira looks up at me and then at the others. "Hey, guys. What?"

She's as bad as Annie sometimes. "Annie. Was she wherever you were?"

"I don't think so, but I was trying to figure out what the lighting tech is trying to do for the soliloquy. She probably could have walked right past me, honestly." Keira makes her way to the table. "She'll be back when the time is up."

Damon turns and heads out into the hallway.

"Where are you going?" I ask, following him.

"Checking the bathroom."

"Seriously?" I shake my head. "She's fine. If you're worried, check your phone."

He stops and pulls out his phone and brings up the app that tracks Annie's phone. It doesn't give an exact location, but it shows her phone is in this wing of the building.

"We're the only ones here. The other play was scheduled for earlier in the day, so everyone could use the larger black box theater. You don't have to hunt her down in the bathroom."

"Fine." Damon walks back into the theater room and calls her phone.

"She's not going to answer in the bathroom." Cam rolls his eyes.

"But she'll text."

The phone goes to voicemail. More people are returning from break. Mark says hi as he passes, but he tends to want to stay in character between scenes.

Damon waits a few seconds and then he pulls up the other app for Annie's ring. It takes a moment to upload. He straightens suddenly. "What the fuck?"

I glance over his shoulder. The dot is speeding away from the theater. I pull up Annie's phone tracker and it still shows her phone here. I press the play-sound button to find her phone. A very slight beep sounds over the people chatting while waiting for the break to be over.

"Keira, something's wrong," I say. "I need quiet."

"Hey, I need everyone to be quiet!" Her yell fills the room.

Crystal stops next to Keira. "Have you seen Chase? He's not in the hallway."

I hit play-sound again.

"It's coming from over here," someone says from near the set.

I lead the way behind the temporary walls. The phone continues to go off. It's dark, so I turn on the flashlight app.

Damon hurries ahead when he sees someone on the floor, but it's clearly not Annie. He picks up Annie's phone and hands it to me. She dropped it or someone might have tried to break it. The screen protector is shattered. He rolls the guy over, and his face is unrecognizable from swelling.

"Fuck, is that Chase?" Cam says.

"Call 9-1-1!" Damon yells, checking for a pulse and breathing, and then steps over Chase. He moves into a small antechamber and pushes open a door below an exit sign. It leads outside.

My heart pounds so loudly in my ears. She's not here. Fuck. I study the surrounding area for any clues to who or what happened to her.

Damon steps outside and looks around. He holds his phone up to see where the dot is and takes a screenshot. "Does someone have him?"

He must be talking about Chase. Mark hovers over him. "Yeah, we'll get him medical attention."

"Good."

"Where's EvanAnn?" Keira asks in a very small, worried voice.

Damon glances at her. "That's what we're going to find out. Hawk, stay here, find out if anyone saw anything. Chase is going to wake up, and hopefully he knows more."

I'm looking around the area with my flashlight when I see a blood smear on a wooden stool. My stomach twists. "Damon."

He turns and looks. He glances over at Chase, who doesn't appear to be bleeding. Whoever took her might have hurt her.

"9-1-1 will send everything. Police, ambulance, fire truck. Tell the police when they arrive. You have her location and ours." Damon clasps my hand. "We'll get her back."

I swallow down the fear and nod. Cam and Damon head out the door and walk around the building. I turn back and look for a stagehand. When I find Rob, I stop him.

"Did someone have this door open?"

Rob opens his mouth and closes it a few times before nodding his head. "It-it gets hot."

I nod. At least that's one mystery solved. Someone left the door open, which might be why Annie came back here. But why was Chase here? Was he harassing her? Did he lead her back here and get betrayed?

I walk through the main area where everyone is gathered. When I glance at Keira, she nods. Practice is cancelled. This is a fucking crime scene.

"If anyone saw anything, please let us know. We all need to stay here until the authorities arrive. Make yourselves comfortable." Keira goes to her desk.

"Hawk?" Sophie tugs at my sleeve before I reach the door to the hallway. I just need a minute to calm myself before I start asking people what they saw.

I glare down at her. I don't have any time for her bullshit. My stomach is in knots. I shouldn't have left Annie alone, but she wasn't. She's never alone during practice.

Sophie wrings her hands and has that horribly guilty look like she did something wrong.

"He told me not to say anything, and then I didn't want to get in trouble. This is my first real break at this school. A junior in a pretty important role." She glances over her shoulder like she's afraid someone will overhear, and I grab her arm to drag her into the hallway.

The door closes behind us, and I release her. "What are you talking about?"

"The rose. I didn't know it was going to hurt her, and then it did and you were so angry. I didn't want you mad at me. I just thought he liked her, and if she liked him, maybe she'd break up with you, and then we could be together. And I know now that was stupid, but he made it sound so fucking easy and real." She's practically trembling.

I take a slow breath. I filter through all the words. "The rose? You put it on the desk?"

She lifts her face and tears stream down her cheeks. "I did. He didn't want me to touch it though, so he gave me a glove. It was odd, but a lot of kids in the art school are odd. Maybe he just didn't want my germs on it. I didn't know. I put the note and the rose on her script so she wouldn't miss it. But when she picked it up..." She covers her mouth, and the tears multiply.

"Sophie, listen to me. You're not going to get in trouble. I need to know who gave you the rose." I keep my tone flat and sympathetic, but inside I'm raging. The temptation to ruin her life pulses through me, but I have other things to focus on.

"I thought he liked her. I thought it was a gift." She cries a little more, wasting precious time. "I wouldn't have done it if I'd known."

"Who, Sophie?"

She peeks up at me. "Brandt."

---

## Damon

There's this tight feeling in my chest, like I can't take a full breath. Someone took her. Someone took her when I was right here. If I'd been earlier. If I'd told her we would be there. If, if, if.

Whoever has her has a lead on us, and they aren't moving slowly. I don't want to think about the blood smear or how badly Chase was beaten up. Is that how they managed to take Evan? They hurt her?

I'll kill them if they hurt her.

"Hey, you okay?" Cam connects to our helmets instead of the phone. He made some calls while we tracked the dot.

"Did you get ahold of them?" I'm not examining that cold feeling in the pit of my stomach. That empty space that Evan usually fills. She's alive. She has to be.

"Yeah, my mom and dad were still at your house. Adam talked to me. Wanted me to send the tracking information so he could let the authorities know."

"When we stop." It's not exactly something he can do while we ride, and we've already wasted too much time.

"That's what I told him." Cam rides alongside me. "My dad can track my phone, so they'll have that."

I have my phone set so I can watch the map. The dot has stopped moving, but it's still too far away for us to catch up quickly. Suddenly, it blinks out of existence. One second it's there, the next second it's gone.

I pull to the side of the road. Fuck. "Pull it up on your phone."

Cam stops next to me and takes off his gloves to use his phone. "No signal for the ring."

"Fuck," I look at the spot where the signal was lost.

"It could pick it back up. Maybe it just went through a bad spot."

"Maybe this whole area is a fucking bad spot." Why did I think I could control this? Why did I think she was safe? Just because I put a piece of jewelry on her and called her mine?

But I didn't think she was safe. She was always with one of us. Always with other people. Fuck, she was with Chase when she was taken. What the fuck was Chase doing with her? Did he set it up and whoever took her fucked him up as payment?

"We're going to find her." Cam's words are low and steady.

"Let's drive to where we lost the signal. Call Hawk and let him know. See if he's found out anything." I put my engine into first gear and shift up as we head down the road. No matter what, I'm going to find her.

---

## *EvanAnn*

My head aches as I try to open my eyes. Whatever I'm on rattles below me and is moving. The road noise next to my ear is constant. When the vehicle goes over a bump, I bounce slightly. I groan as my head hits the solid surface again.

"You awake, pretty girl?"

Jackson. Ice flows through my veins and fear holds my breath. Fuck. I'm disoriented and can't seem to make myself think straight.

"Just a second."

As he brakes, I slide on what must be the floor of a vehicle, but it's not cushioned and it's flat. I clutch at my head, trying to keep the throbbing down. My hand gets wet and sticky. Blood. Fuck.

The engine idles still, but the road noise stops. The door locks engage loudly as he moves around inside the vehicle. I still can't open my eyes, but I know I should. I should fight. Kick his ass and get the fuck out. Run.

"You hit your head on a wooden stool. I didn't think you'd fall, but I needed to make sure that asshole knew not to touch what's mine."

Ice runs through my veins. Gentle hands touch my head, and he even hisses when he feels the lump. I want to flinch away, but I can't. It hurts too much.

"I had to get you away before I could help you." He lifts me to sitting, and my head spins like he tipped me upside down. "You might have a concussion."

I focus on feeling my left hand, scraping my thumbnail against my ring finger. My ring is still in place. I doubt he would have kept my phone, but maybe it's still in the van somewhere. Turning it off would cut the signal, so there's a chance he brought it, and I can get it back. If not, I could take his phone and use it.

I open my eyes a crack, and the pain is harsh, but doable. Worried, dark brown eyes meet mine. I want to scream and pull away, but I can barely focus.

"Just a little bit farther, and I'll get some ice for your head." He reaches into a bag and pulls out a white t-shirt. He holds it against my head, practically wincing from the pain that he's causing.

I barely knew Jackson in elementary school. I barely knew him when I was sixteen. This year, the times I was with him were brief. We tried to know him without knowing him to figure him out.

Now, I have no choice. I need to know him. I have to understand everything about his character. What drives him? What makes him angry? What makes him calm? What is it he wants from me that he can't get from anyone else?

He's jealous of Damon. Did he hook up with Mia or was that a lie? It hurts to think, so I take the shirt and hold it to my head.

"Only a little longer, and we'll be there. I promise I have some ice, and you can lie down where it's comfortable." He moves away, and I watch him through narrowed slits.

I'm in a minivan without seats in the back. Even the carpet has been torn up, leaving the floor bare metal. He climbs into the driver's seat and puts it in drive. There's a green light on the dash.

I'm not bound to anything. My hands and feet are free. I could move if I wanted to. If I could move without my head feeling like it's going to explode. Then reality sets in quickly. I wouldn't get two feet before he recaptured me and decided to make escape impossible.

The van goes down roads in bad repair. My head throbs, and the bumpy road shakes my poor, rattled skull until I want to scream. But I remain quiet, trying to think while also not trying to think.

I cradle my head, praying for the road to smooth out. Praying for the guys to find me. Praying for a flat tire to slow him down. Anything. To give me an edge, because my greatest asset is my brain, and right now, it hurts too much to think.

I must pass out because when I'm conscious again the movement is different. More like rocking, like carrying. I'm being carried. There's fresh air on my face. Maybe one of the guys found me. I sigh, but as I breathe in sharp cologne, my situation reasserts itself. My head hurts, but I remember waking up in the car. The bumps that wouldn't quit.

I keep my eyes shut and try to even out my breathing so he thinks I'm asleep. Fuck, I should look around while it feels and smells like we're outside. My hands and feet are still free. But when I try to open my eyes, all I see is darkness.

It was cloudy earlier, so even the moon doesn't peek through. Forcing myself, I open my eyes wider to let them adjust to the dark.

"I would have parked closer, but it's better if I abandon the car as far away as possible." Jackson talks like we're having a conversation. Like I asked. Is he delusional? Can I play into his delusion long enough to gain his trust?

The rocking makes my stomach churn. Wait, no, my stomach really is churning. When I push away from him and vomit onto the ground, he shakes his head.

"Concussion. You shouldn't have jerked away in the theater." As if it's my fault, he grabbed me. "Ice pack and rest should help."

I drag my sleeve across my mouth and tuck my hands into the hoodie's sleeves. The ring isn't obviously a tracker, but if he thinks it's from Damon, he'll want to get rid of it. And that's my only link to the Devil's trio right now.

I need to keep it on my person as long as possible. If I say it's from my dad, would he be more or less likely to let me keep it?

He keeps walking for what feels like forever. Finally he shifts me against him and says, "Here we are."

I can see the shadow of a farmhouse with an old wooden porch. There are a few open fields around it and trees closer to the house. It doesn't look like any place I've ever been. My heart pounds so loudly I'm sure he can hear it. I swallow down my fear.

This isn't some place I can run from. There's nowhere to hide. The fields have all been harvested, leaving open stretches as far as I can see. I'd have to outrun him. And right now, my head hurts so much I'm not even sure I can stand. The cleared fields also means no one can sneak up on the house unless the occupants are distracted.

My mouth is dry and tastes like sick. If I try to get away now, I won't get very far. And the attempt will cost me the freedom he's giving me. But it's possible that as soon as I'm inside the house, the limited freedom I have could be taken from me. I need him to think I can't move at all, or that it's too painful to move.

Unfortunately, that's a little too close to the truth. I need to keep him focused on me so that if help comes, they have a chance of getting here without him hurting them.

I don't know how I'm going to manage to get out of this. All I can do is hope the ring keeps me connected to the guys so they can find me.

# CHAPTER 44
## *Hawk*

"No one saw anything," I say into the Bluetooth in my helmet connected to my phone. I told them what Sophie said. "Chase wasn't able to give me anything. The police are aware Annie's missing. I'm on my way to talk to Brandt."

"The rose always felt wrong," Cam says. "From everything the stalker did, the rose was the only thing that hurt her."

"Apparently whatever game Brandt was playing wasn't happening fast enough for him." Damon's voice is little more than a growl. It's probably a good thing he isn't coming with me. Though I could probably use someone to hold me back, I'm not sure either of them would be willing to.

They hit a dead end. The GPS tracker is either lost or outside of service, or the asshole who took her brought a GPS blocker. Meaning, even if Damon had tagged her like a pet, it still wouldn't give us anything.

"There isn't much out this way," Cam says. They've pulled up a map to try to figure out what direction the stalker might have taken her. For all we know, he could be driving her out of the state.

I'm sure our parents would prefer us to wait with them and stay out of the police's way, but fuck that. This is our girl. We're not fucking losing her waiting on bureaucracy and fucking warrants.

"We need to find out who all Brandt was using." Damon breathes out. "This could still be Jackson. For all we know, Mia is back and wants to hurt Evan for taking her role."

"I'll find out what Brandt knows." I'm getting close to his house.

"Try to find out before you rearrange his face," Cam says. "There's a few old farms around this area. We'll start there and let you know if we find anything."

"Good luck." I disconnect as I pull up to the gated home. I press the button on the intercom and wait. Breaking in and holding a knife against his throat until he tells me everything would have been preferable and saved time, but also probably would have gotten me arrested. I need to be able to help Annie and can't do that if I'm locked up.

"Can we help you?" The voice in the box is tinny.

"Hawk Wilker. I'm a friend of Brandt's and need to talk to him." Keep it simple.

"Just a second."

I tap my finger while I wait. Every second is wasted unless Brandt gives me information. Hopefully, he lets me in. Otherwise, the knife plan is looking better and better.

The gate buzzes and then opens. I ride up the long driveway to the house. It's opulent and fancy like any rich kid's house. Just a little more over the top. I park my bike and take off my helmet. A girl in a dress stands in the doorway. This must be Elizabeth Stanwell.

She leans in the door with her arms crossed and an arrogant, knowing smile on her lips.

"You're lucky I'm home for the weekend." Elizabeth smirks. "I doubt Brandt would have let you in. But I'm bored and love a little entertainment."

I hook my helmet on my handlebar and walk up the steps. "Are you going to show me where he is?"

She smiles and shrugs. "Probably."

I narrow my eyes on her. "He has information I need."

"Don't we all?" She chuckles.

"I don't have time to play games," I bite out.

"Pity. I do so enjoy games." She backs up a step. "I guess I'll just have to enjoy you tearing my brother a new one. Come on. Mom and Dad are out for the evening."

I pocket my gloves and leave the knife tucked in my pocket. There's more than one way to get information. If the nice way doesn't work, I'm willing to try whatever it takes. Annie is gone. Someone took her, and I doubt they have plans to keep her nice and safe. Time is of the essence.

Elizabeth leads me out to the backyard where Brandt lounges in slacks and a shirt beside the pool. When he sees me, his eyes widen before a smile cuts across his face.

"Are you ready to switch sides then?" Brandt pushes the chair next to him with a nudge of his foot. "I mean, why back a sinking ship?"

I take the chair and lean forward with my hands clasped. I glance at Elizabeth, who watches me with curiosity in her eyes. She wants to know how I'm going to handle this. I doubt she'll intervene unless things get messy.

"I need your help," I say, because everything else I want to say sounds threatening. And I can't do anything to this knob until I figure out where Annie is or narrow down the suspect pool.

"With what? Your lines? Your acting ability?" Brandt chuckles. "I have to admit, you definitely surprised me at the auditions, but this—" he gestures around him. "This is even more surprising. You and EvanAnn seemed pretty solid, so why would you come to me for help?"

"It's not about acting." Though I'm sure these two do more than their fair share of lying.

"Okay? What can I do for you?"

"The rose was you." Fuck this little game. "We have the rose and a witness."

Brandt smirks and holds up his hands like I caught him. "You've got me. What do you want, a confession?" He leans forward and drops his hands. "Actually, do you have me? Or do you just have someone's story of what they said happened? Because my guess is that won't hold up in any court."

He lifts his glass and takes a drink while watching me.

I smile. "You should know by now that we don't use courts."

"Oh, I like him." Elizabeth takes a chair and crosses her legs. "This is the guy who posted the video of Chase, right?"

I glance at her because if I can't get information out of Brandt, she might know enough to get me where I need to be.

"We don't have time to play games." I meet Brandt's gaze and see the slight hint of fear before he hides it. Good, I want him afraid of what I might do to him. He should know I'm willing to do anything for Annie. "Whatever you set in motion now has legal ramifications."

Brandt chuckles and leans back in his chair like he has all the time in the world. "What did I set in motion?"

"Jackson Riordan." It's not unreasonable to think Jackson was part of Brandt's game.

Elizabeth grabs a wineglass from the table next to her and takes a sip. "Some people just don't play well with others."

"Some people don't follow the rules," Brandt says to his sister with a look.

"I mean, Olivia was already a loose cannon." Elizabeth shakes her head with a wry smile. "She drugged a girl to try to get the guy. What did you expect with someone as unhinged as Riordan?"

"He's like the rest—easily controlled." Brandt looks at me like he just remembered I'm in their space. It's fake like everything he does. "So what do you want to know? I'm sure you can keep this between us, right? No need to involve anyone on the rose. It was a little more potent than I was led to believe." Brandt glances at Elizabeth with an admonishing look.

She shrugs. "You're the one that picked a thorny rose. A few thorns would have been enough. Just like I did to Alison. She didn't have to go to urgent care, but she got the point." She winks at me like I'm in on the joke.

"I need to know everything." I glance at my phone. Every fucking second matters and these two will toy with each other indefinitely if I don't rein them in.

"Okay. Everything." Brandt blows out his breath. "That's a tall order." He stands and makes his way over to the bar. "Do you want a drink? Because this could take a while." He holds up a bottle of scotch.

I stand and look at the two of them. "You miscalculated."

"Impossible." Brandt smirks and pours himself a glass. "I'm meticulous about the details."

"I need to know who was stalking Annie." We don't know who took her. We don't know who all is involved.

"The list of suspects is long, isn't it?" Brandt returns to his chair and looks up at me. "Is she spiraling yet? Is that why you decided to confront me? Poor little Annie can't focus on her play?" He scoffs. "I'm usually pretty good about figuring out what's going to happen and who to press to get what I want and how I want it, but the Devil's trio and EvanAnn? I never could have imagined you'd keep her."

"You think all of this is just one huge game?" I'm getting to the end of my rope. He doesn't know who took Annie. He thinks I'm here to press him for information.

"Isn't it?" Elizabeth takes a sip. "Chase was supposed to be the thing distracting EvanAnn. A first boyfriend is ever so distracting. And then her first broken heart would have devastated her, leaving her utterly useless for her play."

Brandt shakes his head. "But he's almost as useless as Sophie. The accident fucked everything up."

"You had to try to divert Damon from his revenge. Give him someone else to focus on." Elizabeth smirks and takes a sip. "Olivia should have been perfect. Except you didn't count on EvanAnn and Damon moving in together."

He tips his glass to me. "An unknown variable that caused quite a bit of problems. But I had an ace up my sleeve, because EvanAnn might not have had a boyfriend before, but she also lacked a friend. Who better to play a friend than an actress?"

"Better yet, an actress who didn't realize she was playing a part." Elizabeth laughs lightly. "She was so easy to push in the right direction. Shame she didn't go for your play though, dear brother."

Brandt shrugs and smiles. "You win some, you lose some. It ended up working in the end though. I met Tanner. Seemed like a decent guy, but he must have pissed off the wrong people." He shakes his head.

"You told Mia to befriend Annie?" I ask, trying to connect the pieces of what they're saying.

He smirks. "I didn't say, hey, why don't you go be friends with that girl." He laughs. "No, but I might have given her a good reason to be EvanAnn's friend. Even if Mia hooked up with her boyfriend."

"It's so hard for a new girl to fit in with a new crowd. Especially a girl like Mia." Elizabeth smiles knowingly. "She knew what was best for her."

"But she wasn't Annie's stalker." I need to keep them talking, make them reveal the whole thing.

"I mean, she could have been." Brandt rubs his fingers over his lips. "But she ended up actually being friends with EvanAnn. I figured she'd eventually sleep with one of you guys and break EvanAnn's heart, but who knew Mia could be loyal?"

"I certainly didn't see that coming." Elizabeth acts like this is some show that she's chosen to watch.

"Back to Riordan," I press.

Elizabeth gives me a little smile. "Now that was an undertaking."

"Almost didn't happen." Brandt nods at her.

"We couldn't have known they had a past. No one did." She swirls her wine in her glass. "Riordan would show up to parties and keep to himself. Our schools are close enough that they intermix. I knew he was in hockey, and you guys had already begun moving in on EvanAnn according to Brandt and his network."

I glance at Brandt and he gives me a cocky grin, raising his glass to me and taking a drink.

"I do so love a good scheme, and it wasn't hard to figure out Jackson hated Damon Storm. A rivalry is always good for pushing buttons." Elizabeth relaxes into the chair and recrosses her legs. "I don't personally follow sports, but once Brandt decided Damon was going to be an issue and Olivia was useless, we had to have something. So I hung out with the hockey team. And boy, did they have a lot to say about Riordan. Not sure anyone on the team actually likes him, but he's too good at hockey to bully off the team."

"That's where I came in," Brandt says and drinks for a dramatic pause. "I needed a rival for Storm and Riordan seemed like the perfect guy. The dislike went both ways. Setting Riordan up with a few coaches was easy enough payment to get him to notice your girl."

Fuck. "You bribed him to go after Annie?" He didn't know about their past at all.

"Bribe? Reward? Po-ta-to, po-tah-to." He shakes his hand in a so-so movement. "It really didn't take much and the results…" He kisses the tips of his fingers. "Perfection."

"Honestly, I think he might actually like her." Elizabeth smiles. "Maybe you guys can add a fourth to whatever you're doing. I mean, the girl has extra hands."

Anger burns through me. I'm almost to the end of my rope, but I want everything.

"The text to Annie's mom?"

"My idea." Elizabeth raises her hand proudly. "We sent some at the beginning of the year to make EvanAnn's mom start watching. But then I saw the way Damon looked at EvanAnn at Tom's birthday party. I'm surprised their parents didn't figure it out earlier. I was hoping he'd go after Chase at the party, but EvanAnn did the honors. The parents were oblivious, and we needed something after the rose, which Brandt took too far." She glares at him.

"I'll do better next time," he says, not the least bit remorseful.

"See that you do," she says haughtily. "It's no good to maim someone. That's not our style."

"But kidnapping is?" I arch an eyebrow.

Elizabeth opens her mouth like she has a snappy comeback, but nothing comes out. Brandt sits forward in his chair. It's the most attention they've given me tonight.

"What?" Elizabeth looks at Brandt with wide eyes.

Brandt presses his lips together. All signs of his smirk gone. So this wasn't part of their plan.

"I wonder if anyone will believe you aren't part of it?" I step over to the bar and hold my phone up, showing that it's recording since I walked in. "After all, you pretty much said you sent Riordan after her."

"What do you mean?" Brandt is pale now. He jerks a little toward me, like he's wondering if he can take my phone from me. But come on.

"I came from the school because Annie's missing. Someone beat the shit out of Chase Chadwick and took her during the break."

Elizabeth sets her wineglass on the table with shaking hands. "Brandt?"

Good, these fuckers deserve to be nervous. Maybe they'll learn that they pushed too far this time.

Brandt stands, but doesn't make a move toward me. "We haven't done anything illegal. We didn't tell him to kidnap her."

"But you basically let a psychopath back into her life. You pushed him to the object of his obsession, knowing it might hurt her, wanting it to, maybe not physically, but emotionally." My words are cold. The anger burns inside me, but I need them to give me something. "He's taken her."

"And how is that my fault? You don't really have anything on me." Brandt tries to sound haughty.

I stop the recording and send it to Damon and Cam. I slide my phone into my pocket and step closer to Brandt, looking down on him. "You know fucking everything, so where would he take her?"

He glances at his sister. She wrings her hands together.

"If I can't find her, I will kill you." I look at him, waiting.

He lifts his gaze to mine and steps back before pretending to be cocky again. There's an edge of fear in his voice though. "And get put away for murder? Even you aren't that stupid."

"What good is my life without her?" And there's the truth. Before Annie, I would have been fine heading off by myself to college, but now that's not an option. Damon, Cam, and Annie are my future. All of them.

"He bragged about a farm his family owned." Elizabeth's voice is small, like she's shed the persona she wears like a shield.

Brandt looks at her. "Liz—"

"No, Brandt." She stands and pulls her shoulders back. There's censure in her eyes. "I saw the way his eyes lit up when we talked about EvanAnn. I've heard rumors of how he treats other girls. This is on us. It's one thing to try to win by breaking her heart. It's another thing to break her. I've seen that coldness in his eyes. He could kill her."

She trembles. So murder is the limit for these two? Or is it because they could be pinned as part of it? How would their father deal with them? How would the media portray them?

I glare at Brandt, waiting for him to break. I'm not opposed to hurting him if he has information that could help us find her. Brandt presses his lips together, but he's not really brave. Under all that sleek veneer, he's a coward who doesn't want to get into trouble. Which is why he makes others do his dirty work.

"He said we could go ATVing out there sometime." He shakes his head. "Not that we wanted to go, but he seemed to think we liked him. We had a good laugh about it, and he even sent us directions."

"I need those. Now!"

## CHAPTER 45
## *EvanAnn*

THE HOUSE IS small with the bare minimum of furniture. The electricity works, so there's light, which hurts my eyes a little and my head a lot after the darkness of outside.

A small galley kitchen. A table with a couple of chairs that look like they might or might not hold an actual person sitting in them. A couple of soft covered chairs in what must be the living room space. An open door leading to a three-piece bathroom barely big enough for a person to fit in. And a closed door I assume leads to a bedroom that I have no desire to explore.

Jackson sets me down on one of the chairs at the table. I put my hands on the table to brace myself for the spinning. He walks away from me and water runs.

When he returns, he kneels in front of me and tips my chin to the side so he can look at the wound. As much as I want to pull away, I don't flinch from his touch. Even though it creeps across my skin like spiders.

"It's not so bad." He dabs at my scalp with a warm washcloth.

I hiss at the sting, but keep my hands on the table buried in my sweatshirt. I don't want to remind him I'm not tethered here. And there's no way I want him to focus on my ring. It's my only hope. My link to the Devil's trio. My link to home.

"That school is bad for you, Evan. You have to know that. It's so fucking toxic with those rich kids who think they can do anything to you and get away with it." His voice is low and soothing. He shakes his head and leaves me. He's in the bathroom rummaging under the sink. "I didn't plan for you to get hurt, but there's a small med kit in here."

I glance at the windows. There are a couple in here and in the living room. Not in the bathroom or the kitchen though. The pitch black of the night presses against the windows, making them reflective of what's happening inside. I don't know how long I've been gone or what time it is.

My head still aches, and my hands shake in my sleeves. I curl my fist around the ring. Damon and Cam have to be back by now. Hawk will have told them someone took me.

They'll find me. I just have to hold on.

Jackson returns and pulls out the chair next to mine. He lays the med kit on the table. My gaze snags on the small scissors in the pack. They wouldn't do much good. The ends are blunt to cut against skin.

He focuses on my head, smearing antibacterial cream on the lump and cut before applying a bandage. "No one was supposed to hurt you. He promised, and then that fucker left that rose for you." He shakes his head as he puts away the supplies. "Blaming it on me like I would ever hurt you."

My heart stops. He didn't leave the rose, but someone else did? We always knew it was impossible for him to have been there and leave unnoticed. But it wasn't even his plan?

"I didn't think you'd hurt me," I say softly. But I did, and I still do.

He'll hurt me if I'm not who he wants me to be. If I make him angry. If I don't live up to whatever fantasy he has for us.

I don't know if I'll make it out of this.

He lifts his gaze to mine suspiciously, but whatever he sees in my eyes reassures him. "They're toxic, Evan. Everyone at that school. We're just a game to them. *You're* just a game to them."

He takes the med kit and puts it under the sink again. He stops in the kitchen and grabs a couple bottles of water from the package on the floor. My lips are dry. But can I really drink anything he gives me?

He twists the top off and takes a quick drink in front of me, not touching the rim to his lips. "It's safe."

He puts it in front of me, and then opens the other one and drinks it down. I lift the water bottle to my lips and drink. It's room temperature, which is a little cool, but it's water and it should help.

He pushes a packet of ibuprofen from the med kit toward me. "For your head."

I take it and tear it open, dropping the pills into my hand. I swallow them with some water and set the bottle on the table, carefully screwing the lid back on so he can't put anything in it easily.

Maybe the pills will help clear my thoughts some. Take away some of the pulsing pain.

"They couldn't protect you, pretty girl." He reaches out and brushes my hair behind my ear.

I force myself not to flinch away. This is just a part I have to play to survive. I have to believe he's my hero. That he's rescuing me from the Devil's trio and from my school.

"They're as toxic as the rest of them. They don't care about you." Jackson leans back in the chair and looks me over.

I'm glad I'm wearing one of Hawk's sweatshirts and a pair of jeans. We rode to rehearsal, and afterward we might have gone to our spot to talk. I even have sneakers on, so if I can get away, I have a chance.

"You know he watches you." Jackson says it low, and he watches my face. "I saw him when we were working out. He has cameras in your room."

I let myself feel the horror of this moment, being held captive by the same boy who forced my first kiss. Letting that horror show on my face, knowing he'll assume I'm thinking of Damon watching me in my private time.

If he wants Damon to be the villain, I can play act that. I need to do whatever it takes to remain pliant, to appear grateful to him if not a little confused. It's the only way to remain free.

I have no doubt he will tie me up to hold me if I resist. The head wound probably helped me out because I might have struggled when he tried to take me.

I would have fought him in the van and on the way here. Which would have forced him to restrain me so I didn't hurt him or try to escape.

I bring my hand up to my mouth to cover it, as if the more I think about it, the more terrifying it is to me. Because the thought of Jackson seeing those private moments would be terrifying.

He shakes his head and puts his hand on my shoulder. I want to pull away, but I stay where I am. "I knew I had to get you away from them. They're toxic, Evan. He thinks he owns you."

I lift my gaze to his and let tears fill my eyes. He wants me helpless. He wants to be my hero. I can let him be that.

"I didn't know what to do." My lips tremble, and he squeezes my shoulder. "My mom moved us in. I didn't have anywhere else to go."

"You're safe now. I've got you. We don't have to see them ever again." He stands and goes into the kitchen. "Did you eat?"

"Yes." I wouldn't eat anything he gave me unless I absolutely needed to for survival. "Won't you see Damon in hockey?"

"Hockey's just a way to get out of this town." He comes back and puts a bag of chips on the table between us. It's the kind he used to bring me at the apartment building. "I'm good at it, but without a scholarship, I won't be going anywhere. Crowne Mawr wants me, but if Damon tells them he doesn't want me there, they'll rescind the offer."

"Why would they do that?" I hold my bottle of water like a lifeline. I can get away without eating, Hawk made sure I had dinner, but without water...

"I'm surprised you don't see it." He shakes his head and eats a few chips. "These rich boys always get their way. Rich girls are just as bad. They think we're usable. Disposable. They laugh at us behind our backs."

He's working himself up, and I need him to calm down.

"Damon said you went out with Mia?" I want to know if she lied to me or Jackson lied about it to Damon.

He pauses and takes a breath before meeting my eyes. "She's not good for you. She's as bad as all the others. But I didn't do anything with her. I used her phone to get your number, but I never texted her. I didn't even see her except those times with you. She's a user. You were better off without her."

Relief sweeps through at the same time as disappointment in myself for not believing in my friend. It can't be helped right now. Right now, I have to do what it takes to get through this. I lift my gaze to the closed door to the bedroom.

I don't know how far I can go with this. If it comes down to it, I might have to fight. Because there are some things I don't want to pretend I'm okay with.

---

## CAM

The directions Hawk sends us aren't far. He's on his way to meet us. It wasn't some place we were already planning on looking, because no roads lead to the house. I text my dad the information. I don't know how long it will take the authorities to get out here, but we have no intentions of waiting.

Every minute is a minute Evan is with that asshole. Under his control. He could do anything to her.

We park and use GPS until we lose the signal.

Damon takes a few steps backward into the woods, and the signal comes back on.

"He's jamming it. That's why we can't find her," I say, and something releases inside me. The part that worried the reason the signal vanished is because she's gone.

"It also means we have to be close." Damon studies the map and puts his phone into his pocket. Blockers don't usually have large radiuses. "How far is Hawk?"

"About five minutes to where we left the bikes." I look at the satellite image of the area. "The house is in the middle of fields. If he looks out the window, he'll see us coming."

Damon rubs the back of his neck. "I'll go in. When the coast is clear, I'll give you a sign."

I nod. When we were kids and playing capture the flag, we always used an owl cry as a signal to each other.

"Wait here for Hawk. That way if Jackson catches me snooping around. We still have you guys." Damon grabs my arm and meets my eyes. "No matter what, get her out."

I nod and clasp his arm.

"Be safe. We've probably got a half hour before the calvary arrives. They'll have to trek in or rough it through the fields." The house is clearly abandoned, with not even a driveway up to it. The fields surrounding it normally would keep it secluded, but with the crops all harvested, it's just barren land.

I'm sure my parents will rally the police, and with someone being kidnapped, they'll do what it takes to get her back safely. But safely can take time Evan doesn't have. There's no telling what Jackson plans to do with her.

Has already done with her. My stomach twists.

Damon sneaks off into the night. I watch his tracker disappear, and Hawk's grow closer. It's torture waiting here, knowing she's trapped in that house alone with someone who's obsessed with her.

But it makes sense to give Damon a head start to make sure he isn't seen. If he gets captured too, then he can distract Jackson while Hawk and I arrive.

The minutes crawl by like hours as I wait, imagining what could be happening to my girl right now while I stand around with my phone in my hand. I look toward the dot heading my way.

"Hey," Hawk whispers.

When he draws near, I tell him our plan. He grabs my arm.

"Let's save our girl."

## CHAPTER 46
## *EvanAnn*

JACKSON SITS NEXT TO ME, eating the chips and not saying anything. It's more nerve-wracking than listening to him talk about how nothing in my life is good. He's mentioned Mia, Damon, Cam, and Hawk.

The blackness of the night closes in on us, suffocating me. The longer I'm here, the more I worry no one's coming to save me. What if they can't find me? What if it's up to me to escape?

The crunching of the chips is the only sound. It's too much.

But I don't want to say the wrong thing. I don't want to upset him or get on his bad side.

"What did you do to tick off Brandt Stanwell?" Jackson says, startling me. He's practically sprawled in the chair. His legs surround the chair I'm on, boxing me in, but I pretend it's not making me uncomfortable. Like he's caging me.

"I didn't do anything to Brandt." I straighten. Maybe I should have pretended to be a little less self-righteous, but I don't know why Brandt decided I was his enemy. I'm his competition. I guess that was enough for him.

Jackson smiles knowingly. "You must have pissed him off good because he wanted me feral when I came for you. I don't usually let assholes manipulate me, but between him and his sister..." He laughs, but there's no joy in it. "They thought they were so much better than me. Smarter too. Thought everything they told me was precious to me. Assholes."

I relax back into my chair. "They wanted you to kidnap me?"

"Probably not." He arches an eyebrow. "But it's not like those fuckers, who claim to be your boyfriends, could protect you. You belong to me. I saw you first. I recognized your potential. They went to school with you for three years before they saw you. Damon acts like you're his property, but you're mine. You've always been mine."

I swallow and take a sip of water. With the medicine kicking in, the fog of pain is receding a little, so I can focus more. "So what's the plan?"

He smiles and eats a chip.

"I mean, you brought me out to the middle of nowhere. You saved me from the evil hockey boys and theater kids of my school to do what exactly?" I glance around the small house to see what there is, and there's not a lot.

The moonless night means beyond the windows is blackness. That should help my guys sneak up or the police or whoever ends up finding me. Someone has to find me. Jackson couldn't have a flawless plan.

I'm not just going to disappear.

"I need to make sure you know you're mine and only mine before we go back." Jackson takes the bag of chips into the kitchen. "I can't risk them turning you against me."

"We are going back though? Because I still want to finish my production or Brandt will win." Maybe he cares about whether or not we win this game. Or maybe he doesn't care about playing it at all.

"This is the problem." He stands in the doorway of the kitchen, looking at me like I'm the one who's broken. Like he needs to fix me. It sends a pulse of fear through my veins.

"The problem?" I tuck my feet up on the chair and wrap my arms around them, like I'm small and helpless. The more he underestimates me, the better.

"They've drilled into your head that you need to win the game. But the game is fixed, pretty girl." He shakes his head and comes over, pulling his chair close to mine and sitting directly in front of me. "They aren't going to let us win ever. Not you. Not me. It doesn't matter that we're better than all of them. The game is rigged. They don't want us."

"What do you mean? You go to a top tier school to play hockey. You were invited to visit a D1 college to play on their team."

Jackson shakes his head like I don't get it. "They didn't do that for me. They don't want me to succeed. They do it to feel better about themselves. See this boy who's good at hockey with the second-hand skates and taped together hockey stick? We can make him look like us, dress like us, and act like us, but we'll always know we're better than him. That the only reason he made it was because we chose him to lift out of the gutter."

Jackson jerks to his feet and walks toward the window, staring out into the night.

"Don't you get it? Don't you see? They're doing the same thing to you. You're like me. We don't have money to do this kind of shit on our own, and they know it. So they see this little girl who can act and they give her her wildest dreams. Hold it out like it's a brand new life. That somehow, we can rise above where our parents had us."

My heart beats a little faster as he gets more agitated. Agitated isn't good. I let the fear trickle into my voice to try to pull him back. "Jackson?"

"Fuck them. They just want to use us. They used you. Don't you see it? Can't you feel it?" He turns and hits himself in the chest with a thump. I try not to startle. "Evan, they want you to almost taste what you can't have unless they give it to you. College, a career, the future. Nothing will be ours, because they gave it to us. And we should be grateful to them because *they* gave it to us."

He crosses the room and lifts me out of the chair, forcing me to my feet. I let out a surprised noise, but don't resist.

"They own us. They want to control us, but we don't have to give in to them."

I swallow as he hovers over me, large and intimidating. My head swims a little from the shift in position. He releases me, and I stay standing.

I collect my thoughts and say, "But what if that's what we want too? What if we're the ones using them to get there?"

His smile doesn't meet his eyes as he slowly shakes his head and closes in on me. I back up. I can't help it. Standing my ground isn't an option. The wall stops me, holding me in place as he hovers over me.

My breath catches in my throat, and suddenly the monster is back. Every nerve in my body is on edge because I recognize this monster. He was hiding, but now he's back. And no one's going to save me.

"That's what they want you to believe." He lifts his hand and slides the back of his knuckles down my cheek and jaw. I control the urge to flinch and squirm and shiver, holding his gaze, trying to play the part when I want to curl up or run away. He wraps his hand around my throat, pushing me back against the wall. There's a wildness in his eyes I'm not sure I can tame.

It won't matter what I say because this is his truth. The monster holding me is the real Jackson.

"Damon took everything from me. He got hockey. He got into the USHL. He got the offer to go to Crowne Mawr." His eyes drop to my lips and his hand tightens around my throat, making it hard to breathe. "He got you."

"But you have me now. You got the offer to go to Crowne Mawr." I resist the urge to grab his hand at my throat. He's not choking me, not yet. I can't give him a reason to. I don't want to be his broken toy.

Broken toys can't run away. My heart trips over itself. My hands shake, but I keep them hidden. They'll find me. They'll always find me, but I have to stay safe while I wait.

He shakes his head and lowers his forehead to mine. "Do I have you, pretty girl? Or are you just an illusion like the rest of it? You were mine years ago. I had you and let you slip from my fingers because I thought I wasn't good enough for you. I saved you from that dumpster fire of an apartment. Made your mom think she wasn't safe there. But I thought if I worked harder I could prove to you that I deserved you. But it wasn't enough. I was never enough."

I want to run. I want to knee him in his junk and bolt out the door and pray someone finds me before he does. But I know I won't get far.

To do this, I need to sink into what he needs me to be. That means I can't be EvanAnn right now.

I close my eyes and pretend it's Damon hovering over me, holding me like this. He's done it before. My hand shakes as I bring it to his jaw and feel the rough day's growth. I try to control the thundering of my heart.

"You're enough," I whisper. "I see that now."

He releases his breath against my lips, and I realize I'm trapped. I'm sixteen again, held against the wall by a boy I thought I liked until he pushed me too far, too fast. I freeze, and there's nothing I can do to stop this.

No mom to save me this time. I can't. I just can't.

"No." It bursts out of my lungs.

He squeezes my neck harder, and I open my eyes to glare up into his.

"You don't get to make me into who you think you'd like better," I say.

He laughs, and the kind mask he wore slips away. A chill rolls down my spine. "I could have pretended for you, pretty girl. For a while." He shrugs. "Guess I don't have to now."

He presses his face toward mine, and I sink my nails into his jaw, struggling to lift my knee between us. His hand tightens, and I gasp to take a breath, but his eyes meet mine as black edges around my vision.

"You don't get it. You're mine, Evan. No one's ever going to take you from me again."

Before I lose consciousness, he releases my neck and I drag in fresh air, too desperate for oxygen to fight. He lifts me and throws me over his shoulder. It knocks the breath out of me, and as the blood flows down to my head, the bump throbs.

He opens the door to the bedroom and tosses me on the bed. My head hurts so bad. I struggle to roll to the side before he can grab me. His hand closes around my neck again, but this time I dig my fingernails into his hands, prying them away.

He slaps me with his other hand, amplifying the ringing in my head. My vision goes black for a moment.

There are ties on my wrists before my head stops spinning. Fuck. He moves to my ankles and I twist and kick, desperate to get loose.

"Let me go," I scream and buck and twist.

A blur of movement bursts into the room, and the hand on my ankle disappears, followed by a loud thud. I struggle to catch my breath and push my body toward the top of the mattress, pulling away from him and tucking into myself. My eyes aren't focusing quite yet, but I see two of Jackson as he falls out of the room.

## CHAPTER 47
## *Damon*

I NEARLY KICKED in the door when he carried Evan dangling over his shoulder into the bedroom, but I needed the element of surprise. I had to wait for the right opportunity.

When Evan screams, I see fucking red and jump him from behind, sending us both crashing into the wall. We fall out of the room and onto the floor of the dining room in a tangle of limbs.

We wrestle for a few moments before I drive my fist into Jackson's gut. He shoves me away and jumps up, racing back into the room where he left Evan tied to the bed. I stagger to my feet and follow after him. In the doorway, I freeze at the horror show waiting for me.

Jackson smiles as he sits on the bed, holding Evan against his chest between us. Her hands still tied to the four-poster bed. He holds a knife with the tip pressed against her heart. His hair and eyes are wild.

"I've been expecting you." He smirks like he's won.

Evan meets my eyes with regret, like she's already lost. But we're not lost until we're dead. And that's not happening. Not here. Not tonight. Not by this asshole.

I wipe the blood from the side of my mouth and look at it on my hand, buying us time. He didn't go through all this hassle just to kill his obsession now. He wants Evan too much to kill her.

Me? He could probably kill in a heartbeat if he could get the upper hand. But to do that, he will hurt Evan to make me heel.

"So what, you're going to kill her?" I hedge that bet.

"No, but you will if you take a step toward us." Jackson's voice is cold. "Haven't you ever heard the saying *if I can't have her, no one can*?"

Evan holds perfectly still, but there's a world of words in her eyes. Things we've shared. Things we still need to share. A life not lived yet.

I need to keep her breathing, keep her whole. He won't take her from me. Even if I have to let her go with him. She'll still be alive, and that would be enough until I get her back. Because he might have been Evan's monster, but I'll be his.

"What do you want?" I ask, tearing my gaze from her to him.

He smirks. "Fucking my girl while you watch could be amusing. I'm sure I could make both of you scream."

I narrow my eyes, unable to control the rage inside me, but keeping my anger out of my voice. "Not happening."

"Did you think I wouldn't have plans for if you decided your whore was worth your time and effort?" Jackson laughs but there's no joy in it. "If you want her to live, sit in that chair."

He gestures with his head to the wooden armchair in the corner of the room.

"Slowly," he says with a sly grin. He turns his eyes to Evan and looks at her with undisguised longing. "I'd hate to make my pretty girl bleed."

Holding my hands up in surrender, I move to the chair without taking my eyes off Evan. I can't tell her help is coming. I can't tell that help to be careful, because he might kill her if he hears them coming. All his focus is on me and Evan. I need to keep it here. I left the door open.

It's the best I can do. Cam and Hawk aren't stupid. I didn't signal the all clear. They won't come in guns blazing. Mostly because we don't have guns.

"So what? You're going to kill me and Evan and run off to live happily ever after in jail?" I sit in the chair almost belligerently, like I haven't a care in the world. Slouching with my legs spread, leaning back.

"The handcuffs on the end of the bed." He nods toward them. "Put them on, threaded through the arm of the chair."

I lean forward to grab them, slowly. If he so much as knicks her skin with that knife, I will make sure he's in ribbons when this is over. The handcuffs are linked together with about a foot of chain.

"You don't want to do this, Jackson," she says as I attach my first wrist and slide the chain under the arm of the chair before attaching the other side.

"Why not? Are you not having fun, pretty girl?" He lifts the knife to her jaw and slides the flat of the blade over her skin without cutting. "Worried your perfect guy won't want you with a scar on your face? I'll still want you, pretty girl."

I hold Evan's eyes, trying to give her the strength to make it through this. There's nothing he could do to her that would make me stop loving her. Nothing.

"You know what I don't get?" Jackson slides the knife back down to her heart. "Why him?"

"What?" Evan is stalling.

Jackson smirks and moves out from behind Evan, taking the knife with him. He stabs the knife into the mattress beside her, and I flinch, jerking on the handcuffs. She gasps in a little breath, but tries to remain calm.

He looks at me with a wicked smile. He wanted to test me, to make sure I was truly bound.

He takes her ankle and tugs her down the bed. He ties her foot to the footboard before going to the other side to bind her other leg. "Why Damon over me?"

She's lying down, spread eagle, but she's still clothed and breathing. I don't like this, but we shouldn't have to wait for long. The guys will assess the situation and pick the right time to take him out. Preferably when the knife isn't in Jackson's hand.

Jackson grabs the knife and sits on the end of the four poster bed between her legs. He studies me like he's never looked at me a day in his life. Like he truly doesn't get it.

"We're practically the same when you break it down."

I arch an eyebrow, but don't say anything. Fuck this asshole. We're not the same.

"Both handsome. Both skilled at hockey. Both have futures in the NHL. Both a little obsessed with you." Smirking, he leans back on the bed. His hand pressing the mattress near her knee. "But when you take away all of those things, the only thing he has that I don't is money."

"I don't care about money," she says softly.

Jackson chuckles and slides the blade of the hunting knife between his fingers. "Don't you?"

"No, I don't." She stares up at the ceiling. There's tension in her arms and legs like she wants to move them. Needs to get away, but can't.

"Don't lie, pretty girl. It doesn't suit you." He grabs her leg and slices the knife down her jeans, splitting them open from the knee down.

She hisses and a small streak of blood appears on her calf.

That's one.

"Careful," he says and glances at me. "I don't want to hurt you, Evan."

I doubt that. He wants to hurt both of us, and he knows hurting her will hurt me.

"See, I could take away his looks." He studies me and leans over to drag the knife along her other pant leg from the knee to her ankle. This time the blade doesn't touch her skin. "I bet if I fuck you in front of him, he won't want you anymore. But I will."

I grind my teeth together. I can't give him anything. He can't know how this is tearing me up inside.

"But he'd still have hockey and the money." Jackson smirks at me before turning to kneel over her on the bed. He grabs the neck of her hoodie and holds it up. "Don't move, pretty girl. I don't want to cut your breasts before I get a chance to play with them."

He slides the blade down the front of the sweatshirt, cutting it in half. She turns her head to the side, and I can see her chest rising and falling rapidly. There are red marks on her neck from his hands.

That's two.

"I can see why they want you." He traces the tip of the blade along her bra. "What do you want, Damon?"

"Her," I say it so she can hear it. So she knows no matter what happens in this room, she's mine, and I will always be hers.

"Interesting." He turns to face me, sitting on the end of the bed again. His dark eyes narrow on mine. "Would you choose her over hockey?"

"In a heartbeat."

She gasps.

"Prove it." Jackson smiles and stands from the bed. "Cut your Achilles tendons and I'll let her go. She can choose whether she wants to be with you or me."

"Give me the knife."

"Damon, no!" she cries out. "We don't settle."

"It would never be settling with you, Evan." I meet Jackson's eyes and hold my hand open for the knife, waiting.

He smirks and reaches into his pocket for a pocketknife. He comes a little closer and tosses it on my lap where I can reach it. "It might take a little bit to really saw into those tendons, but I'll find it entertaining. Try not to bleed to death."

"You'll let her go." I open the blade and glare at him.

"After I get a taste." He smirks, focused on me. "After all, it's only fair if she has to choose that she has all the information."

Evan moves behind him, capturing my attention. Her head is turned toward the door, and she nods. Cam bursts in and grabs Jackson around the shoulders, hauling him backwards. Jackson stabs the knife back toward Cam.

"Cam!" Evan cries out and tugs at her bindings.

With a grunt of pain, Cam shoves Jackson out the door.

When Cam grabs the handle of the blade in his outer thigh, Evan yells, "Don't pull that out!"

The sound of fists smacking into flesh comes from the other room. Cam checks the other room, probably to make sure Hawk doesn't need help. I use the tip of the knife to jimmy open the handcuffs. As soon as I have a wrist free, I go to Evan's hands to cut the rope tying her to the headboard.

Cam sinks into the chair, holding the leg with a knife sticking in it out straight. "Fuck, that's weird."

"Are you okay?" I release her ankles.

"I will be." She takes the knife from me and strides out the door.

"Fuck," Cam says.

Cam and my eyes meet before I hurry after her. Jackson lies on the floor of the dining room, wheezing breaths. Hawk hovers over him with bloodied fists.

"The cops are on their way," Cam yells from the other room. "Don't murder him."

Evan pauses for a second with the knife in her hand, clearly torn, but then she sinks down on the floor beside Jackson. "I'll never choose you."

She slices down through his shirt. He hisses when she cuts him in the process. But it doesn't faze her as she peels his shirt open. Without a word, she carves his chest with the knife. He cries out after the first few cuts, but she doesn't stop until she's written all the way across his chest.

When she stands, her hand trembles, and I take the knife from her, setting it on the table. She turns into my arms and puts her head against my chest with a sob. I close my arms around her as she trembles against me.

Hawk puts his hand on her back. We both look at the words on Jackson's chest. It's written backwards, but it says *NOT YOURS*. Hawk takes his phone out and takes a picture of it.

Guess I don't need to pay him back for hurting my girl.

"Remind me not to piss you off, Annie." Hawk strips off his hoodie and helps her shed the tattered one and put on his, but her arms and her head return to my chest, and I honestly don't want to let her go.

Ever.

"Check on Cam," I say to Hawk as we hear movement outside the house. He disappears into the room as the first cops come into the house.

"Freeze."

Evan looks at the cop, not releasing me. "The guy on the ground kidnapped me. My guys saved me. Cam needs medical attention."

Her voice is strong, but she trembles against me. She digs her fingers into my sides.

I run my thumb over the track of her tear and she looks up at me. "I'm ready to go home now."

## CHAPTER 48
## *Cam*

RIDING in an ambulance driving on fields is a crazy experience. The EMTs decided the placement of the knife wasn't a problem probably, but they still left it in for the ride to the hospital.

Evan sits next to me with her leg bandaged. They looked over the bump on her head as well.

Jackson gets the next ambulance. Damon and Hawk are stuck talking to the police about what happened, but from the look on Damon's face, they'll be with us shortly.

Evan holds my hand like she'll fall off a cliff if she releases it. I'm probably holding her just as tightly. There aren't enough words to explain how I felt when I heard Jackson asking Damon to cut his legs.

Damon knew we were coming, so I assume he was bluffing, but there was such conviction in his voice. Standing outside that room, knowing what was happening and being powerless to stop it, was brutal.

We had to wait for the right opportunity. Wait until the knife was away from Evan. Wait until it was safe-ish. Obviously, I would have preferred not to get stabbed. But when Evan realized I was there, she gave me the signal.

I didn't think. I just acted.

We finally reach smooth highway and speed to the hospital. They unload me first and then help Evan down. I'm staring up at the sky before they push me inside, and then my mom and dad's faces hover over mine.

"Oh my god, are you okay?" Mom grabs my hand and pales as she sees the knife sticking out of my leg. "You were stabbed?!"

"You should see the other guy." I smirk. The knife hurts, but I'm imagining what happens next will hurt more.

Dad shakes his head. "You should have let the police do their jobs."

I turn and see Evan, buried in her mother's embrace while the nurse argues that they need to redress the wounds. Heather just shakes her head and holds Evan so fucking tight. Adam has his arm around Heather and talks calmly with the nurse.

Then I'm wheeled away. It's a while later before I'm in a room waiting. They sliced off my jeans and pulled out the knife before closing up the wound with some stitches. Someone gave me drugs at some point, and I stopped caring what they were doing.

Now I'm in a hospital gown, in a bed, twiddling my thumbs. Dad opens the door and Mom hurries in. She grabs my hand and touches my forehead like I'm sick, brushing my hair away from my face.

"How are you feeling?" She looks over me like she's cataloguing everything is where it's supposed to be. I'm surprised when she doesn't lift the sheets to check that I have all my toes.

"I'm good. How's Evan?"

Dad glances toward the door. "She didn't need stitches. The police were in with her getting her statement."

Mom looks at all the monitors. If there was a clipboard at the end of my bed, she'd be reading that, but all the notes are in computers now. Not that she could make anything out of it. She's not a nurse. But I wouldn't be surprised if she tried to hack the computer.

She finally sighs. "The nurse should be back in a few. The doctor said you'll need to stay off it for a little while, but everything should heal nicely. You'll follow up with our doctor. They're sending you to physical therapy to help with strengthening."

Dad rubs her back. "If it had been anywhere else, you would have needed surgery."

"So I can get out of here soon." I sit up.

"They're going to discharge you instead of keeping you overnight." Dad acts like they really should keep me, but I'm glad they aren't.

Damon opens the door and walks in. "Hey."

I smile and know it comes across a little weird because of the pain meds.

Dad nods to Damon.

"You were a beast." Damon holds his hand out to me, and I clasp it.

I laugh. "You would have done the same."

When he shrugs, my mom makes a noise of disapproval.

"You all could have been killed running into a kidnapping like that." Mom shakes her head and Dad pulls her into his chest. She releases a choking sob.

"He's fine, Lisa." Dad makes soothing noises, rubbing her back.

"He had a knife in his leg! A knife! In his leg!" Mom takes in a shaky breath.

"Give us a minute." Dad nods at me as he leads Mom out into the hallway, speaking quietly to her.

"How is Evan?" I ask. She's safe. That's all I needed to know before.

Damon glances toward the door. "I drew the short straw."

I chuckle. Such a dick.

"Not really," Damon says with a smirk. "I wanted to see how you were doing, so I could tell her when I saw her."

"Always playing the hero." I shake my head.

When the door opens, Dad and Mom move back inside. Mom lowers into the chair and watches me with watery eyes. I hate that I made her worry.

Damon looks me over and his face grows serious. "How is it?"

"He'll be off it for a few days. With physical therapy, he should be back on the ice in a month," Dad says as he leans against the wall next to Mom with his hand on her shoulder. "He should be good by the first game."

Damon releases his breath and nods. "Good."

I didn't even know that yet, so I'm glad Dad told us. "I'm not looking forward to recovery time, but definitely hoping for pampering."

Damon smirks. "Sounds like she might have a concussion, so you might be recovering together."

"She'll make me do my schoolwork," I complain. Though the thought of hanging out with Evan is better than taking it easy on the couch alone.

"I like this girl." Dad chuckles. "Driven, focused. You could do a lot worse."

"I doubt I could do better," I say honestly. I turn to Damon. "I'm good. Go check on our girl."

---

## Hawk

When a voice says to come in, I open the door to Annie's room. She's in the ER. Heather sits in the chair, clutching Adam's hand and looking pale. Annie said before that her mom has hospital trauma. This must be killing her.

"Hawk," Adam says softly. "The doctor said to let her sleep when she can."

I nod to him and go to where Annie sleeps. She wears a hospital gown now. I look her over and breathe. Things were chaotic at the house. Cam held me back from going in so many times. When he threw Jackson to me, I released everything on him.

He's also here, with police standing outside his room. The police weren't happy that we beat them into the house and beat up the guy, but Annie was in danger. And I'm sure my dad will convince them it was necessary force.

Annie's memento was a little harder to explain. The blood was on her hands. Though her, Damon, and Jackson held the knife at some point tonight. The officer who took the report didn't write the carving down, just that Jackson had been wounded by a knife. He mentioned his two daughters were five and three and gave Damon and me a nod of acknowledgement.

The cuts aren't why Jackson's in the hospital.

I put him there. He was beaten worse than he beat up Chase.

"Is it a concussion?" I turn to ask Adam.

"Likely. They're going to get her an MRI to rule out anything major." Adam runs a hand through his hair. "How's Damon?"

"He'll be in. He wanted to check on Cam first." I drag in a breath. "He's good though. Some redness on his wrists from the cuffs, and he'll probably have a bruise on his side from the fight." I smirk. "We're all a little beat up."

I washed my hands and put some antibacterial ointment on the cuts. My knuckles are a little swollen, but I have zero regrets. At least not about beating up Jackson. Not stopping him from taking Annie will haunt me for a while.

She was on my watch. It was stupid. I should have asked someone to stay with her. Not just assumed someone would. I don't know how I'll leave her again without one of the others with her. It's not rational.

I can't be on top of her twenty-four-seven to keep her safe. Not and have a life beyond her. Right now, that's all I want, because it was almost taken away from me.

"Hey." Her voice is soft, drawing my attention to her open blue-gray eyes. She slides her hand into mine. "Sorry, I drifted off there. They gave me some pain meds."

I brush her hair away from her face with my other hand and she smiles at me. "You doing okay?"

"All things considered," she says. She pushes the button to lift her head up a little. "My head hurts. The doctor said I need to take it easy for forty-eight hours."

She frowns. She's probably thinking about the play. I glance over at Heather.

"Did you call Mr. Watson?" I ask.

Heather nods. "Yes, and her assistant director. They know she's not going to be in for a couple days, but they know she's fine."

"I can't take a couple of days off. It's tech week." She reaches for her head as the door opens.

"You can recover for a couple days, Annie. You need the rest so you can blow everyone away with your performance." I smile down at her as her eyes meet mine. So much strength. She closes her eyes and rests her head against her pillow.

Damon takes one look at her and steps in, closing the door behind him. He goes to the other side of the bed and gives me a questioning look.

"Concussion, days off."

He nods because he understands. Out of all of us, he's the one who would have been just as anxious to get back on the ice. But he would have taken that knife if it meant Annie didn't have to. He would do anything for her. We all would.

"Cam's doing well." Damon takes Annie's hand, and she looks up at him. "He had to get some stitches and a couple days off the leg. Probably fully healed in like a month."

"Good." Annie glances toward the door. Her lips press into a thin line. "Is *he* here?"

We all know she means Jackson.

"Until they get him patched up enough to go to jail." Damon glances at his dad. Adam gives him a solemn look. Jackson isn't getting away with this shit.

"He needs intensive therapy." Annie sighs. "Losing time to prison won't help him. It will just ruin all his hopes of a career."

"I don't know a coach who will pick up someone with felonies on their records." Adam shakes his head. "If he wanted a career, he should have chosen that over taking you. There's no guarantee therapy would help him if he doesn't want help."

Personally, I hope the guy rots. I glance at Damon. We still need to do something about Brandt too. He doesn't get away with this without a few scratches.

"How's Chase?" Annie asks. "He was with me when Jackson took me. He tried to help."

Damon releases a breath. "I can find out. He was beat up when we found him, but breathing."

"I'll go find out." I lean down and kiss Annie. Damon gives me a nod when I lift my head. "I'll be right back."

---

## *Damon*

Hawk leaves us alone with our parents. I'm expecting a lecture on how stupid it was to go after her that way. How I could have died or gotten Evan killed. Lisa's words echo in my head. I swallow. She's not wrong and my father would be justified in yelling at me.

Dad clears his throat. I meet his eyes and brace myself.

"I'm so glad you're both okay." He swallows and clears his throat again. Heather squeezes his hand and puts her other hand on his arm as she looks up at Dad. Dad continues, "I can't imagine what you two went through, but I'm glad you have each other. Things could have gone horribly wrong, but they didn't."

I release my breath, and Evan squeezes my hand.

"There's a lot we try to prevent or get ahead of to avoid pain, and I know you guys did your best to protect each other. I'm hoping you'll both take my offer of therapy for at least a month. There's going to be a lot to unpack once you get over the relief of being alive. You both are so driven with your careers it would be easy to just keep plugging away. To say you don't have time, but I want you to strongly consider this as not something you opt out of."

"I think that's a great idea." Evan lifts her gaze to mine.

"Yeah." There's guilt underlying our success. I could see it in Hawk's eyes. "I think we should all go in together a few times too. If that's okay?"

Dad nods. "Whatever you need."

Heather stands and comes over to Evan's bedside. "I'm going to go get some sodas." She brushes Evan's hair a little off her face, careful of the bandage. "I'll be back."

Evan nods, and Heather turns, taking my dad's hand and leading him out of the room, leaving us alone.

I don't know what to say. There were moments I feared the worst in that room, but would have done anything for her. I wasn't sure who we'd be on the other side.

"Would you have?" Evan asks softly, shifting in her bed to make room for me. She tugs my hand, trying to pull me on the bed with her.

I sit beside her. "Would I have what?"

But I know what she's asking. Would I have cut my tendons to save her?

"Given up hockey for me?" There's a hint of fear in her voice.

I shift so I'm lying beside her on the bed, careful of the leg I know was cut. I watched it happen. If she hadn't carved him up, I would have. If she hadn't needed me to hold her, I would have carved him up more.

"Watching him slice open your clothes while you lay helpless on that bed was the hardest thing I've ever had to do." I bring my forehead to hers, careful of her bump. "I would have burned down the world for you in that moment, little devil. Anything."

"And if he had…" The words catch in her throat. A tear clings to her eyelash.

I touch her jaw and breathe her in because we're out of it, but part of me is still in that room, helpless to save her, willing to do anything to spare her pain.

"I would have killed him if he tried. And if I couldn't stop him…" My breath catches in my throat. If he had, he wouldn't be alive, but that's not what she's asking. "I would have held you and helped you heal because you're mine. You're mine to take care of. All of you. No matter what happens to you, nothing will change how I feel about you. I belong to you."

She grabs my shirt and cries softly against me.

"If it meant you lived, I would have gladly given up hockey. He forgot to mention that I'm smart."

She laughs a little.

"I'd just become a lawyer and make sure he spent every day in prison for the rest of his life."

"Maybe with help he could be a good guy." Her watery eyes lift to mine. "As long as it's far away from me."

"I think he got the message this time, little devil." I kiss her forehead. "And if he didn't, he'll be reminded every time he looks in the mirror."

"I still can't believe I did that." Her eyes widen.

"I can. I know better than to get on your bad side, Evan." I pull her into me, and she snuggles against my chest. "I've always known you were a little devil."

## CHAPTER 49
## *EvanAnn*

"Are you sure you're okay?" Lisa sets down two glasses of water on the coffee table. "Do you need anything else?"

"No, thank you," I say.

Cam shakes his head. "One more day and we can both go back to school."

Lisa smiles and shakes her head. She reaches out and cups my cheek. "I'm just glad I get both of you."

Lisa's been kind and attentive. Mom talked about staying home from work, but she has a big project right now. Lisa, Cam's mom, was more than happy to offer to keep both of us during the day. Cam can't move around a lot, and I'm not supposed to do anything mentally taxing for two days and limit screen time.

This is day two, and I'm going stir crazy.

"You just yell if you need anything else." Lisa walks out of the family room.

Cam lifts my hand. "Okay, what can we do that won't disrupt your brain healing?"

"Mom got me a coloring book." I hold it up. "I'd rather work on the pacing of the fourth act."

"Tomorrow."

"It's so frustrating. I know Keira has this. That she can handle two days of practice without me. I'm sure Jason is doing excellent standing in for Desdemona and that Mark is selling the shit out of it. But I hate that I can't do what I'm supposed to be doing." I flick the coloring book back onto the coffee table.

I should be there at practice. Both Chase and I are out. So Jason is doing double time when he can as both Desdemona and Iago. Though he's playing Iago and standing in for me. Even a little beat up, both Chase and I will be back to working. The show must go on.

But right now, all I can do is sit. At least Cam is with me.

Cam holds out his other hand to me. When I give him it, he shifts me in to rest on his chest. He's got his leg elevated. We walked for a little bit to get some exercise, but neither of us is supposed to overdo it.

I rest my head on his chest and pout.

"I know the answer to this, but I'm going to ask anyway." Cam lightly trails his fingers down my back.

"What?"

"If you could be any animal in the world, what animal would you be?" Cam asks it slowly, like it's the most important question he's ever asked me.

I push off his chest to meet his eyes. He's serious.

"You *know* the answer to this?" I arch an eyebrow.

He chuckles. "Of course. Besides, it's not so much what animal but why, so this could take at least an hour of discussion time."

I sigh. "A cat."

"You're too busy to be a cat, goody."

"Okay, what am I then?" I'm expecting to be impressed.

"How about I draw it for you?" He grabs my coloring book and the colored pencils.

I turn so my back is against his front and watch him begin to sketch. Shapes form the outline for his drawing. The scratching of the pencil against the paper is soothing.

"Have you thought about going to college for art?" I ask softly.

"Maybe. I haven't really thought about what I want to do in college. Figured I'd take a couple years to decide." The drawing emerges out of the paper, stroke by stroke.

"I think you should try some art classes to see how you like it." I breathe out as he works and shake my head when I realize what he's doing. "That's not an animal."

"Are you saying humans aren't animals, goody?"

"It kind of defeats the purpose of the question."

"How so? I'm the one who asked it. Why would you want to be anything other than who you are?" He chuckles. "I like you."

"Cheater," I mumble. "But I like you too."

He turns the page and starts drawing the image slightly shifted. Flipping back and forth between pages as he works. I watch as he fills the corners of the pages with images of me. It's relaxing watching him draw. When he finishes, he riffles through the pages and the image comes to life, turning and winking.

---

"What are we going to do about Brandt?" I ask.

Damon and Hawk joined us after hockey practice. I now have a coloring book filled with moving doodles.

"What do you want to do, Evan? He fucked with you." Damon runs his hand through his hair and sets down his chopsticks in the takeout they brought with them. "Whatever you want done, we'll do it."

It's like having a perfectly honed weapon ready to use.

"He tried to take away my future to buy his own." I lean back against Hawk, who insisted I sit with him for dinner. "I could just be better than him."

"You already are, goody. It's why he went after you in the first place." Cam shakes his head and points his chopsticks at me. "Where's the girl who carved her stalker with *not yours*? That's the devious little mind we need right now."

I smirk and take a bite of noodles. "I'm not sure I was really thinking in that moment."

"Whatever you want us to do, Annie?" Hawk kisses my shoulder. "I vote reign terror down on his ass, but I might be partial to a good revenge plot."

"Do you really think anything I do to him in high school is going to stop him from still having a career or life in the industry?" I pick at my food. "This is exactly what Jackson's point was. He'll get punished and his future will be ruined. If Brandt did something wrong, Daddy will bail him out, and he'll end up winning some stupid award. If I screw up, there's no safety net."

Damon tips my chin his way and levels his eyes on mine. "You have a safety net, Evan. You have three who will do anything to keep you safe and whole. Who want only the best for you and will make sure you have it."

My breath catches.

"Jackson will get what he deserves because he tried to take you from us." Damon shakes his head. "He thought he knew better and he didn't. He was fucking bitter and even though he was amazing on the ice, it never would have been enough for him."

I search Damon's eyes.

"Brandt isn't going anywhere." Hawk leans back. "He may eventually have his dad's money or connections, but he's an asshole."

"His own cast hates working with him." Cam points his chopsticks at me. "It won't take long for that to filter through industry circles. He'll kill his own career."

"What I care about is you." Damon narrows his eyes on mine, and I swallow at how much I love this man. "If you feel some way and want him to suffer now, I can make that happen."

"Besides, I have a damning recording of him that he knows I have," Hawk says. "So if he even hints at fucking with you again, I will turn his world upside down."

"Good." I lean in and kiss Damon briefly before returning to my food. "As long as we can make him aware he can't mess with me, or any other ants or we'll wreck him, I'll be good."

"Consider it done."

---

CHASE CAME BACK TO SCHOOL THE SAME DAY I DID. I walked into rehearsal and he was there in front of me. "I'm so sorry I wasn't able to keep you safe."

My mouth opens, but I don't know what to say. I didn't expect him to say anything to me.

His face is swollen and mottled with bruises, but those will all fade and not leave anything behind. He'll be himself before long. But maybe this is the wakeup call he needed.

"I was right there and when you fell, I tried to get to you, but that fucker started wailing on me." He shakes his head and reaches for my arm, but then drops his hand. "Are you okay, EvanAnn?"

I think of all the things he did to me. How he used me and cheated on me and tried to pressure me into sex and started a twisted social media account. But if he hadn't, who would I be right now? What would I be doing?

"I'm good now." I hold out my hand to him. "Thank you for trying."

He hesitates for a moment before shaking my hand. "I'm sorry about the posts."

I release his hand. "I'm not sorry we deleted the account and all the pictures."

"I really need to stay away from Abby." He rubs the back of his neck.

I shrug because I don't care who he dates or what he does as long as it's far away from me. "Make better decisions. Stop trying to take the easy way out and actually be a better person instead of pretending to be."

He nods and for a moment, I think he'll say more, but then he walks away.

Tech week is where everything comes together. I'm back on stage. Cam comes to all the rehearsals since he can't skate, and he makes me sit with him from time to time to give my brain a break. Keira has been a lifesaver.

It's like having another brain, but that one's fully functional. She'll notice when I'm starting to get a headache and call for a quick break before leading me over to Cam. Damon makes sure I eat, and when it gets late, he closes my books and forces me to go to bed with him.

Okay, not so much forces me to, but kisses me until I can't think of anything else.

Brandt has avoided me at school. He doesn't even sneer at me anymore. Word has gotten out about the way he handles his cast, and Mr. Watson has been overseeing his tech week.

No one at school knows about what he did to set this shit in motion. He doesn't come within ten feet of me and never sneers or tries to talk to me. He knows what my guys have on him and that I'm the one not pulling the trigger. Yet.

If he didn't have a whole cast of people depending on him, I would have made everyone aware of what he did behind the scenes. But this is their opportunity too. And while someone could step in and help, it's not fair to everyone who worked hard to make this production a reality.

When Damon explained what Brandt did to his dad, Adam went to talk to Brandt's father. Pretty sure that shut down any other schemes Brandt and his sister might have had. Especially after hearing the recording Hawk took that night.

Things are so chaotic that I don't know which way is up most days.

It's dress rehearsal night. The audience has a handful of people in to watch. Friends and family who know this is a final rehearsal. My mom and Adam sit out in the audience with Damon and Cam.

There's this nervous buzz of energy flowing through me. Tonight, I'm an actor. Keira is helping the backstage manager and will make notes of anything that stands out and needs to be addressed before the show tomorrow night.

I glance back at Hawk who's talking to Chase and give him a quick smile. Hawk winks and a flush of warmth flows through me.

Mark stands next to me. He has his own boyfriend out in the audience watching tonight. "Nervous?"

"Maybe a little," I admit and smile at him. "You?"

"I think I'm going to vomit."

"So perfectly normal then?" I thread my arm through his. "I wish Mia were here."

"Don't want to perform?" he asks.

"I'm excited about performing, but it still feels like her role."

Mark chuckles softly. "It was her role until you took it over. It's your role now, EvanAnn. You've made it yours. We're going to show everyone what a great actor *and* director you are."

I take a deep breath and lift my chin to meet his gaze. "Thank you."

He smiles. "Break a leg."

I walk out on stage to get us started.

"I just want to thank you all for coming tonight. We have an amazing cast and show to put on for you." I see my guys in the audience and smile. "We all appreciate the people in our lives who support us during the crazy schedule of rehearsals and performances. We couldn't do it without all of you. So thank you."

I kiss my fingertips and blow them to the audience.

"Please enjoy yourselves as you watch Shakespeare's *Othello*."

# CHAPTER 50
## *Damon*

EVAN IS amazing at what she does, so I'm not surprised when she gets the invitation to the summer internship *and* gets a call from Sandra Cox. I'm working at my desk on calculus homework when Evan takes the call into her room.

After fifteen minutes, she returns and straddles my lap at the desk. Her stormy eyes meet mine, and I wait.

"She wanted me to do the mentorship."

"That's amazing, little devil." I run my hands over her back. "She'd be insane to pass on you."

Evan sighs and leans back to look me in the eyes. "I told her I decided to go to college first, but that I'd love to try to work something out with her while I attend classes."

"Evan, what happened to we don't settle?" I search her eyes.

"It's not settling if I choose you, Hawk, and Cam. It's not settling to go to a fantastic program at Crowne Mawr instead of straight into industry. It's not settling when I have a summer internship already that I'd have to give up for this mentorship." She threads her fingers into my hair. "I love directing, but I also want to get back to acting. If I do the mentorship, it will be making a choice again. I want the option to act for now. Besides, I can try for the mentorship in a few years if I still want it, but right now, I want to be with you and Cam and Hawk. My career will wait or just be different, but I want to start our lives together."

"You won't regret it?" I have to ask, tucking her hair behind her ear.

"Do you regret this year? I know it wasn't what you had planned. It changed how you were going to get to the NHL. Do you regret it?" She braces herself.

If I had the chance all over again and knew what I know now, would I still choose to go? Would I choose hockey over her, Cam, and Hawk? It's not a choice I really have to make. Everything happened the way it was supposed to happen.

I grab her hips and stand. She squeaks and wraps herself around me, more fully. When I lower her onto the bed, she crawls back as I crawl over her.

"Even if I went, you still would have been under my roof when I came back, Evan. You were inevitable. We were inevitable. I wouldn't change it because I can't. But there's no way in any form of this world the four of us don't end up together."

She cups my jaw and lifts her mouth to almost touch mine. "I'm choosing us. But also still chasing my dream. I earned the summer internship. I earned my spot in the freshman class and the full ride scholarship at Crowne Mawr. Yes, Sandra Cox chose me, and it's a fucking honor and I would spend a year earning her respect, but I'm good with what I've already earned."

"I love you, little devil."

She smiles wickedly. "I love you. Now kiss me so we can get back to calculus."

---

## CAM

I sit next to Evan at the dining room table. Hawk sits on her other side while Damon sits beside me. Our parents are all here for dinner. It's been a few weeks since we last all sat down together when Evan needed a place to stay.

The parents are chatting, but we've got news that we need to share. And I've been designated spokesman for the night.

When dinner is served, the table falls quiet, and I take this as my moment. "As you know, Damon has received offers to play hockey at Crowne Mawr and Yale."

There's a round of exclamation congratulating Damon and Adam.

I clear my throat and it dies down a little. "We were able to go down to Crowne Mawr last weekend to visit." I got to go to the frat and Damon showed us the underground fighting area. We got to tour the drama department. We also looked at housing options.

"I'm going to tell you something, and some of you might be like you're too young to make decisions like this or what if you break up or whatever trite wisdom you think we haven't already thought of between the four of us. We've weighed all the pros and cons. None of us is settling for anything less than we would want for ourselves. But we made this decision together and intentionally."

I stop and look all the parents in the eyes because this is important.

"This is our future and we've decided to make our decision as a group. We want to stay together in college, and we believe it's possible. We know that Damon and Evan both have careers that may pull us in different directions, but we want to spend our college lives together."

My dad meets my eyes. "So you're all deciding to go to either Yale or Crowne Mawr as a group?"

"Yes, and we've decided."

"On?" Adam asks, looking at Damon.

"Crowne Mawr fits all of us better," I say. "It's always been my first choice. Damon loves the team already. Evan will be able to do acting and directing simultaneously. And the pre-law is one of the top programs in the U.S. for Hawk."

I take Evan's hand in mine and she gives me that smile that makes my heart feel like it's going to explode into confetti. Damon and Hawk nod to me. We're a team on this. We'll always be a team.

Dad lifts his glass and nods to me. "To Crowne Mawr."

All the adults lift their glasses and so do we. There's a lot of clinking before everyone takes a sip. To a future together.

## *EvanAnn*

It's the first hockey game of the season and I sit in the stands with Mark and Keira. Mom and Adam are also here, but they're over with Lisa and Alex, and Naomi and Paul. I'm wearing Cam's jersey this game.

He caught me first last night when we went to our spot. It's almost too cold for that kind of play, but we stayed fairly covered during it and still had fun. And more fun when we went home and spent the night together.

"Hi, is this seat taken?"

I look up in surprise at Mia's voice. She's wearing Fletcher's jersey and a decidedly *uncertain of her welcome* smile.

I stand and for a second hesitate before I open my arms and we hug each other. Our words crash over each other.

"I'm so sorry I couldn't talk—"

"I missed you so much—"

"My parents made me stay home—"

"The play wasn't the same without you—"

"I'm still dating Fletcher and Liam and they've been great—"

"Jackson kidnapped me."

"What?" Mia pulls back. "Wait, what? Kidnapped?"

The buzzer goes off, and I pull Mia down to sit next to me. I fill her in on the whole Brandt and Jackson and even Chase drama. Our parents kept the story out of the news, but the rumor mill around school was rampant.

"You know, I forgot Brandt said to be friends with someone like you. That dirty bastard. I didn't even remember him from auditions. And I really didn't fuck Chase, but we did make out a little when I was touring the school. But he didn't say he had a girlfriend. Not that that would have stopped me. I'm a horrible person."

"No, you're not. You're my friend. And I've really missed you." I hold her hand.

"You're too nice. That's why I love you." She smiles softly.

"Are you coming back to Anteros?" I can't help but ask, though I think I know the answer.

"No, with what happened with Tanner, my parents insisted I go to boarding school, Barrington Academy. There's more security and with the trial coming up, they don't want to have to worry about reporters asking me questions. Brandt's sister goes there, but I'll stay away from her. She's a manipulative bitch."

I laugh, and we spend the rest of the game catching up.

When the Devils win, because they always win, we head down to meet the guys when they come out of the locker room. Liam gets there first and frowns at Mia's jersey.

"Kitten?" He pulls her into his arms. "Didn't we talk about this?"

She leans up and whispers in his ear. His grin widens as she speaks. When she turns to me, she gives me a wink.

Damon, Cam, and Hawk come out next. Cam grabs me and spins me in a circle. I barely notice Damon and Hawk greeting Mia stiffly. But it's not like she was their favorite person.

Fletcher joins us and kisses Mia. "You don't know how hard it was to break her free from that boarding school."

"It's called a weekend pass." Mia rolls her eyes. "It's not that hard."

"It will be later," Liam says quietly.

I turn my face into Cam's shoulder and laugh.

"We should go get some dinner," Cam says. "You guys want to come along?"

Surprised, I glance around at everyone as they nod in agreement. I smile at Mia, grateful to have my friend back.

---

CHRISTMAS BREAK IS AMAZING THIS YEAR. NORMALLY, I spend the holiday taking in movies or reading plays or figuring out what to work on next. This year we spent Christmas day with our families and each other, but the day after Christmas we head to Damon's family vacation home in the mountains.

It's just the kind of reset we need. After the semester we had…

In November, I had to testify at Jackson's trial and then present a victim's statement at the sentencing. Hawk and I went over the victim's impact statement a few times. We argued about it. I don't want to ruin his life the way he tried to ruin mine. But I also know Jackson needs mental health treatment to get better.

It feels hypocritical of me to love one stalker and think the other should be punished. Damon and I have talked about it (even in therapy), but what Damon did and what Jackson did aren't different because I liked one of them more. It's why they did it. And yes, Damon did it without my knowledge at first, but now it's just part of who we are as a couple.

Jackson wanted to control me. To make me into who he believed me to be. Damon loves me for who I am. He watches me because he's afraid to lose me like he did his mother.

I do think Jackson should be punished, but I want him to get the help he needs. He'll never have a fulfilling life if his philosophy clings to him.

He's been remanded to a state facility for mental health for no less than three years. He'll be allowed to train while there, so he won't lose his hockey skills. It's the best I can do for him, and I wish him well.

Hawk made sure I'd have a restraining order that's renewable, so Jackson won't be able to go to whatever college I'm at. That was non-negotiable from the Devil's trio. And honestly, I don't know, even after he gets help, if I'll ever be willing to sit in the same room as Jackson Riordan.

Damon and Cam grab our bags from the trunk, and I lead the way to the door, entering the code. It's cold outside, but inside is already warm and the lights are on. Apparently they also pay someone to stock the fridge so we don't have to worry about getting food.

Hawk grabs me and throws me over his shoulder as Cam and Damon bring the suitcases upstairs with us. I'm laughing the whole way and barely get to see the place. Hawk drops me on the bed, and I scramble to sit up.

I glance around the room. It's large, obviously the primary, with a huge bed and a view of the mountains covered in snow. It's gorgeous and feels like a dream to be here with the three of them. After everything we went through, we're stronger than ever.

Hawk sits down next to me and pulls off my shoes before taking off his own. I sit on the bed and watch Cam and Damon putting our stuff away. They took off their shoes downstairs. Hawk lies back on the bed and gives me a smoldering look.

My body heats. We're alone for the first time in forever. Even when we're at our houses, usually a parent or two are home. It's made me self-conscious even if they can't hear us all the way across the house. Because they *know*.

Even though their houses are big, the guys do try to make me scream loud enough to be heard everywhere. It's like a challenge I didn't sign up for but definitely enjoy taking part in. Though I definitely don't enjoy sitting across from a knowing look from parents at dinner.

But here and now, we have the whole place to ourselves with no neighbors in sight. We're in that zone where school doesn't exist for a week, and we have nothing to do but enjoy each other.

"So what do you want to do first?" I turn to ask Hawk. "Movie marathon? Catch up on *Stranger Things*? Oh, read a book? For pleasure?"

Hawk smirks, but doesn't say anything as Cam grabs my legs and tugs me down on the bed. I release a little shriek.

"Did someone say pleasure?" Cam leans over me and kisses me, sending a flood of aching desire through me.

If I thought we'd fall into a routine after the first month or so of fucking, I was thankfully wrong. There's still so much to explore with each other. Cam lifts his mouth from mine. His hands bracket my head on the bed as he looks over my face.

"What do you want to do first, goody? Or should I ask who?" He cocks his eyebrow wickedly.

I can't help but laugh. "I haven't even seen the house yet."

"What's there to see, little devil?" Damon sits on the bed beside us. "We could spend all week right here."

I chuckle. "I thought you wanted to go skiing?"

He smirks. "Not a chance. Too risky. Can't break a leg or fuck up my knee for a little fun. Not when I could spend the whole week buried inside you."

I shift beneath Cam as Damon's words send tingles down to my pussy.

"You want to explore the house, baby girl?" Hawk slides off the bed and strips off his shirt. "We can play hide and seek in the dark. If we catch you, we get to do whatever we want to you."

Damon stands and goes into the closet while Cam helps me stand.

"Hide and seek?" I ask, looking at Hawk.

Cam grabs my shirt and takes it off. "Yeah, why not? It's been too cold to go outside and catch you. It's warm in here, and we can make sure to check off every room on the list while we're at it."

I shiver as he grabs my leggings and slides them down, lowering to his knee to kiss my stomach as I step out of them.

"You want me to run around this house in the dark in my underwear?" I hold my hands out to the side.

Damon comes out, twirling a skirt around his finger. "Not quite, little devil."

I laugh. This time, it isn't my old school uniform skirt. "You're becoming predictable."

He smirks. "I know what I like. Take off your panties."

At least he isn't ripping them off me. As much as I like it, I also like these panties. But I know he'll just buy me new ones too. I slip off my panties and hold my hand out for the skirt. Their eyes devour me, and I already feel like their prey.

"Not so fast." Damon nods to Cam, who spins me and presses my shoulders down. I catch my hands on the bed. Hawk slips closer to me, sitting on the bed between my hands. "We need to get you ready."

Cam thrusts his cock into my pussy from behind, making me gasp at the sudden stretch. My body hums in anticipation. Hawk draws his cock out of his pants and grabs my hair, dragging my head down to take him into my mouth. Resisting a little, I lick around his tip, meeting his eyes. He smirks and pushes my head to take his cock inside.

Cam holds my hips as he begins to fuck in and out of me. We could fuck every day and I wouldn't get tired of this. Hawk matches Cam's rhythm using my hair to guide me over him. Knowing Damon is watching them take me adds a different dimension of arousal.

I'm already close to coming for them. We spend as much time as possible with each other, but this week is ours. And I plan on being very sore and very happy.

Then Damon's fingers coated in lube slide over my asshole before pressing inside, stretching me. I moan around Hawk's cock, but they don't let up. Damon pumps his fingers into my ass in tempo with the others, so they're all fucking into me.

I shatter around them with a moan. Hawk's cum floods my mouth, and I swallow around him. I barely catch my breath before Cam buries himself inside me and groans his release. Then they're all pulling out of me. Damon disappears into the bathroom, and I hear water running and try to slow my breathing. My pussy flutters in anticipation of more.

Cam grabs the skirt and helps me into it. It may not be my uniform skirt, but it's still short. When he takes off his pants, my gaze drops to the scar on his leg. He tips my chin up.

His dark eyes search mine. "I'd do it again. Every fucking time to save you, Evan."

I step into him and hug him, breathing him in. That night doesn't haunt us as much, but there have been nights I reach out, expecting to not find anyone, expecting my wrists to be bound, expecting to be still trapped.

Hawk steps up behind me and wraps around me too. The therapist says the nightmares might fade over time, but return during times of stress. But my guys make sure to keep me close. I haven't slept alone since that night.

"I love you, Cam," I say against his chest. There was real fear that night that what Jackson did was irreparable. But it was far enough away from the artery. He's back on the ice this season, but he's not going to try out for the team at Crowne Mawr.

"I love you, goody."

"I love you, baby girl." Hawk kisses my shoulder, and I lean back into him.

"I love you, Hawk. I don't know what I would do without any of you."

"Get a decent night's sleep for one," Cam says with a chuckle. "Come on, goody. Chin up. We can't keep weeping over wounds that have long since healed."

"Besides, we have things to do." Damon leans against the wall, watching the three of us. "Movie marathons, series to catch up on, a game of hide and fuck."

"You can't just add and fuck to every game." I shake my head as the guys release me and strip down to their boxers.

Damon walks over to me and flicks the hem of my skirt. "In this case, little devil, it fits. Now if we're finished saying I love you for the millionth time and rejoicing the fact we all made it out of that fuck show of a house only slightly scathed..."

I shake my head and wrap my arms around his middle, hugging him to me. "I love you."

He chuckles and wraps his arms around me. "I love you, Evan, but if you don't run, I'm going to throw you on the bed and fuck your ass."

I step back and look undecidedly at the door and then the bed.

"You really don't know what's good for you, do you?" Hawk says.

"Oh, she knows." Cam leans against the bed. "She's just deciding what she wants first."

I wink at Cam and he winks back.

"One," Damon says, and I take off out the door. It doesn't matter where I hide, they'll find me. They always find me.

*Epilogue*

**CAM**

"Third floor, right?" Dad lifts a box out of the trunk.

Mom glances at me as she reaches into the truck to grab something to carry up. I nod. It's move-in day. I glance around the parking lot as Adam pulls in with the moving van, followed by Paul driving a car with Naomi and Heather. Hawk and Damon ride their motorcycles into the parking lot with Evan on the back of Damon's. They park next to mine.

We spent the summer in a sad little bubble. Evan went and did her internship, and Damon went off to hockey camp. He's going to wait a year before entering the draft as a student with the caveat that he wants to finish his degree before signing. Hawk and I went to parties, but it wasn't the same without the two of them. Finally, we're all back together.

And living together. Which was a whole thing with Coach Mitchell, but Damon finally convinced him that while the hockey house might work for some, it wouldn't work for him. Not if he couldn't be with us.

We aren't the only ones moving in today. There's a group of five guys unloading a truck. They're all tall and fit like athletes. An older woman with brown hair, probably one of their moms, stands in the truck directing them.

Evan comes over to me and hugs me. "I'm so excited."

I wrap my arms around her and press a kiss to her blond hair. "I can't wait to wake up to you every morning."

That was a discussion that took days to resolve. One big bed? Multiple king-size beds? Swapping beds? Do we all want to sleep together every night? Do we want our own space? The apartment is big enough, but we decided the one big bed would work and we have a guest bedroom if someone needs space.

Evan beams up at me before heading to the truck where her mom is helping Adam. Damon and Hawk join me. Damon is eyeing the group of guys.

"Football players?" he asks with a suspicious look.

"Maybe." I glance at him. "You worried?"

"If they hit on Evan, we're going to have problems."

Hawk nods. "Better than a bunch of girls trying to pick us off."

We've had enough with other people trying to come between us. That won't be happening here. And if someone tries, our girl is real handy with a knife.

A young woman comes out of the apartment building. She's average height with long brown hair up in a ponytail and brown eyes. She smiles at the group of guys. The biggest guy stalks over and picks her up. She laughs and kisses him before he puts her down.

Another dark haired boy picks her up and kisses her.

"Put me down, Jack!"

But he carries her over to the others.

"Probably won't be an issue," I say and shake my head. "And here I thought we'd be the talk of campus, sharing our girl."

Damon follows after Evan. Hawk punches me in the arm and takes off to join them. This isn't what I thought my first day of college would look like a year ago. Mom and Dad would have moved me into a dorm. If Dad had his way, it would have been Yale, though he's happy I'm at Crowne Mawr.

I would have tried to make friends with some guys on my floor, but it wouldn't have been the same as Hawk and Damon.

And there wouldn't have been Evan.

She turns. "Come on, Cam. We need your help."

Fuck it. I can't wait to see how this year goes. I join my girl and my brothers. Our family helps us take things up to our apartment. Occasionally we'll pass the other group moving in. I give the guys a short nod, but now isn't the time for introductions.

It's a long day of hauling things up and unpacking. Made a little faster with all the help of six parents. My mom orders pizzas and we sit at the table and stools on the island to eat. The apartment is large enough for four people. There's a gym for residents on the first floor, but Damon will have access to the athlete's gym at school for most of his workouts.

Hawk tried out for the team and got on, but I decided against it. I spent most of last year building a portfolio and working with the art teachers at Anteros to get into the art program here at Crowne Mawr.

We set up one of the extra bedrooms as a creative space for Evan and me. The other one has four desks for when we need to get schoolwork done.

After dinner, our parents say goodbye. They checked into a hotel nearby and will head home in the morning. After hugs from everyone and tears from our moms, they leave and we're alone.

"Did you see that girl and her guys?" Evan leans against the counter in the open kitchen. Her feet are bare and there's dust on her pants. "Five guys. Every one of them kissed her too."

"I caught a couple of them making out with her in the stairwell," Hawk says.

"Don't get any ideas, little devil." Damon narrows his eyes on her. "You're stuck with just three."

Evan laughs and holds up her hands. "I'm good with you guys. I can't imagine that many guys."

Her eyes look off into the distance like she's trying to imagine it. Her fingers wiggle.

I shake my head. "That's enough of that."

I lift her against me and she wraps her legs around my waist, focusing on me. Her hands grab the back of my neck.

"Maybe we should remind you how well you take the three of us." I carry her back to the bedroom.

She sighs dramatically. "If you insist."

When I drop her on the bed, she giggles. I can't believe we got here.

That I'm living with my girl and my best friends for the next four years and foreseeable future. About to start our lives in college. When Evan reaches for my pants, I stop thinking.

---

## APPROXIMATELY 13 YEARS LATER

### *EVANANN*

My plane landed earlier than I expected, which means I get to surprise the guys for a change. I sneak into the back of the hockey rink and take a seat in the stands. There are six people on the ice.

Cam, Hawk, and Damon are taller than the other three, but that's not surprising.

"I want to be goalie." Beth whines as she skates circles around her brothers. Her blond hair is tucked under her helmet. Of the three of them, she took to the ice the most. She's still tiny, but fierce with a stick.

"I just started," Keats says and looks to Damon. "Dad?"

Damon shakes his head at Beth, who gives him a pout he's never been able to resist. "Keats is goalie for now. You can be goalie next time."

"We barely have a team." Beth skates to a halt in front of Hawk and narrows her eyes on him. "When are you going to give us more babies?"

Grey's baby laughs fill the rink as Cam holds his hands, slowly guiding the toddler around the rink. He has another year before the guys will put skates on him. Grey's more interested in watching his older brother and sister, anyway. Eight, five, and two.

When Keats was born, it was a big mess trying to figure out how to manage four careers and a baby.

It's easier when it's off season for Damon. This is his tenth year with the Colorado Titans and probably his last. Coach Mitchell is looking to retire and wants Damon to take over for him at Crowne Mawr. We've been talking about it.

I'm usually home between projects, and the kids always visit me on sets when we're filming.

Of course, Cam and Hawk have done the brunt of raising the kids.

Cam works from home most days. His work in animation means he can do a lot from home, but can't always split his focus between work and the kids, so Hawk only goes into work a couple days a week and works from home too. He's a senior associate at the law firm and going for partner next year if Damon retires.

I lean back in my chair and breathe, because this is what I need. I still love being on set. Acting or directing or both, but there are more moments when I'm away that I wish I was here with them.

"Mom!"

Busted. Beth skates to the door in the boards after she spotted me and pulls it open. Keats gives up his goalie position to come over as I make my way down from the back.

Cam lifts Grey to bring him to me as he starts bouncing his knees and calling *mommy*. Keats removes his helmet and his dark hair spills out of it. I tug on the ends. He keeps saying he wants to cut it, but never does.

His green eyes study me intently. Even at eight he's gotten tall. Soon he'll be taller than me.

"Mom, did you see my goal?" Beth scrambles to be in front of Keats.

I meet her blue eyes and shake my head. "Must have been before I got here."

Cam leans over them to kiss me.

"Kiss, kiss. My turn. Kiss." Grey reaches for me and I take him into my arms. He peppers my jaw and mouth with kisses. His little hands hold my face.

Cam laughs. Hawk has skated over behind the kids. Damon picks up some of the cones they had out on the ice.

"Grey's greedy." Cam reaches for him, but Grey wraps his arms around my neck and buries his head against me.

"Does this mean ice time is over?" Beth looks disappointed. Keats shrugs and heads over to help Damon pick up. "But we just got here."

"We've been here for an hour." Hawk chucks Beth under the chin. "You're as bad as Dad when it comes to the ice."

She smirks and straightens with pride. "I know."

She leans in and kisses me before racing around the edge of the ice.

"If we weren't sure on genetics, I'm confident we'd know whose kid she is." Hawk chuckles and kisses me. Grey touches Hawk's cheek.

We both look down at his large brown eyes, and he giggles at us.

"There's not a lot of doubt about these ones." I smile. My trip was quick to do some pickups, so I was only gone a couple days. I sniff Grey's head as he snuggles into me.

"You good with Grey, while we get the others changed?" Hawk asks.

"You want to stay with mommy or go with papa?" I ask.

"I stay with Mommy." Grey clings a little tighter, and Hawk laughs.

"That one though." He shakes his head. "If Cam and Damon could have a kid…"

"My body would be grateful." I arch an eyebrow.

He kisses me again. "Be right back, Annie."

Cam watches him go before stepping in close. "You still feeling sick?"

"No, I feel better." I shake my head. I had some nausea before leaving for this trip.

Cam narrows his eyes on me like he thinks I'm lying. Every time I get sick, Damon worries. He threatens to take me to the hospital for the smallest fever.

"Honest, Cam. I feel fine. Never better." I kiss him. "Go on. I've got Grey."

Cam hurries across the ice to help the others. I carry Grey over to a chair and sit down with him in my lap. The others head to take off their skates and put away their equipment. Beth is the last one off the ice.

"Can you keep a secret, Grey?"

He looks up at me with those dark eyes that make women fall all over themselves already and nods.

"Me too." I tickle him, and his laugh fills the room.

Damon is the first to walk across the ice to me and Grey. "How was Atlanta?"

"Hot." I stand, and he leans down to kiss Grey on the cheek. When I arch an eyebrow at him, he smirks.

"What?" he asks.

I roll my eyes and press up on my toes to kiss him. He chuckles and deepens the kiss.

"Dad!" Beth comes barreling into the back of Damon's legs. "Did you tell Mommy?"

I look at Damon expectantly. He rubs the back of his neck and gives me a chagrined look.

"I'm going to play hockey." Beth smiles so big.

"There's a youth league." Damon runs his hand over Beth's blond hair. "But we needed to discuss it with the whole family first. Since it's a time commitment."

"Please, Mommy. I'm going to be the best hockey player in the world. I'm already better than Keats."

I glance over as Hawk, Keats, and Cam come over. Grey reaches for Damon with the absolute faith of a toddler that he'll catch him. Damon takes Grey and sighs.

"I'm going to be just like Dad and play for the NHL." Beth puffs out her chest and gives me a look that is so Damon I almost laugh. "Daddy said I play just like Dad."

Cam clears his throat. "I believe I said you're as fast as him."

"She's better than any of the boys on my team," Keats says as he leans against the boards.

Beth always tags along to Keats's hockey practice and insists on being on the ice. Since Damon comes sometimes the coach generally lets her as long as one of her dads is on the ice with her.

"Are we going home?" Keats asks.

I look at Beth. "You can do anything you set your mind to."

She smiles and takes my hand. "We need a goalie."

"You don't think Keats makes a good goalie?" I ask.

"He flinches at the puck." Beth shakes her head like he's a disappointment.

Hawk begins to herd us toward the door.

"What about Grey?" I ask.

Beth looks at Grey in Damon's arms. "Maybe. He likes to run around too much to stay still. Unless you guys are holding him and goalies shouldn't be held by their mommy and daddies."

"So what do we need to do?" I ask as we step outside and head for the cars.

"We need more brothers and sisters." She looks up at me expectantly. "But you keep saying maybe."

I clear my throat and smile. "We'll have to see."

Damon's eyes meet mine. We've talked about more kids, especially with his career becoming more stable. We didn't really talk about anytime soon. But a few weeks ago, the kids went to stay with Grampy and Grammy, Cam's parents.

We spent a week just the four of us and didn't take the usual precautions. I don't want to say anything in front of the kids until we're a little further along, but I need to tell the guys.

So we go to dinner while Beth pleads her case to be allowed to play hockey. Keats tells me about this experiment in his science class. And Grey just wants to be loved by everyone.

When they're finally all down for the night, I sit on the edge of our bed and wait for the guys to join me. I finger the rings on my hands. The tracker they gave me in high school is back on my right hand, and the engagement and wedding ring they gave me a year after college are on my left.

We had a commitment ceremony with all of us and legally tied ourselves together, but technically I could only marry one of them. Given Damon's career and the interest of way too many women, he's legally married to me. We all have wedding bands and agreed it's only a piece of paper. What matters is we want to spend the rest of our lives together.

Damon walks into the bedroom first. He sits down next to me on the bed and takes my hand.

"She's really excited for it," he says softly. He doesn't really have to plead her case to me. There's not a lot I could do to keep that kid off the ice.

I smile and bump my shoulder against his. "You had to give her a stick," I tease.

He shrugs. "I tried to encourage figure skating and she'll keep doing that too until she makes a choice."

Cam comes in and sits on my other side. He holds out a pink paper flower. I smile and lean over to kiss his cheek. My collection has gotten ridiculous, but every flower makes this burst of love flow through me.

He also gives flowers to the kids, but they're too impatient and unwrap them like presents to find the drawing on the inside.

When Hawk walks in, he closes the door, pressing the lock. "Are you feeling better?"

I laugh. "Actually, I feel fantastic."

He kneels at my feet and I run my hands through his hair, remembering when he kept it cut short. We've all changed over the years, but this never changes. The way I feel about each of them.

"You each have a little mini me. Do you think this one might take after me?" I put my hand on my stomach with a little wonder. "A little actress with not a lick of athleticism?"

It takes them a minute before they're all talking at once and then kissing and hugging me. When we finally settle into silence, we're lost in our own thoughts.

"You're pregnant." Cam says it like it makes sense.

"Yeah, but it's still early, so we should wait before we tell the kids." I lean my forehead against Cam's. "And this time I want to be here longer."

"If you get that offer though..." Hawk glances at Damon and Cam. "We can take care of things."

There's an opportunity for a franchise. Multiple movies. Acting and directing. It's a dream job, but that's not all I want anymore.

"This wouldn't be settling." I take Hawk's hand and put it over my stomach. "I can make more films later, but they're only little once. And this time, I'm going to choose us."

"We're a team," Cam says. "We can make anything work."

"I know, and that's why I love you all."

Damon nods. He understands. We've had our careers, and yes, there's more to do. There will always be more to do, but we can slow down and enjoy what life and love has given us. These three children plus this one and any more we decide to have are precious to us too. I don't want to just be around for the big things. I want it all.

And with them, I can have it all.

THANK YOU FOR READING THE LUST & LIARS SERIES. I can't believe we've come to the end, but there's always more!

Want more, join my newsletter for an exclusive of a continued Christmas vacation with the Devil's trio and Evan at https://csberry.com/lust-liars-christmas-bonus-scene/.

If you're curious about the horsemen and what happened to Tanner at Mia's old school, you can find out in the Untouched series.

# Meet C.S. Berry

C.S. Berry is a combination of my love for writing and my love for reading. She began as an experiment and took off into something I absolutely adore. It's not often you can do what you love and it works as a career. As for me, I love reading and romance and heroines seriously getting railed. I assume since you've read my books, you do too.

If you want to discuss books or anything with me, come join my Facebook group, C.S. Berry's Spicy Executive Suite. And you can always catch me on Instagram @csberry.

Oh and me, I have a lovely family who aren't allowed to read my books. But are so proud, they keep leaking my pen name. My dog and cats don't care about my writing as long as I sit still long enough for them to snuggle.

XOXOXO,
C.S. Berry

### Keep up with C.S. Berry
View the shop: csberrybooks.com
View the Patreon: patreon.com/csberry
Join her Newsletter on her website
Join the Facebook Group:
https://www.facebook.com/groups/csberryreaders
Checkout her Website: csberry.com

www.ingramcontent.com/pod-product-compliance
Lightning Source LLC
LaVergne TN
LVHW032007070526
838202LV00059B/6328